PANTHER GAP

ALSO BY JAMES A. McLAUGHLIN

Bearskin

PANTHER GAP

JAMES A. McLAUGHLIN

FLATIRON
BOOKS
NEW YORK

PANTHER GAP. Copyright © 2023 by James A. McLaughlin. All rights reserved. Printed in the United States of America. For information, address Flatiron Books, 120 Broadway, New York, NY 10271.

Verse quoted in chapter 66 from "Evening Hawk" by Robert Penn Warren

www.flatironbooks.com

Designed by Omar Chapa

Library of Congress Cataloging-in-Publication Data

Names: McLaughlin, James A., author.
Title: Panther gap / James A. McLaughlin.
Description: First Edition. | New York : Flatiron Books, 2023.
Identifiers: LCCN 2022028772 | ISBN 9781250821003 (hardcover) |
    ISBN 9781250857323 (ebook)
Subjects: LCGFT: Novels. | Suspense fiction.
Classification: LCC PS3613.C5755 P36 2023 | DDC 813/.6—dc23/
    eng/20220624
LC record available at https://lccn.loc.gov/2022028772

Our books may be purchased in bulk for promotional, educational, or business use. Please contact your local bookseller or the Macmillan Corporate and Premium Sales Department at 1-800-221-7945, extension 5442, or by email at MacmillanSpecialMarkets@macmillan.com.

First Edition: 2023

10 9 8 7 6 5 4 3 2 1

For Nancy, of course

When even the bones is gone in the desert the dreams is talk to you, you dont wake up forever.

CORMAC McCARTHY, *BLOOD MERIDIAN*

PANTHER GAP

1

1983

Bowman sat on the floor of the hayloft and kicked his bootheels on the boards to knock off the snow while his father walked downstairs for the eagle.

He wore a green wool watch cap pulled down over his ears, wool pants, a plaid wool jacket. Over the jacket, his father had strapped a baseball catcher's chest pad to Bowman's back and pinned a stiff, poorly tanned Alaskan wolf pelt to the pad. Two half-frozen chicken necks dangled on a leather strap tied to the back of the wolf's head.

Bowman shut his eyes. Wolf-scent from the thick coarse fur of the pelt enveloped him, somehow familiar, triggering what felt like long-ago memories, or the shreds of a dream slipping away in the morning. His saliva flowed at the raw meat of the chicken necks and he swallowed to keep from drooling on the barn floor. His sense of smell was too sensitive, which he thought was strange, but he didn't dwell on it. Instead he leaned over to the hay bales stacked behind him and inhaled the sweet scent of summer afternoons, a mix of brome, grama, wild rye, and bluestem that grew in the high, lush valley his family called Panther Gap. In his mind he left the cold barn and lay on his stomach in the valley, in the breeze and insect buzz, hot under the long sun, watching bison move through tall grass, unhurried as old gods.

Slow footsteps on the stairs. Alecto appeared first, standing two feet tall on an upraised forearm, her head covered with a leather hood Bowman's father had sewn himself. Then his father's thick black hair and graying beard, shaded eyes, a frown of concentration that softened when he saw Bowman waiting.

Bowman rolled to a knee. He and Summer had pulled a lure behind them on a long rope, walking, running, on horseback, teasing the eagle from the sky with a stiff musty fox skin jerked along the ground. But this was going to be different. He knew he should probably be afraid.

The high gable windows showed a blank white sky. Still snowing, the first tracking snow of the season, and when it stopped, he and Summer would walk down into the valley and read the new tracks there. Deer and elk and moose and bison, of course. The black bears were mostly denned up by now, but there would be bobcat, marten, river otter tracks. Maybe they could find the male lion who lived in the valley. A young female had appeared during the fall and Summer was hoping for kittens next year.

Others had arrived as well, animals who weren't supposed to be here, who had come from far away.

Last spring, a pair of wolves had dug a den way up in the old timber at the north end of the valley. In August he'd found a set of long-clawed bear prints in the mud at the head of the lake, a pilgrim from the relict grizzly population up in the San Juans. He'd seen lynx, and at least one fisher cat, and he'd glimpsed a wolverine at dawn in mid-September, disappearing over the high ridge of the Red Creek Range opposite the house.

And there was one other animal, or maybe he was something more, who had appeared in Bowman's dreams, one so powerful and rare Bowman had never even allowed himself to say his name, a massive spotted cat making his way north from the Sierra Madre Occidental, returning home to Panther Gap along pathways forgotten for five hundred years, leaving a trail of carcasses behind him, a trail Bowman would retrace someday himself, following the bones into Mexico.

He hadn't told Summer yet. He wondered where she was now, why she wasn't here to watch.

"You should be moving when I pull off the hood."

Bowman started at his father's voice. It took him a moment to parse the words' meaning. He looked up at the eagle, deep black in the indirect light. It seemed to Bowman that his father had nearly disappeared, had become inanimate, insignificant beside Alecto.

"Will she know it's me?"

"No. She'll think you're an animal. Prey."

Bowman waited. He knew what his father meant by the word, but he was struck by the homophone. There was no church in their lives, no formal religion, but he and his sister had climbed out onto the roof at night and prayed to the full moon. They hid in the willows at the foot of the lake and prayed to the herds of bison and elk feeding in the meadows. And they snuck down through their grandfather's tunnels to the canyon at the edge of the desert and prayed to the ghosts of the Old Ones who roamed the secret cliff dwellings and spoke to Bowman while he slept. They didn't tell anyone they did this, and when they prayed they always asked for things that they knew were going to happen anyway: the sun to come up, the snow to fall and to melt in the spring, their father to kill elk and a bison for their meat, their mother to rest on the east ridge where the sun hit first in the mornings, under the broken stones Bowman had helped to pile on her before Summer was old enough to remember.

"Now," his father said.

He moved fast, crawling on his hands and feet, hunched over, trying to move like a wolf would. He thought wolf-thoughts and loped across the barn floor. He moved in a straight line and didn't turn. A wolf that turned to fight would make the eagle flare and break off the chase. The wolf was only vulnerable when he was running away.

He felt himself change, a little. It puzzled him.

When the eagle hit, it felt like his father had whacked him with a baseball bat instead. His breath went out and he collapsed face-down, his arms protecting his head and face.

He was supposed to hold still, pretend the first impact had

knocked him out, not buck and jerk like a wolf trying to get away. That would be too dangerous, would bring on more killing from the eagle.

Still, she footed him, her first and second talons piercing the pad and pulling and then driving down again, through his skin, between his ribs, and into his chest, teaching Bowman a new kind of pain, an opening up, his guts pricked and held. A boundary so perfect and inviolate that he had never known it was there, broken now, dissolving, as if the eagle had reached inside him and was holding his heart, ungently, intimately. Later he would read that this sort of experience was called a unitive trance, and it was usually brought on by hallucinogenic drugs, extreme religious fervor, or near-death experiences. It didn't often happen to eleven-year-old boys.

His father was speaking. A hollow voice, miles distant. "Are you okay?"

He nodded, not wanting to say anything out loud, to break the wolf illusion.

"Now hold still, let her feed for a moment."

She felt heavier than her fourteen pounds as she shifted, adjusting her grip and picking at the chicken necks. His right side felt punched where the one foot still held him, the other on the wolf's head while she fed. That's the way she was supposed to do it: one foot on the body, driving the two primary talons into vital organs and compressing the lungs, the other on the head to control the wolf's defensive bite.

He had been a wolf for a moment, and now, with the eagle holding him, as he started to bleed internally from two puncture wounds, he was the wolf, and he was the eagle as well. He knew them both. He floated up and impossibly away from his body. He'd read about people claiming to have done this, but had always thought it sounded ridiculous, something they would invent to make themselves seem more interesting. Yet there he was, lying on the barn floor, his point of view unquestionably suspended in the air above, watching as his father approached.

Alecto was mantling, her wings spread protectively over him, shielding her prey.

His father spoke to the eagle in a small voice, in a language Bowman no longer understood, carrying a folded blanket he would use to cover and hide his son as soon as he coaxed the eagle away.

Leo Girard felt an unaccountable foreboding. The short flight had been perfect but Alecto had gone high-strung now. She hissed and glared at him over her shoulder, holding her immense wings out over Bowman. There were no wolves to hunt within a thousand miles, but Alecto was large and fierce enough to take one, and Leo thought he might try her on coyotes later in the winter, when the snow was deeper.

"Easy, big girl."

Leo's great flaw as a falconer was his desire to please his eagle. He knew this, and he fought it, but the little concessions he made had led to a relationship with the bird that was less than ideal.

He would walk out to check on Alecto at night, his boots crunching in the snow, and when he opened the heavy plank door her head was already turned in expectation, eyes shining with reflected moonlight, eyes larger and heavier than Leo's own. He would stand in front of the perch, the eagle's dark form silent, fluffed into a caricature against the cold, and he would feel her looking into him until the things he'd done and seen, the great love he'd lost, his nagging, desperate worry for his children's fraught future, the lives he'd taken, the soul sickness of his already too-long life, it all shrank to insignificance. On still winter nights he stared into those glinting black orbs, thinking there should be some kind of sound emanating from them, a low thrumming hiss like a river in flood. Alecto's eyes were silent in the same way a meteor arcing across the sky was silent, impossibly silent, as if the watcher must have suddenly gone deaf.

"Bowman."

"Sir?"

"Are you sure you're all right?"

"Yes." The boy's voice was weak, muffled, speaking into his arm. "Did I do it right?"

"You looked like a wolf. Even to me." It was more than that, a perfect performance, and it had spooked Leo. The boy had changed into a wolf before his eyes.

Alecto lifted her right foot, the first and second talons shining wet with blood.

"She footed you." Leo moved in closer, reached out with his gloved arm toward the bird. She hissed at him again, the hackles on the back of her neck raised. It was still too soon. Something about this ersatz kill had agitated her. "You're hurt."

"I'm fine. It's kind of hard to breathe."

Leo hesitated. It was risky to try to take the bird off her kill before she was ready.

"Come up, Alecto." He placed a strip of raw chicken on his glove and stepped around in front. His son's face was hidden. "That's Bowman you have there. Let me see what you've done to him."

The chest pad on Bowman's back looked inadequate now—what had he been thinking?—but already he was imagining something more protective, a vest of stiff heavy leather. It had gone so well. He hadn't expected Alecto to take to such a large quarry so quickly.

She held his eyes with hers, her beak open, panting.

"She's not letting me in. We may have to wait a few minutes for her to settle down."

Bowman lay still, the eagle tenting her wings to shadow him, her feathers compressed tightly against her body. She stood like a statue of some crazed angel, her eyes glaring an unmistakable warning.

"You okay for a little longer?"

The boy didn't reply.

"Bowman!"

He heard Summer's frightened "Daddy?" from behind him as he lunged to kneel beside his son's shoulder. The eagle's blooded foot struck at his face like a snake but he was ready, taking the blow with his gloved fist, the thumb talon big around as a pencil going through the leather and into the meat of his palm. Before she could strike again he swept her feet together with his other hand. Her left wing cut a gash in his cheek as he pulled her toward him, folding her against his chest. She weighed no more than a fat housecat, but her power was astonishing, preternatural. Leo Girard had fought men to the death but he had never experienced anything like Alecto's hissing, primal fury, and he knew she wouldn't forgive him for this. He used his weight to subdue her, lying atop her while slipping the hood over her head.

Her struggle ceased as if he'd thrown a switch, and he set her on a pine beam, wrapped her jesses loosely around a peg, and turned to lift his son and carry him to the house. Summer stood wide-eyed at the top of the steps, and he whispered to her, asking if she would please run down and open the outside door.

2

2009

When the sea snakes appeared in the cove, Bowman didn't know what they were at first. A container filled with plastic yellow ribbons must have blown from a ship offshore and broken open, spilled its bright tangled cargo to drift landward, twisting and thrashing in the waves.

Pelamis platurus—the yellow-bellied sea snake—lives in the slicks where ocean currents meet, and sometimes they congregate in staggering numbers . . . to do what? Mate? Migrate? He wasn't sure. Reports by nineteenth century sailors in the South Pacific described living rivers of the snakes that stretched from horizon to horizon and took two days to pass. Hundreds of millions of them. There weren't that many left now, at the end of the first decade of the twenty-first century, well into the amputations of the so-called Anthropocene epoch, but storms off the coast had pushed a modest congregation of yellow-bellied sea snakes into a stretch of Costa Rica's Pacific coast, on the northwest bulge of the Osa Peninsula, and for a few days they swam in the jungly cove where Bowman lived.

In the afternoons, he finned out with his polespear to kill a snapper for dinner, but underwater he was distracted by the psychedelic vision of the yellow-on-black snakes swirling around him, undulating and perfect, like ropes of fluorescent liquid metal poured into the sun-shot water. They weren't shy, and they weren't aggressive. If he held still, they would swim up close. He could reach out and they would slide through his hands, for a moment cold and firm before spooking away with a slap of their paddle-shaped tails.

At night he dreamed his ciguatera dreams, and the snakes spoke to him in the inscrutable language of the Old Ones, dancing weightless in the blue Pacific.

Each morning, a few of the snakes would beach themselves at low tide on the narrow stretch of sand rimming the cove, as if, millions of years too late, they had changed their minds about committing to the sea. Unable to move on land, they lay helpless just beyond the reach of the surf. Eventually they would suffocate like miniature whales, their lungs overcome by the unsupported weight of their own bodies, so he walked the beach at first light and picked up the ones that were still alive and carried them back to the water.

He handled the snakes carelessly though he knew they were venomous and not likely to show any gratitude, and this behavior troubled him. He hadn't survived alone in remote places for so long by being reckless. But he was weary, more so than he'd let himself believe, and he was weak. Before coming to the Pacific coast, he'd lived too long in the Caribbean, subsisting on the fish he could spear, and several bouts of poisoning from ciguatera—a natural toxin that concentrates in the flesh of certain fish species—had damaged his nervous system. During a flare-up, his coordination deteriorated and he would suffer dizzy spells and hallucinations.

These episodes were unpleasant, often involving forced adventures across the perceptual divide into what his more scientific-minded sister would call his own subconscious. He called it *ciguatera city,* a vast and troubled version of reality where the most disturbing truths reared up concrete, animate, revelatory. Last week, while he'd lain in his hammock for a day and a half, barely able to move, his father had walked out of the jungle and sat down right there in the sand where Bowman could see him. Sat cross-legged in the shade, like the sun bothered him. He looked younger than Bowman remembered, and he didn't speak, maybe couldn't speak, was prevented from speaking by some rule applicable to ghosts, and it seemed to frustrate him. Leo Girard wanted to tell Bowman something, and that mute insistence tickled a memory nearly into being.

A memory Bowman sensed he should not have let slip.

He knew it had been important, was important still, and he focused his mind, clawing at this wisp, but the harder he tried to remember, the further it receded. His father watched him struggle, staring his disapproval, a stubborn ghost who sat in the sand for hours, not helping.

Ciguatera city. It was just another trip to the city.

Before dawn on the third day after the snakes had first come into the cove, Bowman stood chest-deep in the cool surf, holding on his open palms a five-foot sea snake he'd carried from the beach, waiting to see if it would revive, when the snake curved back on itself in an otherworldly maneuver and bit him in the web of his palm between his thumb and forefinger.

Mors osculi.

The phrase, from some obscure book of his father's he'd read as a teenager, came to him so quickly he must have been harboring it nearby in his mind.

He shook his hand loose and the big snake swam away.

A death from intense joy; a mystical death, maybe. He didn't actually expect such a thing, but who knew?

He watched the breeze in the leaves at the edge of the rain forest, watched the rippled mirror of the cove break the gold morning sky, and he felt some last resistance he hadn't even known was there let go all at once, crisp and clean, an icicle snapping in his mind. He had determined to live out the rest of his life doing the one thing that remained: bearing witness to *Homo sapiens'* final spasmodic ascendancy from ecological misfit to global catastrophe, the Anthropocene again, a hilariously self-important monkey naming a geological epoch after itself, the epoch in which it finally unmade the world that had borned it, the song-singer eating the world it sang of. That shit had been breaking Bowman's heart for twenty years and he was tired of it and until this moment he'd never found anything for the pain.

The pair of red marks on his hand where the snake had bitten him were no more painful than a beesting.

The ocean's slow push and pull moved his body back and forth until, starting to feel woozy, he left the water and walked up the beach to the grove of tall palm trees where he had lived for the past eighteen months. He sat in the sand, reached out, and drew a wide semicircle with his finger. This particular boundary was one he'd been curious about. Not obsessed with, not like some, but he was going to want to pay attention.

The yellow-bellied sea snake can inject a neurotoxic venom many times more potent than the king cobra's, but the snake's fangs are small and it doesn't often spend much venom on defensive strikes, so its bite is rarely fatal for a healthy adult human.

Bowman, however, wasn't healthy.

He leaned back against a palm, obscure leaf shadows crawling on his skin, and dreamed of his childhood in Colorado. He soared over Panther Gap, watching his mother and father, his two uncles, his younger sister, himself. He saw the myriad Others that lived there. Old Ones stalking the tunnels under the mountain. With Summer on the roof outside her bedroom window, preteens shivering in their sleeping bags, talking quietly. A long-ago December, their father exhaling slow white clouds in a dim room where Alecto stood on her perch like a frozen queen. His boyhood of endless days and nights in the valley, living rough in pursuit of a primitive ideal, his father's ideal, immersed in a sacred world shimmering with life.

The dreams gradually intensified, and he understood he was experiencing something more urgent.

The Sun Dagger at Chaco entered the spiral petroglyph and a fire blazed on a ridgetop.

Summer again, a grown woman, seated at a table in the secret stone house overlooking Panther Gap. She wore a black sweater, her dark hair loose on her shoulders. She looked confident. She reached for a glass of bloodred wine, toasting ironically, smiling at someone.

She thinks she's ready for what's coming.

What he'd forgotten.

A logging camp in the Sierra Madre Occidental, north of El Pozo. The jungle-humid infirmary tent stinking of infection, his father on a stained canvas cot spouting feverish deathbed nonsense, a warning. Bowman had never believed it, had never told his sister, had dismissed it all.

He wasn't the least bit interested in inheritance or family mysteries.

Summer was the far more capable sibling. Their uncles were around to help. By now she didn't really need him, might be better off without him.

But he'd promised. And it was still possible their father had been telling the truth.

He should have warned her.

More images: ravens, dozens of them standing on the ground and perched on stone walls, staring at the round smoldering ruin of a kiva, waiting for it to cool before they fed. A lone, frenzied dancer in a swishing robe of bright tropical red and green parrot feathers, leaping and screeching in the firelight inside a cavernous room, hundreds of bright sweaty faces watching, eyes flashing and rapt. Bowman flew over a city of stone, tiny figures in the streets, people clustering in the plazas, broad roads leading away into the desert, straight lines imposed on the land like spokes, reaching out to other cities over the horizon, armies marching the roads in neat ranks.

Then, finally, Jaguar stretched out on the oak branch, close enough to touch, a map of the universe rippling on his spotted coat, his bright golden eyes like a mirror.

The visions collapsed, and Bowman rolled to his hands and knees.

He'd decided a long time ago that brokenhearted was the only honest way he could live. But it wasn't an honest excuse to die.

Inside his shelter, he rifled his herbal pharmacopoeia for stimulants. His eyelids had begun to droop, and breathing required focused effort, the snake's neurotoxins going to work on his diaphragm. The nearest tourist lodge was twenty air miles to the south, and the Guaymí village near the stone sphere was a dozen miles inland. But a group of friendly Australian surfers were camped two miles to the north. They had a boat, and a satellite phone.

He dug with his hands in the sand behind his shelter and found the emergency dry bag. Inside, his U.S. passport in a plastic case and a dense roll of U.S. hundreds. The passport case also held a photograph of Bowman and his sister on horseback at the ranch, when they were teenagers, in the spring before everything finally went to hell with their father. Summer had given him these things the last time he'd seen her, years ago. She'd made him swear to keep the bag with him. He'd never once unrolled the money, never counted it. But he'd kept it, and there it was, a last tangible shred of privilege.

The dry bag had a belt of nylon webbing and he cinched this tight around his waist. His battered sea kayak was light but he had to stop and rest three times dragging it to the water.

He got himself into the cockpit and paused, feeling a need to say goodbye to this place. It struck him as ironic that he'd come to the Osa in part because it contained one of the last forests in Central America with a reasonably healthy population of jaguars, but in a year and a half he'd never seen one. He'd heard them at night, seen their half-buried kills, and found tracks on the beach near his shelter, but the cats hadn't chosen to engage with him the way they had when he was younger.

He paddled past the breakers and passed out in the kayak, head lolling forward. When he came to, hypoxic and gasping, he was drifting toward the surfers' camp, still a half mile out. His paddle was gone. Then he remembered, he kept it tethered to the boat. It floated nearby at the end of a length of parachute cord. He hauled it in and surfed the kayak to the beach, but he was too weak to get out. One of the Australians lounging near the collection of driftwood logs they'd arranged around a firepit noticed him and called out, "B-man!," then watched in a caricature of stoned surprise as the next wave knocked Bowman out of the kayak and drew him back toward the open ocean.

3

The thirty-first calf trotted through the chute and stuck her head into the headgate, bawling. The veterinarian stabbed a hypodermic of various vaccines while Summer reached out and stapled a plastic tag in the calf's left ear, careful to avoid injuring the veins or the stiff ridges of cartilage giving the ear its structure. She and Uncle Jeremy had brought in thirty-six cows with calves to the handling paddocks just after dawn. She was exhausted and didn't much enjoy this part of cattle ranching—the pathetic traumatized animals lowing and shitting and refusing to believe it was for their own good.

Number 31, at least, was a female—no castration necessary or possible—but the panicked creature still moaned at the painless paint of wormer on her shoulders. Summer was rubbing the calf's nose before releasing her, as if that would help, when the veterinarian yelled, "Here she comes!"

Summer turned around. The calf's thousand-pound mother, crazed with worry in the adjacent paddock, was in mid-leap, snapping the top board as she didn't quite clear the intervening fence, landing with improbable grace, forelegs taking her weight, muscular hind legs following in a seamless transition to a determined charge, no time to get out of the way before her lowered head caught Summer in the ribs and slammed her into the steel frame of the headgate.

She bounced off and fell to her hands and knees, breath knocked out, glad these animals lacked horns. The cow gathered on her haunches for another go, Summer thinking this one must be possessed by her father's ghost, lashing out at her for ruining the land with a bunch of damn cattle. The thought made her angry, angry at the ghost, because she and her uncles went to some trouble to make sure the cattle *didn't* ruin the land. Though she had to admit three dozen artificially inseminated Angus and a hundred-odd seasonal stockers also might not cover the bills, and the taxes, and interest payments on the line of credit that had swollen to an amount inducing 3:00 A.M. panic attacks in Summer and quarterly pronouncements of imminent doom by Uncle Darwin, who kept the books. Running cattle had been her idea, and it did in fact flout a family tradition in place since the seventies, when her father had gotten rid of her grandfather's longhorns, or most of them anyway, and set about restoring the valley's wildlife habitat, turning it into—and this was Summer's gloss, added more recently—a stage on which he could act out his primitivist fantasies. Brother Bowman wouldn't approve of the cattle either, but neither her father nor Bowman had to pay ranch bills, Dad being dead nearly twenty years and Bowman off seeking enlightenment south of the border about that long. So screw them and their judgment.

She managed a half breath and tried to get up off her knees. The calf in the headgate was still bawling, and here came mom again, head down, slobbering, wide-eyed, and Summer thought, *Well, shit,* just as Uncle Jeremy stepped in between like a burly rodeo clown and caught the cow's forehead in his belly, folding over and cursing eloquently as she lifted him off his feet and tossed him to the side, Summer up now, the danger to her uncle triggering adrenaline that hadn't come before. She released the calf from the headgate and dove at the cow trying to stomp on Uncle Jeremy, grabbed both ears and pulled, turning her head in the direction of the calf running out into the pasture, hindquarters kicking up and back with each leap in an exuberant fuck-you to the humans. The cow, seeing this, forgot all about Summer and Jeremy. She trotted after her calf, mooing happily.

The veterinarian had laughed through the entire episode, and for a moment it looked like Uncle Jeremy was going to punch him, but instead he started laughing too. Summer felt like laughing herself, but her ribs hurt too much.

They were finishing up when Uncle Darwin arrived on his four-wheeler. He'd spent last night in Durango—during the winter and summer tourist seasons he cooked three nights a week at a high-end restaurant there. Summer and her uncles had worked jobs off the ranch for years, and it was a challenge to schedule the vet on a day when they could all help. Darwin apologized for being late, said he'd been on the phone with Andrew.

Summer glanced toward the veterinarian, waited until he got in his truck and shut the door and drove east toward the long-sloping left-to-right cut where the road angled up the wall of the valley. He was among the few non-family who knew the way to Panther Gap. Most visitors had to submit to blindfolds.

"They calling the loan?" she asked.

Andrew Coates was a senior V.P. at First Denver Bank & Trust. The family had been making partial payments the last couple of months, and while the bank had informally agreed they could make up the difference when they sold off the stockers in September, this arrangement could be rescinded at any moment.

"Nope."

"A social call?" This from Uncle Jeremy, grinning. Andrew and Summer had dated for over a year before she broke it off last winter.

Darwin ignored his brother. He was acting strangely, even for him.

"He said something from Martin's estate has 'popped up.'"

Her grandfather Martin Girard, née Camboust, a minor robber baron and reputed mob associate, dead since Summer was an infant. First Denver had been co-executor. He'd left some money for the ranch but they'd spent the last of it years ago. He'd also set up a charitable foundation—the management of which was Summer's off-ranch job—but they couldn't tap that for the ranch. Most of his fortune had simply vanished, though a handful of scraps had surfaced over the years—overlooked savings accounts, an insurance policy, stock certificates languishing in a forgotten safe-deposit box, all minor but welcome additions to the ranch checking account.

"Something like what?"

"Wouldn't tell me. He's in town, wants to see you in person. Said to make sure you have your pistol."

She parked her aging 4Runner in a slanted space on Main Street and got out in the afternoon sun, twenty degrees hotter down here than up in Panther Gap. No sign of Andrew's vehicle, but it was seven long hours from Denver, and he wouldn't have driven. Andrew leased a beautiful King Air B300 and didn't need much excuse to fly it. Would've cabbed from the tiny Whitespring airport.

Her reflection floated alongside in plate-glass windows, bootheels thunking on the weathered boardwalk, every second step a concussion firing through her right knee, hip, and into her bruised ribs. She'd swallowed some aspirin but hadn't changed clothes or even washed her face. Inside the Starlight she tucked her sunglasses in a shirt pocket, let her eyes adjust, then, waving at the handful of static human silhouettes at the bar in case she knew any of them, started toward the back. They'd met here on the few occasions she'd invited Andrew to the ranch. The blindfold had never bothered him. He'd just rolled with it as an unsurprising manifestation of her family's paranoia.

He sat in the booth under the inexplicable Rousseau poster—*The Snake Charmer* hanging in an otherwise unpretentious small-town Colorado bar. She'd asked about it years ago and gotten only shrugs.

She tried not to limp, but the first thing he said was, "What happened?"

"Mad mama cow." She slid onto the cracked vinyl bench, holding his gaze while he waited with his eyebrows up. She declined to elaborate. Heard that phrase in her mind: *declined to elaborate.* Keeping her distance, staying wary. This wasn't a date. He got the vibe and didn't press, slid a watery drink in front of her. Another highball glass sat nearly empty at his elbow. Both would be Gentleman Jack on the rocks.

"You're usually on time. I can order another." Andrew was handsome, older than Summer, mysterious about his past. Claimed he'd grown up in Texas and made his "nut" at a hedge fund in New York, gravitated to Denver for the lifestyle two years ago. Bankers' hours, etc., though right now he looked like he hadn't been sleeping much.

"It's fine." She raised the glass and drank a third of it down. Crushed a diminished ice cube with her molars. The whiskey scoured her dry throat and she shuddered, expecting Andrew to comment. She could see better now, and his expression was slightly off, tension around his eyes. Not in a joking mood. Worried and trying to play it down.

"Darwin tell you?"

"He said you're being cryptic."

"Yeah, well. You brought the Glock?"

"I keep it in the truck. What the hell?"

He finished his drink and raised a hand to the bartender, looked a question at Summer. She shook her head. When a waitress made her way to their booth, he ordered a pitcher of water and two glasses. The eight-hour rule didn't seem to apply, exactly, but he'd always been careful about flying under the influence.

She waited. Andrew was too quiet, holding back. He usually fell near the loquacious end of the conversational spectrum. She'd teased him about it, told him he wasn't very Texas, was, in fact, the antithesis of a taciturn cowboy, but he'd said she must not know many Texans. Said lots of people from Texas liked to hear themselves talk.

He took a breath and, in a familiar preamble to the delivery of manly wisdom, leaned forward to drop his thick wrists and muscular forearms on the table, rocking it back on uneven legs, unaware of, or ignoring, the teetering salt and pepper shakers, wire sugar-packet holder, and Summer's whiskey all sliding his way. She reached out and snatched her glass.

"Goddammit, Andrew."

"Sorry." Though clearly he wasn't. "So, what I have is mostly good news. The shareholders got a call from some outfit in Switzerland that's been sitting on a secret account of your grandfather's all this time. There's a meeting at the bank day after tomorrow. We'll confirm your identity and they'll hand over whatever it is."

The family had a long history with First Denver Bank & Trust. Supposedly Martin had helped three young ex-mobsters who wanted to go straight set up the bank back in the day. They still owned it now, must be in their eighties, and over the past ten years they'd extended credit they knew the family couldn't repay without selling the ranch. It might be the whiskey, but a flush of optimism took her. A "secret account" from Grandfather Martin could change everything.

"We don't know how much it is," Andrew said, "and there may be some tax complications. Legal complications." His look turned apologetic, or what passed for apologetic in his repertoire, and she recalled his "mostly" qualifier. "Switzerland wants you and your uncles at the meeting, and they say your brother has to be there too."

"That's ridiculous. You know we haven't heard from him for—"

The pitcher of water arrived. Andrew poured their glasses. Summer waited until the bartender was out of earshot.

"I have his power of attorney."

"I know. Tried that. POA won't cut it. And there's more. The Swiss hired professional security, for your protection. A company based in Dallas. They'll escort you from the airport to the meeting, stand guard, and escort you back. You know the name Jake Salifano."

"Isn't he dead yet?" The man was a former mob enforcer, supposedly an old enemy of her grandfather's, prominent in family lore as a kind of bogeyman. Currently serving a very long sentence at Victorville for shooting two confidential informants back in 1980, which should've been the end of him, but Uncle Jeremy kept track, and apparently Salifano had risen to leadership in one of the prominent prison gangs, had a cultlike following inside and outside the system. He and his gang stood as a primary justification for the secrecy she and her uncles still maintained in Panther Gap.

"Sounds like he's too mean to die. The Dallas security outfit is worried about him, they think he might've found out about this account in Switzerland. He'll think he's entitled to it, and he probably has people looking for you already. You and your brother."

"Nobody knows where my brother is."

She remembered something as she said that, a report from Sarge the caretaker that had seemed merely troubling. More of a watchdog than a caretaker, Sarge lived in a house at the unmarked entrance to the ranch and was charged with misdirecting any would-be visitors. Two men in a Hummer had dropped by a few days ago, looking for Bowman. Said they were friends, knew he lived in the area. Uncle Jeremy ran their license plate at the sheriff's office and came up with an anonymous holding company based in Wyoming.

"You told me you'd found him once. In Mexico?"

"It took months. And we were young, I knew him better then." She decided not to tell Andrew about the guys in the Hummer. "There's no way to find Bowman. Not in two days. What happens when he doesn't show up at the meeting?"

"Don't know. Maybe you get half. Maybe nothing."

She dropped Andrew at the general aviation hangar and headed home, watching the rearview mirror more than usual. Sure enough, a large black truck or SUV appeared behind her on a deserted stretch of Route 26 south of town, staying a consistent half mile away. She reached into the glove compartment for the Glock 19 and confirmed a round was chambered.

The pistol had been a gift from Andrew, when they were dating. For her birthday they'd shot targets together at a range in Denver, Andrew testing her proficiency before he sent her off with the new pistol. At the range it came out that he'd served for several years in the military during his early twenties—possibly, she gathered, in some sort of elite capacity. He'd already admitted to being a gun nut, but she was a ranch girl, of sorts, and had been trained by her father in the use of firearms at an early age, and that had never bothered her.

Her Toyota dropped into a slight dip in the road and she braked hard and pulled off, cursing, backed into a grove of cottonwoods, an old cemetery on a creek grown up with willows. She got out and sheltered behind a cottonwood with the Glock in her hand, feeling ridiculous. The other vehicle never appeared. Must've turned off at a ranch gate, probably someone she knew, mending fence, cleaning out an irrigation ditch.

Hours later, she stood on a granitic outcrop on the east rim of Panther Gap and watched the darkening sky to the north, waiting for Polaris to appear. That had always been the sign, every June, on the eve of the solstice. One year—the final year—the sky had been cloudy, and she and Bowman had had to guess when to light the fire. After a long spell when they'd either fought outright or ignored each other, for that last signal fire ceremony they'd managed a truce. They'd laughed about the clouds. Twenty years ago, exactly.

Bowman used to insist it was impossible to actually see the star appear, and in her little-sister determination to prove him wrong she would stare, knowing she was looking at exactly the right spot, unblinking, eyes stinging in the dry breeze until, every time, her eyes somehow flicked away at the wrong split second and there it was, not quite where she'd expected, a pale pinprick in the grand slate sweep of evening.

No staring tonight. She wasn't any less stubborn, but her adult self lacked the patience. A great horned owl hooted its deep, four-note rhythm off to the west and she turned that way, toward the Red Creek Range standing sharp against the soft light of afterglow. In the foreground, blue dusk pooled in the yawning crucible of Panther Gap. The high-elevation valley was a miraculous relict from the last glacial, an ecologically bountiful island out of phase with the desert and semiarid ranchlands surrounding it. Her grandfather had begun assembling the property in the 1920s and had moved here to escape . . . what? A decadent society? The law? Enemies? According to family lore, Grandfather Martin had hated the valley's Anglo name—Sterrett Hole, after the locally infamous outlaw Paul Sterrett who'd used it as a hideout in the 1840s—and he'd started asking Weenuche acquaintances what they called the place. None would tell him, but eventually he learned that an ancient name for the hidden pass, the only access into the valley, could be translated as "Panther Gap." Martin had liked the way that sounded, and he'd started using it for the whole valley, proper topographical nomenclature be damned.

The owl would call again, but before it did, a dozen cows in the valley lowed in a chorus that rose and fell and abruptly ended.

When she finally turned back toward the north, Polaris was there.

She knelt and tucked her hair into her collar, lifted a carved ironwood ember box to her face. She carried a lighter in her pack, but this ceremony called for older tech. Sliding the lid, she uncovered a lump of tree fungus nested in moss. The ember glowed when she breathed on it, and after a few seconds a thumb-sized torch of bundled juniper twigs and shredded bark flared, crackling quietly as she touched it to the tinder at the base of the tepee of larger branches.

Her right knee faltered when she stood, pain knifing in from the lateral ligament, but it held her weight. She might have to get that looked at. Along with pretty much everything else on the right side of her body.

Blue and yellow flames rose from the kindling, seeking the mass of her signal fire, bright-burning scrub oak branches from a big stack behind the barn. Star and Dove, two of Uncle Jeremy's horses, had helped her carry the wood up here. She'd left them with buckets of sweet feed in the old corral she and Bowman had built out of the wind a couple hundred feet below the ridge. Uncle Darwin, descending from his daily walk to the ridge above the house, had stepped off the trail to allow Summer and the horses to pass. Squinting at the precarious bundles strapped to the packsaddles, he'd asked if she seriously thought this was going to work.

Another round of emphatic lowing from the herd. She hated that it bothered her, just a touch, that it struck the residual idealistic girl inside—Leo's daughter and Bowman's little sister—as inappropriate.

Maybe she ought to ride Dove down there and see what was bothering them. So far the cows had impressed her with their determination to protect the calves from the valley's coyotes, black bears, and occasional mountain lion, but a nervous, nearly superstitious tickle in the back of her mind recalled Bowman's insistence that the valley had once harbored more formidable creatures. Grizzly, wolf, wolverine. And when he was younger, he'd dreamed about a particular jaguar so often he'd decided the cat must have lived in the valley in pre-Columbian times, and the old word translated as "panther" in "Panther Gap" referred not to the mountain lion, as they'd all assumed, but to the jaguar. Southwest Colorado would have lain beyond the extreme northern end of their known historic range, but it wasn't impossible, and Bowman certainly believed el tigre's spirit, at least, still inhabited the place. Looking back, Summer suspected he wanted so badly to see these animals that he might have let his imagination get the better of him.

She shook her head to clear it—so much of her brother in there tonight—and stepped away from the crackling, smoking branches. Six miles to the southeast stood Rosewater Butte, where, eight hundred years ago, Ancestral Puebloan people had cut away the equivalent of ten dump truck loads of sandstone to create a notch, a line of sight from this point to another signal fire on Smokehouse Mesa thirty miles farther out. Beyond that were more sites, a chain leading past Mesa Verde to Chaco and beyond, some said all the way to Paquimé in Chihuahua. And to the west, archaeologists had found a signal fire site on Comb Ridge that would have been visible over hundreds of square miles of what was now southern Utah.

The entire Southwest had been networked with interconnecting signal fire sites, but no one knew what the messages had meant, or what had driven people to go to all that trouble. When they were young, she and Bowman had decided the signal fires provided a means of warning against the occasional eruption of mass psychosis and genocidal violence in the south. Somebody down there near Paquimé keeping an eye on things, sparking the alarm when the Aztecs marched north, wild-eyed priests of war god Xipe Totec wearing the flayed skins of their sacrificial victims and playing on musical rasps made of human bones, slaves carrying racks of skulls mounted on poles. Foot soldiers marching along behind. What the fires said was: *Oh shit, here they come again. Watch your ass.*

She'd learned later, in college, that the fires' messages would have been varied and complex, more often tied to astronomical events of ritual significance, and would have fluctuated over the centuries. But still, she wondered if the hypothetical watcher in the south would have had the good sense to light the fire when the Spaniards finally arrived with their alien doom. Not that it could have helped much. She and her brother had lit their first fire here the day their father told them what had happened to the people who lived in the Americas after Columbus's blind landfall in the Bahamas. Summer and Bowman, ten and twelve at the time, experienced a mild form of vicarious PTSD—these were their maternal ancestors, after all—that they expressed in a wordless agreement to meet at the signal site and light a fire. More than a commemoration, she thought of it now as a confused preadolescent protest, an objection, children shaking their fists and screaming, *No!* at a real-life apocalypse perpetrated by humanity upon humanity five hundred years in the past.

The fire burned hot and bright, driving her farther away, eyebrows and hair singeing and stinking, sweat drizzling down her sides in rivulets. Tendrils of flame reached into the dark sky. Sparks levitated, swooping like fireflies before winking out. There was nothing but rock up here, little to burn for a hundred yards in any direction, but she watched for spot fires. One year, must've been the mid-eighties, a dry wind had surprised them after they lit the fire and she and Bowman had run around stomping out flames that snuck up in tufts of bunchgrass. She'd ridden her pony back to the house to get their father and uncles to come help.

She dozed, then woke with a chill. The waning moon had risen, must be after midnight. She added more wood. The fire bloomed and brightened, a hissing, guttering throat-song in the blue-orange coals at its center. Bowman used to hear a voice in the fire, a booming drum of a voice singing in a language they'd never been able to identify. He'd written down some of the words phonetically and he and Summer had read them to their uncles, to local Weenuche, Navajo and Hopi and Pueblo acquaintances too, but no one recognized any of it.

Summer had never doubted her brother back then.

Goddammit, she thought. *So long ago.* She'd arrived at an age when the acceleration of time made her angry. Eventually, she suspected, she would find it terrifying.

She sat facing away from the fire, close enough for therapeutic warmth on her sore back. Off to the southeast, invisible now, was the notched butte and, beyond that, the next signal site, unlit for centuries. She watched, but no answering fire appeared. Lower, but still far away, a dim glow moved across the plain, headlights creeping along one of the BLM roads. Some rancher from over by Tomwater, taking the long way home.

4

Sam was lost, driving not-quite aimlessly through moonlit desert somewhere north of the Four Corners. Mac had climbed in the backseat with
Melissa, and the two of them were working their way through the apparently bottomless bag of cocaine she said she'd stolen from her ex-boyfriend.
Their manic, inane conversation didn't include Sam. He tried to focus on
the astringent scent of sagebrush blowing through the open window, the
antique country music playing on AM radio. Melissa wanted a ride to
Moab. He didn't know where they were, but they were still a long way
from Moab.

"Walt Whitman," she piped up from the back, apropos of nothing,
"makes me horny as a goat."

Sam peered in the rearview, but it was dark and he couldn't see what
was going on. He and Mac were too old for this sort of thing. He was
drunk and he found the whole scene shabby and amusing.

They'd discovered Melissa in a café at some unpronounceable crossroads in northeast Arizona earlier in the day. She was a nervous sprite in
her mid-twenties with too-blue eyes and slick blond hair to her shoulders. A drive up to Moab had sounded fine. He and Mac were on a kind
of abbreviated walkabout, five days with no particular plans.

Walt Whitman, he remembered, was Mac's pretentious code for cocaine. It had something to do with lines, maybe long lines? Sam had never

thought it was clever, and anyway he'd put the cliché of attorney-on-cocaine behind him when he'd turned thirty. Mac, demonstrably, had not.

He glanced at the fifth of Maker's Mark propped up in the passenger seat, reached for it, had himself a snort. That's how he described it to himself: a snort. It sounded vaguely cowboy, decidedly western. When he drank alone he sometimes entertained himself via self-mocking role-play.

I'm loster'n shit, he thought.

He hadn't said anything about being lost to Mac and Melissa. The skein of secondary and tertiary roads he'd traced with his finger on the atlas back at the Four Corners monument had become irrelevant after six, maybe seven unmarked intersections, and the roads kept getting worse: potholes, washboards, patches of drifted sand where the trusty Subaru—after only a few days he thought of it as trusty—wallowed, hesitated, lurched ahead. He drove with artificial confidence, steering by the only light he'd seen for hours, a flaring yellow and orange beacon suspended on the crest of a ridge off to the northwest. It flickered and danced, waxed and waned, someone stoking a bonfire and lighting up the night. Whenever he had a choice—that is, every time he came to an intersection, where one nondescript dirt road crossed another—he turned toward the light on the mountain. It kept him from driving in circles.

By the clock on the dashboard it was 1:17 in the morning, and the last radio station had faded away. A pair of headlights appeared in the rearview, so far away they nearly merged. Then they vanished. Sam watched but they didn't reappear. It might have been a trick of his mind, or a reflection from inside the car. They hadn't passed another car since nightfall. He drove on, fighting to stay awake. Mac and Melissa jabbered intermittently. In the café, as they were eating BLTs in their booth, Mac had pointed his finger at Melissa slouched alone at the bar sipping coffee, big yellow backpack at her feet. She looked tired and unbathed and beautiful, like a swimsuit model ready to check into detox.

What Mac had said was, "That, my friend, is our destiny."

But Sam had seen this before and he knew she was only Mac's destiny, and only for a while. Mac had found his destiny at least twice in Las Vegas over the weekend. Sam checked the dark rearview mirror again. They'd been quiet for longer than usual. Mac was handsome past a fault, famously smooth, and when he was in pursuit of a new female he tended to become single-minded and inconsiderate of his friends.

The road ahead split into two roughly parallel dirt tracks, two lights on the mountain, four lines of fence posts connected by too many strands of barbed wire to count. Sam shut one eye, which eliminated the double vision but made him sleepy. After he dozed off a second time, he gave up and pulled onto a flat patch of dirt and gravel next to the road, declaring they would spend the night here.

Mac and Melissa set up the tent while Sam gathered a few sticks of dead sagebrush, some paper trash from the car. Melissa wanted to lock her heavy yellow backpack in the Subaru and wouldn't let him do it for her, so Sam handed her the keys. They tried to maintain a conversation, Melissa asking where were the tall trees, where was the babbling brook.

He constructed his campfire, willing unsteady hands to cooperate, but before he could light it, a gust of wind lifted the paper tinder and scattered his broken sticks across the dirt road and into the brush on the far side. Probably best. He didn't want to spark a wildfire. He raised his headlamp and started to apologize to Melissa, but Mac had her up against the car with her shirt unbuttoned, his mouth on her neck. Her bra was long gone, and she had one hand in Mac's short black hair.

Sam carried his pack and sleeping bag into the sagebrush, looking for a place to sleep. He pinched off some leaves and held them to his nose, rolled them back and forth between his thumb and forefinger. A heady scent, sharp up close. He pushed through the stiff branches, remembering a friend's story about a backpacking trip in southern Idaho that had been cut short when they'd found the area populated by small aggressive rattlesnakes that climbed up in the tall sagebrush to wait like miniature mambas, rattling and striking at hikers as they passed. The friend, an experienced outdoorsman, made the point that being surprised by a thin papery sizzle at waist level was qualitatively different from hearing the same thing at your feet.

Sam's headlamp cast a glow barely brighter than the moonlight. He held his hands out in front of his face and tried to focus on his ghostly white palms.

At the fence, he stood and stared for a moment, stymied, then turned and walked alongside until he found a small meadow of sparse bunch-grass. He unrolled his backpacking mattress and spread out his sleeping bag.

The night air was calm, and from his makeshift camp he could hear Mac and Melissa screwing noisily in the tent, at one point setting a family of coyotes to howling up on the ridge. He sat up and drank the rest of the bourbon, staring at the quarter moon that dimmed and brightened as silvery mackerel clouds blew across the sky. He sang every one of the seven or eight songs he knew by heart.

After he'd finished the bottle, Mac and Melissa were still going at it. Must be the cocaine.

Sam stood up with a handful of pebbles and started winging them at the tent, which was about a hundred feet away, a light blue blob unsteady in the moonlight. He'd always had a good arm and the first two stones clattered into the road, but his third toss sounded like it hit a hubcap on the rental, and the fourth went *swat* into the side of the tent. Melissa squealed, and Mac spoke up.

"Stop throwing rocks, fucker."

He hurled another one that pinged off the roof of the car. He held his fist over his head, stumbling a little. "*The arm of Zeus*," he growled.

"Don't make me come out there."

Sam answered with a wolf howl and jogged once around his sleeping bag. That made him dizzy and he sat down on the bag, hoping he wasn't in for a night of the bed-spins. The coyotes answered him, yipping and yowl-ing, sounding now like they were being beaten, now as if the moonlight had driven them mad with ecstasy. He could pick out four, maybe five in-dividual voices. Some sounded like pups. He decided he liked coyotes. On the ground beside him he found the bourbon bottle. He lifted it, toasting the moon, the coyotes, the desert at large, then tipped it back for the last drops tingling on his tongue. Finished, he held the bottle at arm's length and let it slip from his fingers. It fell back to earth with a hollow *chink*.

Hunh, he thought. *Gravity*.

The coyotes quit singing. Crickets chirped nearby, and for the first time he noticed the wind's sad moan way up in the cliffs on the mountain. He searched the ridge for the light that had led him here, but it was gone.

Then Mac and Melissa started up again. Godalmighty. He remembered his earplugs and, using the headlamp, fished around for the Dopp kit in his pack. He rolled the orange foam into slender cylinders and shoved them in his ear canals, lay back in the expanding silence, the moon bright overhead and moving magisterially across the sky.

Three subadult coyotes arrived at the fence, attracted by the strange sounds coming from the humans. No one ever camped in this area, and the coyotes' fear of roadside shooters had given way to curiosity. They could easily leap over the fence or dig and wriggle underneath the bottom wire, but they stood on the far side and watched Sam, inert in his sleeping bag. Mac and Melissa inside the tent were quiet by then as well. One of the coyotes lay down and rested her chin on her front paws.

Eventually a vehicle approached on the road. It was loud, the muffler rusted out, and the driver slowed and cut the headlights a quarter mile away. The coyotes waited, holding very still.

A tan Ford Explorer with New Mexico plates coasted to a stop behind Sam and Mac's rented Outback. Two men got out and approached the tent, one carrying a small flashlight. He unzipped the door of the tent and lit up Mac and Melissa, both nude and trying to cover themselves with Mac's sleeping bag, squinting at the light, Mac promising to kick Sam's bourbon-drunk ass.

The man with the light said he had a gun and Mac stopped talking. When the man asked where their friend was, Mac said he didn't know, that he'd walked off toward that mountain to camp by himself.

The man told them to lie on their stomachs and put their hands behind their backs. While he held the light, the other man bound their wrists with zip ties, Mac's first, then a strip of duct tape over his mouth, wrapped around his head. He bound Melissa's wrists and began pawing at her butt, speaking to the other man about what it was going to be like when they fucked the skinny woman. She kicked at the man and turned and spat and when Mac got up on his knees the man in the tent hit him with a short punch to his right kidney and he fell flat again. There was some laughter. The man duct-taped Melissa's mouth and crawled out of the tent with an armful of discarded clothing. He stood with the other man, rifling pockets.

While the second man walked over to the Subaru with the keys, the first man stepped to the edge of the gravel and made a perfunctory search for Sam with his flashlight, but he was unwilling to walk into the thick sagebrush. Then he returned to the tent and peered in. Mac and Melissa were sitting up and she was leaning against him. Naked and bound, they made themselves as small as possible, knees drawn up, heads bowed. The man asked where the package was, a rhetorical question, as his captives were unable to reply, but Mac's eyes widened and he looked sharply at Melissa, who closed her own eyes in response. The other man called out from the Subaru that he'd found it locked inside, and that it was very heavy. The two inspected Melissa's backpack with the flashlight, both of them laughing and exclaiming. The second man carried it to the Explorer.

When he came back he entered the tent again, lit by the first man's flashlight, and forced Mac into a kneeling position, facing away. He drew a small semiautomatic pistol from the pocket of his jacket and held it against Mac's head, behind his right ear. Melissa had worked with her tongue to loosen the duct tape, and when she screamed the volume and pitch were startling, and the three coyotes waiting beyond the fence all answered at once with delighted yips and howls. As if this were why they'd come, what they'd been waiting for. They were even louder than Melissa, and they sounded like they were standing just outside the tent. The man with the gun left Mac and Melissa and stood beside the man with the light. They tried to find the coyotes in the sagebrush, but they were invisible as banshee spirits, and they didn't stop, and after a moment the men spoke with their heads close together.

Sam heard the coyotes too, a distant clamor through his earplugs, and this triggered a dream in which he watched a wolf pack running through a snowy moonlit forest. He turned in his sleep and slung his forearm over his eyes to block the moon.

The second man put the pistol back into his pocket. He told Mac and Melissa to get out of the tent. He gathered the clothes he'd dropped in the gravel but smiled again at their nakedness, especially Melissa's, and at their hands still bound behind their backs. The men followed the naked couple as they limped barefoot across the gravel to the Explorer. The rear cargo door opened and the interior light came on, and after a wide-eyed moment of hesitation, Mac nodded and Melissa sat her bare bottom on the edge and wriggled backward into the plastic-floored space, Mac waiting until she was out of the way before doing the same thing. The men watched, not helping, looking pleased with themselves. They tossed the clothes in, and the man with the light shut the door and went back to the Subaru and started the engine, pulled around, and drove back the way they had come, the Explorer following.

The coyotes sang until the vehicles were too far away to hear.

5

1984

Leo built the crate from quarter-inch plywood and chicken wire, feeling almost as if he were making a coffin. But that was ridiculous—the eagle would be fine—and he was only burying his own hopes of flying her. He would trap another young eagle in the fall, but Alecto was special.

As he'd feared, when he'd forced her off of Bowman in the wolfskin, he had offended her so deeply she would become enraged and physically violent every time she saw him. For a while he had to let her bate to exhaustion before he could hood her, a completely untenable situation that drove Leo into dark psychological territory.

It was Bowman who'd provided a partial solution to the Alecto problem. As soon as he'd recovered from his chest punctures, Bowman, with Summer's help, took up the eagle's care and training with enthusiasm. It was remarkable that not only did Bowman not fear Alecto, the experience seemed to have affected the eagle as well, creating a strong bond between the two.

Still, living on the same property with an eagle who wanted very badly to kill him was not ideal for Leo, and over the past months he'd tried everything he could think of to ease her enmity. Finally last week he'd consulted with an eagle falconer he'd found

in Montana, and the man insisted the only sane course was to release her somewhere far away.

Bowman had been even quieter than usual after Leo had told
him the plan, so when he opened the door to Alecto's stall in the
barn, he wasn't surprised to see the boy standing there. A little
surprising was Summer, standing there too, the children flanking
Alecto on her perch.

Thankfully, they hadn't removed her hood.

"Et tu, Summer?"

She didn't respond. She folded her arms against her chest, imitating her brother.

Alecto fluffed her neck feathers in irritation at the sound of Leo's
voice.

"You can't take her," Bowman said.

Leo told him the eagle would be more happy in Montana. Free.
She would find a mate and raise generations of healthy young eagles. One might fly down to Colorado someday and they would
catch her and hunt with her. He said he would take Bowman up to
visit her territory, the best, most remote eagle habitat in the lower
forty-eight.

Bowman was quiet for a moment, considering this information,
Summer and Leo both watching him.

"Not yet," he said.

Leo decided he couldn't force this. Keeping Alecto would be
difficult, even dangerous. But it made him proud that Bowman—
and Summer—felt so strong a connection to her that they were
willing to stand up to him.

"She'll be your responsibility."

"I'll help."

Summer, he saw, addressed her brother, a promise of support to
him rather than a promise to Leo intended to bolster their case. It was
a subtle difference, but it pleased him. After their mother died and
their uncles left the ranch, he had had some difficulty placing these
two into healthy social interactions, just as his own father had when
Leo himself was a boy on this ranch. Martin had eventually solved
the problem by sending Leo off to boarding school. If Summer and

Bowman remained this close and mutually supportive, Leo hoped he would be able to avoid doing the same.

"I'll save the crate," he said. "We'll need to let her go eventually, and unless she changes her mind about me, we'll have to take her far away."

Bowman's shoulders relaxed a little.

"You should fly her now. Down in the valley. Take the fox lure. Give me time to get back to the house."

Bowman didn't bring Alecto into the valley. He carried her on the T-stick up the ridge behind the house, Summer helping when she could. The eagle was hard to hold up for long and they had to stop and rest several times on the way up.

"Why fly her up here? Dad said to take her down to the valley."

"We're going to see if she wants to stay with us."

"But if she gets away, she'll try to kill Dad."

They both worried about their father. Bowman knew this was probably normal. Their father was all they had.

"If she decides to leave, I don't think she'll stay around. She'd go off exploring."

He stood on a rock for height and held the leather tab on top of the eagle's hood in his teeth, both hands supporting the post of the T-stick. When he reared his head back, it was like uncovering a bright bulb, the eagle's attention—her presence—charging the air. She looked back at Bowman, holding his gaze for a moment, then a glance over her left shoulder at Summer before her wings opened, flapped once as she dropped off her perch, dipped close to the ground, and was over the lip of the nearly vertical rock face to the east, turning into the wind and lifting, rising, carried up overhead, not deigning to flap her great wings again, still and fixed as a kite but—Bowman felt this as an otherworldly tingle and shift in his own phantom wings—the living mobile sheath of feathers covering her body executing hundreds of tiny adjustments every second. A thousand feet overhead, her mind filled with details—what she saw, what she felt in the invisible medium of air—alien impressions trickling into Bowman's consciousness as he opened up to her.

"Can I swing the lure?" Summer's voice was distant.

"Wait a minute," he said.

There was something he needed to see. Far below, two upright figures, primates, humans, walking side by side on the long driveway in their impossibly slow, plodding way.

Summer managed thirty seconds of the minute.

"What is it?" she asked.

He released his connection and fell from the sky. The stones and bent stunted junipers trained eastward by centuries of prevailing wind from the Red Creeks—his skinny, wild, incorrigible little sister standing there beside him—all of it so close as to be nearly claustrophobic.

Looking at Summer, he grinned. This was good news.

"Our uncles are back."

6

Bowman couldn't speak.

He could purse his lips, sort of. Open and close his mouth. He could hum. His legs and arms moved. The nurse nodded and told him in Spanish the doctor thought it would wear off before long. It was the venom from the snake, she said. She brought him a pad and pen and he started to write in Spanish but caught himself, wrote: *What day is it?*

The nurse looked at the pad and frowned. *"¿No hablas español?"*

Bowman shook his head. Ignorant tourist. The nurse left the room. He dozed, and dreamed he and Summer flew hang gliders near the ocean, though he had never done such a thing in his life. As they soared out over the water, Summer said everything was going to be okay, and when he asked what she meant, she told him when they die they're going to turn into eagles. They flew back from the open ocean and landed in East Canyon at the ranch, where the cliff dwellings were filled with dusty old books no one had read in a long time. He opened one at random and read a passage: *I have been to the edge of the world, and I looked across to the other side, and there is nothing there.* This woke him up.

Same hospital room. Dim fluorescent lighting, no windows. Old-fashioned privacy screens made of fabric on either side. No idea how much time had passed, but he felt better. All these dreams, though, like the residual sea snake venom was holding open a portal to ciguatera city.

When he raised himself up on his elbows an IV shunt bit into his left forearm. Past the foot of his bed was an open door leading out to a brighter hallway.

He gave his voice a go. "Hello?" Hoarse and weak, pitiful. Tried again. A different nurse appeared, then went away as quickly. Someone in the hallway said something about the American, and after a moment a woman in street clothes came in, not smiling, followed by the nurse. She crowded the bedside and leaned over him, darkly curious. She was heavyset and looked like she would be a pleasant sort of person in a better mood. She said her name was Luisa, asked in English if she could help him.

He struggled to make his words. "I need to know what day it is, the date, June . . . ?"

"Twenty-one."

The solstice already.

"I need to leave," he said.

Her look darkened even further, she didn't like that idea at all. "You aren't well enough. And you have to pay."

He asked where his bag was, a small bag with a strap. She turned and told the nurse, *He wants his bag, the one with no money in it.*

The nurse reached under the table next to his bed, produced Bowman's dry bag. He unrolled the top. His passport was inside, the cover and pages warped and wrinkled from multiple saltwater intrusions over the years despite the supposedly waterproof case Summer had given him, but Luisa was right, no cash. They'd already checked, of course. He'd ended up in a private hospital, and Luisa must be an administrator of some sort. She didn't like him because she'd seen indigent broke dirtbag tourists before, people from wealthy countries who expected health care and then claimed they had no money.

A doctor walked into the room then, a woman, and Luisa translated her summary of his case. He had lost consciousness and almost stopped breathing. The oxygen they'd given him in the Puerto Jiménez clinic had saved him. By the time he got here, there was no point in administering antivenom, and they couldn't confirm the species of snake anyway. She said not many people react like that to sea snake venom.

Bowman showed no comprehension when the doctor spoke, waiting for the translation of each sentence. He wanted the staff to speak freely around him. There might be some things he should know, things they wouldn't tell him.

He explained about the ciguatera poisoning, and as Luisa translated, the doctor's face lit up, a puzzle solved. He said he'd been getting better. He was used to these spells, and he could function. Again he insisted he had to leave right away. Luisa told the doctor, *He wants to leave.* The doctor said, *The snakebite might make his ciguatera symptoms worse, at least for a while. He needs another day in bed. Maybe he has family with money? Maybe,* Luisa said. *He doesn't look like it.*

When the women left, Bowman opened his dry bag. *This is how you know you're crazy,* he thought. Looked inside again anyway. Passport still there, money still not. Every caretaker in his chain of custody must have looked in his bag, and while at least some of them had taken money, every single one had seen the passport and left it there, and had gone to some trouble to make sure the bag stayed with him. He had no idea how much money had been in that roll, or whether he'd overpaid for his rescue. Probably not. He remembered surfing his kayak to the Aussies' camp, then he was in and out of consciousness on a long, jarring boat ride to Puerto Jiménez. He didn't remember the clinic there, or the lifesaving oxygen. Now that he was concentrating, he did recall asking someone to get him on the plane to San José, and telling them he had money in his bag. A noisy aircraft after that. An ambulance to the hospital.

Summer would be pleased when he told her she'd saved his life with that ridiculous wad of cash. She'd given it to him six—seven?—years ago. He'd been convalescing in a town clinic in the Sierra Madre of Chihuahua. That was the last time he'd spent any time in a medical facility, albeit one much smaller than this one. He'd been shot in the chest. A dark time of threats and violence. The local police had insisted a family member collect him.

He opened his passport case to the plastic window in the back, where Summer had tucked the photo of the two of them at the ranch. Happier times. The photo had struck him as unusually sentimental. As if he would be more inclined to come home if he saw this image of the two of them at the end of their idyllic childhood. Not like Summer at all.

But it might be in there for another reason completely. For the first time, he tried to pull the photo from the sleeve, but it stuck to the clear plastic. He peeled it away, trying not to damage the image, turned it over.

ABA number, international routing number, account number, First Denver Bank & Trust. "Password is our real name."

That was the Summer he remembered.

Luisa brightened at the mention of a bank account. She brought a phone and a laptop and they determined the account was held jointly with his sister. Summer had told him Uncle Darwin had set up an "education fund" for each of them with a life insurance payout after their father's death. She'd spent hers but his was sitting there in the bank, and she'd threatened to steal it and spend it on the ranch if he didn't come home. He knew she was mostly kidding but he'd told her that was exactly what he wanted, to please take it and use it to help out. She'd brought papers for him to sign giving her power of attorney, which meant—so she claimed—that she'd be able to rob him blind, but judging from the account records Luisa pulled up, Summer had been bluffing. There'd been no withdrawals for years, though interest had gradually accumulated, compounding, and the account held just over a hundred thousand dollars.

The balance seemed large to Bowman, but his entire adult life he'd lived on barter, foraging, and the small amounts of local cash he earned, and he had no frame of reference. Luisa was impressed enough that she became more polite, slightly formal, and the transformed social dynamic made him sad. He was another rich gringo after all. They arranged for a wire to the hospital's account to cover his bill plus eight grand to get him home. It sounded like a lot, but Luisa talked him into it. She also pointed out that as co-owner, his sister would be alerted to the transaction. Bowman hadn't thought of that. He didn't mind Summer knowing, but he hoped no one else was watching the account.

A courier accompanied by a bored, unarmed guard brought the cash from the hospital's bank up the street, a couple thousand dollars' worth of Costa Rican colones and the rest in U.S. hundreds. Luisa dressed him in scrubs and paper slippers and released him before the doctor could find out and object. Outside it was morning, a busy noisy smelly city street. He hadn't visited a city of this size in years, and for a moment he nearly panicked. He stood frozen, people walking around him, staring at the tall skinny man dressed like a doctor. He was too conspicuous, and intensely conscious of the packet of legal tender in the dry bag strapped under his shirt. He picked a direction and started walking.

7

Sam woke to a hot morning, almost nine-thirty by his watch. He pulled the earplugs and stood, blinking in the light, his whole body vibrating unpleasantly. No morning birdsong. A warm nervous wind hissing in the sagebrush. The trusty Subaru had disappeared but the tent was still set up in the flat spot next to the road. He carried his things through the brush to the roadside, crawled in through the tent's mosquito-netting door, and sat on the thin foam mattress. Inside it stank of sweat and sex.

He kicked Mac's tangled blue sleeping bag into the gravel and lay back, glad to be out of the sun. His head, though. Someone drilling into his right temple. Closing his eyes only made it worse, so he stared up at the glowing baby-blue nylon dome. Leaving him here was probably Mac's revenge for the rock-throwing last night. He would show up eventually with a lukewarm extra-large coffee and a bag of greasy fry bread. Melissa may or may not still be attached. Sam and Mac were an unlikely pair, functioning as temperamental bookends for their group of friends from law school, but they had spent a lot of time together in the past year. They were both single—Sam newly so—and they both worked in D.C., where Mac was a trial lawyer at an insurance defense firm. Unlike Sam, he hadn't married, had never even seemed tempted.

Sam woke again at eleven, the tent a blue-fired kiln. He crawled into the open air, snatched his hands away from the sun-hot gravel, and got himself up on his hind legs, feeling pretty much as he had before his nap. All alone in a too-bright scorched landscape. No Subaru, no Mac or Melissa.

He repacked his daypack and struck off on his own, following the dirt road northward through the desert. Still angry, still hungover, he walked at a pace he hoped would sweat the alcohol from his body. He drank his first liter of water too fast and up it came, pale thin bourbon-stink puke in the ditch beside the road. He hadn't even made a mile.

Chastened, he sipped from the second liter. He swore off whiskey forever. Given the geometry of the Four Corners, this had to be either Colorado or Utah, but he wasn't sure which. A mile or so to the west, the mountain rose up like a wall. He scanned the ridges and canyons, hoping for an RV or a pickup truck, or the line of a road cut into the slope that would lead to whoever had built the bonfire he'd seen up there last night. He would hike in and bum a ride to the closest town. Then he could rent another car and finish the week traveling by himself.

He drank the last of his water just after one, noting the time because it seemed like a fact that could become important. The sun bore down. He probably should have left a note for Mac at the tent.

A half hour later, he stopped in a sandy dip in the road. Water had flowed here, but not for a long time. His petulance spent, he took out his cell phone to call Mac—the firm provided him with a so-called smart-phone but he refused to bring it on vacation—and shaded the little screen with his body so he could see, but of course there was no signal here. He turned it off to save the battery.

The hot breeze sliding off the mountain felt like a blow-dryer, the back of his neck hot with sunburn. He imagined himself desiccating, venting moisture with each breath. His eyes stung and he pushed his sunglasses tighter against his face to block the wind. A quick inventory: he wore light canvas shorts, a short-sleeved cotton shirt, new socks, and good leather hiking boots. Besides the two now-empty liter water bot-tles, in his pack he carried a couple of protein bars, his phone, wallet, nylon Dopp kit, matches, sunscreen, a clean T-shirt, a change of socks and boxers, a light rain shell, and a fleece sweater.

The road ahead ran relentlessly flat and straight northward, its sides converging on a classic vanishing point in the heat-shimmer distance. To his right, the dry plain stretched away to the eastern horizon, broken by a single orange butte some miles away, huge and squat in the flat hot light. There were no cattle, no houses, no telephone poles. On his left, the wash snaked through sage-covered flats that rose from the foreground to a wall of sheer rock, split by a canyon with umber sandstone cliffs disappearing in shadow. Lower in the canyon, a patch of sunlit green glowed among the dry reds of rock and earth, the dusty sage. It looked like a small cotton-wood tree, which might mean the stream was flowing there. Should at least be a seep, or wet sand he could dig in. He could use his shirt to strain the water.

He stood in the road and tried to think clearly. The sun was sapping him out here in the open. If he turned around now it would take him three hours to walk back to the tent. Three more hours walking in this sun, with no water? On the other hand, he could easily walk up the dry wash to that canyon. He felt it pulling him, an uncanny sensation he attributed to the heat. Even if the creek was dry, there would be shade. He could rest until it cooled off this evening.

At the fence, a metal POSTED sign confronted him. The sign was unambiguous, but wasn't necessity a defense to trespass? Grinning at his own recklessness, he climbed over and started up the wash.

The sand and loose gravel was frustrating stuff to walk in, and be-fore long his stride deteriorated into a miserable shuffle. After an hour, the mountain didn't appear to be any nearer. He walked on even though he knew he'd made a mistake. Eventually, he slowed to a stop. The walls of the wash were higher here and closer together, kind of a trench, so that his view of the desert was ground-level, looking up at sparse bushes and thorny scrubby trees and cacti. The hot blue sky. No vultures cir-cling him, not yet. This perspective, it was like he'd been buried up to his neck. He remembered a scene in a movie he liked, a guy buried that way, as a form of torture. He couldn't remember what happened, or the name of the movie, which was unlike him. He stood puzzling over this longer than he should have, given the situation.

What, exactly, was he doing here? When cajoling Mac into giving up a week of golf and singles bars in Las Vegas for a random camping trip across the desert, he'd been unable to describe what exactly he was after, saying he hoped that if he got himself back out into the wide-open West he remembered from camping trips with his family when he was a kid, then something real would happen to him. Mac had rolled his eyes but it was the best he could come up with.

Was this what he'd imagined?

A tingling in his neck and along the backs of his arms. Not cold, obviously. Maybe a symptom of heatstroke? No, someone was watching him.

Ahead, upstream, a pair of curious amber eyes. They blinked, suspended in the air. Then a twitch of an ear, and a coyote face materialized around the eyes, then the rest of her, exactly the color of the stone and sand. He knew the animal was female, without knowing how he knew. She was small, slender but healthy-looking, standing about thirty feet away. Her tail hung down behind her, richly furred and lively, a luxurious thing that twitched and curled while he watched. She seemed proud of it. She lowered her head, not losing eye contact, then turned in a fluid motion and levitated to the rim of the wash and trotted away.

She might be one of the coyotes he'd listened to last night. The notion gave him renewed energy, a feeling he was not alone, that he'd made a connection. Maybe Coyote was his power animal. The Trickster. He walked on. Time passed. He didn't stop again, and when he finally reached the mouth of the canyon, the small cottonwood at the base of the cliff turned out to be a grove of ancients, and blocks of stone he'd assumed were modest boulders towered several stories high.

He moved his hands over the cottonwoods' deeply corrugated bark, listening to the liquid sound of leaves quivering in a light breeze. The wash, though, was as waterless here as it had been out on the plain, and when he urinated at the base of a tree his piss was the concentrated dark yellow of dehydration. His head throbbed. The pack had chafed his shoulders. He set it on the ground and tried to dig with a flat stone in the creek bed. After a foot of dry sand, he hit packed gravel, and for the first time today he felt a little clench of panic in his guts.

Stay calm, he thought. *There'll be water in the canyon.* He listened, hoping for the sound of splashing, trickling, the buzz of insects attracted to wetness. He sniffed for water on the warm stony breeze. There was something, a presence, perhaps of water. An attraction. He shouldered his pack and allowed himself to be drawn shambling into the canyon.

The antler nearly tripped him. It lay in the loose sand of the wash as if it had recently fallen there, a startling object that looked like a curved ivory ladder with one side-rail missing. He squatted and reached out to touch it, afraid it was a hallucination, which would tell him he was in more danger than he'd thought. But it was solid, and he lifted it. An elk antler, lighter than it looked. He glanced around to see where the thing might have come from, and there, forty feet up the far canyon wall, was its twin, still attached to the skull, which hung askew from a loop of rusted cable bolted to the rock. Below the skull was an arched opening in the native stone. To the right, another ledge, a course of masonry, then more, parts of an old wall, then all at once a small village materialized, built on several levels of ledge and running maybe three hundred feet left to right—cliff dwellings and granaries cleverly concealed in the nooks and shadows of the cliff face. The genius of it stunned him. You could walk through this canyon ten times and never notice anyone had ever lived here.

He backed to the opposite wall, scrambled up on the broken boulders at its base for a better look. Back in the shaded gloom of the shallow grotto, underneath the skull, he could make out the weathered planks of a massive wooden door.

A door leading into a cliff? The place had felt desolate, but now he studied the narrow canyon with new eyes, squinting at shadows where someone might be lurking, watching him. He was trespassing, after all.

He staggered along the base of the cliff, looking for a way up, but the stone was unclimbable, so smooth it had to have been polished. Voices were whispering, the wind again. A dizzy spell hit him and he sank backward into the branches of a green willow. Far above, blue sky and a crescent of red sandstone bright in the sun faded away.

When he came to, the breeze was stronger, cool air from higher in the canyon. He felt better, still woozy but no longer panicked, his consciousness expanding, recovering from the brute effort to survive that had consumed him throughout the afternoon. The effect was disconcerting. Was he a tax lawyer on vacation, or was he a hunter-gatherer waking up from a dream of America? He mulled over his dreamed self, Sam Hay, discontented Of Counsel at the upper-second-tier Stratton Weyland LLP, his divorce recently final. Chafing for a change, he'd listed his small house on a pleasant, wooded lot in an expensive Alexandria neighborhood at 20 percent above market. He lived with two spoiled SPCA cats his ex-wife had dropped off in January.

His butt was cool, moist. He was sitting in a seep. He turned and pawed at the coarse sand, which smelled of algae. Bare hands weren't doing much; he needed something to dig with.

The antler's tines gouged furrows in the sand—a moose antler would have worked better as a shovel. He loosened sand with the antler, scooped it out with his hands, then plowed with the antler again. After a while he straightened, his back sore. The hole he'd dug was about a foot deep in damp sand, but no muddy water was collecting in the bottom. He would have to hike back out to the road. The air was cooler now, but he wasn't sure he could make it. When he checked his watch it was blank, the digits gone. He rapped it with his knuckle, pushed a few buttons to no effect. He wished he had a fancy steel dive watch like Mac's. It didn't need a battery, as Mac often pointed out.

He turned and leaned backward, stretching his lower back. The wind blew sand into his face and he covered his eyes. When he pulled his hand away, a woman stood in the arched grotto, looking down at him. He shut his eyes, but she was still there when he opened them, the toes of her boots poking over the edge.

8

Summer called the San Jose bank as soon as Uncle Darwin told her about the wire from her joint account with Bowman. Then she reached out to Hospital Biblica Clinica, eventually speaking to the comptroller several hours after her brother had walked out the front door. He was sick. He'd been bitten by a sea snake. More surprising, he was planning to fly to Colorado. He must have somehow found out about the inheritance, though it was a stretch to imagine Bowman suddenly cared about money. Maybe, as Darwin had suggested, deadpan: her signal fire had worked.

Her uncles were acting cagey. Darwin, skeptical as usual, pointed out there might not be much balance remaining in an account left unsupervised offshore for thirty-five years, decades of fees and depredations, the inevitable thousand cuts inflicted by a succession of anonymous, sticky-fingered managers. And Jeremy naturally worried about the implications for family security. The mention of Salifano had put him on edge.

A stack of foundation paperwork waited for her in the office, two dozen funding applications from charities and landowners in Colorado, New Mexico, a few in Wyoming, but she was too distracted to work. Bruises were appearing on her thigh, hip, ribs from where she'd connected with the headgate yesterday, and she told herself sitting at her desk was the worst thing she could do. Instead, she ate some more aspirin and rode Dove down into the valley, where she helped Jeremy and his dog move two groups of steers to fresh grass.

Still avoiding the office in the afternoon, she walked the long dark steps through Grandfather's tunnels down to the AP village in East Canyon. She always spent time here on the summer and winter solstices, and with Bowman on his way home she'd decided it would be a good place to prepare herself to see him for the first time in, how long had it been? *Seven years,* she thought. He'd been shot, in Mexico. She'd flown down to collect him from the hospital.

So when she opened the door and stepped to the edge of the alcove and saw a long-backed, slender man scraping in the wash with an elk antler, for an awful moment she thought it was her brother, and that something was terribly wrong with him.

But it wasn't Bowman.

The man noticed her, stood there gaping like he didn't think she was real. She shouted over the gusts blowing downcanyon.

"What are you doing here!"

He took a step, unsteady on his feet, and tried to reply but failed to make a sound she could hear. He cleared his throat. "Hello," he called out. He waited for a moment, as if he expected her to disappear. When she didn't, he looked down at the antler in his hands. "I found this in the sand. I was digging for water." He ventured a painful-looking smile.

"Where did you come from?" She and her uncles had opened up parts of the property to the Weenuche, but the appearance of a stranger in this canyon was more than unusual—she was reasonably sure it hadn't happened in her lifetime. "How did you find this place?"

"We camped beside the road last night. We were lost. This morning my friend ran off with his new girlfriend and stranded me. I was walking on the road when I saw the cottonwoods at the mouth of the canyon." He walked closer, until he stood directly beneath her, twenty-five feet down. "I was looking for water."

She carried a water bottle, something she wasn't about to mention, though he was obviously dehydrated, his lips dry and cracked and inhibiting his facial expressions. His hiking clothes were dusty and sweat-stained and clashing with his primitive digging tool. Like a refugee of some sort, a bummed-out granola recreationist from Durango, fleeing the apocalypse.

Wild speculations sprouted in the paranoid corners of her brain. The man's timing was certainly suspicious. Could he have anything to do with the inheritance from her grandfather? Had he been sent by the sinister Jake Salifano? Or was he undercover law enforcement? Maybe an IRS agent looking to infiltrate the Girard compound?

She let the delusions pass without engaging them, and the reflexive Girard paranoia eventually subsided into something more rational. That one about the IRS agent made her smile, but the man didn't see. He was gesturing upcanyon, wearily, his arms heavy, shoulders slumping.

"I thought someone might live up here," he said. "I saw a light last night, on the mountain, a big bonfire. You could see it from a long way off. It's what led me here."

"What do you mean, it led you here?"

She spoke sharply, and the man frowned, wondering what he'd said.

"It's just, when I was lost, and driving around on those dirt roads, I kept turning toward the fire. Otherwise, I would've—" his voice faltered, like he'd run out of energy. He apologized for trespassing, and turned to walk back the way he'd come.

"Wait," she said.

She was safe here, felt the invulnerability the builders of this settlement had intended, and she had to consider the possibility that this man could be a physical threat, a violent criminal, maybe mentally unstable. But he didn't look dangerous. His face was lean but kind, his eyes amused even in his current condition. He spoke with a hint of a southern accent.

A thick hemp rope, knotted at three-foot intervals, was attached to the back wall of the alcove and coiled at her feet, what she used to climb down into the canyon and back.

His comment about her signal fire was powerfully intriguing, and she didn't want him to leave before she had a chance to better understand the person she'd lured.

She was curious, which probably made her reckless.

She squatted on her heels and tossed down the rope.

"Do you think you can climb up here? This was a late settlement and the APs used wooden ladders they could pull up behind them. They didn't cut steps into the cliffs because they were afraid of cannibals."

The man rested the antler across his upper chest like a yoke, the middle tines on either shoulder, and began climbing. The cliff was nearly vertical, and he must've been a Boy Scout or something because he knew to lean back and walk his feet up the face. Still, he was weak, and by the time he reached her he was out of breath, his expression frantic, and she grabbed his arm with both hands and hauled him up and away from the edge, catching the antler as it slid from his shoulders.

She backed up a step, holding the antler with the tines pointed out, settling her weight evenly on her feet, lowering into a slight crouch, adrenaline erasing the pain in her knee and ribs. *Gut check,* she thought. The very real risk she was taking sank in, and she watched the man for any sign of aggression. If she kept her center of gravity low, she could push him back off the ledge. The antler would be useful.

But the man dropped to his hands and knees, exhausted. He wore a small backpack. After a moment he lifted his head, sat back on his haunches. The look he gave her was open, grateful.

"That was close," he said, trying to shape his chapped lips into a grin.

She leaned the antler against the back wall, next to the big eyebolt attaching the rope to the rock.

"That elk skull has been hanging down here as long as I can remember, probably my father's doing, though he never said why." As she spoke, she reached into her jacket and brought out her steel water bottle. He took it, thanking her, unscrewing the top.

"I'm Sam Hay." He tipped back the bottle and drank.

"Summer Girard," she said. She hauled up the heavy rope and laid it back down in coils on the floor of the alcove. When he tried to return the bottle she told him to go ahead and finish it.

She pulled open the thick door, silent on its hinges, ponderous like the door of a safe, to reveal a rock-walled landing and a flight of stone steps. "You should come up. We'll get some more water."

He stepped inside. Turning to her, he said, "This is awfully strange."

"I suppose it is." The body of the door was steel, and he helped her pull it shut. She relocked the deadbolt and dropped two steel crossbars into brackets on either side of the doorway, switched on a small flashlight. The air in the tunnel was still and cool. "We used to have lights in here, but the wiring went bad a few years ago."

"I have a headlamp." He shook off his pack and found it, adjusted it on his head. The beam was a weak flood but sufficient for the tunnel. She motioned him up the stairs and fell in behind.

9

Summer opened the old gas-powered refrigerator in the barn and pulled out a thawed whole chicken—feathers and guts and everything—and carried it into the horse stall where Alecto stood on her perch, chirping at Summer like a gigantic songbird. She laid the chicken on a rough plank platform as Alecto hopped up, trailing her long leash, and began happily plucking. Feathers drifted to the floor while Summer raked up sawdust caked with the eagle's mutes—like most birds, she pooped and peed in one go— and dumped it into a bucket. She changed the drinking water and cleaned and refilled the shallow pool outside where Alecto bathed. The day was hot for October and the sliding door to the stall was open so Alecto could spend time in the grass or on her perch beside the pool, restricted by her leash. If Summer's father walked by, he would have to be in disguise, usually a hooded jacket with the hood up and obscuring his face. No one thought the disguise actually fooled Alecto; rather, she seemed to accept it as a show of respect for her rage.

She and Bowman usually did this together, but he'd left last night on a solo camping trip. Her father took care of the other two eagles he'd captured after Alecto turned against him, but if he walked in here, even with his hood up, Alecto would consider it a mortal insult and she would try to attack him. Uncle Jeremy and Uncle Darwin had learned how to help with the eagles, but today they were with her father, working on the water pump down in the valley. So Alecto's care fell to Summer alone.

She only minded because it meant her brother was off in the mountains without her. On Bowman's fourteenth birthday, her father had announced he was going to start "differentiating" their education and training regimes. He spoke like that to his children, always had, and they'd worked to keep up with his vocabulary. Summer didn't like this differentiating. It wasn't fair. She was as good as Bowman at almost everything, even though he was two years older. There should be no differentiating. She'd raised this objection but her father smiled and said it had nothing to do with how good she was. It wasn't a punishment of her or a reward for Bowman. It was simply a recognition that Bowman had reached an age where a young man had to encounter certain things. Summer would encounter other things, eventually. He'd always taught them boys and girls were different but equal. This was the different part.

Summer wasn't fooled by her father's happy horseshit—a phrase she'd recently learned from Uncle Jeremy and said to herself several times a day—and she wasn't going to put up with it.

The library doors stood open and as she walked in she bowed to the huge stuffed hyena and leopard standing guard, frozen forever and lifeless but still emanating power that demanded acknowledgment. She nodded as well to the giant black bearskin hanging on the wall above the mantel. Then she emptied her pack of books on the table beside one of the big leather armchairs flanking the fireplace: natural history, ecology, novels by James Oliver Curwood and Jack London. Her current favorite was the slim paperback *Why Big Fierce Animals Are Rare,* even though it was technical and she was pretty sure at least half of it went over her head.

She and Bowman had been immersed in natural history since their earliest memories, taught about the plants and animals, encouraged to seek them out, understand them as fellow beings, name them, draw them, find new ones, figure out how they related to everything else. Their father thought this was important because, he said, the human mind evolved at least in part to make taxonomic distinctions and perceive ecological relationships. Cataloging the components of an ecological system, and seeing how living things related to each other, was highly adaptive for a wide-ranging omnivore facing repeated climatic stresses.

So her father's emphasis on book learning—accompanied by relentless criticism of the assumptions authors always made without saying so—was relatively new, and Summer loved it. Books suited her just as well as the outdoor adventures. Bowman was less patient. He read fast, too fast, she thought, to enjoy the experience. Then he was out the door.

Bowman had left during the night, after she'd gone to bed, and without telling her where he was going or what their father had told him to do when he was out there. It was the first time he'd cut her out, the first real break in their mutual commitment to share everything, the solidarity they'd formed to survive their father's overbearing, loving, sometimes frankly insane approach to parenting. Things had been a lot better since their uncles came home to the ranch, but it wasn't like suddenly she and her brother didn't need each other, was it? When she'd first realized this morning that Bowman had ditched her she'd been hurt, then pretty quickly she got mad. By the time she'd finished breakfast she'd decided to confront him, and she wasn't going to wait until he got back.

She opened a book by Loren Eiseley—a he or she, she wasn't sure, because she hadn't started it—and laid it in the chair. A half-finished glass of water she left on the table next to the books. She'd had to pour it from a jug in the kitchen instead of using the tap because her father and uncles had shut down the water pump three days ago and the holding tank was empty. The pump had been losing pressure for the past week, and she'd heard them arguing about whether to repair or replace it. There were new, more efficient pumps. It was hard on the old pump, pushing water all the way from the valley floor up to the tank buried in the slope above the house. If they could afford it, a solar-powered pump would be best. They could get rid of the propane tank and the noisy generator in a shed down in the valley, and the propane company's truck wouldn't be driving up the hidden driveway quite as often. But of course they couldn't afford a new pump, much less a solar-powered setup, so the three men were taking the old one apart.

Her backpack was lighter now without the books, but it still held a rain jacket, knife, flashlight, fire-making tools, tarp, and so on, the usual kit they all carried when out in the valley. From the pantry she added a pear, an apple, some jerky, and filled a canteen from the ceramic jug. Out the French doors and up the hill, cutting off-trail to stay low on the slope, watching over her shoulder to make sure she kept a tree or a rock outcrop between herself and the little pump house down in the valley. Once she found the trail leading along the ridge above the house, she could jog north and then west, making good time, well hidden all the way to the forests across the valley. She would've ridden her pony, or maybe the mare Bowman usually rode—Milly might've been some help in finding him—but sneaking out was harder on horseback.

The northwest corner of the valley was Bowman's favorite because it was the most remote part of their property, where the rarest, most secretive animals could be found, black bears and mountain lions and bobcats, as well as the more exotic animals Bowman claimed to know about.

She made good time, and an hour and a half later she cut his tracks, going northwest into mixed pine forest at the foot of the Red Creeks. She walked easily on the mat of pine needles and twenty minutes later she heard the sound of a person being sick. It stopped, but it troubled her, and instead of running to meet her brother, she snuck uphill to a better vantage, moving silently through a grove of huge ponderosas, slipping from one trunk to the next until she came to an outcrop looking over a small clearing in the brush below.

In the clearing was Bowman, completely naked, his arms, face, chest, and legs painted with a muddy red pigment. She almost laughed out loud when she saw he'd painted his uncircumcised penis and scrotum too. He was walking in circles in the dusty clearing, which looked like a nearly dry bison wallow. She saw no pack or tarp or fire or any other sign he'd made camp.

She was ready to call out and make fun of him when he fell to his hands and knees and vomited again. Not much came up, just some water. He stood and resumed walking.

Something told her to stay quiet. Bowman's behavior had shifted in her mind from silly to alarming. Or maybe he knew she was there and was teasing her? No, this was too elaborate to be a prank, and he couldn't have known she was on her way. Could he have poisoned himself? She knew the medicinal plants better than he did; maybe he got into something hallucinogenic like jimsonweed, or he might've found some coprophilic psilocybe mushrooms and eaten them on purpose.

He disappeared into the brush. She could hear him thrashing around, and when he came back he carried a heavy stick in each hand that he used to support himself as he continued making his circles, leaning forward, like he was trying to bring his posture closer to that of a four-legged animal.

She watched, fascinated and starting to feel guilty about spying on her brother. He was so serious about whatever this was. It was something private, not for her to witness.

He stopped and vomited a spray of clear liquid between the sticks. Then a guttural vocalization that couldn't have come from her brother. She looked around for . . . what? a moose? . . . but then he did it again, and she felt a chill and ducked down a little lower, hiding herself behind the rock outcrop before she knew she'd done it. For some reason it mattered now that he not know she was there.

She thought about what to do next. Shadows were starting to lengthen, and she guessed it would take two hours to hike back to the house. She didn't mind walking in the dark, but didn't want to alarm her father and uncles. This, she realized, was the sort of consideration that would be unthinkable to her brother. She wondered if it made her weak. Maybe she should be naked and hallucinating too, and the fact that she wasn't meant their father had recognized in her a limitation Bowman didn't share.

She would have to think about that. She was no longer jealous; she felt no inclination to join her brother. This strange thing he was doing was not something she wanted any part of. That was a new feeling, and it made her sad. She turned and started back the way she'd come, preoccupied with the implications of this fundamental shift in her universe.

Her steps were slower as she walked away, feeling defeated and walking along in a bubble of her own thoughts and emotions, at a low level of engagement with the world around her. This was both disrespectful and dangerous, but she couldn't help it. Just before she turned eastward onto the shaded part of the trail, she stopped at the base of a stone pillar lit in the last sun shining through a gunsight canyon to the west. She leaned against the warm stone and took a bite of the pear she'd brought.

The pear came from a small orchard near Whitespring. Her mother had loved the admittedly non-native fruit and tried to grow a few trees near the greenhouse on a terrace below the house, but the winters, bugs, and meager water had doomed them. When they finally died, three years after her mother, her father had cut them down and burned them, weeping. She remembered the trees with clarity but possessed only a handful of shadowy memories of her mother. The difference between being five and eight, she supposed. Summer treasured those few memories of Anna, not because their content was particularly rich, but rather as evidence that she, Summer, had once been present in her mother's mind, her heart. She liked to put herself in her mother's place, to imagine what she must have thought and felt—the smell of Summer's hair, the weight of the little girl in her arms, the things Summer must have said. She couldn't know her mother, but her mother once had known her. It was something.

Halfway through the pear she stopped, a sudden sickness rising up. She looked at the pear. Nothing wrong with it. Could this be a delayed reaction from seeing Bowman vomit? But it wasn't quite nausea. She recognized it now: the intense, unnerving certainty that another animal—something formidable, dangerous—was unseen but close by. A prey species' reaction to the terrifying smell of a predator. She remembered the big tom lion she and Bowman had seen last winter, but she'd never felt this kind of threat from a healthy mountain lion.

Bowman had told her there were other, rarer animals hiding out here.

Trying not to make any sudden movements, she looked all around, scanning the trees, then the rocks nearby—maybe a rattlesnake?—even the sky overhead. There, at the top of the pillar, Bowman's red-painted face staring down at her. She stepped away for a better view.

Forty feet up, he was perched on the top of the rock spire. It couldn't have been an easy climb. She waved, impressed.

He didn't wave back. His eyes were flat, and his whole posture was off, not Bowman. She felt again the chill, and more than that, the nauseous shift that came with the realization that something was wrong in the world. Should she fear him? The thought had barely crossed her mind when it angered her.

She cupped her hands around her mouth and shouted, "I'm not afraid of you!"

Bowman backed away and disappeared over the edge of the cliff. A moment later he appeared lower down, closer, going on all fours.

He was hunting her.

As long as Summer could remember, their father had encouraged fantasy, imagination, role-play, but always with a key admonition: It must be a way in, not a way out. Never a soporific to escape the pain and tedium and terror and inconvenience of everyday life, but a tactic for expanding your mind, enriching experience, transcending barriers, inhabiting the perspective of the Others.

She had to believe that's what this was about. She also believed Bowman might be taking it a little too far. He would never hurt her, and whatever animal he was imitating probably wouldn't either. But what of the hybrid? An unpredictable and unnatural mapping of unbounded human intention on a wild, nonhuman Other? Later, she would learn what a therianthrope was. A subset of therianthrope was lycanthrope.

She ran.

10

2009

Sam's right calf cramped and after limping a few steps he stopped on a nar-row landing where the stairs turned. The woman, Summer, stepped be-side him in the dark stairwell, into his space. She was tall, strong-looking, dressed in jeans and a faded canvas jacket that might once have been black. Her broad face was vaguely Asian or Native American. Straight, dark hair in a simple shoulder-length cut. No makeup. Turquoise stud earrings. Older than Sam had thought at first, thirtysomething. She was striking, a little bit exotic, and in the light from his headlamp her dark brown eyes were so searching, so curious, that he had to look away.

"Leg cramped up," he said. "I'm fine."

Her close proximity was setting off biochemical flares in various parts of his person. He was self-conscious of his sweaty stink but he caught a whiff of her as well, like she'd been working with animals, a ranch smell. Not unpleasant, quite. Leather and horse sweat. He rested, hoping she would go on ahead.

"It's not much farther." She reached for a metal railing—no wedding ring, he'd already checked, a new reflex for him—and continued past him with her flashlight, her footsteps quiet, scrape of boot sole on stone. She had a slight hitch in her step too. Maybe she was making fun of him.

He thought of the "walk this way" scene in *Young Frankenstein*. There, he was back to recalling movie titles, a sure sign of recovery.

"My grandfather hired miners to dig tunnels in this mountain back in the 1930s. I still haven't explored them all." She waved her hand at a dark glass wall sconce. "We have our own electricity: solar panels, generators. Never have been on the grid, though we get propane delivered a couple times a year."

"Who lives here?"

"My two uncles and me. We work some cattle, try to keep the place up. Which means we all have part-time jobs off the ranch."

Sam trudged up the steps. His stomach bloated uncomfortably and he wished he hadn't chugged her water all at once. If he threw up here in the tunnel with this woman it would set a new low-water mark for him socially. He asked Summer about her family, how long they'd lived here. She said her grandfather had emigrated from France in 1898 with a modest fortune and invested in mining, timber, railroads. He transformed himself into a rich American capitalist, then he went back during World War I and joined the French army.

"Wait, your grandfather was alive in the 1800s? My grandparents were born during the Depression."

"My brother and I come from a long line of late breeders."

After Verdun, she said, and the pandemic that followed the war, her grandfather decided he wanted nothing more to do with the twentieth century. He returned to the States and bought this remote ranch, built the house and stockpiled supplies, made his life as self-sufficient as possible.

"I told you earlier he had miners dig these tunnels in the mountain, but they got carried away. Like the dwarves of Moria, they delved too deep and awakened something, the spirits of the APs, maybe, something that infected Martin—and our family—with a profound paranoia."

"APs?"

"Ancestral Puebloan. It's the PC alternative to Anasazi, which is an insulting Navajo term."

They passed a couple of landings with doors leading into the stone wall, and the rough stone treads gave way to smooth flagstones; a peeled-pole railing appeared, then a few dusty Navajo wall hangings. The walls were tightly fitted stone blocks, and up ahead, tall windows let in late-afternoon desert light.

A man stood at the top of the last flight of stairs, a thickset silhouette against the bright windows. Sam and Summer squinted, their eyes still adjusted to the dim tunnel. She waved but the man disappeared before they reached him.

"That was my uncle Darwin," Summer said. "I think you surprised him. He's my mother's brother, one-half Native American, tribe unknown."

Sam wasn't sure what to say to that. He wanted to ask why they didn't know their tribe but decided it would be presumptuous. They walked through a hall, passing French doors on the left that led out onto a gravel-and-sandstone courtyard. The kitchen was high-ceilinged, with commercial appliances from the sixties and countertops of dark stone, cabinets of unpainted wood. A rustic plank table in the middle with chairs and a big butcher-block cutting board. He dug into his pack for his water bottles, and Summer filled them at the sink.

He remembered he should call Mac again. Summer offered the landline, but he needed to check his messages too and didn't know how to do it without using his cell. She said she could usually get a signal on a ridge above the house, if he was up for more hiking.

Before he could reply, the uncle bustled in and without a word pulled a tray of marinating meat from the refrigerator, gathered vegetables on the table: tomatoes, an onion, some sort of squash. He had ruddy skin and stiff dark hair cropped short in a military-looking flattop. A wide, creased forehead rose over his rounded nose, soaring cheekbones, square chin. Dark brown eyes. He looked robust, probably in his sixties. Sam saw a similar ethnic influence, but other than that there wasn't much family resemblance with Summer.

"Uncle Darwin, this is Sam Hay. I found him down in East Canyon. He was dying of thirst."

"He looks okay to me." Darwin spoke to his vegetables.

That made Sam smile. He walked across the kitchen, reached out his hand. "Pleased to meet you."

Uncle Darwin had pulled a chef's knife from a wooden block. After a moment he put down the knife and shook Sam's hand with a big firm

grip. Frowning, he looked like he thought Summer was playing an unpleasant trick on him.

"Summer gave me water, probably saved my life. I feel better now,
thanks."

Darwin lifted the knife and turned back to the vegetables. "Another
yuppie."

"I'm not a yuppie."

"Usually it's a creative. Or an *intellectual*."

"And I'm not her—"

"There was a cowboy phase. You got to admit she looks like a model
for the Sheplers catalog."

I actually like this guy, Sam thought, trying to imagine where Summer
would meet creatives and intellectuals around here.

Summer herded him out into the hall, leaned back into the kitchen
doorway. "You should be more polite. We're walking up to the ridge so
Sam can use his cell phone."

"Ha!" said the uncle.

11

Fleeing the kitchen and Darwin, she opened the door for Sam and they stepped outside into the longest day of the year, the red sandstone pillars that loomed over the courtyard throwing off stored heat. She led him to the trail curving up the slope behind and they climbed out of the shadow of the house, past the array of solar panels on metal posts. The panels gleamed black in the sun, which was finally falling toward the jagged Red Creeks. The hillside was hot and xeric, the vegetation prickly pear, bunchgrass, low sagebrush.

The trail cut to the right in the first switchback as the slope steepened. She set a moderate pace and when Sam flagged halfway up she stopped to let him rest. Her knee had started to swell from all those steps and she reached down to massage it while Sam turned to look back the way they'd come, held out his hand to shade his eyes.

The sprawling house hunkered among red boulders on the slope below, roofed with sand-colored tiles to camouflage it from the air. Beyond and another few hundred feet below the house, Panther Gap ran four miles to the southwest, green as an oasis. Hidden between the cliffs and ridges visible from the public road and the Red Creek Range in the west, the valley was watered by streams that hung like silver threads on the far slopes, runoff from the mountains feeding a kidney-shaped lake, the headwaters of Red Creek.

"This is amazing," Sam said. "Reminds me of Ngorongoro Crater, except for the cows. If you squint I guess they could be wildebeest."

"Ngorongoro was kind of the idea, at least for my father. If you look past the cows . . ." She pointed to a meadow a mile away where a handful of bulky dark shapes moved almost imperceptibly against the green. She'd never been to Africa, but her father had shown her his pictures. This valley was smaller, and more hidden among the surrounding geography—desert mesas giving over to the alpine uplands of the San Juan and La Plata Mountains—and the shape wasn't a perfect bowl, rimmed all around by cliffs and steep mountain slopes rather than volcanic crater walls. But like Ngorongoro, Panther Gap had a feeling of almost magical enclosure, of a world lost in time.

"Are those bison?"

"My father brought them here in the seventies, from South Dakota. There's a wild herd now of about thirty head. He was into that sort of thing, reintroducing native species, especially the kind he could shoot. He'd been to Ngorongoro in the sixties, and when he came home he wanted to replicate it here. He got rid of Grandfather Martin's longhorns, though a few escaped the final roundup. Now they're like aurochs, another wild species out there with the elk and bison."

They crested the ridge into a sparse grove of leaning junipers, paused beside a stone bench on short pillars. Eastward the open plain was a vast carpet of dun and pale dusty green, Rosewater Butte still lit red by the lowering sun. The road a pale line, no cars, no dust plume in either direction. The wind, always strong up here, pushed at their backs. Sam opened his pack and produced a fleece pullover. She watched him. Too much sun would make you more susceptible to feeling cold, but she didn't think it was more than a moderate case of heat exhaustion.

He switched his phone on, waited while it searched for a signal. She thought he might get one bar up here, two bars if he pointed it northeast. He noticed her staring and glanced up from the phone.

"Are you a lawyer or something?" she asked.

"God, it's that obvious? I do tax work, mostly."

"Tax work?" She laughed out loud. On the day before she was supposed to claim an inheritance with, as Andrew had put it, *complications,* her signal fire had lured a tax attorney.

"Why's that so amazing? I sit in my office, I stare at my computer."

He turned back to his phone. After a minute he said, "Shit," and held it to his ear, listening, facing away. He didn't speak again, must be a message. His body language turned confused, puzzled, then alarmed.

12

Bowman stood at the Delta ticket counter, eight U.S. hundreds in hand, explaining to Chloe, the young CUSTOMER SERVICE REPRESENTATIVE—according to her name tag—that he did not have a credit card with which to purchase his ticket to Colorado. She mumbled something about an extra fee, and a delay before he could fly. She peered at his passport.

"There's, like, water damage or something?"

He sighed and opened the dry bag, reached in for more cash, fingertips brushing the bound sheaf of hundreds. Stopped, because this was Miami, in the U.S. of A. Because Chloe the Delta customer service rep was not soliciting a bribe.

A man's voice from a loudspeaker in the ceiling reminded Bowman he shouldn't leave the luggage he didn't have unattended. The din of human voices rose up again, so many at once. Thin futuristic televisions were everywhere. He'd slept on the flight from San José but his mind still fogged up intermittently, he guessed from the insidious combination of sea snake venom, whatever chemicals they'd given him in the hospital, and the sensory assaults of civilization generally.

"I've been living in Central America," he said. "Off the grid. My passport got wet. And credit cards are not useful in the jungle. I need to fly home for a family emergency."

The rep squinted at this strange man who was complicating her day.

"The manager's at lunch? For about an hour? No flights leave for Denver before three anyway?"

He hesitated, not sure how to answer Chloe's questions, but she was finished with him, signaling eagerly to the next couple in line. He stepped back out into the stream of walking humanity and let it carry him.

His stomach rumbled, reminding him it was empty, and he began moving with purpose, hunting something to eat. He saw signs for a FOOD COURT, which sounded promising, but before he got there two men were following him. The old paranoia washed over him for a moment, but they were so obvious about it they had to be low-level airport security, operating on the premise that if he knew they were watching, he would behave. In a men's restroom he used the urinal, washed his hands. His escort waiting outside. At the mirror he splashed water on his face. A truly sane response to the insane milieu of civilization would read as schizophrenia to the good citizens around him, so he'd tried very hard to compensate, to pass. He didn't think he'd acted unstable. Must be his appearance that had attracted the guards' attention. People had been staring at him all day: raggedy beard, long ponytail, sun-darkened face. Tall, skinny. Weird. He'd bought a cheap pair of shorts and sandals on the street in San José and changed in the cab to the airport, but he still wore the scrub top Luisa had given him. He smelled of antiseptic and body odor.

He nodded to the two guards on his way out and crossed the hallway to a high-end men's store. His father had brought him to a Brooks Brothers store in Denver when he was sixteen as part of his accelerated—in retrospect, possibly panicked?—attempt to civilize his feral son. This looked like that place, but more self-consciously hip. The salesclerk hovering near the entrance blinked and took a step back. Of course he did.

There'd been a couple of problems with his father's training. First, the abrupt and disturbing switch in emphasis from the wild to the civilized coincided with the hormonal surge generally associated with teenage rebelliousness. His father had apologized for this, saying circumstances had forced him to depart from the timeline he'd planned on, which made zero sense to teen Bowman, who preferred the former program where he got to camp out by himself for weeks at a time. And second, father Leo's own time in civilization before returning to the ranch—roughly 1951 to 1971—had been spent entirely in the employ of the U.S. government, first as an army sniper and then as "a diplomat in Central Africa," which young Bowman had assumed was a euphemism for "CIA field agent," so the civilizing skills imparted to Bowman had been those a retired Cold War warrior would deem necessary—to wit: deception, acting, manipulation of others, how to hide, escape, kill. Not all of it had suited Bowman's nature.

Nevertheless, he thought. *Nevertheless. This is nothing but role-playing. You can do this. Is there a name tag?* Yes, of course, they were ubiquitous now, a sensible development. He focused on the man's dark eyes, still in his twenties, self-confident.

"Hello, Tommy," Bowman said. "I hope you can help me out. I've been on a really long surf vacation in Costa Rica, I mean years, and I had to leave today in a hurry. Family emergency back home in Colorado, if I can get the nice lady at Delta to sell me a ticket. But right now I've got security following me around the airport because they think I'm a homeless person. I need to get cleaned up." He let that sink in for a beat.

"Not that there's anything wrong with being homeless," Tommy said.

No, Bowman thought, wondering where this was coming from. He waited. For the past twenty years he'd lived pretty much as a homeless person himself.

"These days, anyone can become homeless, just like that." Finger snap.

The recession, then. And a recent vogue for facile social consciousness among young people. Everyone was performing, all the time, and he was already tired of it. He gave the store a quick look, the racks of shirts and suits, the shoes, the smelly soaps and colognes and shaving supplies. All this *stuff.* Expensive stuff.

From his dry bag he withdrew a rubber-banded stack of bills and, without looking at it, laid it on a walnut-veneer side table. The intentionally dramatic deployment of all that lucre made him a little sick, but he heard his father saying you have to inhabit your role, no matter how distasteful, and instinctively he'd queued up an uber-capitalist staging his reentry from a spiritual sojourn in the so-called third world.

He smiled again, thinking of the word "wolfishly" and how wrong that adverb was versus the real *Canis lupus,* but also thinking the nursery-rhyme version did describe the effect he wanted.

He hated this, hated himself thinking this way. The sudden reinsertion into American clamor and commerce had triggered a sense of dislocation, as if he'd teleported to a different dimension where he didn't even know himself. This perception, he knew, was false. The urban setting, air travel, the enclosure of the airport's four walls, the technological soup, it was all of a piece with hanging suspended ten feet underwater, holding his breath, watching the yellow-on-black sea snakes swim in the cove. It was all real, all part of the same terrible, magnificent world. It wasn't something you could leave or return to. You were always in it.

For years he had lived simply and alone in remote places, all the while fully aware in "a sardonic and even humorous declining of self-delusion"— their father had insisted Bowman and Summer read Faulkner in their teens—that he could never really escape, never accomplish the kind of freedom humans experienced before the hegemony of the agricultural-industrial state overspread the planet. For example, he'd remained free from oppression in "his" cove on the Osa only because the Costa Rican government had remained uninterested in his presence. More broadly, his—everyone's—very existence depended on various global superpowers managing through dumb luck and cynical self-interest to avoid immolating the planet with nuclear weapons. And his well-being—tied so directly to the well-being of whatever remote ecosystem he happened to reside in—would inevitably deteriorate as unchecked global warming and other anthropogenic devastations continued to wreak their changes on the earth.

After a short discussion, the money lying on the table between them, glowing and shimmering with its bizarre power, Tommy got on the phone with a hairdresser in Concourse D and talked her into meeting Bowman at the Admirals Club later, after a meal and a shave and shower. The security team finally lost patience and entered the store. Bowman assumed they were going to ask something cliché, like, *Is this man giving you any trouble?* But instead they stood and watched Bowman step into the changing booth with an armload of expensive boxer shorts, jeans, and shirts. He heard murmured conversation, the words "report," and "behavior," and "no problem." Tommy was waiting alone near the cash register when Bowman came out wearing a maroon polo and the first pair of jeans that had fit. The jeans, Tommy explained, cost extra because they were made in Japan, which Bowman found amusing, and because they'd been washed and tossed about and strategically abraded so as to look exactly one year old.

"I think those guys were just bored," Tommy said. He tugged at the shoulders of Bowman's shirt, checking the fit. He led the way to a rack of sport coats. "But there was another guy." He tossed this back at Bowman, his manner studied-casual. "He was walking by when you pulled that roll, and I noticed because he did a major double take. Then he came back when I was talking to the rent-a-cops. I got my phone like I was reading a text and tried to take his picture." He repeated this action, pointed it at Bowman, who reached out, palming the device. He knew about digital cameras and these newly ubiquitous "smart" phones from the tourists and surfers he'd met.

Tommy took a sharp breath and his eyes got big, must not be used to people touching his things. "I wasn't gonna . . ." Bowman pushed the phone down, let go when it was no longer aimed at him.

"Okay. Anyway, I tried to take his picture but he knew exactly what I was doing, and like that"—another theatrical finger snap—"he turned away, walked out."

"Did you get one of his back?"

Tommy the resourceful retail salesman pressed a couple of buttons and turned the screen toward Bowman. "He didn't look like a thief."

Square-shouldered man in loose khakis and tight T-shirt, headed for the door. Sandy blond hair, nondescript. Bowman knew it had been a risk wiring that money. Summer and Darwin would have tried to keep the account secret, but if any of his father's paranoid imaginings turned out to be true, others might have been watching as well.

"Dude might be law enforcement, higher up the food chain." Clearly Tommy didn't believe Bowman's rich surfer story. He wanted to show he was hip to the life. Bowman fought a smile. *So much for my acting skills. He thinks I'm a drug dealer.*

He stared at the image on Tommy's phone. Yeah, not a thief. A cop wouldn't run off like that. He was something else. Or maybe he was nobody. Tommy watched him expectantly.

"How about shoes?" Bowman asked. "I don't think I need a sport coat."

Tommy's disappointment at being rebuffed lasted about half a second before he recovered his professional mien. "The shoes are the key to the whole thing," he said. "The shoes are where you want to spend your money."

13

Sam held his phone at face level between himself and Summer and replayed the first message, the volume on the speaker turned all the way up.

"*Shit . . . I don't know where he is. Probably doesn't have a signal. Sam, I need your help, man, call my cell as soon as you can, things are really fucked up—Give it to me—Mr. Sam, call your friend back today or he's going to disappear.*"

"Play the others, from his secretary."

"I have to call Mac back. You heard."

"No, call him in a few minutes. You have to be careful, think about what you're going to say. And it might be more important to deal with the secretary first."

Sam stared at her, his surprise at her tone swept aside by the circumstances. He queued Talley's first message, stamped forty minutes after the one from Mac. Almost six hours ago. He held up the phone again so they both could hear the speaker over the wind, their heads close together. His mind spun ineffectively with disbelief and unprocessed shock, like a car stuck in the snow.

Talley's voice was an uncharacteristically shrill falsetto: "*Where the hell are you? Mac has been kidnapped and you have to pick up the ransom money and take it somewhere. They said no police. I opened an account for you at the bank in Whitespring and wired the money there. They're closing in like one hour. He said they'll kill him if you don't do this. Call me!*"

The next one, less than an hour later, didn't add much in the way of content. She sounded near panic.

"Call her back first, calm her down. Tell her you're handling this and under no circumstances is she going to report this to law enforcement or tell anyone."

"Do you know where that bank is?"

"Doesn't matter. It's closed, and you need to get your friend back tonight. The longer you wait, the worse his chances are."

"How can I do that without the money?"

"We'll figure it out, we have some cash here. Call her. She's freaking and you need to stop her from bringing anyone else in. Right now. It might already be too late."

When Sam hesitated, she added that her uncle used to be a police officer in Denver—he had SWAT experience—and he could help.

"The chef was on a SWAT team?"

"No, the other one. I'll call down to the house as soon as you talk to the secretary."

His conversation with Talley went better than expected. She settled down once she no longer bore the sole responsibility for saving Mac. Comfortable in her more accustomed role as facilitator, she answered Sam's questions with gradually decreasing levels of drama. The ransom was fifty thousand, but they could only get thirty-seven from his account on short notice, and the kidnappers had reluctantly agreed to take that amount. No, she hadn't told anyone else. Yes, she promised not to tell anyone. She knew Mac's life was at stake, and what else did Sam need her to do, and so on. She'd already called in sick tomorrow and would do anything to help. It was old news that Mac's secretary was devoted to him in a way that generated rumors, and it didn't help that she was supermodel-skinny, stylish, sexy. For a while Sam had had a crush on her himself, but when she started wearing braces last year it made her look disconcertingly like a teenager and he felt uncomfortable thinking of her that way.

"I'm calling Mac."

"Wait. You have to have a plan." Summer held out her hand for his phone. "Uncle Jeremy will know what to do."

She said almost no one knew the number at the ranch, so as a rule she and her uncles would all jump when the phone rang. Still, it must have rung ten times before the chef—Uncle Darwin—picked up, and he had to track down the SWAT uncle and get him on the line. Sam could only hear Summer's side of the conversation. Clearly the uncle was arguing with her until she told him she didn't have time to debate the merits and reframed the situation as a hypothetical. Then she listened for a long time. She thanked him and hung up and began coaching Sam. It was basic stuff: be agreeable but firm, ask for proof of life, clear up any ambiguities in the kidnappers' demands, be sure you don't hang up without a specific plan for exchanging the ransom for the captive, and so on.

"Put it back on speaker," she said. They'd moved east over the lip of the ridge into the lee, where the wind was calmer.

Sam dialed.

"Finally you call!"

"Who is this?"

"I'm who is going to cut your friend's head off if you don't bring us the fucking money."

The harsh malignance—the venom—in the man's voice took Sam aback. This was worse somehow than the message. Live, he didn't sound like an actor pretending to be a criminal in a movie, which was Sam's only reference. He sounded like a person who habitually hurt other people, who liked doing it, whose life had been defined by his willingness and ability to hurt others. The vast majority of people weren't like that. Certainly no one Sam had ever known was like that. He felt childish and naïve, stripped naked, even over the phone.

Summer caught his eye, mouthed his first line.

"Let me talk to him," he said. He thought this was a cliché because it was what they always said in the movies, but Summer nodded encouragement. There was a pause, some rustling, murmuring in the background.

"Sam?"

"Yeah, I'm here. Are you hurt?"

"No, I'm fine. Did you talk to Talley?"

"Of course. It's all taken care of." Summer had said it was important to reassure both the kidnapper and kidnapped. You didn't want to roll over for every demand, but the kidnappers should feel you were taking them seriously, reacting with specific action, not stonewalling. The idea was to stay calm, to alleviate the fear that was always thick in the air, though Sam thought Mac sounded more tired than scared.

"Can you get the cash?"

"I got it already." He and Summer had come up with a story that sounded more plausible than the real situation. "A local gave me a ride into town and I was a block from the bank when I got a signal, got the messages. They weren't going to give me the cash but Talley got on the phone with the bank manager, said it was an emergency, a gambling debt."

"That's good, Mr. Sam." This was the other voice; he must've reclaimed the phone, or maybe they had theirs on speaker too.

"What about Melissa? You have to let her go too."

The man laughed.

"What the fuck? We'll pay. Just let her go."

"Melissa? Was that her name?"

"Oh hell, what did you do?"

Summer frowned and shook her head. *Don't.*

No reply. Sam swallowed, made himself keep going. "I have the cash, and I'll meet you tonight. I'm at somebody's ranch now, he'll loan me his truck. I can find the tent, where we camped last night. I'll meet you there in four hours."

"No, Mr. Sam. I tell you where we meet, when we do it."

They haggled over the time and place, Sam objecting that he didn't know the area, that he couldn't ask the rancher for directions without letting him know what was going on. This was all part of the strategy from the uncle, framing the negotiations while allowing the kidnapper to feel he still had the upper hand. Sam eventually agreed to meet them at 2:00 A.M. at a remote crossroads southeast of Whitespring. Summer nodded again, she knew where it was.

After he hung up, Sam sat on the bench in the dark and half listened to Summer's reassurances. Her uncle knew how to manage this sort of thing, he would make sure Sam was safe and could collect his friend, it wasn't Sam's fault, and so on. Eventually they started back down the trail, Summer leading. She described the SWAT uncle's background, how her father had first trained him when he was in his early twenties, and then he'd left the ranch after Summer's mother died to join the Denver police.

Sam wasn't paying a whole lot of attention because he knew she was just trying to reassure him, but then her tone changed, like she was slightly embarrassed, genuinely apologetic, asking *him* for a favor. There was a meeting tomorrow at a bank in Denver, something to do with her grandfather's estate. The uncles were going, and her older brother was supposed to be there, she hadn't seen him in years but he was on his way from Costa Rica, they needed money for the ranch but the situation wasn't straightforward and it worried her. Their grandfather had been a questionable character, and the guy she knew at the bank was acting squirrelly.

He didn't know why she was so insistent on telling this story. Almost like she was talking it out, trying to convince herself of something. Eventually a long silence fell and he thought she might be waiting for him to reply.

"What, you want me to represent you? At this meeting? Tomorrow?"

"Nothing formal. Just come with us. Consult. I'll feel better with you there. Everything will go fine tonight. I know it sounds crazy but I think this is why you ended up in the canyon, why I found you there. My uncle is uniquely able to help you get your friend back, and you're uniquely able to help us with this inheritance. It's the clearest case of serendipity I've ever experienced."

He started to object that he didn't do much estate and gift tax but lacked the heart to discuss it. So he agreed, distracted by the conviction he might not survive the night anyway, and by the need to step carefully on the barely visible trail lest he tumble into the cactus he'd seen growing alongside earlier.

14

1986

Today Leo was flying Horkos and Hesperus while Alecto remained in the mews. Summer and Bowman brought the horses around and they all rode down into the valley, Leo and Jeremy carrying the two eagles on T-sticks wedged into their stirrups. Summer and Bowman followed behind on their mounts, all of them bundled against a November cold front. Darwin was working in Durango today. He didn't often hunt with them anyway.

Within the first couple of hours, the eagles had killed two jack-rabbits and a blue grouse on the snowy sagebrush slopes at the southeast end of the valley. Then it was quiet and for a while they hardly saw any animals at all. They rode on, the horses' footfalls muffled in the snow. Leo thought they might roust a fox down here, but he'd given up hoping for coyotes anywhere on the property, and had to drive the eagles south to Weenuche land to find them. He knew why: a pair of wolves had taken up residence in Panther Gap, driving out the smaller canids. The wolves were determinedly crepuscular, nearly nocturnal, which helped explain how they'd made it here from wherever the hell they'd come from. Alberta, he supposed. Their presence was remarkable, beyond explanation, and he pretended not to know they were there. Bowman was secretly shielding them, always contriving to steer the eagle hunts away from the northeast corner of the valley where the wolves had dug their den. Leo wouldn't hunt the wolves anyway, they were far too rare, too special, but he let Bowman believe they were under his protection.

Jeremy had transferred Horkos on his T-stick to Bowman and now he ranged ahead on his bay mare, trotting back and forth in a fast zigzag, trying to flush something for the eagles. He frowned in concentration the way he did when undertaking any task, but the man was happiest when on horseback, and bird-dogging on that feisty, athletic mare was probably what he'd been looking forward to all morning. Leo smiled, watching him. For the thousandth time he silently thanked his brothers-in-law for coming home.

Leo knew now how poorly he'd understood these men, despite having lived with them on the ranch for years, despite having fallen in love with and married and fathered two children with their sister. When he'd left government service and returned to the ranch in 1971, he'd been amazed to find his father, Martin, had taken in a new family, must've gotten lonely after Leo's mom passed away in the late fifties. Darwin, Jeremy, and Anna St. John were the children of the foreman at Martin's sawmill in central Oregon and his Indian wife, whose tribe identity was somehow lost after a gang of drunken locals who disapproved of miscegenation tossed a Molotov cocktail in the window one night. The dad got the kids out but he went back in for his wife and neither of them made it. When Leo had come home, the three St. John kids had been living at the ranch for thirteen years, and to them the place was as much home as it was to Leo.

Leo had been glad for the life and energy the youngsters brought to the ranch, and, in retrospect, he knew he'd been naïvely enthusiastic about their indigenous heritage. Still intoxicated by the revelations that had come to him during his time with several tribes in Africa who still lived the old way, he'd romanticized his young quasi-siblings and probably made an ass of himself on a regular basis, though it hadn't put off Anna sufficiently to make her refuse his proposal when the time came.

Jeremy and Darwin had left the ranch after Anna's death, gone off, Leo assumed, to seek their true heritage, find out who their people were, join the tribe. But his offer of investigative help was declined, and during what turned out to be a five-year sabbatical, Jeremy had become a Denver police officer and SWAT team leader, and Darwin had learned French cuisine and made a living and a reputation in the New York restaurant scene.

They'd returned a year and a half ago, together and without warning, apologized for ever leaving, asked Leo's permission to move home even though his father had set things up so they were legally entitled to live there. Within a couple of months, Jeremy and Darwin had bought a half section of irrigated farmland near Whitespring with money they'd inherited from Martin—Anna had left them her inheritance as well, at Leo's insistence—and last summer they'd planted alfalfa, contracted with a local to help them cut and bale on shares, and sold their hay to horse people over near Alamosa, contributing the profits to the ranch account. Leo put in his pension, and there was enough, barely. He had trouble grasping the fact that his government pension, which seemed to him a lot of money, wasn't enough to carry the ranch, but Darwin had shown him the books. To bring in more income, Jeremy was talking about joining the county sheriff's office as a part-time deputy, and Darwin had already started working weekends at a restaurant in Durango.

After another hour of riding complicated patterns in the sagebrush without flushing so much as a sparrow, Jeremy gave up and turned his horse, rode in like a frustrated English setter. He grinned at the others, signaling it was time for Leo to issue his usual challenge: if Bowman could evade the two eagles for five minutes, Leo would grant some reward he knew the boy wanted. Today it would be a surprise: he planned to take Bowman and Summer to Chaco Canyon for the winter solstice, something they'd both been asking for. Leo wasn't knowledgeable about the history of the place, but Bowman had been reading about it in the Whitespring library and wanted to see it, to spend the night there; apparently some of the structures at Chaco had been built to honor various celestial events, including the solstices.

Summer and Bowman dismounted, opened their bulky saddlebags. Cordial to one another, but cool. This coolness had set in after Bowman's long solo in the fall. Summer was jealous of the turn her older brother's education had taken. Maybe the trip to Chaco would help.

Bowman put on the leather jerkin, turned his back so Summer could attach the wolfskin and a piece of raw chicken using the rawhide ties. Leo had stitched the jerkin himself, three layers of full-grain bison leather. It had a high collar in the back, a soft fleece lining. For the impenetrable armor it provided against the eagles' talons, the jerkin was light, and it gave Bowman freedom to move, to run and dodge.

Bowman was so serious today, almost reluctant to play the game. Leo asked if he was feeling all right. They didn't have to fly the eagles to him; they'd flown enough at the grouse and jackrabbits earlier, but Bowman shook his head, as if Leo's words were flies, bothering him.

"He's like this," Summer said, sotto voce, "because he thinks he's about to turn into a wolf."

Bowman shut his eyes, exhaled a long slow breath, making a show of his forbearance.

Leo had seen in his son a marked turn toward the metaphysical. Both children had always been curious about their Indian heritage, and they were fascinated by the mysterious Anasazi people who had once lived in the area. For years, they'd been following their grandfather's tunnels down to East Canyon to explore the hidden settlement there, and they'd dabbled in various Native practices they'd read about and seen among the local tribes. Their uncles couldn't help because Leo's father, Martin, had brought them up as whites and had never tried to find out what tribe they came from; they'd attended school locally, posed as the caretaker's adopted children. Long after the fact, Leo had apologized to Anna for the way his father had raised her and her brothers, but she'd only shrugged. Martin *was* white, she'd said. What else was he supposed to do?

More recently Bowman had taken to describing his experiences with the ghosts of the Anasazi—he called them the "Old Ones"— and he claimed he could enter some kind of alternate or enhanced reality, sometimes involving direct communication with wild animals. Maybe Summer was right, and Bowman did think he was going to turn into a wolf. He certainly could act like one for the eagles; his mimicry was uncanny, had been ever since that first time in the barn three years ago. Leo suspected Bowman watched the wolf pair when he was allowed to spend nights out in the valley, and recently he'd become more wolfish in his movements generally, aping their fluid stealth and light-footedness. Or maybe that was Leo's imagination, and the boy was just growing.

So far, Leo had neither encouraged nor discouraged Bowman's spiritual investigations. He'd raised both children with a strong emphasis on direct experience of the physical world, of wild nature in particular. After nearly a year in a tent in the valley, they lived in the house most of the time now, but the real world, the important world, was always outdoors. An intense and constant immersion in natural history, in unmediated contact with the ecological systems of Panther Gap, had taken the place of religion and simplistic superstitions. Leo's teaching of history started not with the Mesopotamian city-states but encompassed the past million or so years of primate evolution, with "civilization" and widespread agriculture characterizing only the most recent post-glacial moment, a calamitous leap from free-ranging social primates toward what he feared would be a hive-mind future, humanity reduced to termites in a global termite mound.

Their unusual education, he hoped, would grow a robust and grounded worldview in Summer and Bowman, a heightened awareness that would be useful in the life he knew was coming for them. As for Bowman's recent turn, he supposed it was possible his son's experience of an immanent universe had led naturally to a discounting, or dismissing, of the boundaries of Leo's reason. If Bowman experienced the world as alive and sacred, why insist on the limitations of current scientific understanding? That line between real and not real would appear arbitrary. If that's what was going on, Leo decided, he would let the current phase of Bowman's maturation play out. Without Leo's interference, the boy might achieve a level of awareness beyond what Leo himself could even imagine.

He wondered, though, why Summer hadn't followed her brother

in this. She had imitated him in nearly everything else ever since their mother had died, but they were different, these siblings, and they were drifting apart. Summer was less dismissive of human relationships, less willing to sacrifice or damage them in the service of a high-minded quest for personal growth or spiritual journeying. She was more mature than Bowman in that sense. Leo could tell she'd been hurt by her brother's increasing tendency to leave her behind in the last year or so, and especially his more recent—and hardly unusual or unexpected—teenage boy's desire to spend time alone. In turn, Summer had redirected more of her warmth toward her father and uncles. Leo treasured this attention from her, but he hated to see the rift between the siblings who had been so close for so long.

An only child, Leo worried about the bond between his children. He had no experience with such things. A long time ago Anna had told him not to worry, that surely they would fall in and out of each other's favor many times as they grew up. What concerned him, though, was a certain time far into the future, when the solidarity between these two would matter a great deal.

He realized they were all watching him—his children, his brother-in-law, the horses, the eagles. He smiled, shaking off his misgivings, and handed Summer the stopwatch. If Bowman lasted the appointed time she would blow the brass whistle she carried and Bowman would collapse facedown in the grass, the eagles pouncing and scrabbling over the meat until Leo and Jeremy arrived to calm them. It was like riding a bull in the rodeo: Bowman could beat the eagles for only so long. He tired before they did, just like the coyotes. In open country, the eagles always won.

Bowman smelled the wolf fur, and he began to lose his mind.

His speaking self receded and the world exploded with texture, information, story.

He held himself still, trying not to betray to his family what was happening. One of the horses shied from him and the others watched with ears forward. He heard them breathing. He smelled his sister's hair, his uncle's sweat. The sagebrush and bunchgrass moved without moving, shimmering in place even though the wind was light today. Every blade of grass, every vole tunneling under the snow, even the rocks that would try to trip him—everything, plant or animal or otherwise, had a story, and a self of some kind. A life.

Summer was looking at him skeptically.

Only last week, she'd finally admitted she'd intruded on his solo back in October, and what she'd seen. At first he'd thought she was making it up, but then as she went on it was like a dream he'd forgotten. He apologized for frightening her, and he asked her not to tell their father.

"Did you take something?" she'd asked. "Mushrooms? Sleepy grass?"

"No." He was sure of this. He'd only wanted to be with the wolves, for them to let him into their world. "I wanted to approach the wolves, and I got the idea of masking my scent with mud. I found a bison wallow and took off my clothes. Then it was like I'd jumped off a cliff, into something unknown. I don't really remember anything after that." He'd been halfway home when he'd realized he was still naked. He ran back and found his clothes, his backpack. He'd never even unpacked his sleeping bag.

"Did you ever see the wolves? I bet they ran away from you all painted up with red mud like a crazy person. Like I did."

"I think I did see them." He remembered two pairs of piercing yellow eyes, two spectral forms running fast alongside him, through the forest at night. Another dream, maybe.

She looked at him for a long moment. She seemed so sad. But when she'd finally spoke, her tone was resigned, and firm. "You're going to a place I won't follow."

"I know," he'd said. And he'd felt sad then as well. "I'm sorry."

The memory dispersed as he walked away from the others, his feet punching through the crust on the snow, his body beginning to quiver. When Summer blew the whistle, he fell to all fours and went straightaway through the sagebrush, loping, seeking speed and distance. A wolf would try this first. Wolves were easily killed from aircraft because they had not had to worry the past million years or so about danger from the air. Eagles killing wolves was an aberration occurring so rarely in the wild that it had had no effect on the wolves' evolution.

A hiss of air in feathers. Bowman feinted left, slid right, and Horkos shot past him, braking frantically, turning to correct his course, but he'd lost his speed and Bowman was away. Where was Hesperus? He stopped and scrambled backward, not taking the time to look for the second eagle, but he heard him in time and dove to the ground, rolling and then back up, moving low behind a thick line of big sagebrush, ducking into an old wash, using the contour of the land. The eagles were rushing, not coordinating their hunt, making mistakes Alecto would not have made. Female eagles were much larger than the males, and Alecto would have taken him on that first rush, waiting to commit until he tried his evasion, then dropping on him without velocity, relying on her strength to subdue him.

He heard one of them coming and rolled again, back on all fours, going another direction. Eventually he grew winded, his leather-gloved hands sore and cold, feet grown stupid, catching on stones and sagebrush. The wolfskin was losing its power, and as it did he regressed, back into an exhausted teenage boy. He listened for Summer's whistle.

15

2009

"Where is he now?"

"Taking a bath. Calming down. He's exhausted and he feels responsible. I told him to try and sleep until you all head out."

Jeremy unclipped the lead rope from Star's halter. She trotted into the dim paddock, turned, and reappeared in the glow from the awning lights and began slurping from a stone water trough. Summer and her uncle watched without speaking. She knew not to press him on family security, which was what this came down to. Jeremy's dog was loudly crunching kibble somewhere in the barn. Half-jokingly, because she knew her uncle's nature, she told him fate had delivered in Sam the perfect representative for the family, that you couldn't ignore this kind of serendipity.

"I didn't think you were so superstitious. That was Bowman's department."

She let that pass. There was a gray area where someone like Bowman would say a thing is magic and she would say the same thing is a natural phenomenon, and they wouldn't really be disagreeing. When she'd told Jeremy about the wire from Bowman's account and her conversation with the comptroller at the hospital, he'd put her in touch with a private investigator in Denver who would intercept Bowman in DIA before his flight to Whitespring and take him to a motel, where they could pick him up in the morning on their way to the meeting.

"See," he continued, "this coincidence, this fella showing up the day before the meeting, you're telling me it's happy fate. Divine intervention or whatnot. You know I'm going to see it as damned suspicious, with Jake Salifano's name coming up. And those two fellas looking for Bowman the other day."

Summer almost laughed. Sarge had described the men in the Hummer as "possibly ex-cons." Sam couldn't be *less* ex-con.

"Wait until you meet him. He's sweet. He's a guy who got lost and wandered into East Canyon. Who happens to be a tax attorney. Whose friend happened to have got himself kidnapped."

Jeremy hefted the saddle off the top rail of the paddock fence and when he turned to walk past her and into the barn he gave her a look she'd seen now and then since childhood, the look she got when she transgressed beyond the bounds of reasonableness so completely that he could hardly believe they were related. He spoke over his shoulder.

"And to get this sweet lost attorney to fly with you to Denver, you plan to hand him thirty-some thousand dollars, and you want me to drive him out into the desert and help him give that money to a bunch of armed drug runners. How much cash do we even have?"

"About that much."

Like any rich paranoid worth his salt, sometime after World War II her grandfather Martin had bought a big safe, hidden it in the tunnels, and stocked it with cash and twenty-dollar Saint-Gaudens gold coins. The hoard was for "real" emergencies—the apocalyptic variety—and long-standing tradition prevented anyone in the family from raiding it to pay the bills. Summer had only dipped into it a few times. Uncle Darwin had pointed out that while the gold had done okay, the cash had suffered decades of inflation and wasn't nearly the haul it had been in the fifties and sixties. She'd once looked into the potential collector's value of the old bills themselves, but they had none beyond their face value.

She followed her uncle into the tack room. Her father used to keep eagle paraphernalia in here with the horse tack. Jeremy had taken it over after Leo's death, filled it with Old West memorabilia. Antique

Winchesters in racks on the wall, bleached animal skulls, Native tapestries. He was vain about his saddles and bridles, though he rode his ATV as much as the horses these days.

"He's not a pro," she said.

"Who?"

"The kidnapper. The one Sam talked to. Nasty as hell, but he's not a cartel enforcer or anything like that. He sounded high, twitchy. I assume there's more than one, they're probably street gang opportunists who had a rich lawyer land in their laps. I'm certain they killed the hitchhiker. Sam's friend wouldn't last the night, and I don't trust them not to just kill Sam and take the money."

He slid the saddle onto an empty rack and hung the bridle on the wall. Sprayed saddle soap on a rag and began wiping down the leather.

"Sam and his friend are good for the thirty-seven thousand," she said.

"No doubt. It's not the money I'm worried about."

No, she thought, and it wasn't the personal danger she was asking him to walk into either. Secrecy was the Girard family religion, and Uncle Jeremy was the high priest. In extending her family's help to Sam and his friend, she knew she was breaking unstated generations-old rules, making a leap of faith based largely on superstition, on her conviction that because of the circumstances and timing of his appearance, Sam would somehow be important in whatever drama was about to unfold for the family.

"I took his phone," she offered. This prompted a short laugh and she could feel her uncle about to criticize someone who would let her do that, but he stopped, knowing how persuasive she was. His shoulders relaxed and he gave a fatalistic huff and shake of the head as if understanding in that moment he had been persuaded as well. She was glad she wouldn't have to insist on going with Sam herself.

"No police," he said, reasserting some semblance of control. "Other than me. No FBI. He knows?"

"He swore it."

"And I'm going to handle it the way I handle things."

"I wouldn't have asked you otherwise." She was throwing Sam to the proverbial lions here.

Jeremy brushed past her, out of the tack house, and back toward the barn, probably looking for his dog. "You know what we're risking for these strangers," he said. "Even if I'm careful, there's no good result for us."

"I know," she said.

16

Bowman paid the cabdriver, adding a hundred-dollar tip for his patience. Their first stop had been a big satellite parking lot near DIA, where Bowman pretended to have forgotten where he'd parked. They drove around the lot until he realized it was too well lit, with cameras on every third light pole, so he'd acted confused and told the driver he wanted a cheap motel where he could get some sleep and try to find his car tomorrow.

After the cab drove off, Bowman drifted away from the motel's front office and into the shadows to watch the lot. A couple dozen cars of various vintages were parked there, but any recent tech would defeat his dated skills, so he marked the older models. Had to be near midnight by now, and the place was pretty quiet. Two floodlights dim and flickering, leaving big pools of shadow. No slim jim, so he had to find an unlocked vehicle. He would start with the most-shadowed, most nondescript car, a light blue Toyota Corolla with a Christmas tree deodorizer hanging from the rearview, and work his way through the lot.

A stout woman in a flowered robe emerged from a ground-level door and walked out to an SUV, rummaged around, returned to her room. He waited. He reached up and rubbed his hair for the twentieth time. He'd had long hair since he was a kid.

"Make me look like a banker on vacation," was what he'd told the stylist, an exuberant young woman from Venezuela. They'd exchanged a few phrases in Spanish but again he hadn't let on he was fluent. Walking through the airport showered and clean-shaven, wearing tastefully distressed jeans, a shirt that fit, and the Hungarian-made chukkas that so excited Tommy the clothes salesman, Bowman had felt like an alien in his own skin. People were noticing him again, men and women, but differently. There were smiles, furtive glances. He wasn't blending in very well after all. The Delta rep who'd given him a hard time before had gone home, but the manager took his cash and issued him his ticket to Whitespring via Denver, telling him he looked "just like" some celebrity Bowman pretended he'd heard of.

In the Denver airport, he'd picked up another person following him, not airport security this time. He'd slipped around behind the man, and at the last moment decided to walk past the gate for his flight to Whitespring. If people were looking for him, the one flight to Whitespring would be too obvious a choke point. They'd be waiting for him on the other end; they could abduct him, kill him, or—worst of all—follow him to the ranch, where Uncle Jeremy would kill him for compromising security.

His father had described the state of mind currently possessing Bowman as "constructive paranoia." He would say Bowman was already playing into "their" hands by flying directly to Colorado, that he was acting too predictably. He would insist that the only way to evade them now was to do something off-kilter.

Like steal a vehicle.

This was too much thinking about his father. Might be the start of a ciguatera episode. Surely Leo Girard wasn't about to show up in person. Driving his old Willys jeep, top down, windshield folded forward onto the hood. Dad loved that vehicle. He had a big ventilated crate bolted to the back for the eagles.

Bowman walked through the dim parking lot, trying doors and windows on all the older cars, setting off a sophisticated car alarm that had been installed on a restored '77 Coupe de Ville and necessitating a quick scurry into the dark vacant lot next door. Leaving only a badly rusted Ford pickup from the late eighties, which he'd saved for last because its tires were bald and he had serious doubts about its roadworthiness. The headlights might not even work. He knew he could steal it because the passenger window had already been broken and was patched with duct tape and translucent plastic sheeting. The plastic was sun-hazed, the tape frayed and dusty. The owner didn't have the cash to put in a new window, and who would steal a truck like this anyway?

The doors were unlocked, and he'd found a sharp Ka-Bar knockoff in the glove compartment and was about to start stripping wires when he remembered to look for the keys, which were under the driver's side floormat. He used the knife to switch plates with a car across the lot. In the dim interior light, the registration said the truck belonged to Sherman K. Carver of Longpoint Highway in Bird City, Kansas. On the floor, a heavy leather tool belt caked with gypsum dust. He left this on the sidewalk with silent apologies.

He drove into the night, navigating by the Front Range rearing up on the western horizon. Seven hours to Whitespring, give or take. Bowman wasn't proud of himself. Wearing clothes the price of which would have fed him for months in Costa Rica. Stealing the property of a broke sheetrock hanger from Bird City. There was some consolation in knowing he would ask Summer or Uncle Darwin to go into that bank account and make sure Mr. Carver was anonymously paid the cost of a better truck, but deploying his family's advantage ex post facto to justify unethical behavior left him uneasy, a voice in his head telling him this was exactly why he'd stayed away for so long.

17

1986

By the time they finished setting up the new wall tent, her father had apologized twice for the fact that the campground was so crowded. He'd had no idea, he said, there would be so many winter solstice enthusiasts willing to drive the awful roads to Chaco and spend the night outside in the cold. Summer didn't mind—they so rarely saw strangers, it was interesting to watch their behavior—and Bowman had put on his usual stoic equanimity and didn't complain either.

Bowman had originally proposed they sneak up Fajada Butte to see the famous Sun Dagger site, where in late morning two shafts of light would bracket the same spiral carved into the rock that received the single "dagger" on the June solstice. Leo had noticed Bowman's use of the word "sneak" and looked into it himself, finding the Park Service had prohibited public access to Fajada Butte because so many visitors were damaging the Sun Dagger site. Instead they planned to walk from the campground to the Wijiji great house, which had been built, presumably for ceremonial purposes, precisely in a spot from which you could watch the sun rise in a notch on the distant horizon the morning of the winter solstice.

Their tent was big, with plenty of room for the three of them, but Bowman insisted on staying outside despite predicted lows in the single digits. This made Summer suspicious, and sure enough, when she and her father woke two hours before dawn, Bowman had disappeared, his sleeping bag and ground tarp rolled up and tucked under the jeep.

Leo said he was sure Bowman had gone off "to climb that damn butte and get arrested," but when they went to track him with flashlights they saw his prints headed up the trail toward Wijiji. By the time they got to the great house, a handful of visitors had already gathered, not including Bowman, and Summer eventually found his tracks continuing off-trail up Chaco Wash. After another mile they found him in an alcove at the base of a cliff wall. There he sat, glassy-eyed and semi-catatonic in the pale predawn light. Summer wanted to interrogate him but her father said they should sit with Bowman and wait for sunrise.

She sat cross-legged on Bowman's left, mocking his self-serious expression, amusing only herself. Their father had gone to some trouble to bring them here, and Bowman sneaking off alone to find his own special site where there wouldn't be any tourists struck Summer as rude. Still, he had left tracks they could follow, and clearly Leo didn't share her outrage, so she kept her mouth shut. Ten minutes later, the top arc of the sun appeared, perfectly aligned on the right side of a notch in a butte far to the east.

They were all quiet, squinting at the yellow orb erupting in slow motion, a big bright mushroom pushing its way up from the horizon. Summer was dressed warmly but she always shivered in that last coldest breeze of dawn.

When the sun was two fingers over the horizon, she stood and stretched. Behind her, her father stood as well. He made some sort of exclamation, not a curse but an expression of surprise. When Summer looked, he was pointing at the rock wall behind them, shadowed before but illuminated now by the sun: spirals, handprints, an upright humanoid with an elk's head.

That last one gave Summer a chill despite herself.

"How did you know this was here?" she asked.

Bowman took a moment before he answered. "I didn't."

They all stared at the images. Summer felt they were being a bit theatrical in their utter amazement, but she also knew she was being defensive. She had accepted Bowman's uncanny sensitivity to a more expansive conception of reality, as well as her own lack thereof. But her father, she thought, was overly impressed by her brother's talent, or whatever it was, and he tended to give Bowman the benefit of the doubt when he was rude and selfish. The dynamic struck her as unhealthy, not likely to turn out well.

"What are you after, son?" Leo asked.

Summer started to roll her eyes at her father's over-earnest question, but she wanted to know too. Bowman had told her humanity had gone mad at some point, probably more than once, and he wanted to know why, how, when. He showed her the charts and maps he'd drawn, tracking human migrations and various cultural and technological developments, mapping them in time and geography versus known mass extinctions and landscape-scale anthropogenic ecological disruptions.

As before, Bowman thought about his answer for a while. They waited.

"There's something in these ruins. It's similar to what Summer and I feel in the Old Ones' village back home, and in the tunnels." He paused again, the slow conversational rhythm and the obvious effort to include her all part of a performance, but then he actually seemed to be struggling with his words. Which was unusual.

"There's a residue," he continued, "something sticky, from what happened here a long time ago. A transformation of some sort. I think it has something to do with how people went so wrong in the first place."

He was looking for the Fall. Which presupposed a Garden. Summer didn't think he was going to find it.

18

2009

Sam woke in the guest bedroom, still dressed. Took a few minutes to figure out where he was and what was happening. That it hadn't been a bad dream. How long had he slept? His watch was still useless, and Summer had taken his phone for some reason, but it must be nearly time to leave with the ransom.

He walked into the quiet house. Soft sconce lights like the ones in the tunnel lit the halls. At the main entrance hall the stucco walls were smooth and curved, beams of some rough dark wood exposed on the high ceiling. A heavy wooden front door that reminded him of the one he'd first seen in the canyon. He was about to open it and look outside when he heard something in the hall to his right, fast clicking steps coming his way. Like a child caught snooping, he stood there more or less paralyzed until a huge white long-haired dog trotted around a corner, its toenails tapping on the stone floor.

The dog slowed. No growling. No tail-wagging either. Male for sure; he stopped and gave Sam a searching look with hazel eyes big as half-dollars. A long, feathered white tail curled up over his back like a cobra. Sam swallowed hard and dropped to a knee, looking into the dog's face. The dog looked back. When he reached out his hand and asked, "What's your name?" because he couldn't think of anything else to say, the tail relaxed and swished slowly back and forth. The dog sniffed his hand.

"That's Marco."

Sam stood and turned. Uncle Darwin had snuck up and was standing behind him, dressed in jeans, scuffed boots, a denim shirt with the western-style yoke over the shoulders.

"Marco," Sam repeated. "What kind of dog is he?"

"Big mutt."

"Where's Summer?" As he asked this he realized how absurd the question must sound this time of night.

"Bed, I guess." He raised an eyebrow, but Sam couldn't tell if it was meant to be suggestive in some way.

"I'm supposed to go with you all later. To a meeting in Denver." Why was he babbling about this? Probably because if he started talking about the ransom exchange his voice would quaver.

"I heard that. You want some eggs?" Darwin smiled at him, like they were pals now. "She said for me to fix you breakfast before we head out."

"You're going too? For the ransom?"

Darwin nodded. "Let me show you something first." He walked down the stone-paved hall, Marco beside him. Sam followed, nonplussed. The uncle opened a set of heavy double doors and clicked on the lights inside a large wood-paneled room. It was like walking into the mammal hall at the Smithsonian, or maybe a Cabela's store. Animals stood on the floor and stared down from the walls between bookshelves. Marco trotted into the room and stood very still, face-to-face with a massive-shouldered hyena, as if the last time he'd checked, this hell-dog was dead, but it didn't hurt to make sure. A tremendous black bearskin hung head-down above the mantel, but most of the animals were African. To Sam's left, opposite the stone fireplace, a deep alcove contained a diorama of six African antelope in full-body mounts.

Darwin flipped another switch that lit up the antelope as Sam approached. He recognized a kudu with graceful corkscrew horns twirling up toward the ceiling, a reddish bongo, an oryx. The largest was a dark chestnut animal the size of a horse with a black-and-white mane under its neck and twisted horns as thick as Sam's leg. Its plaque said LORD DERBY ELAND (*TAUROTRAGUS DERBIANUS GIGAS*), ZEMONGO, C.A.R., 1962.

"Summer said you've been to East Africa. I thought you might be interested."

"Who shot them?"

"Summer's dad, Leo. He spent the sixties over there working for the government. Must not have been much work to do, seems like all he did was hunt. Those antelope were all either world records or number two at the time. This guy"—Darwin stepped toward a Schwarzeneggerian leopard crouched on a weathered log beside one of the two big windows, rubbed it between its ears—"would be the world record now if the Central African subspecies was still recognized."

Marco became interested in the leopard and stepped over to carefully sniff its left ear, Darwin's gesture possibly bringing it to life. The dog was unwilling to let his guard down. Probably he wasn't allowed in the room very often.

"They're all starting to fall apart and it costs a small fortune to get 'em spruced up. I told Summer she should give this stuff to a museum, but she's sentimental about it."

"She wasn't even born when her dad was in Africa, was she? Did they ever go back?"

"Never did. Leo gave up trophy hunting. Said he put it behind him, in his youth where it belonged. Summer hunted with him here on the ranch for meat, but that was later."

Sam crouched down in front of the leopard, stared into its shiny glass eyes. "So Summer and her brother grew up with all these animals in here?" The lips were drawn back to show the two-inch-long yellow-white canines. "This must have been incredible to a kid."

"This whole deal was. Can you even picture growing up in a place like this?" Darwin patted Sam's shoulder companionably. "Come on, you skipped dinner last night. Got to eat something. Can't face those drug dealers on an empty stomach."

Marco followed them into the kitchen and curled up under a window. Darwin poured beaten eggs sizzling into a huge black cast-iron skillet on the gas stove. Sam's stomach made quiet noises. Last night he'd been too nervous to eat anything other than his last protein bar before he'd passed out on the bed.

After a few moments, Darwin set a plate on the table with a mound of steaming eggs and warmed-up sausage and a thick slice of dark, rustic bread. His bushy eyebrows waggled up and down. "Toaster's over by the coffee maker—that's a fresh pot if you want some."

Sam poured dark coffee into an old-fashioned white ceramic mug heavy as a hammer, added what looked like whole milk from a glass jar. The eggs were delicious. Fresh and steaming but not runny. Sam hated runny scrambled eggs. He added salt and pepper and some hot sauce from a little bottle on the table. Darwin stood at the sink scrubbing dishes, talking about how they used to have chickens up here, but eventually gave up trying to protect them from the twenty-one different predator species that lived in Panther Gap, every damn one of them bent on the chickens' total destruction, and now they bought their eggs from a family that lived down in the low country near Whitespring.

Sam thought about that for a moment, started trying to count predator species in his head but didn't get very far. Maybe Darwin was pulling his leg. Then he realized something else. He swallowed a long pull of the strong coffee, set the mug down on the table with a dull clunk.

"You're Uncle Jeremy, aren't you?" Sam said this half to himself.

The uncle heard him and laughed but didn't reply.

19

Bowman drove south of the city on a new bypass and turned in to the dark mountains, headed in a southwesterly direction, hungry again, starting to imagine he might actually arrive at the ranch in time for breakfast, when he noticed the engine temperature needle was in the red zone. He pulled off to let it cool. An hour later it happened again. He waited longer this time, his hopes for breakfast evanescing. The truck overheated twice more over the next couple of hours.

On the climb out of Creede, steam issued forth from under the hood. He steered onto the dirt shoulder and switched off the engine, the head-lights. Sat and listened to the faint gurgling hiss from the radiator. The sweet-metal stink of vaporized engine coolant caught in his throat.

He should have stolen a better vehicle.

The road he'd ended up on was not well traveled at this hour. He waited in the dark. The driver's-side window was down, and over the diminishing noise of the radiator he heard the rush of a creek not far away. The sound of the water grew louder, impossibly loud, and his head expanded like a balloon. He held the steering wheel to keep from float-ing up and out the window into the night.

It sometimes started like that, a forced entry to ciguatera city. This felt like a bad one, and a sweat ensued, soaking his new shirt. He got out, still feeling he might lose contact with the ground at any moment, and unlatched the hood, propped it open. He would need a rag for the hot radiator cap. Surely Sherman Carver from Bird City had faced this problem before. There should be spare coolant somewhere in the truck. Though, come to think of it, driving from Bird City to Denver wouldn't involve a lot of steep climbs. A couple thousand feet of gain over a couple hundred miles, then a long gentle descent home after Mr. Carver finished a job. Bowman had transgressed the truck's accustomed and agreed-upon limitations by bringing it up this steep canyon into the mountains. He apologized out loud to the old Ford for his ignorance and insensitivity.

He turned away from the stinking, ticking engine. To his right, the dark canyon fell away from the blacktop to the noisy creek. He breathed deeply, slowly.

"I'm talking to a truck," he said.

Back in Costa Rica, he'd learned to adjust to the way ciguatera warped his mind. In the jungle beside the ocean, the potential for bad decisions—the trouble he could get into—was predictable and relatively easy to understand. Things were different here.

Had he been influenced by the oncoming episode when he'd stolen this truck? Possibly. What about in the airport, when he'd abandoned his flight to Whitespring? Hard to say. Those decisions might not stand up to scrutiny by someone like Summer, but they still felt right.

He was probably fine. Light-headed, feverish, but fine.

Where was he, though? According to the stars he could see, this highway was still going in the right direction. The light from a distant ranch house shone dim yellow in the notch of the canyon back the way he'd come, miles away.

Behind the seat he found an old towel stained with what smelled like motor oil. Wishing he had a flashlight, he squinted at the junk in the bed, began feeling around in there with his hands. Mostly construction detritus, probably salvaged from sites where Carver had worked, stuff he thought it was a shame to throw away, stuff he could use someday. Then, shock-corded into a corner, two empty gallon milk jugs. He freed them and stepped to the edge of the shoulder, peered down the steep slope to the dark line of brush along the creek.

He felt hot, like his skin could ignite, so he took off his sweaty shirt and hung it on the crooked passenger-side mirror to dry. In the men's store in the Miami airport, Tommy had assured him the ankle-high boots were fine for hiking, but the soles were smooth, no traction, so he took them off, stuffed the socks inside, rolled up the cuffs of his new blue jeans, and made his way down the slope barefoot, his feet tough from life in Costa Rica. Turning sideways to force his way through the willows, he felt mud between his toes and then he was kneeling beside the busy creek, melted snow from the high country tumbling happily over a bed of broken rock. The sound enveloped him, soothing but also preventing him from hearing anything else. If he had time, he would wait here for a lull in the ciguatera episode, all night if necessary, trusting the water spirits to protect him as he crossed over to the city, sliding from memory to vision to paranoid fantasy, hoping to learn something or achieve some new insight by the end.

Instead, he filled the two jugs with cold creek water and climbed back toward the road. Halfway up he stopped and crouched. A long dark SUV had pulled behind the truck. It waited there with its lights off. After a moment, a figure appeared on the shoulder.

Bowman waited, hoping he hadn't been seen, but a flashlight stabbed at his eyes, then switched off.

A friendly male voice called out, "Oh hell, sorry about that!"

He blinked at the bright afterimage.

"Are you okay down there? I stopped to see if you need a hand!"

Still he didn't move, considering his options. Decided he had none. Shouldn't have left the damn hood up, wasn't that some sort of signal that he wanted help? Or, much worse, could he possibly have been followed? Through the airport, on the cab ride to the motel, someone parked out on the highway, watching him with night vision as he stole the truck, and then trailing expertly several miles behind? Now finding him broken-down and vulnerable.

He tried to focus but his mind kept slipping. Usually this wasn't a problem, but with so-called real-life exigency pressing on him to react in certain ways to the world, he found the slippage impossibly frustrating, like he was using a pry bar with the pointy end bent the wrong way. There was no dig, no catch.

Eventually he managed to get his feet moving again and made it to the shoulder, where he stood with his dripping water jugs, shirtless and shoeless, squinting in the dark at a man leaning under the open hood. The flashlight illuminated the truck's engine.

"This thing's an antique, I mean, that's good, you can see what's what in there. The new Chevys like mine, it's all computers, you can't work on your own car anymore."

Bowman watched his face in the spill of light. The man looked a little older than Bowman—early forties, maybe—a clean-shaven white guy with a strong jaw. Good-looking, fit, muscular but not overly so. He wore casual civilian clothes: khakis and a black shell jacket over a dark T-shirt. Red baseball cap, newish running shoes. He remembered the stranger in the men's store in Miami, in the photo Tommy had shown him. Similar build, but different hair.

"You got a rag or something for that radiator cap?" The man smiled. Bowman's state of undress didn't seem to take him aback. In fact, the pricey ensemble that had allowed him to function at the airport would have clashed suspiciously with Carver's pitiful truck. "When I was a kid my daddy got second-degree burns on his arms in a situation just like this."

"Thanks for stopping," Bowman said. He remembered to throw some rural Colorado into his voice. The plates he'd stolen were Colorado, which he was thankful for because he had no idea what a Kansas accent sounded like. "I got a rag but I'll wait a bit, let her cool down some more. The old girl does this all the time." He held up the two heavy jugs. "A little creek water'll fix her up, get me over the pass. It's downhill from there," he added cheerily, wincing, afraid he might be overdoing it.

"Well, okay," the man said. "I don't mind waiting along with you. In case you can't get started again." He stepped away from the truck and switched off his light. Bowman could make out his head turning left and right, considering the empty highway. "You might be out here all night."

"Wouldn't be the first time I slept in the truck," Bowman said, laughing. The man stood there, nodding his head. Big grin. Bowman realized the only way he was going to get rid of him was to start the truck. He put on his shirt and shoes and socks, found the oil-smelly rag, and focused on opening up the radiator cap without burning his arms. Poured both jugs of water in.

"Give her a crank," the man suggested helpfully.

Bowman sat behind the wheel and gave her a crank, but nothing happened, just a faint electrical clicking noise. The man was looking under the hood with his flashlight again. Then he came around to the driver's-side window.

"I believe your thermostat's busted. Good thing I waited."

"Should still crank," Bowman said.

"Don't know what to tell you." The hint of menace in his voice might be Bowman's imagination, or the man might have snipped a wire when he was messing around under the hood. He might be armed. Leo Girard spoke into Bowman's ear, telling him to play along, to find out what this stranger was after, to save his move, be it fight or flight, for the proper moment.

"I'll give you a lift to Stumptown. You can call a tow truck in the morning." And with that, the man got back in his vehicle. The headlights came on with the engine, a bright soulless ice-blue, must be some new kind of bulb. He drove up beside Bowman, the Suburban pointed west. The passenger-side window lowered silently. "Hop in."

Bowman felt the steep, irresistible slip-sliding of fate, a sense of predestination. He glanced around the dark cab of his stolen pickup truck. Couldn't imagine anything in here he wanted. He felt for his dry bag, still strapped to his waist. It contained the rest of his cash—an unknown but large amount, he hadn't really kept track—along with his passport. He remembered that in Miami he'd bought three snack bars made of nuts and peanut butter and chocolate, which sounded delicious to him just then, but it didn't feel like they were in the bag, so he must've eaten them.

"You coming?"

Bowman said goodbye to Sherman Carver's truck and got out. The moon hung above the crest of the mountain, shimmering like a flag in the wind, which meant his fever was worse than he'd thought. To the east, the dim down-sloping country was open, its vegetation sparse, moonlight revealing the rock bones of the land. No sign of dawn. He had to get to the ranch today. Summer was in danger. Once again he regretted not warning her when he'd last had the chance, seven years ago.

Setting aside his qualms, he opened the Suburban's passenger door and slid onto the plush leather seat. The man extended his hand.

"Bickford Rangely," he said. "But call me Bick."

Bowman hesitated, thinking it sounded like a made-up name, then, knowing he had to go ahead and ride this out, he reached over and shook hands, introducing himself as Sherman Carver.

20

Jeremy, Sam, and Marco rode down a narrow road switchbacking off the ridge in a big open ATV. Jeremy said the family only used ATVs and horses on the property, and they kept their trucks in a barn way down at the caretaker's house near the public road. The eighteen-wheelers that brought in the stockers—Sam gathered this was a kind of cattle— couldn't go any farther than the caretaker's house, so they unloaded there and Summer and the uncles drove the herd several miles up the driveway, over the mountain, and into the valley the old-fashioned way. Same thing in reverse come fall.

The first stretch cut through a deep trench in the rock, but as they descended, the way became more exposed, the drop-off on Sam's side of the vehicle precipitous—the moon shone now over the butte off to the east— and he tried his best not to look down. The dog, who'd become fascinated with Sam for some reason, kept pressing his wet nose into Sam's ear and giving a loud huff, Sam nearly leaping from his seat every time.

They stopped at a massive metal gate, where Jeremy used a key on three deadbolts, releasing a heavy steel bar connected to a cable on a windlass. Sam helped him raise the bar from its brackets, and they swung the left side of the gate outward. After they drove through, Jeremy stopped the ATV and they both went back and reversed the process. When Sam made a comment about the security, Jeremy said it used to be better, which Sam took to mean more secure. He said it was harder to hide out now with satellites taking pictures and putting them on the internet.

"Visitors usually get blindfolded driving in and out," he said. "You already know where we are, so I'm making an exception."

Sam laughed, then reconsidered. Was he serious?

After another ten minutes on a rough dirt track, a small ranch house appeared on a knoll set back fifty yards from the public road. Sam guessed it had to be the same road he'd been walking on yesterday. Another few miles and he would've been knocking on the door of this house. Instead of Summer, he would've met Sarge, the family's caretaker. He would've given Sam a ride to Whitespring, dropped him off at the airport. Where he would've picked up Mac's calls. Sam would be trying to handle this situation on his own. He started to appreciate Summer's claim of serendipity.

They drove into the barn behind the house, triggering a floodlight inside that illuminated a dusty Toyota SUV and two pickups, a newish black Ford and an ancient Dodge. Jeremy parked beside the Dodge, explained that he didn't need a fancy vehicle, didn't have to drive very far to get to work. Summer traveled the most, he said, back and forth to Denver or the airports in Whitespring and Durango.

"She said you all have jobs off the ranch."

"Got to, anymore. Cow bidness sure don't pay."

Sam noticed the uptick in cowboy-speak but saw no indication the uncle intended any irony.

"She said you work in law enforcement?" No response. "Said Darwin's a chef, and she works with some sort of nonprofit, but she didn't say what it does. What its mission is."

"You being nosy?"

Sam was taken aback. "Just making conversation."

"That's all right, I can tell you. Her grandfather set up that charity way back when, and Summer gets paid chicken-scratch to fly off somewhere every month and give money to other ranchers doing the same things we're doing here."

Sam imagined a family foundation. There were rules now on how much family members could get paid. He lowered the tailgate while Jeremy pried open a big rusted steel toolbox bolted in behind the cab and loaded a long plastic case and a duffel from the ATV. Marco gathered himself and leaped onto the tailgate; in the truck's bed, he hopped his front paws up on the toolbox, stood tall as a man with his head above the top of the cab. Jeremy tucked the paper grocery bag of thirty-seven thousand dollars cash behind the bench seat like it was their sack lunch and they headed out in the old truck.

The meeting place was nearly an hour away and remote enough that, Summer had said, the odds of anyone observing them at two in the morning were inconsequential. Jeremy stopped the truck at a dip in the road. He cut the headlights and jumped out with a screwdriver he used to jimmy open the toolbox. Removed a bundle of clothing from his duffel. When Sam rounded the rear of the truck Jeremy wore a headlamp throwing a dim red glow and was stepping into the pant legs of a set of camouflage coveralls. In the bed, Marco stood close to Sam and breathed warm dog-breath into his ear. Sam reached up and absently scratched the dog's huge head.

"Can you trust your friend?" Jeremy asked, somehow satisfied with Sam's own trustworthiness. "He can't report this to the police. And you can't tell him anything about us. No names, nothing about Summer or the ranch, he can't see my face, the truck license plate, nothing."

Jeremy reached into the toolbox and brought out the rectangular case. He unsnapped the latches and produced a black assault rifle with a bulky black scope on top. Pulled out a silencer the size of a cardboard paper towel tube and attached it to the barrel.

"Whoa," Sam said. Jeremy had brought a small cooler with Coors in cans and they'd each had a few on the way. Despite the beer, Sam's butterflies had been slowly morphing into nauseous abdominal pit bulls, and the sight of this serious version of Uncle Jeremy with a military rifle was downright calming. "Is that night-vision?"

"You can drive a stick, right? I'll be on overwatch, out in the brush, up that rise north of the road. Give me a ten-minute head start, then drive until you see their vehicle, be maybe a quarter mile. Stop a hundred yards back and kill your lights. Walk halfway with the bag and make them show your friend's alive before you toss the bag. Don't get close to them, step back, let them count the cash if they want. When they let your friend go, get him into the truck and wait for them to leave."

Sam nodded, not trusting himself to produce a calm vocalization. Jeremy spoke to Marco, telling him to stay, and disappeared into the sagebrush. Sam counted to six hundred and started the truck. It had been more than a decade since his last experience with a clutch and he stalled twice before he was able to get the truck moving along in first gear. The red reflectors on a vehicle appeared in the distance and he braked, stalling again, switched off the headlights, got out, and pulled the money-heavy grocery bag from behind the seat. Feeling one hundred percent sober, he stood beside the hot ticking hood of the truck.

The other vehicle switched its lights on. Sam realized he'd forgotten all about the rented Subaru. What had they done with it? Two figures got out, their heads sleek and black, must be wearing ski masks. His stomach went watery and he managed to keep his legs from buckling only because he knew Jeremy was watching.

Okay, he thought, *I have thirty-seven grand in a bag and I'm taking a step toward a couple of drug-dealers-slash-kidnappers. But I'm not the one kidnapped. That would be my friend Mac. So this is for Mac, Mac is the one in trouble.*

He felt stronger. Another step.

The men moved forward a few yards and waited for Sam to close the distance. Sam was going to have to break the ice. How to say it? Surely he'd seen this in a movie, but he couldn't recall a single specific scene, a proper challenge uttered by some coolheaded hero.

"Where's Mac?!" he shouted. That might've been too loud. To the point, though.

"Mister Sam! Where's our money?!" It was the voice from the phone, mocking, imitating his nervous shout. Both men laughed. Sam held up the bag, and the one who'd yelled nodded to the other, who walked back to the SUV and bundled a third person out of the raised hatchback, wearing a hood, taller than the other two but hunched over, gradually straightening as he was led forward. At least he could walk on his own. They pulled off the hood and shone a flashlight in his face: Mac, taped across his mouth, beaten up but recognizable. He was wild-eyed, shaking his head, yelling into the tape, trying to tell Sam something. The hood fell over his face again.

"Give us the money, Mister Sam!" Still making fun of him. Sam tossed the bag.

As the second guy bent to pick it up, Sam asked, "What about Melissa?" The man with the bag looked up at the other and they both shrugged theatrically. They had a flashlight, and peered into the bag. A low, almost whispered exchange Sam couldn't make out, then they turned and ushered Mac back toward the SUV.

"That's thirty-seven thousand, you can count it . . . Hey!"

They pushed Mac into the back of the vehicle. Both men were laughing.

"Hey, you got the money, bring him back!"

Backlit by the headlights, the two men moved toward Sam with startling aggression, each pulling a weapon of some sort from his belt.

Sam couldn't move. His mouth fell open and he couldn't shut it. This embarrassed him but there was nothing he could do. Closer now, both men were definitely pointing pistols, demanding something, Sam's ears ringing, the men closing until Marco roared from his perch in the bed of the truck, hardly even sounded like a dog. They hesitated, and something swatted into their heads—first one, then the other—and they fell unstrung to the gravel road. Some of what had been inside their heads, expressed as a spray and backlit by the headlights, took longer than the bodies to sift to the ground. Fascinated, Sam watched it fall.

The sound of galloping behind him. Marco appeared and sniffed at the two corpses, his tail up high. Uncle Jeremy jogged into the road, kicked the pistols away, and gave each of the kidnappers a shove with his foot, then approached the SUV with his rifle at his shoulder. When he'd confirmed no one was in there but Mac, he turned off its lights.

The dark was sudden, Sam's eyes gradually adapting to the moon-light.

Jeremy returned, guiding Mac by the arm and speaking in a voice too low for Sam to hear.

Sam realized he hadn't moved his feet since he'd thrown the bag of money, which Jeremy carried tucked under an arm.

He managed a few steps. He stood beside Marco, rested a hand in the thick fur on the dog's shoulder. This was oddly comforting.

"Sam?" Mac spoke from under the hood. Jeremy had been serious about not letting Mac see his face, though he'd removed the tape from his mouth.

"I'm here. You okay?" Sam stepped over one of the kidnappers and took hold of Mac's shoulder. It was shaking. Jeremy had left his wrists zip-tied. "Can we untie his fucking hands?"

"They were going to kidnap you too, to get more ransom. They would've killed us both."

"I got that impression. What about Melissa?"

"She's dead."

Jeremy had collected the pistols and was ungently searching the kidnappers' pockets. He didn't answer Sam's question about freeing Mac's hands.

Mac spoke again. "This guy says he's helping us but he won't take my hood off."

"He's pretty paranoid. But he saved our lives. Just do what he says."

"You ain't paranoid if they're really after you," Jeremy said, cornpone again. He was wearing the dim red headlamp and he opened a leather wallet Sam recognized as Mac's, checked the driver's license. Handed the wallet to Sam and walked to his truck, opened the toolbox, and put away the rifle and the camo, and when he came back the bag of money was gone, so he must've tucked that in there too. Without speaking, he knelt and lifted one of the kidnappers in a balletic fireman's carry, headed to the SUV.

When he hoisted the other, beefier kidnapper, grunting this time, Sam asked if shooting them was the plan all along.

"Hell, no. Dead gangbangers are a pain in my ass."

He shut the hatchback on the bodies. Then he rummaged around in the SUV, doors opening, slamming. When he returned, he was carrying Melissa's big yellow backpack.

"This it?"

Sam nodded.

"Shit."

"What?"

"It's heavy. Twenty-five, thirty pounds."

"She said it was mostly books."

"Ha." He opened the top and looked inside. Stared for a moment, closed it back up. "Makes no damn sense."

"What makes no sense?"

"Well, last time I checked, this particular narcotic was eighty dollars a gram wholesale, maybe one-eighty street. There's four hundred and fifty grams in a pound, and if you've got ten pounds of coke, that's forty-five hundred grams." He paused, figuring in his head.

"Three-sixty-K wholesale," Sam said. "Eight-ten street. Twice that if it's twenty pounds."

Jeremy cursed again. "Those two idiots weren't working for the real owners. I don't know how they found you. And I don't know how whoever the owners did send haven't caught up with this pack yet."

"Melissa said she took out a tracking device."

Sam and Jeremy looked at each other, then at Mac's hooded head.

"She admitted some stuff to me. They taped our mouths but she could still talk."

Sam's outrage finally boiled over. "Can you please cut that fucking plastic thing off his wrists? This is fucked up, it's like he's our prisoner and we're interrogating him."

Jeremy pulled a folding knife from his pocket. "Leave the hood on," he said as he cut the zip tie. The sudden release of his shoulders unbalanced Mac and he stumbled forward. Sam caught him, held his elbow. Jeremy was bouncing on his toes now, antsy to go, but he asked Mac if the girl had told him anything else.

"Yeah, it was like she was confessing, she felt guilty for getting me in trouble. Her boyfriend was a big deal in one of the Mexican cartels, he worked in Phoenix. They had an argument, he was abusive, she thought he might actually kill her this time, so she attacked him with a golf club. Knocked him cold. He'd been acting weird, paranoid about the backpack, so she grabbed it when she took off. She ditched his Porsche at a truck stop and started hitchhiking. She'd been around the business long enough to know she should look for a LoJack, and she got rid of it."

"Not a LoJack," Jeremy said. "Some kind of GPS transmitter. So how'd they find you?"

"Word got out. She said the cartel would've offered a big reward. Those two must've stumbled on her in the café where we picked her up, or maybe before that, and followed. Dumb bad luck. They got greedy, decided to blow off the reward and keep the coke so they could sell it themselves."

Jeremy thought for a moment. "What's your phone look like?"

Mac described his BlackBerry. Jeremy returned to the SUV and brought back two phones and the BlackBerry, muttering about the god-damn battery being dead.

"Where's the charger?"

"I don't know. Probably in the rental."

"Your car. What happened to it?"

"They sold it to somebody."

"Probably a chop garage."

Jeremy stood behind Mac, lifted up the hood, and showed Mac the BlackBerry in the light. Mac nodded and Jeremy removed the dead battery, tucked phone and battery into a pocket. He tried the other two phones but they were locked.

"They use these other phones to call your people?"

"I don't think so. They used the contacts on my phone."

"They call anyone else on it?"

"No . . . I don't know. I don't think they did."

"You need to make sure. As soon as you can get the battery charged, you turn it on and look for outgoing calls, write down any numbers. Then turn it off again and take the battery out." He took Mac's arm with surprising solicitude and led him toward the SUV. "Sam, you and Marco follow in the truck. Let him ride in the cab with you. Road's gonna get rough."

Sam followed for more than an hour, eventually getting used to the clutch, Marco hanging his head out the passenger window. They drove a bewildering tangle of barely passable back roads, then a mile or so off-road through the desert with their headlights off, churning in low gear along a dry creek bed, nearly getting stuck half a dozen times, finally stopping at the mouth of a box canyon. Jeremy got out and walked hooded Mac back to the truck.

"You two wait here for me. Don't follow." And to Mac, "Keep the hood on for now."

As soon as Jeremy drove away, Sam told Mac to take the fucking hood off, but Mac refused. They waited in the truck with the dog sitting hugely on the bench seat between them, snuffling Sam's ear when the notion took him. Mac answered Sam's questions in a heavy monotone, saying he'd already had to tell the other guy all this stuff. The two kidnappers had driven

Mac and Melissa to an abandoned building near a railroad somewhere. They'd raped Melissa and shot her in the back of the head. Mac managed to convince them he was a valuable hostage, an opportunity to make some quick easy cash that would set them up for selling the coke. They'd forced him to dig a grave in the dirt lot behind the building and bury Melissa there. He said the masks and the hood at the exchange were all for show. He was sure they never had any intention of letting Sam or Mac live. He apologized for nearly getting Sam killed.

After that, Mac didn't want to talk anymore, and Sam felt it was too weird talking to his friend in a hood anyway, so they sat in silence, listening to Marco pant. Eventually, orange light flickered on the walls of the canyon.

"He's burning that SUV. I'm going to get a better look." Sam slid from behind the wheel, eased the truck door closed, and climbed out of the creek bed, careful in the dim moonlight. The SUV was parked on a slight rise in the tight box canyon, enveloped by hyperactive reddish flames twisting and jumping raggedly downwind. It reminded him of Summer's bonfire and he experienced a moment of dislocation, remembering his former self driving drunk through the desert, using the fire as a beacon.

Jeremy had picked a good place for this. The inverse of Summer's signal bonfire, Jeremy's pyre couldn't be seen at a distance from any direction, and it didn't look like there was much brush in there to catch and start a wildfire. Must be BLM land, or maybe the remote corner of a reservation. Then he noticed Jeremy sitting at the edge of the light, upwind of the burning vehicle, messing with Melissa's backpack. He pulled out four rectangular packages one by one and stacked them on the ground beside him. He sat with the empty pack, staring at the packages.

He sat there long enough that Sam worried there might be something wrong with him, like he'd had a stroke or something, but finally he seemed to come to a decision, replacing the packages in the pack, closing the flap, and instead of hurling the pack into the fire he slung it over his shoulder and jogged back the way he'd come.

21

1987

On the flight to Mexico City, Leo sipped a whiskey in the aisle seat and watched his children sidelong, Bowman staring out the window, Summer leaning over to see past his shoulder, calling out anything she recognized: the Sky Islands in southern Arizona, the vast Chihuahuan Desert, the Sierra Madre Occidental a vague etching on the horizon to the west. Bowman endured silently, his thoughts to himself. Leo knew he was traveling the country below in his mind, imagining the plants and animals and rocks and rivers, the people there and how they lived. What they believed. Who their gods were, their ghosts.

When the plane descended to circle Mexico City and the Valley of Mexico, Summer quieted, silenced by the urban spectacle, this tiny patch of the planet where fifteen million people made their lives.

Neither child had ever seen anything remotely like it. They were used to Whitespring. Durango was their big town. Leo had driven them the long hours to Santa Fe a few times to visit museums and galleries, but this was different by orders of magnitude.

He might have waited too long. It might be too much of a shock.

Thirty-five years, his father had said. *You have thirty-five years to*

teach them whatever you want. I'll be long gone and you can make them
ready, as you understand what that means.

This was Martin Girard on his literal deathbed, a cold November day in 1974, telling Leo he was throwing all his hopes for a dy-
nastic legacy on a two-year-old and an infant. Leo hadn't even been
offended. So long as the ranch was secure, he'd never cared what
the old man did with the rest of his wealth. Leo had his government
pension, which was plenty, and he knew how fortunate he was to
be able to raise his children in a place like Panther Gap.

He had put the inheritance out of his mind. In the seventies, the
year 2009 smoked distant in the future, merely notional, a science
fiction fantasy. He and Anna would raise Bowman and Summer at
the ranch to honor her indigenous heritage as well as the wisdom
Leo had learned so late in life in Africa. The kids' reality would be
grounded in the vast, immersive community of the Others before
they were exposed to modernity. But Anna was gone so soon, and
overnight Bowman and Summer had morphed into these inexplicable
beings called teenagers, forming opinions about the world, opinions
he quickly figured out he not only couldn't control, but had, in fact,
almost no influence over. His father had known this, had experienced
it with Leo himself. Leo felt foolish for assuming otherwise.

Anna had always insisted the day would come when they would
have to disappoint the idealism they were fostering in their children. Without her to insist, Leo had put off that day for too long.
He wouldn't be able to determine their stance versus the world,
but he could make sure they saw more of it before their characters
calcified. He would, as his father had suggested, try to make them
ready.

Leaning toward the window, his face close to the backs of his children's heads, smelling their unaccustomed soapy scent, Leo watched as
the plane banked over a green mountain range where the city washed
up against the steepest slopes like flotsam. They descended, flying over
hyperdense slums and city buildings and broad highways and wooded
neighborhoods, a land populous beyond imagining.

"How could there be so many people?" This was Summer, her
usually confident voice small and shocked.

Bowman was silent, his nose nearly touching the window. They both seemed to be having the reaction Leo had feared: not awe and amazement but horror. That wouldn't do. Too strong an aversion to cities would hamstring them in the future that was coming.

His own ideal of human potential had gelled around the difficult, urgent, wise, and spectacularly conscious lifeways of the independent forager and hunter-gatherer tribes he'd lived with in Africa, but that ship had sailed for the rest of the species a very long time ago. So he launched into an unplanned lecture about the importance of remembering that cities were as much a part of the world as the ranch, the desert, the mountains. This was a beautiful, highly cultured, cosmopolitan place with a deep and complex history reaching back hundreds of years before the Spanish came. He said many of the people were desperately poor, cut off by the injustices of society from so much that was essential to a fulfilling life, facing challenges every day that Summer and Bowman couldn't imagine. He droned on until the flight attendant took his glass of watery scotch, and the three of them watched in silence as the urban tableau gradually rose up to meet the plane and the pavement slammed into the landing gear, breaking the spell.

In the mornings they got up early and were out in the city all day. Leo brought them through poor neighborhoods, middle-class neighborhoods, downtown, talking to people on the street, improving their colloquial Spanish in conversation with everyone from policemen to beggars. He also tried to show them what a contented urban dweller would consider to be the city's attractions: staying in a hotel downtown, eating in restaurants, music, art, museums, shopping, haggling with street vendors, traveling by taxi and bus, the pervasive humming energy of it all.

Summer liked the museums. She said they were like funnels concentrating human endeavor and knowledge in one place where you could soak up a lot at once. Bowman was dismissive, said her "funnels" served primarily to concentrate formerly living beings as well as artifacts created by indigenous peoples, all handily removed from their context so that narrow-minded Western humans could experience them in isolation and cook up reductive analyses rendering both the Others and indigenous humanity as objects rightly to be dominated.

This rocked Summer back, but instead of lashing out she gently called Bowman a goddamn stick-in-the-mud and said she was mainly talking about the modern art anyway. They were being civil and more or less respectful, so Leo let the two of them argue.

Part of each day was spent on urban survival skills: how to achieve situational awareness in a loud, busy, distracting environment, what to do and where to go if you perceive a threat, how to follow someone without being noticed, how to notice someone following you and evade or confront them. They practiced blending in: dressing local, obscuring their features, mimicking local behavior and movement. Once in the outskirts of downtown they had to defuse a confrontation with a knot of hostile teenagers, but otherwise the training proceeded uneventfully.

By day five they were all weary, and Bowman's mood especially had darkened. The city had provoked a physical reaction, the skin of his arms and shoulders red and welted, his nights sleepless, his critiques nearly constant.

"Everything is people," he said. "They live indoors, and when they go out it's walls and buildings and streets and more people. No quiet, no space. No sky at night. No wild animals, no aloneness. How can anyone live like this? The ones who aren't poor, they could live somewhere less crowded. Is this what they want? It doesn't even seem real."

Leo was sympathetic, but he said, "This *is* what's real, to most people. They would say you're the one who can't see the real world."

"There are some who can live without wild things, and some who cannot." This was Summer, reciting his favorite Aldo Leopold quote. He'd known it would be a struggle to convey to his children something he himself comprehended only with difficulty: that for thousands of years, billions of humans had managed to live rich, fulfilling lives in cities. Summer appeared less troubled by this than Bowman.

The point of their expedition was urban experience, but Leo had chosen Mexico City partly because they could spend time in the large parks and relieve the tension of city life if they had to, so they spent their sixth day in Chapultepec and the nature reserve on the UNAM campus. This rejuvenated all three of them and led to a chance meeting in the Botanical Garden with an old associate of Leo's, a former spook who'd landed a desk job at the U.S. embassy. They had dinner together that evening, and when he offered to arrange a private tour of the tunnels under Teotihuacan, both children wanted to go.

Their host also mentioned in passing two notorious strongmen who had recently come to power in the African countries where he and Leo used to work. Leo thought he'd hidden his surprise, but on the way out the door the former CIA officer took Leo aside and told him to forget about Africa. There was new thinking in the State Department about these things, and it wasn't right, but there wasn't anything to be done.

That night he stayed awake, preoccupied by the news, worrying about the people he'd known there, and wrestling with the first sneaky tendrils of a paranoia he hadn't felt since leaving the service and moving back to Panther Gap.

On the bus ride to the ancient city of Teotihuacan, Summer and Bowman sat together in the seat in front of Leo, and he could overhear them talking, arguing, Bowman providing an exegesis on pre-Aztec religion and mythology, his fascination with these people and how they understood the cosmos and their place in it bringing him out of his funk. Typically, Summer interrupted constantly with pointed questions, but Bowman kept his temper and answered without pique. He described commonalities among chthonic representations in various pre-Columbian cultures of the desert Southwest. He spelled the word for Summer, who claimed she already knew what it meant and how to spell it. He spoke of the Aztecs' idea of an underworld from which humanity was said to have emerged after an older world had been completely destroyed, and he speculated it might be a reference to a physical disaster, or a cultural one, a shift from a better way of life people had lived before, maybe a real-life utopia at Teotihuacan.

He said after the tunnels he wanted to see the jaguar head sculpture, and the jaguars on the murals. To try to understand the way

people responded to the jaguar back then. It was the land, he said—
the local geology and ecology—that gave the people their gods,
like terroir. And it stuck, it still mattered. Pantheism persisted, even
today, because it answered a basic human need. Scratch any great
world monotheism and you find under the skin the ancient gods, the
dualism of good and evil forces. Always, he said, the devil was there.
Leo found this last bit chilling, an uncanny echo of the memories,
the dormant, bone-deep pessimism that his old CIA compatriot had
awakened, that had kept him up last night.

Summer climbed down a ladder to a floodlit chamber, the staging area for archaeologists where their guide, Julio Cesar, waited.
Bowman followed, and before their father joined them Bowman
whispered that he was going to look around on his own some, and
not to worry about him. She'd thought that was a bad idea, but kept
quiet even after Julio warned them: "Stay together, it's easy to get
lost down here."

After half an hour of wandering around the tunnels, Summer
watched Bowman sneak off. She let him go. Residual sibling loyalty,
she supposed, and if Bowman wanted to spend a little time alone,
time to concoct a mystical experience unavailable to the shriveled
imaginations of his sister and father, who was she to stop him?

She counted to one hundred before staging a dramatic look all
around, her headlamp doing little to light the walls of crumbly-
looking aggregate, the dusty rock floor.

"Where's Bowman?" she asked.

The chamber where they stood wasn't as grand as the one with
the restaurant for the regular Teotihuacan tourists, but it was big
enough that a half-dozen passages branched out from it in various
directions. According to Julio, the interconnected tunnels and caves
east of the Temple of the Sun had barely been explored. These were
the upper levels, rough tunneling in poor stone left by the Aztecs
who, five hundred years ago, may or may not have found access to
the older, more extensive tunnels rumored to exist farther down in
basaltic bedrock.

"Bowman!" Her father's shout was harsh up close but went nowhere, absorbed and muffled by the dark mouths of the other passages. Followed by the fretting Julio, she and her father backtracked to where Bowman's footprints in the dust departed from theirs. He hadn't left much of a trail, probably on purpose. Soon, though, his prints changed, no longer heel to toe but up on the balls of his feet, and farther apart.

"He's running," she said.

Julio moaned unhappily and said something about open pits and weak ceilings. A passage had caved in recently. People had been hurt.

"Wait here." Her father started off down the passage. Summer glanced at Julio, lighting the side of his face with her headlamp. He took off his backpack and pulled out a spool of fine white string on a spindle. He held it up by its handle.

"We're required to bring this with us down here, but I've never used it before. I didn't understand its utility. If you get lost, it's too late to start leaving a string to show you the way back out." The end of the string was tied to a big aluminum nail, which he pounded into the floor with a loose stone. "But we should use it now."

Deploying the string, they jogged after Leo, following the glow from his flashlight.

Summer understood time passed differently underground, had noticed it whenever she and Bowman explored the tunnels underneath the house in Panther Gap. Still, it felt like Bowman had run a very long way, and Julio Cesar's spool of string was running low when they emerged from the tunnel into a chamber larger than any they'd seen so far.

Bowman lay on the floor in the center of the room in a fetal position. Leo's fingers were on his neck, feeling for the carotid as Summer ran up to him, waiting for his nod: *He's alive.* His hands moved around Bowman's body, searching for injuries. Finding none, he asked Summer to help prop her brother in a sitting position so he could hoist him onto his shoulder. Bowman was tall and strong but thin, and Leo carried him easily. Bowman stirred and began to speak without waking up.

Later, in the cab, Bowman raised his head from Summer's shoulder and asked where they were going.

"Hospital," Leo said. "What happened to you?"

"I don't know." He said he felt light-headed, but not sick. He was fine. No need to visit the hospital. He slipped back into a slumber but was able to walk through the emergency entrance. Summer sat with him in the waiting room while their father spoke to an attendant.

"What did you see?"

"I don't remember. A voice called out and I ran to it."

"You didn't see silver pools underground, a night sky with stars, metallic balls?"

He frowned, confused.

"No jaguar?"

He shook his head.

"When we found you, you said that's where you were going. A jaguar was going to take you. We didn't see anything like that, it was just another chamber. Nothing in it but a bunch of rocks."

Now she saw he did remember, and the remembering gave him gooseflesh, a flicker of fear on his face.

"I could see it in my mind. It's way older than anything the Aztecs did, a place the ancients made to call up the chthonic gods. They thought it would bring them power and knowledge. But the city burned, the people burned it fourteen hundred years ago. What came up from the earth wasn't what they expected. I wanted to know what it was. It was important. A tall human figure met me in that chamber. It morphed into the shape of a were-jaguar, like it was mirroring, or trying to show me the jaguar that has been in my mind. I didn't think it would hurt me."

Summer scoffed. And regretted it right away. It felt defensive. He scared her, and she didn't like that. She started to apologize but now he was staring at her, a surprised, hurt look on his face.

"Or maybe it was all a hysterical fit," he said. "Or a scorpion sting." His voice was flat, like he was resigned to his own sister not believing him anymore.

22

When Sam walked into the motel room with his paper bag—two Bud tallboys, corn chips, and mixed nuts from the convenience store—Mac was sitting up in the far bed, glassy-eyed, watching CNN with the sound off. He raised his hand and gave Sam a blank look, his forehead and left cheekbone decorated with butterfly bandages. Jeremy had administered first aid by the light of his headlamp but had vetoed an ER visit.

Was that what a thousand-yard stare looked like? Mac had been through trauma Sam had trouble imagining. He started to ask if he had anyone he could talk to back in D.C., but stopped himself because telling a therapist about the kidnapping, rape, murder, and dual more-or-less justifiable homicide followed by the incineration of the bodies—none of which anyone had reported to the police—raised implications he wasn't prepared to contemplate.

"I have beer," he said instead.

Mac reached out, his hand a grasping claw. "Give." He took a long gulping pull, followed by a low burp. This was standard Mac behavior and Sam felt better about him.

He tossed the bag of chips to Mac and sat on his own bed with the nuts. Per tradition established on the long drives since Las Vegas, they would each eat half and then switch. A commercial for some sort of blood pressure medicine played on the TV. Sam opened his beer, which he was almost too tired to drink.

"You get a flight?"

"Seven forty-five out of Durango," Mac said. "Dallas to Reagan in the afternoon."

Sam found the keys to his car in his pack. They'd parked at Reagan, in a covered lot. He searched around in the interior pocket where he was sure he'd left the receipt.

"You remember where we parked my car?" He tossed the keys to land on the bed. Mac stared without picking them up.

"I tried to make a reservation for you but they wouldn't let me."

For a moment Sam worried about his friend's hold on his memory, on reality. "Jer— . . . the guy who helped us is picking me up at six, down the street, we're meeting someone at the Whitespring airport. I told you."

"What does she look like?"

"That has nothing to do with it. I gave my word."

"He said he's her uncle."

"Uncle SEAL Team Six."

"Uncle Fucking SEAL Team Six." Mac repeated this without much humor. Sam wondered what Mac and Jeremy had talked about during their time together in the kidnappers' vehicle, Mac still hooded and two recently dead bodies lolling and jostling and leaking fluids in the back.

Sam slid onto the other bed. They sat in silence for a while. Sam finished his beer. He shouldn't have let Mac and Melissa get kidnapped in the first place, though he wondered what he would have done if he'd been awake when the kidnappers showed up at their campsite. Thrown rocks?

"I'm sorry." He said this before he realized he was going to speak out loud.

Mac didn't reply and Sam looked over, expecting he'd fallen asleep, but he still stared at the TV. Replaying, Sam imagined, the horrible shit he'd seen. Rape and murder.

"For what?"

"Sleeping through those guys kidnapping you and Melissa. I'd put my earplugs in."

Mac seemed to think that was funny. After another long pause, he spoke again in that flat voice.

"As soon as I realized they were dangerous I started doing telepathy, telling you to stay out of sight. I thought you were being smart, that you would call the police."

"Guess not." The gap between Mac's hope and his own ridiculous actions made Sam even more miserable.

"But you did better than that, Sam. You brought Uncle SEAL Team Six. He said his niece has got you involved in something important, and that you're not allowed to talk about it, and I'm not supposed to try to get you to talk about it."

"Yeah. She thinks there's something special about me because I showed up at their place when I did. I don't know what the hell is going on. They're pretty paranoid."

Mac wrenched his attention away from the TV screen. "Fly back to D.C. with me, man. You know damn well we're already accessories after the fact to a whole bucket of felonies. Plus, I spent some time alone with Uncle, and I am currently more afraid of him than I was of the kidnappers."

Sam set his empty beer can on the bedside table. Mac was right. Jeremy was scary. Summer was scary, a little. The fact that Jeremy hadn't burned the cocaine worried him.

He should go home. He should call that regional airline, though he'd have to borrow Mac's phone—he hadn't cared about handing his over to Summer when there was no signal, but he wished he had it now—and get a seat on the plane with Mac. He should return to Alexandria and take his quaint little house off the market, feed his two affectionate cats, scoop the litter box. Shave the ugly stubble from his face and take a shower and put on one of his conservative not-extravagant but respectable suits and drive his secondhand BMW into the city, ride the elevator, plunge back into the diverting, challenging, complex, and ultimately meaningless tangles of the Internal Revenue Code.

And know for the rest of his life—what was the phrase?—that he'd been weighed and found wanting.

"I have to stay," he said.

On the TV, an advertisement featuring a long sequence where the

camera, which must have been on an aerial drone, followed a man running and jumping through a city, gymnastic, running up walls and vaulting over things and leaping rooftop to rooftop. Urban environment as
obstacle course. He'd heard of this but hadn't seen it. There was a name,
sounded French, that he struggled to recall. Parquet? No. Something like
that. The guy was amazing, and Sam's mind dropped into a half dream,
the images on the television smearing into a parodic Walter Mitty scenario where Sam romped through a city like Batman, agile, powerful,
courageous. He woke with a start when he realized he was trying to find
Summer.

23

"You're bringing her?"

Bowman hadn't expected to find his uncle waiting for him, but he supposed it was fair, since he'd asked to borrow the man's truck. Uncle Jeremy stood just inside the open door of the barn at the caretaker's house, in the shade, wearing his canvas coat. It was early afternoon and sunny, but a line of thunderstorms had blown through the night before, trailing a cold front, and the air was cool for late June.

Bowman dismounted and wrapped Milly's reins around the horizontal peeled pole outside the barn, holding on to Alecto's T-stick with his other hand. Then, with both hands, he lifted the stick with the heavy eagle from its boot. She was hooded but didn't like being jostled. Her feathers fluffed and one wing flung out partway for balance.

The mare sniffed at Alecto's tail while Bowman set the base of Alecto's stick on the ground. He rubbed Milly's nose and thanked her for carrying human and eagle down the mountain. All of the horses on the ranch belonged to Jeremy, but Milly liked to hunt with the eagles and Bowman rode her almost exclusively.

"Bird's not going to take a shit in my truck, is she?"

Bowman didn't respond. His uncle knew he'd stored the transport crate Leo had built for Alecto down here in the barn. It fit, barely, on the truck's cracked and stained vinyl bench seat.

"You won't find much to hunt over there. Jackrabbits, maybe."

"I know. But she'll get to fly around in a new place." He set Alecto on the low padded perch inside the crate. When he turned around, Jeremy had unstrapped the overnight backpack from where Bowman had lashed it to the saddle and was tying Milly to a hitching pole beside the barn.

He came back with the pack, deposited it in the truck's bed, and watched Bowman adjust the mirrors.

"Gas tank's almost full. I checked the air in the tires. Couple of cans of oil behind the seat. Won't be any filling stations between here and where you're going."

"No police either." It would only be about a hundred miles round-trip.

"If you get caught by a statie or a res cop, I'm telling Leo you stole my truck."

"I know." Bowman found himself smiling at his uncle, admitting to himself for perhaps the first time in his life how much he loved the man. How good and strong and complicated—and completely different from each other—his mother's brothers were. He pictured trying to tell them that, which made him smile even wider.

Uncle Jeremy was giving him a quizzical, suspicious look.

Bowman's eyes stung and he turned away to check on Alecto in the crate. It hurt, as he'd known it would, to even imagine saying goodbye.

His experiences last year in Mexico City had upended a fair number of naïve assumptions about life in general, and had kindled a growing realization that Leo had raised Summer and him to know and love a world that had died or was dying everywhere else, a world few people could ever experience. The luck of living in Panther Gap had been as invisible and assumed as the air they breathed, as the gravity holding them to the earth. He didn't know what to make of that. It seemed wrong, but he couldn't quite put his finger on why or how. He struggled with whether it was okay to live like this when so many people couldn't, and he'd begun to suspect he might not be able to stay at the Girard ranch forever.

The drive to the base of Smokehouse Mesa took just over two hours. The BLM roads were in bad shape and he didn't pass a single vehicle, certainly no state trooper or reservation police. Not that they would really have given him a ticket or even called the ranch. Jeremy St. John's nephew driving the old truck around without a license wouldn't have bothered them much.

Nothing but a skinny pull-off for parking, still muddy from the storms, the day finally heating up well after noon. Reaching into the crate, he unthreaded Alecto's jesses, leaving only her cuffs, and brought her out on a glove, speaking in a low voice, telling her this was practice for him but if she wanted to leave, he understood. He removed her hood and looked into her eyes and told her she was the finest eagle in the world. Maybe the best bird who had ever lived. The eagle stared back, unmoved. Her nictitating membranes flicked milky-white across her eyes. Summer would make fun of him if she heard what he said to the eagle when they were alone. He cast her up using both hands and watched until she flew out of sight.

Shouldering his pack, he found a faint game trail he hoped would lead to the hidden road he'd read the Old Ones had cut, switchbacking only once on the way to the crest of the mesa. There wouldn't be any trailhead map or helpful signposts here, partly because BLM didn't want to make it too easy for people to find the signal site.

Several times on the way up he caught glimpses of Alecto, high and wheeling, watching him. He didn't flush any jackrabbits or anything else but still she stayed close, and she permitted some of the old connection, unwavering even when he couldn't see her. She wasn't leaving him yet.

The Old Ones had built their signal site at the northernmost tip of the table-flat top, a vertiginous place where sheer sandstone walls on three sides fell five hundred feet to the sloping base of scree and broken stone blocks. The firepit itself was similar to the one on the Girard property—hundred-pound stones arranged in a rough circle six feet across—except here he saw no sign of recent fires, no charcoal, only shiny, blackened shapes on the stones' inside surfaces. A sheltered rock wall nearby was marked with a spiral, a hand, and three ambiguous figures he couldn't quite make out. He thought there must have been a dwelling of some sort here, shelter for a rotating crew of watchers, but if so, it had been dismantled long ago.

Off to the southeast, a long, low plateau lit red and green in the setting sun. He tried to pick out the ridge where the next signal site had to be, but it wasn't obvious. He turned northwest and shaded his eyes. Thirty miles off, Rosewater Butte stood a deep shadowed red, blocking the paler rock face of the escarpment guarding Panther Gap, six miles farther on. The notch in Rosewater was invisible at this distance, but the top of the butte stood directly in front of the highest part of the escarpment, where Summer would be arriving about now. Farther yet and rising another several thousand feet, the dark forested bulk of the Red Creek Range. And in between, hidden as always, lay green Panther Gap, a place he still loved with every molecule in his body.

At the panel of rock art, he examined the marks more closely. There were several faint handprints he hadn't noticed before, and some small geometric petroglyphs he didn't recognize. No human-animal hybrids were depicted on the rock, which was a relief. He'd been leery of therianthropes ever since Teotihuacan.

The were-jaguar—that's how he had come to think of the spirit that assaulted him under the Temple of the Sun—had tried to lure him to the old underworld with intimations of wisdom, revelation. Now he suspected there was no wisdom there after all, no guidance from a prior, more humane civilization, nothing but the timeless, abyssal depths of human misery, human arrogance.

A half-serious theory he and Summer had cooked up when they were younger was that the spectral beings humans called gods and devils had spontaneously appeared as epiphenomena of the planet's first biological activity—the green emanations of photosynthesis, the early neural flashings—manifesting through some quirk of quantum mechanics beyond the reach of science. The more prevalent and destructive gods came later, when humans evolved and spread their influence over the planet. The human gods were not to be trusted because they were never content with what they had, and they were especially dangerous when they tried to assume the power of nonhuman animals. Were-jaguar, for example, contained only one aspect of Jaguar, the power of a ravening predator, perverted by human goals and failings.

For a moment he wished his sister were here to argue with him, but the new Summer had no patience for this sort of thing. When he'd asked if she would light the fire by herself so he could drive down here and confirm the story about the Old Ones excavating the notch in Rosewater Butte, she'd told him she'd agree to it only if he promised not to do anything "weird."

Now the sun was well down, and the air had begun to cool. He put on a wool shirt from his pack. Soon it would be dark enough. He and Summer had collected the wood and built the bonfire two days ago. He'd told her they would be connected by the signal, linked across the miles by a communications technology thousands of years old.

Where was Alecto? He could feel her still, but hadn't seen her since he'd topped out on the mesa. He should try to bring her in. She knew he had food, three whole quail wrapped in newspaper in his pack. Frozen when he'd left the house but thawed by now.

He unpacked the lure, a retrieving dummy for waterfowl dogs with a mallard skin sewn on, attached to a long cord. He swung it around in a circle, gradually paying out the cord. He watched the sky. For such a large bird, Alecto could sneak up and take the lure before he even knew she was nearby. The duck wings were attached loosely, and they fluttered and spun as Bowman swung the lure faster. There she was, not sneaking this time, coming in on a steep glide over the long bulk of Smokehouse laid out to the southwest. When she took the lure he let go of the line and she carried it nearly to the edge of the cliff.

She hopped from the lure to his glove, looking into his face with unusual curiosity. All this was different. A new place, and time to fly around on her own. Melancholy in Bowman's face, his distant demeanor.

Probably she just wanted her dinner. He leashed her and set her on a rock, tumbled the quail from the damp newspaper in front of her, and she began to feed.

A handful of stars were shining now. Jupiter too. No Polaris. A sharp breeze blew dust across the top of the mesa, cooler, almost cold. He lay back against the warm stone slab where Alecto was lingering over her quail, the plucked feathers skidding downwind and vaulting over the edge. Even in the twilight she stopped often in her feeding to look around, seeing things he couldn't. He'd never brought her camping with him before. She seemed to like it.

The next time he checked, Polaris shone pale in its accustomed place in the north. Summer hated the bow drill, so she would be fiddling with her ember box now, trying to get the fire started without using matches.

He stared, his eyes watering in the dusty wind. Then, as if he'd conjured it by his own insistent will, a yellow light flared on Rosewater Butte, Summer's fire shining through the notch, dim at first but growing as bright as any star, then brighter than Jupiter, its color warming, now red as Mars, a hot orange jewel set on top of Rosewater. He smiled. That was his sister, reaching out to him.

But there was something else, too, not coming from Summer, a signal detached from her intention.

He felt a warning, ambiguous but chilling. Like when some older part of your brain lights up at the buzz of a rattlesnake in the half second before you recognize it.

In his dreams, the Old Ones feared a threat from the south. Centuries ago, the watcher's job here was to pay attention to the horizon and pass any warning along to the ridge above Panther Gap; from there it would be passed to Comb Ridge and beyond. Word would spread quickly, everyone could get ready, carry provisions to the hidden cliff dwellings, gather defensive weapons, take in whatever harvest was available, and—maybe most importantly— begin the right ceremonies to counter what was coming. Because the threat was always more profound than enemy raiders or war parties. Something like the being he'd encountered under Teotihuacan. A force derived from humans but not controlled by them.

Summer's fire was telling him something new. The threat would come from the north?

Or from everywhere?

He should pass the warning along, but he'd promised Uncle Jeremy he wouldn't build a fire here. Standing and rifling through his pack, he brought out Jeremy's heavy Maglite and flashed it toward Summer, then turned and pointed it toward Mesa Verde, flashing again. Afterward, he felt unsatisfied, worried. The warning he'd felt was profound and powerful, but he hadn't understood its meaning. He knew he hadn't done enough.

Alecto chirped softly, her eyes shining wet, reflecting the afterglow in the west, looking at him with what felt to Bowman like sympathy.

She'd finished the quail and jumped up on the T-stick he'd secured upright with slabs of stone. He considered whether he should hood her for the night. He thought not.

After Summer's signal fire went out, he lay his sleeping bag on the smooth stone next to Alecto's perch. A waning quarter moon rose to reveal her silhouette against the sky. He woke several times during the night from troubled dreams about the warning in the signal fire, and each time, when he opened his eyes, Alecto was there. He knew she slept but he couldn't help feeling she watched over him.

24

2009

Bick Rangely was a talkative man. Talkative, Bowman decided, to the point of catastrophe, his logorrhea riding to the very brink of ruin.

His own overreaction might have something to do with his fever spiking again. He tried to block out the friendly man's voice long enough to give that notion a sober analysis, force a bubble of quiet space in his mind, something that would allow a few seconds of careful thought.

Failed.

The man's voice was unblockable. It flowed freely through Bowman's undefended consciousness, triggering the most basic, instinctive cognitive responses: pity at first: *This is what Americans make of their overprivileged lives?* Then: *This is what humanity has come to?* Followed by revulsion, pain, and, eventually, paranoia. He sat rigid in the leather upholstery of the recent-model Suburban and listened, suffering.

Bick Rangely talked about himself. Bick Rangely talked about his family. His family back in Arkansas. His wife of twenty-two years and their three daughters, all in their teens, all "big into cheer," whatever that meant, the A-frame vacation house on Lake Dunwin—a lake that probably didn't even exist—the five-bedroom brick home in a Little Rock neighborhood with quiet streets and big trees, his job as a health care admin, his coworkers, the office politics, lots of office politics. His wife's charity work with the church, Bick himself a pooh-bah of some sort in the Loyal Order of Moose. It was at this point, when he launched into a detailed explanation of what had to be completely fabricated Moose rituals, that Bowman decided Bick wasn't just playing a role, trying to lull Bowman off his guard. No, his performance was too on-the-nose. He knew Bowman, knew his history, the way he'd been raised, his philosophical leanings, the extreme measures he had taken to live a certain kind of life. Bick was torturing him intentionally.

"I guess I'm a pretty ordinary guy," he said, slowing his cadence, deepening his voice to a portentous pitch as if delivering the ultimate result of a long bout of come-to-Jesus self-analysis, an adamantine gem that Bowman, for his own good, ought to pay attention to. "But I'm proud to be a man, an American. I work hard and I provide for my family. I do right by my community, my country. I don't believe there's any higher calling."

He looked over to see how Bowman was receiving this hard-won wisdom. Bowman blinked, and nodded, but was too punch-drunk to reply.

At the one stoplight in Stumptown, Bick declared the town to be sleepy.

"I don't know if you'll be able to find a tow truck here after all. Motel either."

There was a closed Kum & Go and a little post office that looked so picturesque, so nineteenth century, it had to be ironic, possibly Potemkin. A few tiny, well-kept houses. A trailer park farther on. Then more dark road.

"No, I suppose not," Bowman managed.

"Where do you want to go, then?" Bick left the SUV idling at the now-green light. They were the only people awake in Stumptown. "Back to your truck? Or we can keep looking for a tow. Next town is"—he reached to the glowing screen on the dashboard and punched some buttons, moved his fingers around, and a map appeared—"Marlton. Might have better odds there."

Bowman capitulated. "I don't really need to go back to the truck. I think you know that."

Bick blinked stupidly in the light from the map on the dash. His persistence made Bowman angry. There'd been no mention of the fact that they both happened to be driving around rural Colorado at four in the morning. Only the excruciating details of Bick's life in Arkansas.

"When did you start following me? At the airport?"

The smile he gave Bowman was sly, crocodilian, like he'd given up trying to stay in character but would continue his charade purely from a perverse desire to annoy. "Now, why in the world would I do that?"

Bowman regained some self-control. He let it slide. Shifted back into his role as Sherman Carver. "Okay, then, where were you headed? Where would you be going if you weren't helping me out?"

"Just driving around. I pick a state and explore. This is my third time in Colorado. And I like to drive when no one else, or almost no one else"—here he glanced companionably at Bowman, his fellow traveler in the wee hours—"is out and about. I thought I might end up in Durango. I hear the historic hotel there is pretty good. What about you? Where were you bound?"

The Suburban accelerated, put the town behind them. Bowman stared straight ahead, thinking the word "bound" sounded wrong coming from Bick. Maybe he was dropping some kind of clunky threat. He couldn't get a fix on the game Bick was playing. He wished he hadn't been so reckless, hadn't gotten into the Suburban with Bickford Rangely without a fight. Woozy again, he watched the blacktop rush toward him in the light from the headlights, the highway climbing now into a medium-sized mountain range, he didn't know which, had really no idea where they were. Bick took the curves fast, expertly.

"Whitespring," he said, under his breath.

"Whitespring? Never heard of it. Where's that?" Bick fiddled with the map on the dashboard again without waiting for Bowman to answer. Like he'd asked the dashboard device instead of Bowman. The screen filled with contours, roads, place names.

"Hell, Whitespring's not too far out of the way." Bick's finger traced a roundabout route that would add two hours at least to the drive to Durango, running northwest and then looping around to run for a dozen miles on the north side of the Red Creek Range before dropping down into Whitespring. That route only made sense if Bick was making an educated guess at the location of the Girard ranch.

"What about your truck? You gonna go back for it?" Bick was enjoying himself now. "That truck's a classic."

"That truck is dead," Bowman said.

Three cow elk bounded into the road. Bick braked and swerved to the left, surely about to clip the trailing cow but at the last possible second she dug hard with her hind legs, muscles bunching, throwing herself out of the way as the front right bumper nearly grazed her flank. Bowman watched as they passed her by, her head back, eyes wild and flashing in the bright blue wash of the headlights.

The Suburban fishtailed on loose gravel, drifting too far to the left, a gray rock pillar looming on the narrow inside shoulder.

The lead elk had dropped over the right side of the road and disappeared. The other two followed and Bowman saw through the eyes of the last one, the one they'd almost hit: a steep slope of loose scree, dust kicked up in the moonlight by the first two running down. Dark foliage along a creek in the bottom.

Bick steered coolly into the skid, braking, slowing until Bowman guessed their speed at twenty-five miles per hour, dropping to twenty, then fifteen as Bick corrected course and got the vehicle pointed in the right direction again.

In twenty seconds he could vanish completely: a jump, a roll into the gravel on the shoulder, then up and sprinting downhill after the three elk, sliding in the scree, following them into that cover. Bick would know enough not to chase him on foot, but he would make the mistake of waiting on the road, driving back and forth, looking to catch Bowman as he inevitably returned to hitch another ride. But Bowman had seen the map on the dashboard, and the moving green dot representing the Suburban, and he knew roughly where they were now. He would walk into the wilderness. Even weak and hallucinatory with ciguatera, even if he found nothing to eat, he could walk the ten, maybe twelve hours cross-country to Bear Creek Pass. He could catch a ride from there to Whitespring. He would make it to Summer as fast as he could. *Better late,* he thought, *than never.*

He thumbed the release button on his seat belt and with his other hand he lifted the little plastic lever on his door to unlock it.

Nothing happened. He grabbed the door handle itself and pulled, but the door was locked. Bick accelerated to fifty miles per hour. Bowman still held the end of the detached seat belt in his left hand. An electronic chime had started going off somewhere.

The chimes came slowly, one every second and a half. Then they started coming faster. Or that might have been his imagination.

He reinserted the metal tongue of the seat belt into the holder at his left hip. It clicked into place and the chime ceased.

Bick let forth with an exaggerated sigh of relief.

"Funny how those critters can come out of nowhere like that."

25

Sam showered, shaved, and snuck out the door while Mac was still asleep. Outside, the sun was barely up on a clear, brisk mountain-town morning. He found Jeremy's truck parked on the street near a busy diner, Marco sitting in the bed and watching Sam approach. A heavy, new-looking chrome padlock now secured the lid on the old rusted toolbox. He stopped to rub the big dog's head. His eyes, light brown with gold and green flecks in the morning light, weren't really dog-like, and not human either. Sam got the sense Marco saw something good in him. It was a peaceful, settling experience.

He tore himself away and opened the passenger door.

"Can we get some coffee?"

But Jeremy was on his phone, frowning at Sam's intrusion, waiting for someone to answer. He shook his head no and reached for the ignition. Like Sam, he wore the same clothes he'd had on earlier. Must not have made it back to the ranch. He looked ragged, his eyes red-rimmed and tired, more than tired, like killing the kidnappers last night might have had more of an effect than he'd let on.

As they drove down Main in Durango, everyone—from preppy middle-aged recreationists to pierced-and-tatted dirtbag enviros to bearded resource workers in giant pickups—everyone waved, happy to see them. Sam waved back, puzzled. Jeremy spoke without any long pauses, must be leaving a message, mumbling quietly into his phone like he didn't want Sam to hear, which caused Sam to pay close attention. He heard the words "chatter" and "wild-goose chase." Jeremy recited his ten-digit number and ended the call.

"Good morning," Sam said. Jeremy ignored him.

"For a paranoid recluse who lives in a camouflaged house in a remote valley, you sure have a lot of friends in town."

"I don't know those people. They just like Marco."

Sam twisted around and looked out the back window. Marco was standing on the toolbox, front paws on the cab. Sam could only see his hind legs and tail but he could imagine the picture: decrepit pickup truck; huge white happy-looking dog up there smiling at the world. Most of these mountain towns were dog-friendly to the point of fetish.

Jeremy took a turn to cross a bridge over a picturesque western river and the dog's claws screeched on the metal roof. Then came a bang as he jumped down into the bed and prepared for the curvy highway going west. Jeremy said Summer had convinced the bank to put off the meeting until later today, so they could take a later flight. She wanted to give Bowman more time to show up. In the meantime Sam would have to tag along while Jeremy ran some errands.

"You got your backpack of cocaine locked in the toolbox back there?"

Jeremy sighed. "I knew this whole deal was a bad idea from the get-go."

"You mean helping me save Mac from the kidnappers."

"Yep."

"I need to look in the pack."

"Why?"

"I think we should let Melissa's family know she's dead."

"Absolutely not."

"Well, try this, then: Shouldn't we at least try to figure out who she was? So we have a better idea what to expect? Maybe she's the estranged daughter of a hedge-fund billionaire who's going to move heaven and earth to find her. We'd want to know that."

"I already looked."

"Humor me."

Jeremy was quiet, thinking it over.

"Hey," Sam added, "I'm a lawyer, I might see something you didn't." This was bullshit and Jeremy surely knew it, but he pulled over and got out with a key for the new padlock. He opened the toolbox, talking to Marco about something or other. Then he set the heavy yellow pack on the seat between them and drove on without saying anything.

Inside, the brick of cocaine that Melissa had been raiding for her party with Mac had been duct-taped shut. Sam lifted out all four, placed them carefully on the floor at his feet. The pack itself was nearly new, nothing special, what you'd buy at Walmart. He went through all the pockets and compartments, all of them empty, had probably never been used at all. He sat back in the seat with the pack in his lap. In frustration, he shook it, drawing a frown from Jeremy. Something was still in there, some mass in the bottom third of the pack that went beyond the empty fabric, black straps, foam padding.

Reaching in from the top, he felt around and found that the divider between the main top pocket and the one at the bottom was padded, but there was no reason to have anything but a lightweight layer of fabric there. He fetched the headlamp from his own pack and peered in. The stitching on the divider was similar to that on the rest of the pack, but less perfect. He picked at it with a fingernail, got a thread to come loose.

"What are you doing?" Jeremy asked. "Don't mess with it." The highway followed the big river they'd crossed, winding through a green, gradually narrowing valley. Their windows were open and the cool morning wind rushed in.

"I might've found something. A secret compartment."

Jeremy sighed. Kept driving.

Sam worked on the thread. He could feel the end of a packet of some sort, and when he'd removed enough stitching he worked it back and forth until it came out. Held it up: roughly the size of a legal pad, two inches thick. Jeremy glanced over.

"That's tamper-evident tape."

Sam turned the package over in his hands. "Don't you want to open it? Maybe it's cash."

"Do not break that tape."

"Okay, keep your shirt on. Actually it feels more like documents."

Sam thought about that. "You know, it might be bearer bonds. That'd
be old-school, but they're still out there." He felt the implication sink in,
a disorienting shift into more dangerous potentials.

It was two inches thick.

The package grew heavy, too heavy to hold up. It collapsed into his
lap. He made himself take a deep breath, then another. When he'd managed to reunite corpus and psyche, he spoke carefully.

"If that's what it is, um." He breathed, breathed. *Strong voice,* he told
himself. "It could be worth a ton of money, I mean like tens of millions."

"Which is why I say don't open it. Put it back."

Jeremy pulled into a decrepit strip mall and parked in front of what
looked like the only storefront still in business. The logo in the window
was a stout bear standing upright with two pistols in shoulder holsters:
AUGIE'S GRIZZLY ARMS. It seemed early, but two weather-beaten Harleys
were parked outside next to an antique diesel International Harvester
flatbed with Arizona plates.

"You need more guns?"

"Ammo," Jeremy said. "Let Marco out."

Sam lowered the tailgate while Jeremy unlocked the toolbox, pried
open the top, and heaved in the yellow backpack, which glowed in Sam's
imagination with something like radioactivity, the rusty toolbox and
even the truck itself beginning to glow too, Jeremy and Sam and Marco
all affected by it, marked for anyone driving by to see.

Jeremy reached into the paper bag of ransom money and stuffed a
substantial stack of bills in his jacket pocket. Seemed like a lot for ammo,
but Sam didn't mention it.

The store was tiny inside and smelled of cigar smoke. Sam and Jeremy and Marco barely fit in the narrow space along the glass-topped
counter. Handguns were arranged on poorly lit shelves under the glass;
rifles and shotguns and such hung from pegs on the wall behind. At
least three sophisticated-looking cameras surveilled the small space. A
grandmotherly woman sat behind the counter, watching them, unim-
pressed with Jeremy's friendly greeting, but she buzzed them through
a back door and they walked into a spacious, high-ceilinged garage. A
cloud of smoke obscured several men moving away from a rough board

table strewn with empty beer bottles and a dozen handguns. On the wall behind them, a series of monitors showed views of the parking lot, what must be the back of the building, and the front part of the store.

A short, stocky man stepped toward them, must be Augie. "What's that damn dog doing in here?"

Marco stood close by Jeremy, who laughed and continued with his friendly act, shaking hands, accepting a lukewarm morning Budweiser that he handed to Sam. The other men had drifted into another part of the garage without being introduced, one sinewy, tatted white guy hanging back a little longer than the others. When Sam looked around again, they had all disappeared. Some preliminary gun talk ensued, but Jeremy said they were on a tight schedule and only needed a couple boxes of .45.

"I got something you'll like," Augie said, and pulled a black plastic case from a shelf under the table. Inside, a big black pistol nested in a foam cutout. Two extra magazines, a laser or flashlight or something, and a fat matte-black silencer sat in their own cutouts.

Jeremy lifted the pistol and opened the slide, glanced in, let it slam shut. The pistol filled his big hands. It had tall sights and the barrel stuck out a quarter inch past the end of the slide.

"That's the finest production .45 on the planet," Augie said, grinning at the expression on Jeremy's face. "Brand-new. Outfit in Utah made the suppressor. Maybe fifty of these got commissioned for a unit you've heard of. I could sell it on the internet for five, six grand."

"I know what it is. Where'd you get it?"

"That's the thing. Boy had funny-looking teeth."

"So it's hot, and you can't sell it on the internet for a damn thing."

"I'll let you think about it." Augie disappeared into the main store.

"What are we doing here?" Sam handed the unopened beer back to Jeremy, who set it on the table. "Are you going to buy a stolen pistol? And you need a tax stamp for that silencer."

"How the hell do you know that?"

Sam figured it was his turn to shrug. Years ago a wealthy client of the firm had died with a safe full of Title II weapons and no gun trust—machine guns, silencers, short-barreled rifles—and Sam had been enlisted by a senior partner to figure out what the family should do with it all.

When Augie returned with two boxes of ammunition, Jeremy pulled the roll of hundreds from his back pocket and started counting. He laid a stack on the table. "Three grand for the HK and the ammo." He counted out some more. "Two grand for the information you're about to give me."

All at once Augie went tense, angry. And disappointed, like Jeremy had tricked him, had violated some unspoken rule of engagement between them.

"You know I ain't a snitch."

"I know. It's for me, not the sheriff. It's personal."

Augie waited.

"I need to talk to someone with authority. There's something they want real bad right now and I know where it is."

Augie's eyes widened before he could control himself.

"You looking for a bust or a reward?"

"Neither. I want to talk before they start doing stupid shit."

"I can't reach 'em," Augie said. "They call me, give me a new phone every time." He reached into a drawer and produced a cheap cell phone. "Look it over." He reached the phone out to Jeremy.

Jeremy gave an almost imperceptible shake of his head and Augie put the phone in his pocket, then he shut the plastic pistol case, snapping the latches closed.

"You still want the HK?"

Houses and businesses began to appear on both sides of the road, and they passed a sign at the eastern edge of Whitespring, pop. 7,787. Jeremy drove impatiently, ignoring two stop signs, eventually parking behind a diner called the Chicken Neck.

He pointed down the street to a convenience store. "Go buy me three disposable phones. Nobody knows who you are. It makes you useful. Pick up a car charger too. And some cold beer."

"What are you going to do?"

"Coffee's cheaper here than in that Durango tourist trap. And I'll pick us up something to eat. You got any dietary restrictions I can ignore?"

The truck cab was locked and Jeremy was still in the restaurant when Sam returned with the phones, the charger, and the beer, so he sat on the tailgate, drinking a liter bottle of water he'd bought and scratching

Marco's neck, his hand buried in the dog's thick white mane. A six-pack of Tecate and a bag of ice sat in wet spots on the pavement at his feet. It was hot in the morning sun and he fed Marco a few pieces of ice from the bag but the dog promptly threw them up, along with what looked like a breakfast of kibble, in the truck bed.

"Are you all right?" he asked. Marco came back and begged for more. "Jeremy's gonna kill me." He scraped the vomit onto the pavement with a scrap of cardboard and found what had to be the dog's water bowl overturned in a corner of the bed, poured in the rest of his bottle.

The noise of the dog slurping obscured the sound of the motorcycles until they were pulling around behind the Chicken Neck. Two loud bikes, Harleys, headed Sam's way. Marco raised his head, two-foot-long strings of drool hanging down from his lower jaw. Tail up.

The bikes slowed and came to a stop behind the truck. One biker hung back while the other, a wiry, tanned white guy in a black Rockies baseball cap and dark wraparounds, eased up close and shut off his engine. He wore a light brown leather vest with some sort of insignia on the chest, his arms dark with intricate tattoos.

"You were at Augie's," Sam said.

"I was. I heard y'all talking." He glanced at Marco, who'd started growling, like he was imitating the Harleys.

Sam felt the man's eyes drawn to the glowing toolbox, enough money in there to buy a small island. He fought the impulse to turn and look at it himself, wished Jeremy would come out of the stupid restaurant. When the biker reached under his vest Sam thought he was about to be shot, but it was a cell phone. He caught the underhanded toss without bobbling.

"Tell Deputy Sheriff St. John to expect a call. Might be a hour or so."

He started the motorcycle up again with a low rumbling cough.

"Who are you?" Sam shouted.

"Just a concerned citizen," the man said, chuckling. He turned his machine and he and his partner rode back out to the street and accelerated with the usual Harley roar.

26

First light, gray predawn. Through the window inches from his nose, Bowman watched center-pivot irrigation rigs spray groundwater on fields of alfalfa. His head still throbbed, and he'd dozed in his reclined position. After the near-miss with the elk in the road, Bick had turned contemplative and managed to stay quiet for a good long stretch.

The plush passenger seat in the Suburban was undeniably comfortable. He felt around on the side next to the door for the recliner switch and a nearly silent electric motor eased him upright, facing the windshield. When he moved his feet, he kicked three empty Red Bull cans rolling around in his footwell, all Bick's. He'd called them "energy drinks."

"You talk in your sleep."

"What did I say?"

"It was gibberish."

Then, as if Bick had opened a door, Bowman's dreams came to him in a rush, a wave of hopelessness. The worst kind of ciguatera dreams, feverish and terrifyingly incoherent, the infant's nightmare of towering amoebic demons, a rudimentary consciousness seized by terror and anxiety but lacking any sensible narrative or language with which to process the fear. The nihilistic dreams of every sleeping life-form that had ever lived, the primitive ur-nightmare of the earthworm, the crocodile, the alien creatures of the Cambrian explosion. Half a billion years of suffering in the night.

He shook it off. The places his mind sometimes went during an episode. It troubled him that his ciguatera-brain was getting worse, not better.

He reclined his seat again, turned to the window. Rural Colorado passed by.

A hand on his shoulder. He flinched and woke up. They were parked at a gasoline pump in a garish yellow establishment with a half-dozen pump islands and a convenience store. The sun was up, and Bick was grinning at him.

"You got any money for gas?"

Bowman unrolled the top of his dry bag, slid a hundred-dollar bill from the stack, and handed it over.

"That'll do 'er," Bick said. He opened his door and stepped out, waving the bill in the air. "You mind pumping?" He walked across the parking lot to the convenience store, leaving Bowman alone.

He tried the door. It opened. The place was moderately busy, several other cars gassing up. He smelled fumes, burned coffee, fried food. He blinked and turned in a circle, checking the surrounding landforms. Definitely Whitespring: Mirror Butte loomed in the east, and in the hazy morning sun he could make out the faint shadow of the tall Red Creeks way off to the southwest. The sight of those home mountains surprised him with a sharp thrill of recognition.

He could head home. Clearly Bick had left him unattended. Should he run? Was he really some sort of captive? His fever had subsided some during his second nap, and with it his earlier panic. His determination to open the door and jump out of the Suburban when they'd nearly hit the elk felt far off and hard to fathom.

Bick was waving to him, leaning out the front door of the convenience store, giving a thumbs-up. Bowman stepped around the vehicle to the driver's side. The small door to the gas cap was already open. Bowman fussed with the pump, pushed some buttons, got the gas flowing.

A whirring, high-pitched whine emerged from the background

noises. Not a sound he could recall hearing before. It seemed to be coming from the sun. As he faced east and raised his hand to shade his eyes, a tiny helicopter with four rotors descended to hover over the parking lot nearby, about twenty feet up. Must be a remote-controlled toy of some sort. He couldn't avoid the sensation that the thing was looking at him. It hovered in place, buzzing angrily, annoyingly, for another ten seconds or so, adjusting its position when a breeze threatened to push it toward the store building. Then it abruptly ascended and flew away to the east.

The pump slowed and stopped at $91.33. He had never seen anyone spend that much on gasoline. Bick appeared, walking fast across the lot with two Styrofoam cups and a white paper bag.

"Breakfast!" he said, then, "Where do you live? I'll drop you off."

Bowman thought about that. He wasn't going to lead Bick to the ranch entrance, but it shouldn't be too hard to find someone in town to give him a ride out there.

"The library is a few blocks north," he said. "I'll catch up with a friend there."

As they drove through town, Bowman finished the egg and cheese sandwich Bick had handed him, surprising himself with his own hunger, though he worried what this food would do to his system. Continuing to act against his better judgment, he also drank the black coffee, and sure enough he felt his temperature spike again.

In the nearly empty library parking lot, Bick slammed on the brakes.

"Shit."

He leaned forward over the steering wheel and squinted up at the sky. Another small aircraft, or the same one, showed in a quick glimpse as it passed overhead and moved to the other side of a cottonwood tree shading the single-story library building. It reminded Bowman of a squirrel hiding on the far side of a tree trunk.

"Shit," Bick said again.

He shifted into reverse and a video picture of the lot behind them filled the screen where the map had been. He watched this rather than the mirror, driving fast through the library parking lot in reverse. The rear tires gave a short screech as he accelerated back toward Main Street.

"Sorry about that," he said. "I think we better find another place to drop you off."

"What was that thing? There was one at the gas station too."

Bick shot him an angry look that Bowman read as genuine, a rare crack in the man's performance. "Why didn't you tell me? Did it see you?" When Bowman didn't answer, Bick added, "They have cameras."

"Yeah. Definitely."

Bick ran a stop sign and headed for the main highway through town. A guy with a bushy white Santa Claus beard driving a new Mercedes wagon honked and gave them the finger. They backtracked past the gas station and shot out of town on Route 26, headed south. Toward the ranch.

Bowman watched the passenger-side rearview. "There's another black Suburban following us."

Bick's eyes didn't leave the road ahead. "That's weird," he said, in a voice that implied he didn't think it was weird at all.

"I was fine at the library."

"No, you weren't. We need to get you home. Just sing the fuck out when we get to your turn. I'm serious."

Thirty minutes later, the Suburban blew past the modest brick rancher and cluster of outbuildings at the entrance. A rough track led from there to the big gate at the base of the escarpment and the driveway cut into the rock face of the mountain, designed by his grandfather and his mining engineers to be both defensible and nearly invisible from the public road. Even from the air it looked unremarkable, like an old mining track.

Bick showed no flicker of recognition, no letup on the gas, not a twitch on his face. Bowman sat back, relieved but still wondering who the hell Bick was and what he wanted. They were moving along on the gravel road at a pretty good clip, fishtailing now and then.

"Have you kidnapped my sister too?"

No reply.

"Are you police?"

Bick smiled at that.

Bowman gave up and watched the escarpment rising in the west. He had known the land so intimately, so long ago. He still knew it. Familiar ridges and outcrops and gorges unfolded in a slow-motion tableau as they drove southward. The pull was physical, iron filings under his skin reacting to a giant magnet. He'd once told Summer he would never come back to Panther Gap, that he wouldn't let the gravity of the place rule him. But the family always came back. Jeremy had even brought Leo's body from Mexico to bury on the ridge.

Bick noticed him staring. "You're not going to show me how to get in there, are you?"

He gave Bick a dopey look and turned in his seat to look out the back. The trailing Suburban was still there, holding a steady position at about a hundred feet, barely visible through the dust.

They thumped over a bridge and Bick braked, sliding into a hard right turn and accelerating on another road that ran upstream alongside Red Creek. Swallows stormed out from under the plank bridge and slipped low over the surging blue water. The powerful stream, incongruous on the xeric plain, drained from the lake in Panther Gap, snowmelt off the Red Creek Range. This gravel road would follow alongside the creek for about ten miles before veering to the south. Some sort of willow, probably invasive, had grown up in a thicket along the banks, hiding the creek itself from view.

The road began climbing out of the creek bottom on a narrow side cut. A burst of static sounded from somewhere on Bick's torso. He reached into a jacket pocket, pushed an earbud into his ear. Bowman turned to look behind them again. The other vehicle was farther back, maybe a quarter mile, and Bick had a conversation with what Bowman presumed was the driver, conducted in grunts and monosyllables—*yeah, no, don't.* Then, his voice sounding tighter, "I see it. . . . I don't *know* how."

A rooster tail of dust hung off to the southeast where another gravel road intersected in a T with the road they were on. Eventually the dust resolved into a silver dually pickup truck that turned to come at them head-on. A wide black military-looking SUV pulled out from behind the truck and accelerated to run alongside it. They blocked the road ahead completely.

Bickford breathed out a long sigh and turned toward Bowman with the kind of wide-eyed drama the old Bick would have shown. Probably about to say something ornery about how they wouldn't be in this mess if Bowman had only shown the way to the ranch. But all he said was, "Hang on."

The vehicles ahead maneuvered so that when they stopped, their front ends were pointed inward, forming a chevron. Their dust cloud overtook them and obscured both vehicles before blowing away in the westerly crosswind. The effect, to Bowman's now unsubtly fevered mind, was eerie, portentous, the two vehicles smoking with malice.

The driver of the military vehicle opened his door but then thought better of it as Bick accelerated, steering right onto the narrow shoulder, the Suburban tilting to the left as he got the right tires up on a low berm guarding the drop-off to the creek, Bowman's view obscured by the brush off the shoulder, the vehicle loud and straining, bouncing and heeling over dangerously, stripping willows as they went.

A man with a submachine gun jumped up in the bed of the pickup and fired a burst at the Suburban's front tires, but Bick was going too fast, his maneuver catching them by surprise, and he would've made it too, if the military vehicle hadn't reversed hard up onto the shoulder in a perfectly timed ram into the rear quarter panel of the Suburban as they passed by. The impact pushed both rear wheels in a hop up onto the berm and Bick lost control.

At that point Bowman, who had never experienced an automobile accident of any consequence, noticed a severe time dilation, probably exacerbated by the ciguatera episode, and later he would be able to recall the wreck in great detail and from several points of view that he couldn't have actually experienced himself, especially since most of the time his view was blocked by the various airbags that exploded seconds after the other vehicle rammed the Suburban.

The front end dug into the berm and the vehicle launched into a graceful midair flip, slamming down onto its side, sliding down a steep slope toward the creek. A ten-foot stob of tree trunk driftwood smashed through the windshield, nearly skewering Bick to his seat before the vehicle rolled one more quarter turn and landed on its roof in Red Creek, facing upstream.

The airbags deflated and cold creek water rushed through the destroyed windshield, the current pushing the Suburban scraping and bouncing downstream along the rocky creek bed. Bowman unhooked his seat belt and somehow got himself right side up, stealing three raggedy breaths as the vehicle filled with water. He pawed at the fabric of the airbags, uncovering Bick, who was unconscious. The light was dim and greenish, the water shockingly cold, and the sound of the roof scraping downstream was loud underwater. But with his lungs full of air, Bowman was suffused with the curious sensation that all was well. As he reached down to unhook Bick's seat belt he felt confident, even comfortable, better than he'd felt since those troubling visions had interrupted him in the process of dying peacefully of sea snake venom in Costa Rica.

For a moment he assumed he was dying again, that the fever was joining forces with some dire injury, or maybe he'd inhaled water and not air? But his chest started to feel the familiar pressure of carbon dioxide building up in his blood, something he'd felt on a thousand dives with his polespear. He was transported to someplace from his past, his mind full of clear water. He expected a vision of sea snakes, but instead he saw a breeze rippling the water on the lake in Panther Gap, sunlight shattering into diamonds on the surface, a smell of mud, reeds, the vague musk of distant bison.

The effect was coming from the water itself. It carried the old magic of Panther Gap with it. He was home.

He pushed Bick through the broken windshield and followed, swam a few strokes against the current with his arm across Bick's chest before their heads broke the surface. From the road, the sounds of automatic gunfire. Not at them, though; no bullets traced the water nearby. The following Suburban must've pulled up, Bick's associates engaging the other two vehicles.

He sidestroked with Bick to the opposite bank and heaved the man up onto the shore. He pushed on his chest, ejecting a mouthful of water and prompting a spasm of coughing. Left Bick lying on his side as the sound of someone calling Bick's name and scrambling down from the road grew too close. He swam away, bleeding from a cut to his forehead, but he felt no pain. More shooting on the road.

He dove beneath the surface, imagining a thick, sleek river otter, his fur oily and glistening in the sun, extravagant whiskers twitching, tasting home in the water. He stretched his arms out in front and pulled back hard, shot ahead through the current, pointing his toes, elongating. He took another deep breath and swam upstream toward Panther Gap.

27

Summer glanced around the tiny terminal—no Bowman, no Sam, no uncles—and stepped back outside to wait. Her knee was better today, but the ribs were going to take a while. The sun had climbed high, and the heat felt good to her. A quiet day at the Whitespring airport. Most days were quiet here.

She was tired, and hadn't slept much, worrying about Bowman's whereabouts, and Sam and Jeremy's errand with the kidnappers, waiting for Jeremy's call that, when it came, was typically cryptic and not much of a relief: the "good guys" were all fine, but they'd found "some interesting shit." She'd called the private investigator who was supposed to have put Bowman to bed at the Best Western near DIA last night. He answered right away, talking fast, apologizing, describing in way too much detail exactly how her brother had evaded him in the crowded airport.

Bowman was up to something. He should stay in Denver and wait for her, but he couldn't know that. She stepped on her frustration. His snakebite, or some illness or internal demon, some external force, anything could be affecting him, compelling odd choices.

Their plane today was a Great Lakes Airlines Beechcraft 1900D—an hour and change to DIA, then a long cab ride into the city. She liked these regional turboprops, in part because she could imagine herself taking over and piloting the plane in an emergency, which was pretty silly.

Andrew had taught her informally in his King Air when they were dating, and his enthusiasm for flying was so infectious that she went ahead and took lessons, got her license. She stayed current because it was useful to be able to rent a plane and fly herself to far-flung properties where the foundation was funding projects.

She'd called Andrew a half-dozen times this morning, left messages. When she'd tried the bank, they'd connected her directly to Mr. Runnels, one of the three owners, who sounded relieved she'd called. He assured her a delayed meeting would be fine. Andrew Coates, he noted, had been missing and unreachable for two days. Had been acting oddly, in fact, for a week or more.

Sam approached from the parking lot, backlit by the low sun. Tall and slender, a daypack slung over one shoulder. When he stepped up onto the curb, his smile was strained and he started to say something but she stepped forward and embraced him.

"I'm so sorry you had to go through that. We'll talk about it later." She held his shoulders at arm's length. He'd showered and shaved but was dressed in the same hiking clothes. "You're okay? And your friend?"

He was blushing under his sunburn but he managed to nod.

"No Bowman yet," she said. "No Darwin. Where's Uncle Jeremy?"

Sam opened his mouth but nothing came out. Summer felt a little guilty about the effect of her hug. She was going to have to be careful. Another thing to worry about.

"He's out . . ." He gestured toward the parking lot. "There. In his truck. Darwin too, they're talking. Did he tell you what happened? What's going on now?"

"You tell me," she said, and opened the door. "Let's go inside, we board in about twenty minutes." Sam passed through first and she held back, gave one last look around. It was not impossible for Bowman to be lurking out there in the grass, watching, being weird. "I reserved five seats on this flight, not that it ever fills up." She reached into an outside pocket of her worn leather satchel for Sam's phone, handed it over. "I charged the battery."

She bought them each a coffee at the cart in the terminal. Sam started, like he'd suddenly realized something. He looked her up and down.

"I'm not dressed for a meeting at a bank."

She thought about that. She wasn't dressed up, exactly—they were only headed to Denver—but Sam was right. "We'll have time to stop at a store on the way. My treat."

"You're not buying my clothes," he said, but didn't object to the plan.

"Why didn't Jeremy and Darwin come in?"

"Jeremy's not flying to Denver with us." Sam held his coffee absently, too jittery to drink it, like he'd had too much already. "He didn't tell you about Melissa's backpack?"

Summer shook her head, thinking, *Who the hell is Melissa?* Then she remembered, the hitchhiker, with the cocaine, who was presumed dead. They stood in the hallway near the three airline ticket booths. Sam looked around suspiciously. A half-dozen passengers walking through the terminal, ticket agents bored at their computer screens, TSA personnel lounging at the security checkpoint. A man pushing a trash can on wheels and sweeping up invisible bits of litter.

He led her by the arm to a corner behind an impressive ficus plant, speaking low, Summer smiling and about to comment that he was acting like Uncle Jeremy, but the outrageousness of what he was saying stopped her: a burning car, two bodies—"your uncle shot them"—over a million dollars' worth of cocaine, maybe a lot more in bearer bonds, trying to hustle a guy who sells guns to one of the cartels, and then some biker gave them a phone and Jeremy was waiting for a call. Sam had gone wild-eyed.

Great, she thought. *Jeremy's "interesting shit."*

"Won't he take that stuff to the sheriff? He *is* a deputy."

"I don't think so."

Their pre-boarding call came over the loudspeakers and she realized she hadn't bought their tickets. Her uncles had better hurry up. Unless Uncle Jeremy really wasn't coming? Sam's report had thrown her and she needed to talk to Jeremy in person.

At the Great Lakes counter, Sam had handed the ticket agent his ID and credit card, insisting he would buy his own ticket, when her phone rang. A number she didn't recognize, so she declined, but it rang again within seconds. She apologized to Sam and answered.

She heard background noise, wind. She started to end the call, but then Andrew's voice was there, tinny but unmistakable.

"Andrew?"

"Where are you?" More noise behind his voice, a loud motor or something, and the sound was hollow and far off.

"Why, what are you up to?"

"Please, Summer."

She sighed. "I'm in the airport. I talked to the bank. We put off the meeting until later. Where have you been?"

"Shit. Are you through security?"

"Not yet, why?"

"Turn around, make an excuse, say you forgot something. You're in danger, and you need to leave the terminal now."

"Oh come on. Mr. Runnels said you've been acting strange. He's worried about you."

"Summer, you can't trust him, can't trust the bank. I'll explain when we have time, but you have to get out of there right now."

She put her hand on Sam's arm, apologized to the agent. The phone slipped away from her ear as Andrew was saying something about how serious this was and how he needed her to trust him.

"So they changed the meeting again?" She spoke a little more loudly into the phone and raised her eyebrows at Sam. "We need a different flight?"

Sam stood there with his credit card, the now-frowning ticket agent looking from Sam to Summer and back again to Sam. Summer shouldered her bag and headed for the exit, hoping Sam would follow.

"That's good," Andrew said. "Don't trust anyone you don't know. Avoid security cameras. Shut your phone down after we hang up."

"This is ridiculous. What's going on?" There were several security cameras in the terminal, and more covering the street outside. She stopped on the sidewalk and Sam appeared beside her. He looked confused.

Andrew's voice from the phone: "I don't want you driving back to the ranch, it's too dangerous. I have an idea. Walk to the general aviation hangar. They won't expect that. Find what's his name, Stu? Rent whatever he has available."

It took her a moment to realize what he was saying.

"You want me to fly."

"Have you flown at all since . . ."

"Since we broke up. Yes, but only enough to stay current."

"That's fine, you're a good pilot, a natural. You flew all Stu's planes when you were learning. File a plan into . . . I won't say it . . . you remember where we met before we went fishing?"

"What, you think someone's listening in? We're speaking in code now?"

"Please, Summer. Do you remember?"

Andrew hangared his King Air at a municipal airport south of Denver. They'd flown out of that airport in his plane to Cabo.

"I remember. Hang on a second."

She muted the phone and spoke to Sam in a low voice. "I don't know if everyone's gone crazy at once or what, but Andrew thinks I'm in immediate danger and he wants me to take a different plane."

He stared at her. "Who's Andrew?"

"He's an officer at the bank, and a friend."

Sam's look shifted, maybe suspicion? Or disappointment? She might've revealed something in the way she'd said "friend."

"Meet me over at the general aviation building—that brown cinderblock, past the parking lot, there, see it?"

He looked where she was pointing. "Where are you going?"

"I'll walk around the long way. He wants me to stay away from security cameras."

Sam started off. She watched him for a moment, then unmuted the phone as she moved to the left, away from the parking lot and the cameras on the light poles.

"I'm back. Look, this is nuts, Stu might not even have a plane ready. I think I should just head straight home." This would work better for her. If there really was any danger, the ranch was where she wanted to be. It's where Bowman would be headed. Maybe he'd sensed something wrong last night, why he changed his plans. Once he showed up at the ranch, they could handle whatever this was, together with Sam and their uncles.

"No, that's not a good idea." Andrew nearly shouted this, but his voice was more controlled when he spoke again. "They know where the ranch is. You'll be safer in Denver. I won't be able to meet you, but someone I trust will be there. He'll have a placard, with your grandfather's original name on it."

"*Who* knows where the ranch is? Is this about that Salifano codger? And how do you know my grand—"

He interrupted her, saying his associate would help her access the account, insisting it was of utmost importance that she do this as soon as possible. "You'll be helpless without it," he said.

"That makes no sense to me."

"Are you out of the terminal yet?" Andrew wasn't usually so insistent, so brusque. He'd tried to boss her around a few times when they were first seeing each other socially, and she hadn't reacted well. He never tried it again the rest of the time they were together. Watching over her shoulder, she saw Sam stop and stare at something toward the back of the parking lot.

She backed under the overhang at the south end of the drop-off/pick-up lane. No cameras here. Sam had changed direction and was walking toward something hidden from her view by a parked tour bus. She took off her blazer.

"I'm outside, but I'm not flying some rattletrap Cessna to Denver until you tell me what's happening." She dug around in her bag and found an elastic band for her hair. No answer. "You haven't been yourself, Andrew. Are you all right?" Waiting, she thought she could hear him breathing on the phone, but when she looked at the screen she saw they'd lost the connection.

28

The two pickups—Jeremy's beater and Darwin's black Ford—were parked near the back fence, side by side and facing opposite directions so the drivers could talk without yelling across one cab or the other. They were intent on their conversation and didn't notice Sam approaching.

"I'll call Jicky, he owes us." This was Darwin.

A pause. "Nope. Jicky crash-landed over by Pueblo couple months ago visiting his brother's widow. I don't believe he's got it fixed yet."

"Well, I'll call him and ask anyway."

Marco must've scented him. He jumped up on the toolbox, wagging his tail and panting, shaking the old truck side to side. Jeremy frowned at Sam through his windshield. Sam waved and mumbled a hello, unsure how to explain what was going on with Summer.

He turned around, hoping she was behind him, but she'd disappeared. Nowhere in the parking lot. He stood at Jeremy's front bumper, feeling awkward.

Both men watched him, Darwin's eyes blinking slowly in his truck's big side mirror. He wore a handsome black cowboy hat. What a rancher would wear to meet with his bankers in Denver.

"Isn't the flight about to board?" Jeremy asked. "Darwin was going to head in."

Sam nodded. "Um, yeah, but Summer got a call—"

His own phone rang in his pocket, the standard electronic trill that he'd shut off a long time ago. Summer, he realized, must've turned it back on while she'd had the thing in her possession.

He reached into the pocket of his shorts. "This is probably her."

But it was Mac, calling in a panic from the Dallas airport.

"Mac, I can't hear you."

His friend was shout-whispering, and a breeze blew hot fuel-scented air from the tarmac. Sam jammed the phone harder into his ear.

"What?"

"They made a bunch of other calls."

Jeremy's door opened, must've heard Sam say Mac's name. He followed Sam into the lee of Darwin's truck. Sam punched on the speakerphone and turned the volume all the way up.

"You're on speaker, Jere—um, Uncle is here. Who made a bunch of calls?"

"The two guys . . . the fucking kidnappers!"

"On his phone," Jeremy said. "Dammit, you said they didn't. What were the area codes? Were they domestic?"

"Yeah, all U.S. numbers, three of them, seven or eight calls to each one, area codes were Phoenix, Denver, and Albuquerque."

Jeremy went back and grabbed a notepad from his truck. "Read them off."

When Mac finished, Jeremy told him to hang up and turn the phone off again, take out the battery, get rid of the thing.

"I will, but there's something else." Mac lowered his voice, his breathing more pronounced, sounded like he was walking. "There's a guy, Hispanic, waiting for my flight to D.C., he's got those freaky face and neck tats, full sleeves, it's all that death's-head shit. He keeps looking at me and smiling, like he knows something."

"What's he doing now?"

"Hang on." Footsteps, airport noise, a loud announcement. Then, "Ah, he's reading a book."

"What kind of book?" Sam asked.

"I don't fucking know, a how-to-kill-people book."

"Try to get a look at it," Jeremy said.

"Why?"

"Because it's probably a mystery, or some self-help thing, he's probably harmless, and even if he's not there's no way anyone could be following you already."

"Describe him," Sam said.

"He's young, early twenties, wiry, jeans and T-shirt with a logo in Spanish. He's probably good-looking under all the tats. Shaved his scalp so you can see the fucking skulls and shit. A name on the side of his neck, looks like LYDIA. Oh fuck, he saw me looking, now he's pulling something out of his backpack."

"Calm down, Mac."

"It's a big notebook, like a portfolio. I'm going around behind him."

Sam expected an eye roll or a snarky grin from Jeremy, but his face was impassive. A knot of five women approached from the employee parking area, most in some sort of uniform, laughing at something. One broke off, waved goodbye to the others, and walked in between the trucks, put her hand on Darwin's arm resting on the window jamb. Started speaking to him. It was Summer, of course, but she'd turned her jacket inside out, done something different with her hair. She'd even moved differently, loose-jointed, carefree.

Mac on the speaker again, "They're, um, drawings, sketches."

"Of what?" Jeremy had noticed Summer now.

"Animal heads, mostly dogs, some horses." Mac's voice had gone flat, embarrassed. "They're pretty good."

"Mac, hang up, kill your phone, and try to relax. It's too soon for anyone to be onto you. I'll look into those numbers, but we're going to handle this from here."

As Sam tried to reassure Mac and get off the line, Darwin stepped out of his truck and the uncles and Summer put their heads together in a short, intense conversation Sam clearly was not intended to hear. He realized this was the first time he'd seen the twins together. They weren't quite identical, but close enough to create confusion. Now all three of them were staring at Sam. Mac finally hung up.

"What?"

"We've decided we trust you," Summer said, starting to smile.

"You're too random to be connected to any of this," Jeremy added.

"Okay," Sam said. "Thanks." Then, looking at Summer, "Did you tell them about your call from what's-his-name?"

The uncles turned to look at her.

"Andrew's in a panic," she said. "I'm not sure how seriously to take him."

She sounded unconcerned, but obviously she hadn't ignored the warning. Sam thought she might be downplaying it to avoid triggering an overreaction from Jeremy.

"He said I'm in some sort of danger, has to do with the account from Grandfather Martin, maybe Salifano's gang, and he wanted me to leave the terminal." She turned to look back across the parking lot, like it had only then occurred to her to check for someone following. Sam and the uncles did the same.

A couple of hundred yards away, a single taxicab was parked at the far end of the terminal building. At the near end, a woman stood outside the entrance talking on a cell phone. While they watched, a large blue SUV pulled up between the cab and the woman. The rear cargo hatch began to open, must be motorized. Sam tensed, but a woman in a white cowboy hat emerged from the driver's side and met two teenage boys at the back, where they pulled out backpacks and submitted to fierce hugs from the woman before disappearing into the terminal.

Still watching, Summer continued. "Andrew said it's too dangerous for me to go home. Whoever it is knows where the ranch is, they'll be watching. He wants me to rent a plane from Stu's outfit and fly to Denver, to that little airport in Moremount. His 'associate' will meet me there."

"You're a pilot?" Sam asked, but he was ignored. At the mention of a plane, Jeremy and Darwin exchanged a look that, while it seemed completely expressionless to Sam, must have transmitted an extreme reaction.

"What?" This time it was Summer's turn to ask.

"I don't even want to tell you," Jeremy said.

"Why not?"

"You're going to . . . I don't know." He stopped and looked at Sam like he could help explain things.

"They finally called?"

"Yeah. Woman named Mia Cortez. She's number two in the Chicago distribution hub of one of the big Mexican drug cartels. She didn't say which one, but it's not hard to guess."

"And?"

"And I've got to give that shit back. They know who I am, and now we know Mac's phone was a weak link. I bet those numbers he gave us are low-level cartel contacts, the two idiots trying to figure out what they had, what they could get for it. The cartel won't have any trouble finding Mac and his secretary. They'll kill all of us: Mac, the secretary, you, me, Summer, Darwin. They'll kill Marco while they're at it."

Sam's guts went watery again. It was becoming a familiar sensation.

"So give it back," he said. "Like we talked about."

"Not that simple. She doesn't trust me, and I don't trust her. I told her I need to meet with someone whose word will bind the cartel before I hand it over. There's no guarantee they won't just hunt us down and kill us anyway, but it's the best I can do. She's in Mexico now, and she can't convince an underboss to hump up here to pick it up. They're too vulnerable in the U.S. And I'm too vulnerable in Mexico. So we're going to meet at the border, someplace remote. She's hiring me a guide."

No one spoke while this sank in. The sound of a plane taxiing to the runway drifted over from the other side of the terminal. Sam watched as some sort of inscrutable nonverbal communication transpired among Summer and her uncles.

"How're you going to get down there?" he asked.

29

1989

Summer appeared first, as usual, preceded by quick metronomic clip-clops on the stone floor of the hall, those cowboy boots she'd been wearing all year, her face as she rounded into the kitchen guileless and alarmed. Leo had tried to sound casual when he'd knocked on her bedroom door, asked her to meet in the kitchen for breakfast.

"What is it? Is Bowman coming?"

"He's on his way." Leo had found him down at the barn raking out the mews, feeding the eagles. He was in a sullen mood and Leo wasn't certain the boy planned to show up.

"Darwin made us a frittata." Leo's hands shook as he served their plates. He'd faced a hundred armed adversaries with less nerves than possessed him this morning, facing his own children. There would be two schools, on opposite coasts. The high standards wouldn't be a problem. The tuition would be a stretch, but he'd sat with Darwin and figured out a way to pay it.

"I'm not hungry." But she picked up her fork and started eating anyway, frowning. He knew she was gaming out what he was up to. After a few bites, she asked if Uncle Jeremy was sick. Jeremy had been away for a week in Denver, teaching a class at the police academy. Ever since her mother had died of cancer, Summer had worried first about Leo's health, gradually shifting some of that concern to her mother's brothers as she absorbed more knowledge about carcinogens, downwinders, hereditary risk factors.

"Nothing like that," he said.

"But you're worried about something."

A shadow crossed the late winter light filtering in from the hall and Bowman materialized silently behind Summer. She saw Leo's look and turned around.

"Goddammit," she said, but didn't elaborate.

Bowman nodded to Leo and padded sockfoot into the kitchen— he'd shed his boots at the door—and served his own plate from the hot cast-iron pan. He sat down across the table from his sister. He paused—probably a silent prayer of some sort: *Thank you great spirit and generous chickens for this meal*—and tucked in. Leo and Summer watched him eat.

I could simply wait, Leo thought. *Put it off again, not do it at all, ever.* If he invented some other reason for this meeting, right now, their lives could continue as he'd planned, and as they expected.

In so many ways they both were doing fine, better than fine, far better than he had been at this age. They'd fought, of course, but in recent weeks they'd been getting along. Both were passionate, creative, and aware of and engaged with the world surrounding them to a degree Leo himself envied. They soaked up knowledge, questioning everything, and in so many ways affirmed Leo's choices in their education. He had raised them to know the wild, disturbing truth of the world, to know it more deeply than Leo could himself, having glimpsed it only late in life, in Africa. To know it in the old way. To know it in their bones.

But it wasn't going to be enough. Ever since the chance meeting with his old State Department acquaintance in Mexico City, he'd quietly kept track of what was happening in Africa, power accruing to people he knew too much about, and he'd become convinced his own longevity was in some question. If he might not be around to continue Bowman and Summer's preparation for what he'd come to think of as his father's curse, due in twenty years, then some acceleration of their education was in order. He'd taught them what he could about how to function in civilization, but he knew his own limitations. It was time they left the ranch, learned things about the world they could never learn from him.

"We're going to have to make some difficult changes," he began, already feeling he was wrong-noting this. He had their attention, though, two pairs of eyes on him, predators watching a potential threat, or a meal. "In August, you'll both be going away to school."

Summer made a sound like a fox: barking, incredulous.

"That's crazy," she said. "And you're saying it like we don't have a vote. Like you've made this decision for us, like we're little kids."

She turned to Bowman, clearly expecting support, in this dire crisis a return to their old solidarity. But his face was a mask.

"Okay," he said.

"Okay?" Summer's voice ratcheted up an octave, then she seemed to catch herself, or come to a realization.

Leo also found Bowman's acquiescence disconcerting, but he went ahead with the rationale he'd rehearsed—how it was impossible to fully prepare them here at the ranch for the life they faced. How college should be an option for them, and formal preparatory schooling, even for a year or two, would make a big difference to college admissions. They listened, but Bowman's passivity had chilled Summer's outrage. She sulked while Bowman went back to the stove for more eggs and cut four slices of bread from a loaf Darwin had made yesterday, made toast with butter and huckleberry preserves. Summer watched him with an incredulous expression.

"Where?" she asked, her eyes still on her brother.

"Yours is in western Massachusetts. Out in the country. Bowman's is in San Diego. Near the ocean."

"Wait. We're not even going to the same school?"

"The best school for you isn't the best for Bowman." Kentwood was elite, academically rigorous, and more or less conventional. Darcy Academy would be better prepared to handle what he was afraid would turn out to be significant behavioral issues from the much more feral Bowman.

"Why?" Summer asked. "What's so special about me? Or him?"

"You're both very special. But you're also very different from each other." Leo didn't expect any argument to that, and he didn't get any. "You'll both be ahead of the others in your age groups academically."

"But we can't afford it," Summer insisted.

"Darwin says we can." *Barely,* he thought.

At twilight, Summer sat in the big rocking chair in front of the fireplace in the library. Her algebra workbook was open but she watched her brother at the small desk across the room. He was writing something on a notepad. She had no idea what—their educational paths had diverged a while ago. He stopped every minute or so to peer out the window at the falling snow: wet heavy flakes coming down fast, more like sleet. Might be the last big snow of the year. Their father had driven Uncle Darwin down the mountain in the old Willys, which during the winter was equipped with chains and a plow on the front. Darwin would spend the weekend in Durango, working at the restaurant and sleeping on a couch in a friend's house in town.

"Full moon tonight," she said. "Good fresh snow for tracking."

Bowman ignored her, continued his scribbling.

"Awooooooo." Years ago he'd taught her a pretty good wolf howl. His pencil stopped. His gaze was level. She bugged her eyes at him, finally raising half a grin on his face.

"Did you already know about the schools?" she asked. "Did he tell you first?"

"No."

"What are you planning to do?"

"I'm not planning anything."

"Yes, you are. What, are you going to run away? Like a little kid with a couple of sandwiches in a knotted kerchief on a stick?"

This brought on his trademark patient smile. She wanted to smack him.

"When did you start talking like that?" he asked.

Summer fumed. This indomitable air of superiority. But he must've realized he'd made her mad. His face relaxed, a lowering of the mask. She looked away.

"I've missed you," he said.

Was he being conciliatory? He'd kept himself aloof for so long she'd given up on their old close alliance, had settled into a chilly détente. She wasn't proud of that and it made her defensive.

"I've missed our arguments," he said.

She stared at her math problems without seeing them, still too angry to reply. There was so much finality in his demeanor. Things that had always been were coming to an end, and Bowman had grasped that—embraced it, maybe—while she'd been oblivious.

"You're smarter than I am, you know."

This was too much. She looked up but found she was unwilling to meet his gaze, instead staring into the face of the oversized hyena snarling for all eternity on the far side of the fireplace.

"I heard you and Dad arguing in here yesterday," she said.

He closed his notebook with an air of forbearance. "That was an interesting conversation."

"What started it?"

"I asked him why there weren't any primates." He waved an arm toward the half-dozen antelope in the alcove, the warthog, the hyena, the leopard. "Why he never shot any trophy chimpanzees or gorillas or baboons. He said he'd never considered it. That it would've felt too much like murder."

"I missed that part," she said. "I heard him calling you a naïve boy." This had pleased her at the time—her superior mystical brother being called out in terms she thought she might agree with.

But Bowman laughed. "I suggested that societies and cultures sharing an ecosystem with other large primates might have more humility, less of a conviction of human exceptionalism. He disagreed."

She'd heard her father insisting, with some heat, that if people could routinely reduce each other to meat based on meaningless differences in skin color or tribe or religion or nationality, logically they should have no trouble whatsoever doing the same to primates of different species. He'd said in parts of Africa gorillas and chimpanzees were considered nothing more than bushmeat, along with pretty much every other species big enough to make a meal or two.

"You called him a misanthrope."

"Well, he is, isn't he? He's decided people in general are completely hopeless, which somehow justifies us living up here in
idyllic splendor, learning the old ways and expanding our consciousness, while the rest of humanity carries on destroying the
planet and living the miserable fate they brought on themselves."
Bowman had stood up and now he began pacing back and forth in
the library. "You can't dismiss human suffering by saying humanity in general deserves it, that people should never have abandoned
the old ways, should never have taken up agriculture, sedentism,
stratified societies, catastrophic overpopulation. . . . It's all true but
it fails as a personal justification for smug enjoyment of unearned
advantage. For turning away and letting the world burn."

She waited until he stopped and looked at her.

"Is that conversation why he decided to send us off to school,
and why you're not fighting it?"

His face closed down. "No," he said. "He'd already made up his
mind. There's something else going on he's not telling us about."

"You always think there's something else going on." When he
didn't reply, she said, "I don't want to leave here, and I can't believe
you do."

"You'll be glad you did. And you'll come back someday. We'll
always come back."

Hearing him say this stirred a part of her—a selfish part—that had
been secretly excited by the prospect of boarding school in the exotic
New England countryside. But she set it aside. Her father needed her
here. She worried about what would happen to him if she left.

"You're acting superior. And you're not answering my question.
How could you possibly be okay with leaving?"

But their sibling heart-to-heart was over, and Bowman went back
to his notebook. She was far from satisfied, but too proud to beg for
her brother's attention. Something in the pit of her stomach felt a lot
like fear, like what was coming was more than a change, like it would
be the end of everything.

30

2009

Summer sat in the pilot's seat of the thirty-year-old Cessna 185 with her phone to her ear, absently listening to Andrew's line ring. She'd already tried to call the unfamiliar number he'd used earlier. Through the side window, she watched a porta-potty near the chain-link fence marking the boundary of the general aviation section of the airport. She'd used the toilet first and found Sam waiting outside, saying it didn't look like there would be a restroom on that little plane. She liked Sam, but she had to concede his appearance in the AP village might have been meaningless coincidence after all, her assumptions about the utility of a tax lawyer premature. Given current circumstances, her signal fire would've done better with an ex-SEAL. Though, she reminded herself, that was what Uncle Jeremy was for.

After her preflight inspection, she'd had a brief argument with Jeremy about balance, but eventually they'd agreed on Jeremy in the copilot's seat, Sam behind Summer, and their luggage opposite Sam: Summer's leather satchel, Sam's daypack, a hard plastic case for Jeremy that contained weaponry of some sort, and the yellow backpack of cocaine from the dead hitchhiker. The plan was to drop Jeremy and the backpack at an airport near the border, then she and Sam would fly to Denver. Jeremy insisted they not wait for him, that he would find his own way to Denver as soon as he could. Darwin was on his way back to the ranch with Marco in case Bowman showed up, then he would fly out of La Plata tomorrow morning with or without him. Once they all convened in Denver, they would decide how to proceed with the bank, given Andrew's warning.

Jeremy vibrated with impatience, walking back and forth behind the plane talking on his phone. Hopefully he and the cartel person were working out exactly where the hell they were going.

The cartel person. That Jeremy was talking to. Hoping to learn where on the Mexican border they wanted him to hand over a backpack full of cocaine.

She repeated the improbable description to herself twice before Andrew's voicemail finally picked up. Pressing 1 to shortcut his spiel, she left a cheerful message saying she was fine, flying her uncle to Arizona for an errand, and please postpone the Denver meeting again until tomorrow.

Grandfather Martin had waited thirty-five years to lay this account on the family, and she and her uncles agreed he could stand to wait another few hours. Whatever threat might or might not be coming from Jake Salifano would have to get in line behind the decidedly more concrete and immediate danger from the cartel.

The door to the toilet banged open and Sam jogged to the plane. She started to get out, but Jeremy was off the phone now and helped Sam into his seat, showed him how to fasten the shoulder harness. Before she started the engine she instructed them both on how to use the headsets and where they plugged in. Jeremy sat in the copilot's seat, eyeing the yoke in front of him.

"What did she say?" Summer asked over the headset.

"She wants to meet on some hell-and-gone smuggler's trail near the Arizona–New Mexico line. I told her I'd rent a car at the Sierra Vista airport and drive myself but she insisted the guide'll pick me up. Someone's going to call this phone in about an hour or so. I should be able to get a signal if we're near a tower."

Summer opened the throttle, turned the key, and the engine came alive, showing its outrage; to her it always sounded like a large dinosaur waking up in a bad mood. After switching on the lights and radio, she sound-checked their headsets again and asked the tower for clearance to taxi.

At the downwind end of the runway, she rehearsed the takeoff sequence again, taking her time. As Andrew had pointed out, she'd learned on Cessnas like this one, had flown this very plane several times. They were tough, reliable, loud as hell. Not fast, but even at 170 miles an hour they should make it to southern Arizona in under three hours, giving her time to refuel and fly back north to Denver with Sam before it got too late. She could fly at night but she technically wasn't qualified to do so with a passenger on board. It was sinking in that she had committed herself to a very long day of flying.

A new voice on the radio, the airport super this time, Summer thought her name was Misha, ordering her to turn around and return to the general aviation terminal. She was about to ask why when Jeremy pointed out the windshield; an airport security vehicle and a fire engine, both with lights flashing, converging on the Beechcraft still at the gate.

On the radio: *We have a situation here, everyone's grounded.*

"We got to go, Summer." Jeremy gestured impatiently down the runway. "Just take off. Fly south. Tell them it's a medical emergency or something."

She eased the throttle to full.

"Sorry, tower, we have a medical emergency, got to get my elderly uncle with dementia to a hospital, looks like appendicitis." She glared at Jeremy and switched off the radio. Check visibility, check the runway, all clear, check the sky: still no planes anywhere. As she accelerated, she watched the police cars to see if they were going to race after her and block her takeoff like they do in the movies. But they were occupied, had the door to the Beechcraft open and the stairs down and the passengers deplaning in a hurry.

Leaving the earth was a rattletrap, disorienting experience that would have alarmed her if she'd had no experience with this sort of aircraft. The noise from the engine would be deafening without headsets, and even with them there was a disturbing vibration in the bones. She leveled off and made her exit turn, the noise dropping from mind-destroying to head-splitting. Jeremy suggested they fly due south to I-10, then slowly westward along the interstate where he would have a signal for the cell phone.

At a thousand feet, she came around and flew over the airport, tilting to port so she could see. Another fire truck with its lights flashing was inbound from the highway, must be Whitespring Volunteer.

"Doesn't look like anything has happened," Jeremy said, leaning over to see out her window. "No smoke. Nobody was coming off that plane in cuffs."

"So what do you think it was?" Sam asked. "Like a bomb threat?"

Jeremy's pager went off. He read it and replaced it on his belt. "Sam wins the prize. Bomb threat. Sheriff wants me at the airport."

"So that's what your guy was calling about, huh?"

She smiled at Sam's phrase "your guy."

"Who would it be?" Sam asked. "And what would be the point? Of a bomb, or even just the threat?"

"To get her off the plane," Jeremy said. "Put her in a specific place at a specific time, confused and shaken."

"So they want to kidnap me?"

"Rich people get kidnapped all the time."

"Not in Whitespring. And I'm not rich."

"You might be," Sam said. "If this account from your grandfather is dark money, offshore, anonymous, hidden from the IRS, whoever it is would assume you can't go to the police."

This hadn't occurred to her. She didn't see how kidnapping her would allow the kidnappers to steal money she herself had no access to, but Sam was probably right about the police.

Jeremy called dispatch on his cell and by raising his voice was able to report he was unavailable and would be out of the area for an emergency the rest of the day. They flew on. Nobody spoke. Summer automatically noted the conditions, which were perfect. A thunderhead loomed off to the southwest but southward were clear skies, a vague summer haze.

Jeremy's phone started vibrating a few miles north of Gallup. She eased the throttle back as he answered, yelling over the noise again. Both sides of the conversation having trouble. "Coordinates?" he asked. Summer didn't like the sound of that. Coordinates didn't sound like an airport code. Coordinates sounded like a private airstrip. She'd passed her "short/soft" field test to qualify but had been blessed with well-maintained runways ever since.

Jeremy knew this. "How about a municipal airport? Bisbee–Douglas or Sierra Vista, there's a bunch of 'em down there." He listened, looking increasingly frustrated. "Got it, but if we don't like what we see, we're headed to Douglas and you can come get us there. . . . Well, you tell them I said our pilot is not comfortable landing on a crappy ranch airstrip." Jeremy started entering coordinates in the GPS, reading them back to the person on the phone, making sure he had them right. Summer felt a low-grade nausea that she expected was going to last until she and Sam were on the ground in Denver later today.

31

The Jeep came up the switchbacks too fast, sideslipping on the turns, fishtailing in between, raising an obvious cloud of dust. Border Patrol was going to notice, might send someone. They would back off when they saw it was her, but still.

Rice Moore set down his binoculars and keyed the microphone on his radio.

"Slow down."

No response. No slowing down.

He crawled backward from the edge of the outcrop into the shelter of a mesquite thicket. Once he was hidden, he stood and turned and jogged down a steep slope to their campsite.

Apryl had left earlier after a sat text from Jorge telling her to call him ASAP. The closest cell signal was in Douglas, an hour away over shitty roads. After she'd left, he'd finished swapping data cards in their line of trail cameras along a tributary to the Guadalupe, where he'd surprised a group of five migrants under a paloverde, three women and two teenage boys too terrified to run. Abandoned by their *coyote*. He calmed them down, let them drain his water bottle, handed over his protein bars. When he asked them to hand him the wrappers, not leave them on the ground, they didn't understand. The desperation. White dude worried about litter. But Christ, this was a special place.

He and Apryl always offered water, food. Cleaned up the trash they left. Kept a box of thirty-gallon trash bags in the Jeep for the purpose. Apryl chanting, *Fuck this fuck this fuck this I'm not judging but fuck this.*

Not that migrants' litter was the real threat. Not by a long shot. The rugged southern foot of the Peloncillos was a fragile ecological hodgepodge, part of a tenuous bridge between the Sierra Madre Occidental and the Rocky Mountains, where the Sonoran and Chihuahuan Deserts met, where the southernmost reach of many North American species overlapped with the extreme northern range of species found in Mexico and Central America. It had always been too remote and rugged for the feds to bother with, but recently the Department of Homeland Security had started making noises about building a wall here. Rice and Apryl specialized—for several reasons—in biological research along the border, and last year the owners of this property had hired them to build a credible database of species dependent on the ability to move back and forth between the U.S. and Mexico.

They wouldn't log the new images until they got back to Tucson in a few days, a kind of zoological treasure hunt that had become more consequential ever since they'd photographed a jaguar here in March, not a dispersing male but a female of breeding age. The landowners had decided to keep it quiet for now, didn't want the attention a confirmed female jaguar would bring, at least not yet. They wanted more pictures, a pattern of residency. They wanted cubs. Rice wondered how that would play in the fight over the fucking wall: jaguar cubs versus Homeland paranoia.

At their tent, he dropped his backpack and waited, listening to the Jeep's engine rev and back off: frantic frustrated roars and impatient downshifted whines. Apryl's driving voice, unmistakable. She finally slowed when she turned off the main canyon road and crawled in low gear up and over a rise, rolled into their usual parking spot. She got out and eased her door shut quietly the way they always did out here.

"This is fucked," she said. "You need to go scout Los Robles."

Rice swiped dust from the window and looked in. Plastic shopping bags on the backseat. A new cooler had displaced some of the junk in the back.

"Now?"

"Yeah. We're supposed to guide some dude to the border later today. Jorge's all excited, this thing is coming from important people. But then he says, 'You have to hide him from the Patrol.'"

"We can't. They're all over the place. Randy drove by with some new recruit while you were gone."

"I told Jorge we'd dress the guy up as a birder." She emptied Walmart bags onto the ground: XL camo coveralls, boonie hat, cheap binoculars, energy bars, a green plastic tarp. They usually bought their equipment at the military surplus store in Tucson, where they could blend in with the preppers and militia types and military buffs. Now Apryl would be on the CCTV at the big box store buying camouflage. Not a big deal, but something to keep in mind. At least they had a cover story.

"In back of the parking lot I had to rendezvous with a ten-year-old kid who ran up to the chain-link fence with this." She held up a high-end satellite phone. "Called our package on the way back. Told him where to land."

"You using the Baker strip?"

"Yeah, he's on his way, I got to turn right around. The best part is his pilot's a newbie."

"That's not good." Rice had flown into that strip once before with a friend of Apryl's, an expert pilot, and had sworn it wouldn't happen again. "If he's so important, why didn't they find him a decent pilot?" He and Apryl had always carried packages, never people, but he knew sometimes a known honcho, or a family member, couldn't chance a more conventional return to old Mexico and had to be snuck across.

"It sounds like he's coming on his own. He's not cartel, he's meeting with cartel. We walk him to the border, they have a powwow, then we bring him back and drop him off in Douglas."

Rice slid the heavy cooler from the back of the Jeep. "That's not what we do."

"Jorge says they're tripling the fee, close to twenty grand for a day's work, so I said whatever, Jorge, we can do that, but he didn't answer, he just sighed, sounded almost apologetic, like he felt bad, and Jorge never feels bad."

Apryl got back in the Jeep, eased the door shut again.

Rice leaned down, spoke through the open passenger window. "Our new gig, guiding bird-watchers on the border."

"Yeah, it would be pretty funny. But."

She started the Jeep.

"But," he prompted.

"Before he hung up, Jorge goes, 'One more thing, *mija,* bring your guns. This man will be carrying something of great value.'"

32

Biting insects, hot sun, cows lowing. More biting insects. Bowman lay facedown in grass and gravel, his legs in water. Small fish nibbled at his toes. He was unsurprised to find he was completely naked. In his bones he knew the long-ago gravity of home, but he wasn't sure why he'd been away, for how long, or where he'd been, who he'd been. How he'd come home. None of that was worth puzzling over right now anyway.

The bugs, though. The bugs demanded his attention.

He was used to bugs. They didn't often bother him.

But these were bad. Bites like needle stabs, falling like rain.

He brought his palms up, worked them under his shoulders, managed a push-up. A cut on his forehead stung and throbbed with the effort, and his left shoulder ached but held his weight. A fresh trickle of blood ran down into his eyebrow and dripped onto the gravel shore. He held himself there in what his father had called a plank. Painful and unsteady at first, but he drew strength from the earth. Blackflies, that's what these were, now they bit his nostrils, lips, eyelids.

No memories of home matched this pestilence. A panic to escape stuttered and swelled in his chest. He'd read about herds of caribou driven mad by these insects, running until their hearts burst or they drowned in snowmelt-swollen rivers, their helpless calves exsanguinated.

He crawled backward, back into the lake, an evolutionary reversal. The

drop was steep and he sank to the gravel bottom. Turned onto his back underwater, ears popping, all blurry blue above, distant sun, bubbles rising. A
far-off background roar, the waterfall where Porcupine Creek fell into the
lake over on the western side. Cold down here. No bugs. Relief and respite.
He could hold his breath for a long time, but he couldn't stay forever.

The insects were on him again as soon as he surfaced. They were
blackflies mainly but also horseflies and the usual mosquitoes too. Cows
lowing again. A stink of livestock. *Cows? What are they doing here?* He
waded through knee-deep water to a stand of horsetail at the mouth of
a small stream feeding the lake, where his feet sank into fine silty mud.
Dragonflies and damselflies rose from the tall green stalks. Swallows
swooping and dipping in the water nearby.

The cool mud smelled of decomposing plant matter and drained
splashing from his hands as he rubbed it onto his chest and shoulders, legs,
groin, buttocks, painted his face and head, glopped handfuls onto the bank
and lay on his back. When he had caked his entire body, he walked away
from the lake into the tall grasses of the meadow until he came to a chest-
high fence of light woven wire, held up by flimsy-looking plastic posts.
An electromagnetic field emanated from the wire, so he avoided touching
it. On the other side was the source of the lowing and, presumably, the
reason for the plague of insects. Dozens of black cows grazing peacefully,
picturesquely. A few younger animals noticed him and shied, then the
grown cows decided he was not a normal two-legged after all, all of them
now moving away, their lowing more emphatic and alarmed. They were
a quarter mile to the west, near the far end of their enclosure, before they
began grazing again, two of the older cows still glowering his way.

He turned northward and left the paddock behind, the stench and
blackflies diminishing. Soon every barefoot step felt familiar. The sounds
and scents drew him more deeply into an old version of himself, one
that included and depended upon—blurred with—this particular land, the
space that enveloped him. Light fell onto his retina, images fitting the spaces
etched there in a former life: the dry slopes and red cliffs to the east, green
mountainside to the west, meadows and forest alternating on southern and
northern exposures, post-alpine scree higher up, peaks of broken rock. It
all felt like a gigantic, complicated key finding its matching tumblers inside
Bowman, turning, unlocking someone he used to be.

There were Others, he remembered, who should be here. They took shape in his mind, the ghosts of the Old Ones, the bison, the scattered wild longhorns. Elk and deer and moose and pronghorn, coyotes, lions, owls, falcons. A family of wolves. The black bears, the compact furtive grizzly, the wolverine. The eagles. Where was Alecto now? He knew he'd set her free, like he'd always meant to, but he couldn't remember doing it. He watched the sky: a deeper darker blue at this elevation, darkest in the north. Swallows over the lake. A pair of redtails circling in the south.

The faces of his parents came to him then, their rock mounds on the ridge. More faces: Uncle Jeremy, Uncle Darwin. He saw Summer, no longer a girl but a grown woman. Were they here?

The wolf den would be off to the north, in the heaviest timber, old ponderosa pine and Douglas fir. They'd made a home up there, hunting at night, keeping themselves to themselves. After a long period of suspicion, then wariness, then a kind of initiation, they had accepted him. He remembered wanting to stay with them, never returning to the house and his human family. But he'd always gone back.

He would check on the wolves. He'd been away for a while, so they might not welcome him right away. He would be stealthy, out of respect.

In the forest, the light changed along with the scents, the birdsongs, the insect buzz. He knew these entities—the trees and shrubs and the small plants crushed under his feet releasing a more astringent scent, fourteen different insects now, eight birds, all of them cataloged in an old corner of his mind, but the more he strained to bring forth their names, the more frustrated he became. Each entity had many names: the names they gave themselves, the ones he and his sister had made up for them, the colloquial and Native names, the official titles and scientific Linnaean compound names intended to illustrate where they fit in the family of life, and finally names describing their roles in the complex biota that even now was beginning to absorb him, to pull tufts of consciousness away—he was a ball of thistledown with no core, no center, surrendering himself to the breeze and sunlight, to the utterly improbable and perfect meaningless sufficiency of existence.

On his hands and knees, studying the old side-cut stream bank, dry for generations after the stream changed course, where the wolves had dug their den. He sniffed, his mouth partly open. The den itself had caved in and the old stream bank was grown over. No wolf scent at all.

The leaden weight of years—of decades—settled on his shoulders, pressing him facedown into the soft forest floor, pine tags loose over matted forest duff slowly accumulating. He dug into it with his fingers, pulled away a handful. The decomposing forest detritus was cool, pungent. How far down would he have to dig to reach the bed of needles he'd last rested on here? A boy lying on his stomach, watching the single surviving pup disconsolate at the mouth of the den, his sisters dead of some virus, growling at Bowman's slow crawling approach, the mother sitting alert but tolerant in a patch of green-filtered forest sunlight twenty steps away.

Those three wolves—small parents, smaller pup—he'd known their names once. Had the pup lived a full life here? He was smart, Bowman remembered. Strong and quick. Had he wandered off somewhere else to live? Had the pair raised others? Where were their bones?

Sadness and loss. So much time had passed, so much more time than he'd realized. Such a great long gout of time, the weight of it again, forcing his face back into the soil. Most of those beings he'd known in this valley would be gone now.

He'd been a teenage boy, an absurd creature in any context, and what the land told him now was that he had broken faith. That he'd been wrong to abandon Panther Gap, to wrench himself away and follow the jaguar south. There would be no forgiveness for his misguided, petulant idealism, for his intentional severing of the old bonds.

But I'm back, now.

Couldn't he just stay here? Live here alone and relinquish his human ego. A kind of penance for ever leaving. He could survive easily enough, knew where to find water, dig roots, feed alongside black bears on wild berries, set snares, ambush a young elk. He could live on, his body growing stronger while he forgot and forgot, an inexorable cognitive entropy shredding the self he'd made during his years away. Like fingers picking at the thistledown until the final strands parted and drifted away in a breeze. Leaving only empty space.

33

Summer banked the plane almost vertically and Sam woke up, gasping, neck tweaked from his usual chin-on-clavicle airplane sleeping position. He didn't think he'd dozed long, but Jeremy pointed out the window and said something about a green tarp being the all-clear signal. They were only about a thousand feet up and Sam could see a vehicle, looked like a Jeep, someone leaning over, staking out a lime-green tarp next to it. A small wind sock hung limp from a pole at the end of what he guessed was their landing strip, a narrow lane bulldozed through the brush years ago.

"Why won't they just shoot you and take the pack?" Summer asked.

The person next to the Jeep stood up, clearly a woman. She got back in the vehicle and left the driver's-side door open.

"The cartels don't kill people like me if they can help it."

"People like you?"

He ignored her. "Remember you've got to turn this thing around right quick. We're a good ways north of the border, but you still want to get the hell out in case the Border Patrol shows up." He turned to squint at Sam. "Now, if they come in a bum rush when we land it means they're trying to kidnap us. Hand me up that pistol."

Summer leveled the plane, then banked again into a tight circle around the tiny airstrip. Fighting the g's and his lurching stomach, Sam managed to twist around in his seat and slide the case forward. An edge caught Summer in the head when Jeremy reached back and brought it into his lap. She readjusted her headset without comment.

"What do you think?" Jeremy asked.

Summer was watching out her side window. "It's long enough, but the sun's still too high, I can't see shadows. I'll make a low flyover but there's no way to know exactly how rough it is until we feel it."

"You'll be fine."

Sam peered down at the ground and tried to think of something encouraging to say. There were no vehicles in sight other than the woman's Jeep.

After the flyover, Summer made two approaches, coming in with the nose up, aborting both, cursing. On the third try she pulled the yoke all the way back to flare, and the fat tires settled down for a few seconds before they hit a big bump, bouncing the plane back into the air. She corrected, cursing again, controlling the plane, and they had room and were going to be fine, except the wind sock at the end of the strip suddenly inflated and stood out at a right angle, a freak crosswind that caught the plane in a moment and the tires hit with a slight twist and something in the undercarriage snapped and the plane listed to the right, scraping along until Summer was able to get them pointed in the right direction and shut off the engine as their forward motion stopped and they all shot forward into their harnesses, then back into their seats with a bounce, and it was over.

"Shit," Summer said. "You guys all right?"

Jeremy grunted and popped the latches on the pistol case, pulled the pistol out, and pointed it at the floor. They all watched the Jeep where it was still parked about two hundred yards back. The woman stood beside it with her hands on her hips. Then she got back in and started driving toward them on the airstrip.

"Here she comes to kidnap us," Sam said.

"We're not flying out of here," Summer said, opening her door. She sounded disgusted with herself. She stepped out with her hand on a wing strut, wincing with pain, and bent down to look under the plane.

The Jeep skidded to a stop. Jeremy replaced the pistol in its case, and he and Sam climbed out of the plane into the intense afternoon heat.

The landing gear struts were both bent and the right wheel was cocked up almost ninety degrees.

"Nice landing," the woman said. She stood in front of her Jeep looking at the three of them and their crippled plane like they'd flown four hundred miles with the sole purpose of ruining her day. She was lean, young, probably early or mid-twenties; long black hair, dark eyes. Dressed to hike in the heat: shorts, boots, green tank top. She didn't look particularly friendly.

"Nice landing strip," Summer said. "Has anyone actually ever landed a plane here before?"

The woman stared at her with the beginnings of a smile. Sam sensed the woman was attracted to Summer, and before he could tamp it down he suffered a flush of jealousy.

Summer wasn't fazed. Either she was used to that kind of attention or hadn't seen it.

"Can you give us a ride to Douglas?"

"No. Which one of you is Jeremy?"

Jeremy had climbed back into the plane and unloaded their bags onto the ground and was on his belly now dragging out Melissa's heavy pack. Sam turned and pointed at his legs and butt.

"Let's go, Jeremy," she said.

He emerged with the yellow pack, red-faced from effort and the unreasonable heat.

"What's your name again?"

"Apryl."

"What's going to happen to them if we leave them here, Apryl?"

"They'll wait with the plane until someone who gives a shit drives by. Or maybe someone noticed your aerial display. Border Patrol gets a call and later today a couple bored agents show up. These two'll sit in a holding facility near Sierra Vista while the Patrol takes the plane apart looking for contraband."

Summer stepped forward. "We absolutely have to get to Denver tonight. I'll pay you extra."

"Summer, we can't take this stuff"—Jeremy pointed to Melissa's backpack—"anywhere but straight to the border." He picked up all of the luggage at once and walked to the Jeep, started piling bags into the cargo space through the open rear hatch.

Sam didn't like the idea of riding around in a Jeep with the radioactive backpack, but waiting here would be worse.

"We should go," he said. "We don't want the Border Patrol to pick us up. We're taking a chance the longer we wait."

"Bowman could be at the ranch by now," Summer said.

Jeremy seemed to think that was funny. "Darwin'll take care of him."

"That's what I'm afraid of. And shit, I have to call Stu about his plane." Summer shook her head like she was trying to clear it. "All right, we should all get out of here. We can figure out how to get to Denver later." She turned toward Apryl. "You got room for us in the Jeep?"

Apryl seemed to think this over while she gave Summer another long, appraising look. She looked over at Sam, then at Jeremy coming around from the back of the Jeep. Seemed to resign herself.

"I don't know what you're into, or what's in those bags, and I don't want to know. We're probably going to run into Border Patrol in the canyon, but they know me. I'm supposed to be guiding a birder. Now you all have to be bird-watchers. Can you do that? We're looking for an elegant fucking trogon. Can you pretend to know what that is?"

They all nodded.

Apryl unlatched the driver's seat so it flipped forward. "Get in if you're coming."

34

1989

Summer caught Milly and rode bareback up to the ridge where her mother and grandfather were buried. Uncle Jeremy had said her father needed her help, was out looking for Alecto, and he wanted Summer to meet him at the graves. She'd searched the barn for the fox lure, but it wasn't there.

There was more going on than the missing eagle.

Last night Bowman had come to her bedroom and they'd crawled out the window onto the roof, the way they had when they were younger. He told her he was worried their father was unstable, that he might be losing his mind. She started to ask what he meant but there was a knock on the door and their father called Summer's name. They'd made it back through the window when their father entered the room. He'd stared, his face hardening. In a cold voice he'd asked Bowman to go with him.

She hadn't seen Bowman this morning. Darwin was in Durango. Neither her father nor Jeremy had been at breakfast. She had fed herself and gone back to her books in the library until Jeremy found her there.

Summer dismounted and wandered around looking for the perfect rock to add to her mother's grave. How many hundreds had she added since the first one she'd placed the day they buried her? She'd been five years old, and she didn't even know if what she had was a memory of a memory, or of something Bowman had told her. They all visited the graves from time to time, she and Bowman and their father and Uncle Jeremy and Uncle Darwin, and she wasn't the only one who kept adding stones—both mounds were chest-high now.

Milly nickered softly, and her father's horse answered from the slope below. She would wait to turn around until she knew he was behind her, and catch him sneaking up. He and Bowman and even Uncle Jeremy took perverse pleasure in sneaking up on Summer, but recently she had trained herself to maintain what Uncle Jeremy called "situational awareness" and she'd begun catching them before they could surprise her.

She turned, smiling, but her father wasn't playing today. Frowning, his eyes red. The inscrutable dread she'd sensed growing in him over the past year seemed to have suddenly multiplied.

"What happened?"

"Your brother released her."

He sounded distracted, and Summer thought again that Alecto flying around free was only a pale shade of whatever the real problem was.

"Where is he?"

Her father shrugged. More than worried, she realized. Angry. About the eagle? Bowman could recover her easily. Summer could do it herself, so long as her father wasn't nearby. Alecto's hatred of Leo had not changed or diminished after five and a half years. Which was why her father would ask for her help.

"Do you have the lure?" she asked.

"In my saddlebag. And a gauntlet."

"She won't come to you."

Her father didn't reply. He looked out over Panther Gap, not really seeing, not registering what he saw.

"We argued last night."

"Where's Uncle Jeremy?"

"Checking the south line. Darwin's on his way home. When he gets here he'll start driving the roads."

This troubled her. It wasn't unheard-of for Bowman to disappear on unplanned camping trips, but he always stayed in Panther Gap because that's where the wildlife lived. Ever since Leo had decided to send them off to school, she and Bowman had been enjoying each other's company, all spring and summer. They'd lit the signal fire on the eve of the solstice. She'd let herself believe he wouldn't leave before the fall.

"You think he's out there." That was the phrase—"out there"— her father had used to refer to the world beyond the boundaries of Panther Gap. A notion of insularity that she had come to understand was at least problematic if not pathological. The crash course in so-called civilization Leo had imposed over the past two years had made that clear.

Her father shrugged again and motioned for her to follow.

"I want you to find Alecto, bring her in if you can. We'll split up at the fork and I'll ride the ridge, look for tracks."

He seemed reluctant to say Bowman's name. They mounted their horses and rode northward along the narrow trail below the crest of the ridge, hidden from view to the east, Summer scanning the sky over Panther Gap, when the sound of ripping canvas came sudden and violent in the air to their right as Alecto swooped up from behind the ridge and slammed feet-first into her father, knocking him from the saddle. His horse spooked and Leo rolled twenty yards downslope to a juniper snag, where he lay supine, unmoving. Chirping madly, Alecto pitched up and swung around to the west before turning to stoop at Leo. Summer shouted and slipped off of Milly, started toward her father carrying the heavy leather gauntlet he'd given her, as if it would work as some kind of weapon, but she was going to be too late. Her father was stunned but conscious, watching Alecto come, when at the last moment she flared her enormous wings, braking as she touched his face with a closed talon, and landed in the skeletal juniper above him, where she immediately relaxed and began to preen.

When Summer reached her father, he had sat up and was watching the unconcerned eagle. His arm and shoulder were bleeding from deep gashes.

"I'm okay," he said.

She held out the gauntlet and whistled, but Alecto ignored her, resumed preening.

"I'll get the lure."

"No," her father said still staring at Alecto with a relieved but melancholy look. "He cut her anklets. She's free. We should let her go."

"But what if she does that to you again?"

"She won't. I think we're even now."

Summer too watched Alecto in the tree, thinking, *You magnificent creature, I fed you and cleaned up after you and helped to train you. I'm going to miss you.* The eagle glanced at her, then down at Leo. She launched with a single great flap of her wings, the branch shaking as she left it, and glided out over Panther Gap.

"What about Bowman? Where is he going?"

Leo shook his head, a darker, more frustrated gesture. "I don't know. And I don't know if he's coming back."

35

2009

A muscular, fight-scarred tom bobcat rose up and stretched on the deadfall where he'd stopped to watch a strange creature moving through the forest. It was human but going along on all fours, making quiet sounds of distress more like a coyote, its breath hot and sick, the rest of it reeking of frogs and turtles and mud. It had fallen face-first to the ground. It didn't get up.

The cat dropped noiselessly from the bole of the old pine and approached the prone creature, circling it twice before sitting nearby. The thing twitched and huffed in unknowable dreams. Then it was still. He approached and sniffed its foot, then turned and shot a stream of acrid urine splashing onto the creature's heel, dug up a small mound of loose duff to pile on its foot before walking off to the west without looking back.

An hour later, Bowman stood and shook himself. The mud on his skin had dried and was flaking off in places. He felt strong, but sad. He knew where he was, but he struggled to remember how he had come to be here.

A memory assembled itself in his mind, maybe a dream, recent, terrifying, *a cool green rush of river water, the otter clambering onto a warm gray boulder, his oily fur wet and glistening, turning to look downstream at a man lying on his side on the grassy bank, bleeding, coughing, and retching. A short loud burst of popping sounds, danger on the opposite bank. The man struggles into a sitting position, searching for the source of the noise. He looks upstream directly at the otter but he doesn't see.*

More of the noises, and the otter is about to return to the river when another sound intrudes: a terrible clattering coming fast from downriver. The shooting stops abruptly and a flying machine appears, slows, and settles down behind the screen of willows on the far bank. The otter dives into the water.

A hundred yards farther upriver, the otter turns to look. Other men are wading into the water, swimming the deep part. They speak with the man on the bank, and one of the new men hurries back and soon the flying thing is in the air again, over the river and going low and bringing a tornado gale, the noise and stink of the end of the world. The otter dives to the cold quiet slippery stones at the bottom of the river. The machine passes back and forth three times before flying away downriver. The otter makes his way to the foot of the mountains. The water there is colder and clearer, calling him upward.

The scent of the old ponderosa pines heating in the afternoon sun brought him back, a faint vanilla sweetness. The huge trunks all around, yellow plate bark, two-hundred-foot trees standing in greenish filtered light. These were familiar, unchanged, his twenty-year absence unnoticed. The trees blinked and there was Bowman, back again. This perspective calmed him. His thoughts grew more rational, a blooming orientation in time and space. Worries, concerns, curiosity. He'd been sick with ciguatera, fever. Better now. As details filtered into his consciousness he began to feel some urgency. He still didn't know who Bickford Rangely was, or what he wanted, or why the people in the truck and SUV had shot at them and run them off the road. After the wreck, there'd been more gunfire. And, if his otter dream could be trusted, a helicopter.

Were they fighting over him?

More important now: Where was Summer? Was she safe? So far he'd failed to do her any good whatsoever. The best thing now would be to find her.

He walked southeast, down from the slopes and out of the forest. He walked into the hot sunlight and stopped in a meadow of tall grasses. A place teeming with memories. They'd lived in a wall tent here, at the center of the meadow. He kicked around in the grass until he found the stone fire ring they'd used, sunken into the ground.

After his mother died, after Darwin and Jeremy had left, Leo had moved the remaining family of three out of the house to live in the valley, away from the stone walls, the rooms he could no longer endure. Nine months here, living on fresh meat, foraged greens and roots, sharing a makeshift privy near the forest edge, bathing in the lake, returning to the house only for blankets and warmer clothes as winter came on. All of it had seemed a fine adventure to Summer and Bowman, had eventually become normal life to them, but now he knew their father hadn't been well. Their diet deteriorated as winter set in, and all three were beginning to suffer from malnutrition when, right after Christmas, a heavy snow collapsed the tent, the potbellied stove was knocked over, the canvas caught fire. They'd nearly asphyxiated. This precipitated a retreat to the cold, dark house, which was less comfortable than the tent but at least provided a solid roof overhead.

He stood in the footprint of the old tent and studied the high slopes to the east. Searching for the horizontal roofline, a few right angles that were too perfect. You had to know where to look. A window flashing when the light was right. It wasn't far.

He knocked, then after a few minutes he did it again, more loudly, for the first time in his life using the brass wolf's-head knocker that had been on the door since before he was born. He doubted anyone else had ever used it. Its very existence struck him as amusing, always there and never questioned, Grandfather Martin's ironic decorative gesture lost on two generations who failed to even notice, until now, until Bowman came home after twenty years away.

His musings were interrupted by the sudden swinging inward of the front door to reveal Uncle—had to be Darwin—standing there in new blue jeans and a dark red button-down shirt, holding the collar of an enormous white long-haired dog, its ears cocked forward and glorious white plume of a tail held high.

When he'd stopped to greet Jeremy's horses in the paddock on the way up, they'd shied away, and now the dog whined and tried to lunge. Darwin held on, barely. The dog wasn't aggressive so much as intensely interested. Darwin was less so. He watched Bowman with a gaze so level, so drained of emotion, emitting an air of such profound disappointment, that Bowman gradually awakened to a rudimentary self-awareness, a social primate seeing himself mirrored in the eyes of another social primate, a novel perspective indeed, still naked and covered with dried mud.

"Look at you," Uncle Darwin said, his voice deeper and more mellifluous than Bowman remembered. "All grown up."

36

Sam was starting to get carsick. They'd been driving for more than an hour on the worst roads he'd ever seen, twisty and rutted and potholed. Dust puffed through the front windows that Apryl insisted on leaving open because she said the AC didn't work. Summer, sitting beside him in the cramped backseat, leaned to the right and peered out her window at the outcrops looming above the road, tried to clear the plastic with her hand, but most of the dust was on the outside. Apryl sped up a steep washboarded slope, the Jeep loud and rattling like it was about to disintegrate.

Summer reached forward and put her hand on Apryl's shoulder.

Apryl jumped at her touch. "What?"

"Please stop."

"We're almost there. What is it?"

"There's a man with a rifle up on that cliff. He's watching us."

Jeremy cursed and leaned over to look out his own open window, unlatching the pistol case he'd set on the floor at his feet.

Apryl slowed and the Jeep's trailing dust cloud billowed through the open windows. Sam coughed and pulled up his T-shirt to breathe through. As it cleared, they all squinted and blinked, searching the cliff where Summer pointed.

"What did he look like?" Apryl asked. "Hispanic? White guy? We get cartel scouts here."

"White guy. Wearing camouflage. He had binoculars. He's big, dark hair, brown backpack."

A sophisticated-looking handheld radio that had been bouncing around in a bin between the two front seats squawked with static, and a male voice said, "Why'd you stop?"

Apryl picked it up. "You just got made by one of our clients. You're a scary-looking motherfucker." She let off the brake and accelerated, spraying gravel from all four tires.

"I don't think so," the voice said.

"Sorry about that," Apryl said. "Rice is my partner. He's been scouting the route to the meeting site on the border."

Five minutes later, they turned onto a barely visible two-track, climbed up over a small rise, and stopped near a campsite: tent, gas camping stove, big water jugs, a cooler. They got out, pulled their bags from the back. Apryl held up a set of camouflage coveralls and a hat.

"I bought these, and binoculars, but there's no fucking point dressing up just one of you. On the other side of that thicket there's a tarp under some camo netting." She nodded toward their bags lying in the dirt. "Put all your shit under the netting."

Sam picked up his bag and Summer's, and followed Jeremy toward the line of brush.

Behind them, Apryl called out, "It's fucking hot, so stay in the shade, drink more water than you want to, don't exert yourselves. We walk out of here in thirty-five minutes."

When he turned to look, Summer had sat on the cooler and, as he watched, Apryl handed her a metal water bottle covered with arcane stickers. She unscrewed the top to drink, Apryl staring at her, saying something Sam couldn't make out. He turned to follow Jeremy, who found a faint trail and pushed through, using the pistol case to push aside thorny branches. They didn't speak as Sam lifted one end of the desert camouflage netting so Jeremy could stash Melissa's pack underneath. Summer's leather satchel followed, but he paused, holding Sam's pack.

"You mind if I hide the pistol in here?"

"No. I was about to ask you if you trust her. I guess not."

"She's cartel."

"Good point."

"This means we trade packs. If there's a problem, I'll need to be able to move. Get to the pistol quick. I'm asking a lot. You'll have to carry the big pack to the border."

Sam swallowed. He'd assumed he and Summer would wait here. But he said, "Yeah. Of course."

When they returned, Apryl was loading water bottles in her pack. She inspected everyone's shoes, making sure they had decent footwear even though the hike would cover only a couple of miles each way. She handed out protein bars and passed around the water bottle she'd given Summer, insisted everyone eat and drink. Sam forced himself, without appetite in the heat, to eat a chalky chocolate bar and wash it down with Apryl's bottle. He walked over to a blue jug on a folding table to refill the bottle from a spigot, tilting it to drain the last of the water, and when he turned back toward the others he saw with a mild shock that a fifth person, dressed in camouflage fatigues and a sweat-stained T-shirt, had joined them and was standing next to the Jeep, head down in conversation with the much shorter Apryl.

Summer and Jeremy were staring as well. The man drew the eye despite his cryptic clothing. Not because he was all that good-looking—it was something harder to describe—the word Sam came up with in the moment was "density."

Apryl looked up and noticed, seemed to realize social convention called for an introduction. She spun the man around by the elbow.

"This is my partner, Rice." Pointing at the others, she called out their first names in turn. Jeremy gave him a laconic, manful nod. Summer managed a distracted hello and squinted at the man like she was trying to remember where she knew him from. Sam, the only one standing, and the only one from the South, felt he ought to walk over and shake hands. They were of a height but Rice outweighed Sam by forty pounds, his advantage all bone and gristle rather than weight-room muscles. His hand was big and rough, his dark eyes amused and at close range warmer than Apryl's.

"You the one who saw me up on that ridge?" Rice asked, in a way that Sam was a little bit glad it hadn't been.

"No, that was Summer."

Rice turned toward her, his half smile fading as they looked at each other.

"Good eyes," was all he said.

"We have a situation you need to know about." Apryl spoke to Jeremy. "We were hired by the people you're meeting, but we're also interested in self-preservation, and we figure we have an obligation to keep you safe."

Jeremy frowned at her grudging promise of protection. Apryl looked at Rice, who had tried the empty water jug. He lifted another full jug to the table and began filling his water bottle before speaking. "I watched a guy with a scoped rifle set up on a slope near the meet site, on the Mexican side. He wasn't a cartel scout."

"Sniper?"

"I assume so."

"Did he see you?" Jeremy asked.

"No."

"You're sure."

"Yeah." Rice shut off the water and smiled at Jeremy's insistent interrogation, but Sam got the sense it wouldn't be smart to push much further.

"We should go ahead anyway," Jeremy said. "It's only security."

"You don't think it could be a third party?" Rice asked. "Someone after whatever it is you're carrying?"

"Unlikely," Jeremy said. "My contact has serious weight in the cartel, and our communications have been clean, at least on my end. She promised to bring an underboss, so I'd be surprised if they didn't take precautions. They need what I have, and they're not going to just shoot—" But Rice shushed him, listening, squinting, his head turned quarterwise to the left, then turning back to the other side. Sam didn't hear anything.

"Patrol," Rice said, and Apryl started to herd the others toward the brush line at the back of the clearing but Rice stopped her. "Too late."

"I don't hear what you're hearing," Summer said.

Apryl shut her eyes, as if gathering herself for a great effort. When she opened them, her demeanor had changed. Almost pleased about the intrusion.

"Their exhaust systems are muffled, and Rice is weird. He's like an owl or something." She pointed at his head. "See, his ears are even offset like an owl's, one's lower than the other. It gives him three-dimensional auditory perception."

They all turned and looked at Rice's head, Sam thinking, *What the hell?*

"They've turned off the main road," Rice said. Sam heard it, a low-frequency throbbing, hard to say where it was coming from, then two ATVs appeared, cresting the hill that hid the camp and rolling to a stop behind the Jeep. The riders wore helmets with dark face shields.

One called out to Apryl, asking with a laugh what the hell she was up to in this ungodly heat.

Apryl stepped forward, her aspect open, gregarious, friendly. . . . This was what she'd been doing, morphing into the agent-whisperer.

"Hi, Randy," she said. She worked up a big grin. "We're bird-watching today. Where's Marcia?"

"She got moved over to Nogales. Rookie Julio riding with me now."

They removed their helmets. Randy was a round-faced white guy with a goatee and an open aspect. Apryl introduced the "bird-watchers."

Julio looked about eighteen and was trying to act tough, like Randy's friendliness was embarrassing him.

Randy asked to see IDs and they began fishing around in pockets. If the Patrol had found the plane, Sam thought, they might be in trouble, or if the Whitespring airport had reported Summer . . . she must've committed a nontrivial crime taking off like that.

Still as chirpy as a high school cheerleader, Apryl explained guiding paid a lot better than the science work. The agent didn't like the idea of their party approaching the border, said he'd heard all the birds were in the canyon itself, near the water, but Apryl said she and Rice had found a male elegant trogon in that thick oak grove up Simmons Wash a couple of days ago. It was clear neither Randy nor Julio had any idea what an elegant trogon was, but given the outlandish name they seemed to accept the notion that someone might travel in order to look at it.

Jeremy handed Randy his driver's license and another card. The agent brightened. "You're a sheriff's deputy."

"Ex–Denver Police. Part-time now with Sheriff Sartoris up in southwest Colorado, Mirador County. Helps pay for the cattle ranching."

After handing Sam's license back to him, Agent Randy launched into a lecture about the gray area on either side of the border being a lawless no-man's-land, a combat zone that they should stay away from, rare bird or no, said it wasn't worth getting killed or kidnapped over a bird, now, was it?

Sam was starting to chafe at Randy's irrelevant patronizing bullshit. No one said anything for a moment, not even Apryl, as if she'd exhausted her bonhomie, battery run dead. It was Rice who spoke first.

"I'll be watching," Rice said. "I'll stay up high, and I'll radio Apryl if I see anyone. They'll turn around and come back."

"You'll be up there with the cartel scouts high-pointing on the hill-top, then?"

"Yeah, don't shoot me."

Randy nodded, as if acknowledging these fine American citizens were stubborn and foolish but at least they were in competent hands. "I'm going to catch hell if any of you get hurt."

After the two ATVs had disappeared over the berm, Apryl glared at Jeremy. "You're a fucking *cop*?"

37

She'd cut her hair. That was the first thing Leo noticed. All her life she'd worn it halfway down her back but now it hung in a thick dark curtain to barely brush her shoulders.

He waited with his back against the far wall of the concourse, obscured by a narrow pillar and a sign in English advertising a guide service for tourists. Scanned the other passengers coming out of the gate, regular folks arriving in Hermosillo for the Christmas holiday. No one who looked out of place. No one obviously watching Summer. But they wouldn't be obvious, would they?

Without thinking, he reached behind his right hip to brush the leather concealment holster on his belt. Empty. Jeremy and a DEA contact had arranged a pistol for him, a new Glock, had even concocted an official-looking permit, but bringing it into an airport in Mexico would be more than foolish, so he'd left it hidden in the truck. Odd that he felt so naked without it. After nineteen years of not having to carry, in just a few weeks he'd regressed to the kind of weapon dependency that had defined too much of his life.

Summer stepped aside from the deplaning queue and searched the concourse. Leo stayed hidden. He wanted to be sure.

He hoped this wasn't a mistake.

Almost four months had passed since the day Bowman set Alecto free and left Panther Gap. He'd taken his backpack with camping gear, some food, and his passport from the Mexico City trip, but he couldn't have had much money. The cash and coins in the open safe had been undisturbed. Jeremy had found tracks through East Canyon, so Bowman must've paid his respects in the cliff dwellings before heading out. A dozen Weenuche friends and acquaintances searched the reservation nearby and found nothing. The Mirador County sheriff and deputies spent an otherwise slow week driving around looking for him, and Jeremy had quietly requested all the sheriff's departments in adjoining counties to keep an ear out for news.

In early October they got a postcard, sent to the ranch P.O. box in Whitespring, salutation "To Summer, Dad, Jeremy, & Darwin," saying he was fine, not to worry, that he was "following the jaguar." Postmarked in Rodeo, New Mexico, thirty-four miles from the Mexican border.

Leo had called the school in Massachusetts and read the card to Summer. What did it mean? She said the closest good habitat was in the northern Sierra Madre Occidental. Of course, Leo said. But it seemed to him more like a metaphor, some kind of spiritual quest. Was there someplace else he would go? Any particular prehistoric ruins, or some holy site?

Summer had laughed. "He's looking for jaguars, Dad. He used to think there was one in Panther Gap."

Leo had asked his friend in the embassy in Mexico City for help. A six-foot-three, long-haired seventeen-year-old was going to get noticed on his way to the Sierra Madre Occidental, and sure enough, within three weeks he had some sketchy reports of such a creature appearing in small towns along the Sonora-Chihuahua line. Headed for the mountains. Leo had flown to Chihuahua and was driving a rented pickup truck on back roads through the northern Sierra Madre by November. He'd had some near misses, and now suspected Bowman was intentionally hiding from him.

His eyes fell back onto his daughter, her expression so serious. She looked older, noticeably taller than she'd been in August, gangly and bony, but she still moved with a girl's careless grace.

He'd told her on the phone he was looking for Bowman in dangerous territory. The Sierra Madre backcountry was still relatively lawless, and drug gangs were becoming more prevalent. He'd even offered to come home to be with her at the ranch for part of her school holiday. She'd shot down that idea—he couldn't afford to let the trail get cold—and pointed out that she knew Bowman better than anyone.

She would be safer at the ranch—that was inarguable—but Leo had convinced himself he could protect her here. She really might be helpful, and he wanted the time with her, and was gratified she wanted to be with him. He'd missed her. Jeremy said his judgment was clouded. He'd come right out and called him irresponsible, and he was probably right. But when Leo had suggested that he and Darwin try to talk Summer out of this, Jeremy laughed and said, "No thank you. She's your daughter."

Summer spotted him, the old familiar smile lighting her face as she raised her hand to wave. Before he could signal for caution, she broke through the crush of passengers at the gate and ran to him. So much for stealth. Her hug enveloped him, strong and unselfconscious, his fifteen-year-old daughter murmuring happily into his shoulder that he shouldn't worry, that they were going to find Bowman and bring him home.

She seemed to think this was going to be an adventure.

But Summer had in mind not so much an adventure as a game, a test of wits with her annoyingly invincible brother. She and her father spent the first night in a hotel on the west side of the northern Sierra Madre, and as they drove into the backcountry the next day she studied the map he'd marked with a grid, points where Bowman had been seen, arrows showing his movements. The people in the mountains were friendly and open, and apparently fascinated by the two Americans, the father and his young daughter. Summer had brought more photos of her brother and they showed them to anyone who would look, asking about Bowman. They asked about *el tigre*. At night they camped beside the truck.

By the end of the first week, though, Summer had begun to

question the fundamental premise of their quest. Based on their conversations with people who'd encountered him, Bowman was doing fine. He was, in fact, avoiding them.

Her father, on the other hand, had suffered multiple bouts of irrationality that frightened her. He repeatedly hinted at some shadowy threat that could be stalking them as well as Bowman, and he insisted on carrying a pistol he said the DEA office in Chihuahua had given him. She remembered what Bowman had told her that night in August before he left, that the family paranoia had, in their father, advanced to a delusional state. Bowman hadn't had time to explain, and she'd dismissed his concern as paranoid or delusional itself, another ride on the crazy-making Girard family merry-go-round.

Now she wasn't sure.

And she'd come to believe her brother was doing exactly what he wanted. She told her father Bowman was not the one he should be worried about. She told him he needed to come home and let Bowman finish whatever it was he was up to.

But Leo said he couldn't leave Bowman here, he had to find him, convince him to go to the school in San Diego, or at least stay at the ranch. The relative lawlessness of this part of Mexico left him vulnerable. Vulnerable to what? she'd asked. His answer was confusing but it had to do with people who had grown powerful in the years since he'd left the State Department, dangerous people who might not sleep well at night remembering what Leo knew about them. He worried they would capture Bowman and use him as leverage.

Sometime after midnight on their tenth night in the mountains, Summer woke up, her father's hand on her shoulder, shushing her. Headlights swept over them from the road, reversed, swept back, stopped.

She felt Bowman nearby. She was out of her sleeping bag, already in pants and a T-shirt, socks. Pushed her feet into hiking boots. Her father had insisted they sleep fully dressed, in case something happened.

Something was happening.

"Get behind the truck, behind the engine block."

"I know," she said.

Her father tossed their sleeping bags and tarp into the back of the truck. Every night he packed up their food and cooking gear before bed. He joined her, crouched next to the front tire in the truck's shadow. His pistol in his hand. The vehicle on the road hadn't moved, its bright headlights on the trees around them, lighting the small creek where they'd camped the past two nights, her father cursing himself for being lazy and not finding a new spot.

"Bowman is here," she whispered.

"He's up there?" Meaning the car with the headlights.

"No, I don't think so. I was dreaming about him." She looked around. There was a grove of big pines on the other side of the creek. He could be there.

Laughter from behind the headlights. The engine revving, then a door slamming.

"I'm getting you out of here," Leo said. He opened the passenger-side door and crawled through to the driver's seat, staying low, telling her to get in, ease the door shut, curl up on the floor.

He started the engine and accelerated, the truck struggling up a short embankment, fishtailing in the dirt, finally lurching onto the road and speeding away. Leo switched on the headlights and drove fast down the mountain, watching the rearview, making her stay on the floor until he was sure no one followed.

On the drive back to Hermosillo, he apologized, said he was angry with himself for exposing her to danger. Given his mood, she refrained from pointing out she'd never seen any sign of this danger other than headlights and what had sounded to her like drunken teenage laughter. They found a hotel in the city and the next day he put her on a flight to Dallas, then on to Massachusetts, even though she still had four days left in Christmas break. He told her she would be safest at school.

She knew he was feeling like a failure as a father, and she did her best to convince him he wasn't, but by the minute he was taking on more and more of the paranoid sniper-spook persona. In the airport he was quiet and scary, and Summer hated herself for it but she was glad to get away from him.

38

2009

Rice jogged along the brushy crest of Jonas Ridge, moving faster than he liked to in this heat, struggling to keep Apryl and the others in sight as they followed a foot trail winding up Simmons Wash toward the border. He stopped every few minutes to scan the trail in front of the others—and the dry, sparse slopes above them—first with just his eyes, then with binoculars. In another quarter mile he would come to the ridge where he'd hidden earlier and watched the sniper set up his shooting position, and he was careful not to blunder into the man's view.

He heard an aircraft and fell down on all fours to scramble under a scrubby pine, keying the mike on his headset. This was reflex, he realized, no real reason to hide when the Border Patrol knew they would be in this area. Still.

"Drone," he said. "Maybe light airplane."

The sound of the engine passed over, following the border to the east. He never got a glimpse of it.

"Gone," he said.

Apryl's voice, angry: "Little more warning next time."

He stood and watched the group emerge from behind rocks, reassemble on the trail, and continue southward. He and Apryl had been sleeping together for a few months now, but she was technically his employer, on both the licit and illicit sides of their business together, and giving orders came naturally to her. Chiricahua Apaches had dominated the Peloncillos for at least a century until they were illegally displaced by the U.S. Army, and half-Apache Apryl affected a proprietary stance. She said Rice had to obey her orders here because she was the boss and "this is fucking Apacheria," the old stomping ground of Mangas Coloradas, Cochise, Geronimo. She was mostly but not all the way kidding. Sometimes he did what she said, and sometimes he didn't.

The four figures continued up the trail, Apryl leading, the attractive and mysterious Summer following, then the lawman, Jeremy, carrying a small daypack Rice was certain contained a weapon. The other guy, Sam, some sort of adviser, slogged along in the rear burdened by the larger, heavier yellow backpack that clearly contained the very valuable "something" Jorge had warned Apryl about.

Rice watched until they disappeared under a canopy of acacia and mesquite. Higher up, the trail entered an oak grove in the saddle separating Simmons Wash from Arena Wash, then led through an open meadow to the slack, ragged barbed-wire fence representing someone's long-ago notion of the border between the U.S. and Mexico.

He jogged down a steep slope into shadow, losing the trail, thrashing through thick mesquite in a rocky side canyon, and climbing the far ridge before pausing below the crest, in the sun again, sweating, kneeling in the dirt, waiting to catch his breath. Somewhere in the past few minutes he was pretty sure he'd crossed the border. He put on his leather gloves and scarred tactical kneepads before crawling the last few yards to the top.

Apryl and her party were off to his right, waiting at the edge of the oak grove. The landmarks he'd used earlier to mark the sniper's hide looked different through his binoculars from this vantage, and it took a while to find him, but there he was, prone, watching the saddle, the border fence. Apryl and the others would be exposed to his fire if they continued on the trail. It would be a long shot, not anything Rice would try, but a skilled sniper could kill all four of them.

He spoke into the microphone again. "He's still there. Same place." Apryl keyed her mike in reply. They drifted back into the scrubby forest, where they would wait in the shade, hidden from the sniper. If the other party showed up—Jeremy had mentioned a cartel rep named Mia

Cortez—they'd go ahead with the meeting. If not, they would assume the whole thing was a trap for Jeremy and fall back to camp. Apryl would contact Jorge and explain their repertoire of services didn't include delivering sheriff's deputies to be shot by cartel snipers.

Rice still couldn't see the approach from Mexico, so he dropped to his belly and wormed through a thicket of yucca, tarbush, and grama grass, not the safest thing to do in this country, but he hadn't seen a rattlesnake all morning. Which was a little unusual. He'd come across at least a hundred individuals of six different species down here over the past couple of years. He was so used to watching for them that he did it unconsciously.

Now he had a clear view all the way down Arena Wash to a larger canyon where an old jeep trail from Highway 2 terminated. The Mexican access to the border was short—only a few miles from the major east-west highway—but the extreme ruggedness and remoteness of the country on the U.S. side made this route, known on both sides as "Los Robles," unattractive to all but the most hardy, or desperate, migrants and smugglers.

Behind cover, he removed his pack and pulled out his carbine and unfolded the stock, then crawled forward, easing aside a patch of bunchgrass with the barrel to clear his view. The time of day was lucky, the sun behind his right shoulder, so he wouldn't be flashing his location off the scope or his binoculars. He laid the gun on its side and scanned with the binoculars, checking on the sniper first, then working his way from the border fence down Arena Wash, where most of the trail was obscured by thick oak and mesquite. On his third pass with the binoculars he noticed two vehicles in the canyon at the far end of the trail, maybe three-quarters of a mile away, jacked-up four-wheel-drive pickups parked under an overhang and camouflaged with netting.

A human figure appeared beside the trucks and stood watching the dirt track behind him. He was carrying a weapon, and at this distance it was hard to tell but it looked like a thick-barreled submachine gun, probably suppressed, hanging from a sling muzzle-down below his chest. That kind of weapon was a troubling sign, but the man was relaxed. He leaned back against one of the trucks and lit a cigarette.

Rice had switched on the voice-activated microphone so he wouldn't have to move to communicate. For the first time he appreciated the fancy radios with their tactical VOX-capable headsets and rolling encryption.

When Apryl had proposed the investment, Rice pointed out they almost never said anything suspicious on the radio, and if she wanted to buy another expensive toy they should spend the money on night-vision goggles. But she was the boss, and here they were, able to speak freely in a heavily surveilled section of the border. He had gotten it in his head that the mike took a moment to switch on and would clip the first thing he said, so when he used the VOX he sometimes started his sentences with a triggering syllable, like "um" or "ah," which drove Apryl mad.

"Uh, two vehicles parked in that canyon where Arena drops out, one guard left there is well armed, so the others will be too. Assume they're on their way up the wash. I'll let you know as soon as I see them."

"Got it."

Apryl carried her little Woodsman .22 pistol in a holster, and Jeremy had whatever it was he'd stashed in that daypack, but they were going to be outgunned if it came to a firefight.

The sun hung well above the ridge to the west, firing the spot where Rice lay, heating the air. Even in the shade, sweat dripped stinging into his eyes. He pulled two brown bandannas from his pack and tied one around his forehead, laid the other close by to mop his face.

A nervous-sounding rattle behind him, just a few pops, reacting to Rice's careful movements. Not alarmed. Not angry. But close. Dry scrape of scales on dead leaves. He held himself very still.

Then, a gentle weight on his left Achilles' tendon. Heavier. Now it was on his right calf as well.

It stopped. The urge to move his legs was almost irresistible. Slowly, slowly, he turned his head to look. A Mojave? Not huge, but big enough, and thick, better than three feet long. He couldn't see the striped tail, so it might be a diamondback, but the diamonds running down its back were distinct, more like a Mojave. A Mojave would have fewer, larger scales between its eyes. He squinted.

Yeah, Mojave.

A fascinating fact: The Mojave rattlesnake was capable of producing an intensely toxic venom that shut down your nervous system. It was also capable of the usual rattlesnake venom that destroyed blood and tissue. No one knew why, or exactly what caused snakes in a given area to possess more of one type or the other.

"Hello, Mojave," he whispered. "Hemorrhagic or neurotoxic?"

No reply. Either one would suck.

The rattlesnake lay on his legs like a housecat.

He slowly lifted his right calf, hoping the snake would decide to leave. It rattled again, somewhat more annoyed, and he lowered the leg. Mojave proceeded another few inches forward until nearly all of its weight was on his legs. It stopped again.

Rice tried not to think about it. Watched the trail, the border fence, the sniper.

This time of year, in the oven heat before dusk, the desert was so still that any movement leaped out at you, and the slow-walk of three human beings coming out of Arena Wash on the Los Robles trail was so obvious they might as well have been waving flags. Careful not to disturb the rattlesnake, Rice raised the binoculars. The three paused at the edge of the thicket, then the smallest walked forward on the trail, into the open. A woman, must be the Mia Cortez Jeremy had mentioned. The other two waited, watching, carrying suppressed submachine guns like the guard back at the trucks. Rice was not a firearms expert but he'd picked up a good bit of lore in the past year, and he recognized the weapons as German HK MP5s.

"Shit," he muttered.

"What?" came back from Apryl.

"She's on her way up. Two dudes with MP5s are hanging back." Only serious operators in the cartel carried high-end firepower like that. You had to have balls and connections. In a normal transaction, where they weren't actually expecting someone heavy, if he saw a suppressed MP5, he would call it off and pull Apryl back ASAP. Weapons along the border were used as much to signal as to shoot—Rice's own SCAR 16s, a new military-style carbine made in Belgium and chambered in 5.56mm, was a good example, a major investment that had already paid off several times without his ever having to point it at a human being.

Apryl's voice on the radio: "Okay, we see her. Can you describe the other two?"

"Young, unamused, well-armed Mexicans. Not street guys. Disciplined."

Rattling from Mojave. The snake was deaf in the usual sense, but intensely sensitive to vibrations, and it didn't like Rice's voice.

The woman marched up the trail like she was out for her evening hike. She had nothing in her hands, no pack, no obvious weapon.

"Jeremy wants you to confirm there's no one else with her."

"Can't do that," Rice whispered. "Might be others behind them. No way to know. But even if there's no one else it's a lot of firepower."

"Why are you whispering?"

"I'll tell you later."

After a moment, Apryl spoke again. "Deputy J's not worried about firepower, he's looking for another party to the meeting. The underboss. Might be waiting, back in the trees. He wants to go ahead."

Rice shook his head. There's no way an actual underboss was going to show up. Jeremy was dreaming. But this woman was clearly important in her own right, enough to make Rice edgy.

He heard Apryl say, "It's not negotiable."

"Ah, what's not negotiable?" But she didn't reply. Jeremy and Summer were arguing with her in the background, she must've turned on her voice-activated mike, then it shut off altogether. Ten long seconds of silence, the cartel woman approaching the fence, the two guards moving now, flanking her at a distance to keep her in view, a practiced choreography.

"Apryl? Shit." He shifted the binoculars in time to watch her step out of the oak grove and walk toward the woman at the border fence. She held her hands up. No holster on her belt. She walked the same way she always walked. Smooth, quiet, assured. She hit a switch on her headset with her left hand, and ambient sounds came through his earpiece again, breeze, footsteps, breathing.

"What the hell?"

"I'm making sure she knows we're not to be fucked with."

"Apryl," he hissed, still trying to whisper. "She's cartel. *She's* not to be fucked with."

"I understand that."

She slowed as she approached the fence. Stopped a few feet away. The two guards were alert but not moving forward. The woman stood on the other side of the old border fence, hands on her hips, anger and frustration in her posture. She was about Apryl's height, ten years older, slightly heavier. Rice could barely make out her words over the radio.

"Where is he? What the hell are you doing?"

Apryl stood still, somehow managing a defiant posture despite still holding her hands away from her body.

"I'm clearing something up first. We know there's a shooter, right over there." Apryl gestured vaguely to the slope to the southwest. "He's been up there for hours, probably needs to take a piss. If he's not yours, we need to abort right now." When the woman didn't react, Apryl continued. "If he is yours, we assume he's there for security, but you need to know we have a shooter too, listening to me on this radio." She inclined her head in Rice's direction. "For security."

"You're forgetting who hired you."

"We were hired to see a person safely to and from the border, and that's what we're doing. We're not setting him up for you to assassinate."

Silence. A show of teeth, something over the radio that might have been a quiet laugh. "I just hope he has what he says he has."

Apryl said she didn't know anything about that. She said she'd send him out. She was walking away when Mia called out to her, but Rice couldn't make out her words over the radio. Apryl stopped and turned and was silent for a few moments, then she gave Mia her name: Apryl Whitson.

Even Jorge didn't know their full names.

Rice shifted his carbine toward the sniper. In the low-power scope he could make out the pattern of rock and bare pine branch he'd memorized through the binoculars, so he knew where to aim even if he couldn't actually see the man himself.

He realized he'd forgotten about the rattlesnake. The weight was gone. He shifted his left leg. Three emphatic pops of the rattle. *I'm still here.*

The snake had curled up in the space between his legs.

With both eyes open he could watch Apryl's agonizingly slow progress toward the shelter of the oak grove while keeping the scope's little yellow chevron aiming point on the sniper's position.

"Um, why'd you tell her your name?" he asked.

He counted three, four, five strides before he got an answer.

"She asked."

39

Bowman rinsed off with a hose outdoors and toweled dry before Darwin let him in the house. His uncle sat him down and silently bandaged the deep cut on his forehead and sent him to his father's old bedroom to "find something to put on." Opening Leo's closet, he momentarily slipped into what felt like his father's consciousness—a place of loss, longing, hope, shadowy monsters just out of sight. He recoiled, feeling a pang of sympathy.

Dressed in Leo's musty Wranglers, long-sleeved plaid flannel shirt, and leather work boots, he sat at the old plank table in the kitchen working on a cup of Uncle Darwin's strong black coffee, which might be helping or might be hurting. The big white dog sat at attention in a corner across the kitchen, staring at him.

Darwin cut a bright red tomato into thin slices, his movements precise and economical. Said something about Summer flying an airplane somewhere. She was a pilot, but she hadn't flown for a while, and he sounded worried. He paused.

"You need to snap out of it."

Bowman thought his uncle was probably right. "Is she married?"

"Who, Summer? No. Pay attention." Darwin pulled some things from the refrigerator. "Are you on drugs?"

Bowman didn't answer. A series of items appeared briefly on the cutting board to be dismantled: radishes, carrots, a hard-boiled egg, three different kinds of lettuce, sausage, fresh thyme, rosemary.

"So how'd you get here?"

"I don't remember. I must've come up Red Creek."

Darwin looked like he wanted to object, but held back. They both knew the course of Red Creek off the escarpment was all waterfalls and narrow rocky chutes.

"Before that."

Sitting in the kitchen fully clothed, drinking coffee and watching his uncle fix a salad, he felt more lucid, and he cast his mind backward, to the time before he woke on the lakeshore to a plague of blackflies.

"I flew from Costa Rica to Miami, then to Denver, but someone was following me, so I didn't get on the plane to Whitespring. I stole a truck, and it broke down. A guy gave me a ride."

A long silence followed, Darwin waiting for him to elaborate, Bowman mesmerized by the *tap-tap-tap* of the slicing, vegetable pieces piling up in a pottery bowl he recognized from childhood, big as a hat. His bowl. He'd had an awesome appetite in his teens. Darwin had done most of the cooking, and Bowman had never thanked him. He wondered what else he'd neglected to do, what he was neglecting now.

"He said his name is Bickford Rangely. I don't know who he really is, or what he's up to. I don't trust him. He pretended he didn't know me at first, but then he wanted me to show him how to get to the ranch. I'm pretty sure he was trying to protect me, but not out of altruism. Men with machine guns blocked the road, I have no idea who they were. They rammed our vehicle and we wrecked, almost drowned in Red Creek."

Without comment, Darwin brought out a jar of dressing from the refrigerator, shook it and poured some on the salad, slid the bowl across the plank table, followed by a fork and a plaid cloth napkin. Bowman stared at the careful arrangement, the rich colors, sniffed the green vapors, the crushed raw garlic.

"That's beautiful."

"Just eat it."

After silently thanking the plants and animals composing his meal, Bowman picked up the fork and started in. It was the best salad he'd ever eaten. He made sure to thank his uncle, receiving a grunt in reply. His report about Bick and the violent encounter earlier had had an effect, like Darwin was unsure whether to believe him, didn't want to believe him, but kind of did believe him and disliked the implications.

Darwin changed the subject, leaned back against the counter beside the refrigerator and tried to explain why Summer and Jeremy and some new person Darwin didn't like had all flown to southern Arizona. The coffee made Bowman jittery and he had trouble following—Summer had asked Jeremy to help out someone who'd been kidnapped, and Jeremy found a big stash of cocaine, and now he had to give it to a woman from a Mexican cartel so the whole family wouldn't be murdered.

He held a slice of sausage from his salad down low beside his chair. Over in the corner, the dog's ears perked up. He waved the slice back and forth. The dog stood.

"Neither one of 'em's answering," his uncle said. "Probably no signal, but when she calls I'll tell her you're here. See what she wants to do. We could get a flight ourselves or she could stop and pick us up in Whitespring."

Finally the dog approached, stiff-legged. Darwin watched as Bowman held out the piece of sausage and the dog sniffed at it. They'd never had dogs while Bowman was growing up because his father thought that kind of domestic animal would warp his and Summer's understanding of the Others, but dogs were everywhere in Central America and Mexico, and he'd found he enjoyed their company.

"That's Jeremy's dog. Marco."

Marco took the sausage gently with the small teeth in the front of his mouth, then returned to his corner, chewing and keeping his eyes on Bowman.

"I've never seen him act like that. He's either friendly or if he doesn't like someone he ignores them."

"Where do you want to fly?"

Darwin gave him an impatient look and Bowman gathered he must've already gone over it. "To Denver, to meet with someone from the bank. They'll turn over the account, from your grandfather. That's why you're here. You knew about it all along. Leo told you."

Bowman nodded. "He said it would be dangerous. That I had to warn Summer. He said Grandfather Martin was involved with criminal organizations, and as soon as we had the money his old enemies would come after us. I didn't believe him."

Darwin watched him, a little warily.

"But now I know he was right, and I came back to warn Summer not to take it."

Darwin's look sharpened. "You can't do that. I don't even know if there's much left after all this time, but we need whatever we can get. The ranch needs it. That's what your grandfather wanted."

"Dad said it's too dangerous. That it wouldn't be worth it."

"It's been thirty-five years, Bowman." Darwin nearly shouted this. Then he calmed himself, almost looked like he was going to apologize. "Martin thought it would be long enough. He thought they would all die, or forget."

A loud ringing, the phone in the hall. Darwin stood, saying they finally must've gotten a signal. Bowman knew communications technology had changed since he'd left the ranch, and he found it calming that his family still used the same telephone in the same hall alcove that he'd grown up with. In fact, almost nothing about the house had changed. Even the kitchen appliances were the same.

He heard Darwin say, *I can't reach him either. You should tell Sheriff Sartoris. I know what he said, you should tell him anyway.* Long pause. *Well, all right.* He was shaking his head when he walked back into the kitchen.

"Come upstairs. I want you to look at something."

Except for the computers on the two desks, Grandfather Martin's expansive office looked as unchanged as the kitchen, at least until Darwin opened the sliding door to a big built-in cabinet on the south wall, revealing five video screens.

"That's new."

"Jeremy," he said, as if that explained it. Which Bowman supposed it did.

It was a big room, the biggest in the house, a bank of windows looking west across Panther Gap to the Red Creek Range. Two desks, one with a phone. Before Summer was born, Martin had bought a second mahogany desk and set it up in here for Darwin, the only other member of the family who'd shown the slightest interest in business.

Darwin picked up a complicated remote control and one of the screens on the wall lit up with an image of the entrance and the front of the caretaker's house. Then six small pictures with dates on a black background. One of those expanded to fill the screen: the same image of the entrance as before, but in morning light. It looked static until a pair of crows floated past. Tall grass shifted in the breeze.

Darwin did something with the remote and the crows flew backward across the screen, then nothing for a while until a big black vehicle with tinted windows—like a child's exaggerated idea of a military jeep—backed in from the public road and parked in front of the caretaker's house. The driver and a passenger got out and walked backward toward the front stoop where a sturdy dark-skinned man, presumably the caretaker, stood with his hands on his hips. Darwin halted the video and zoomed in, but the visitors seemed to know where the camera was and kept their faces obscured by the bills of their baseball caps.

"Do you know these men?"

Bowman sat down in his grandfather's old office chair, smell of old leather and a faint musky perfume. Summer's chair now.

"I know that vehicle. It nearly killed Bick and me today."

"They stopped by a few days ago. They told Sarge they're friends of yours."

"They're not. What'd Sarge tell them?"

"Same thing he tells anyone: nobody lives up here anymore. That was Sarge on the phone, he saw the same Hummer again in town today. It followed him from the grocery store to a gas station. Looked like it had bullet holes in the driver's-side door. It drove off when he tried to take a picture with his phone."

A deep sharp bark from downstairs. Marco had snuck out of the room unnoticed. After a moment, three more.

"He doesn't bark at nothing."

Bowman jogged downstairs behind Darwin. Marco stood at a French door with his tail curled, ears forward, listening. Darwin opened the door and Marco charged into the stone courtyard and around the side of the house. Bowman and Darwin followed, found Marco near an array of solar panels, looking at the sky above the ridge. A tiny helicopter buzzed there angrily, moving forward, then being swept back, fighting a strong wind guarding the valley. Marco barked again.

"I saw one of those this morning."

"It's a drone. Never seen one here."

The thing stabilized and lost altitude, flying along the ridge to a point above where the two men and the dog stood.

"I'm not sure we should let it see us."

"Too late," Darwin said. "It's trespassing. I'm going to shoot it down."

40

"Why is he taking off his clothes?"

Sam's voice struck Summer as incredulous, in extremity, as if seeing her tough uncle unbuckling his belt and pulling off his Lee jeans to drop in the pile next to his boots and blue chambray cowboy shirt, standing there in his boxers while a very serious-looking woman nearly a foot shorter walked a circle around and patted down his bottom and privates—as if this might just be the final bizarre vision, the proverbial straw laid upon the poor camel, reducing Sam to a gibbering victim of too much weird shit happening in a single thirty-six-hour stretch.

"She's looking for a wire," Apryl said.

"Oh, right," Sam said.

Summer glanced his way. He looked numb, but calm.

The woman, this Mia Cortez, who'd agreed to bring someone with more authority in the cartel—someone who so far was not in evidence—stood next to the run-down border fence and watched with her arms crossed while Jeremy took his time dressing, showing her he wasn't rattled.

Jeremy, Summer marveled, hadn't been rattled all day, even when she'd nearly killed all three of them with that landing. Sam had held up remarkably well too, showing some strain only when Apryl had threatened to pull her pistol on Jeremy and shoot him "in the fucking face" if he didn't let her arm go. When he did let go, she removed her holster and handed it to him with a grin before walking out into the sniper's line of fire to confront the woman from the cartel. To warn her against assassinating Jeremy. To tell her they'd deployed what Jeremy called a "countersniper."

Referring, of course, to this man Rice, Apryl's partner, who was another kettle of fish altogether, an insistent presence in her mind ever since she'd somehow perceived him from the Jeep, and especially since he'd looked at her in camp like he knew her. Even now, she caught flashes through his eyes, hidden on a ridgetop watching over them with binoculars and a desert-brown carbine. Bowman would say these were visions, but she preferred the only somewhat less disturbing notion that she was losing control of her imagination. She was pretty sure Apryl and Rice were a couple, though they didn't act like it. . . . Anyway, that situation didn't bear thinking about, which meant she would probably obsess over it.

Suddenly Jeremy and Mia were shouting at each other, gesticulating, it was hard to make out what they were saying at this distance but Summer thought she understood Jeremy saying, *My only goddamned condition,* then Apryl said, "Oh fuck," and walked back out into the open, drawing the pistol from the holster she'd reattached to her belt.

Summer saw then what Apryl had seen: on the far side of the open scrubby meadow, the two guards Rice had described were trotting toward Mia and Jeremy with submachine guns pointed discreetly, and doubtless temporarily, at the ground.

"What the hell?" from Sam, who started forward after Apryl, digging into the pack Jeremy had left behind and coming out with Jeremy's pistol.

Summer caught up with him. "You know how to shoot that?"

He held it in both hands with a reasonably competent grip, trigger finger pointed straight and not curled prematurely around the trigger.

"In a general sense," he said, voice definitely shaking now as they moved farther away from the trees, trailing along behind Apryl. Summer was feeling fluttery herself, acutely aware of the sniper over on the Mexican side. She searched the slope Apryl had pointed to earlier but the sniper was hidden. Instead, she saw Rice in her mind, felt his adrenaline spike as the three of them walked toward Mia and Jeremy, Mia's guards raising their guns.

"Go back," Apryl hissed, but then she saw the pistol in Sam's hand. "Fine, but stay calm and don't bunch up, spread out, give them multiple targets."

She gave Summer a sharp look, the only one unarmed. "You should go back."

"I'm not doing that."

Jeremy and Mia were focused on their argument and hadn't noticed them, but the two guards had, and now there was a hitch in their progress, seeing a new threat, and they adjusted quickly, professionally, the appearance of armed interlopers ratcheting up their intensity. The one closest turned his weapon to cover them, changed his angle of approach, moving to put himself between them and his boss. Apryl held her small pistol pointed at the ground in front of her. Sam did the same with his. Summer walked on. She felt like she was floating.

Sam said something off to her left but she couldn't make sense of it. She wished she'd brought her Glock. For some reason she imagined holding her right thumb and forefinger in the universal hand sign for a cocked pistol, then realized she was actually doing it. If she raised her hand and pointed her finger-pistol at Mia, she mused, would the sniper shoot her?

41

"You know I've been looking for you. Did you know your sister was with me?"

Bowman nodded. Nearly two moon cycles ago. He'd hidden in the forest and watched them, wanted to talk to Summer but hesitated when he saw how much she'd changed. When the other truck pulled off the road and lit up the campsite, he'd heard the young men laughing, his father suddenly spooked and Appaloosa-eyed, pointing his pistol at every little sound. Bowman had been sneaking up, wary of being shot, when his father and sister piled into the truck and drove away.

He squatted at the edge of his father's campsite. Leo had been backpacking in the wildlife reserve, and he was sick, some intestinal parasite, and Bowman had watched for two days as he'd run out of water, too weak to climb a mile down the steep thrashy slope to the river, too ignorant to know a sweet rill burbled quietly a few hundred yards to the north.

"Where is she now?"

"Out East. Back at school." His father sat up in his hammock, grimacing. He sipped again from the tin canteen Bowman had brought him. A heavy pistol hung in the hammock beside him, something new, Bowman didn't recognize it.

"You sent her anyway," he said. "Even though I was gone."

His father stared for a moment, then sighed. "I should have explained the danger. . . ." His voice trailed off. Bowman remembered he'd tried, on that last night at the ranch. He'd sounded crazy.

"What about Alecto?"

"She forgave me. She passes through now and then. I released Horkos and Hesperus too."

Bowman was glad.

"Did she want to go?"

It took his father a moment to figure out he meant Summer. "Not at first. I sent her because it was safer. Bowman, I need to tell you some things. I should have done it a year ago, should have told you and Summer both, but I was hoping to protect you for a while longer, and that was a mistake."

He stopped when he noticed Bowman shaking his head.

"What is it?"

"You need to pack up," Bowman said. The apparently wealthy American wandering around in the mountains asking questions about a missing teenager had finally attracted the wrong kind of attention. The only thing that had saved him so far was being too weak to start a fire.

His father caught the meaning in his tone. He didn't ask why. He finished the canteen and stood with the hammock supporting his back, then shuffled ahead until he was on his own. Took a deep breath. As far as Bowman knew, this was the first time he'd stood in two days. He'd been crawling from his hammock to the edge of the small clearing to shit and piss and vomit. The place stank from it.

He stood unsteadily but without leaning on anything.

"Can you help me?" he asked.

42

Darwin rummaged around in a closet at the far end of the office, looking for his "elk rifle."

"Wouldn't you want a shotgun?"

"I don't believe that thing'll come close enough."

The one lit video screen now showed a live picture of the entrance and the front of the caretaker's house. Bowman watched with trepidation.

"You should call the caretaker. Warn him."

"Warn him about what? The drone?"

"The people in that truck are dangerous. I think it's their drone. Wouldn't they have to be somewhere close by?"

"Sarge can handle himself. He's ex-military. Jeremy hired him."

Darwin laid a tan leather gun case on his desk and zipped it open. A sleek bolt-action rifle, dark timeworn walnut and silvery blued steel.

"I remember that rifle."

Darwin's glance was defensive. "He gave it to me. Before he left to go chasing after you. He gave away a bunch of things, like he knew what was going to happen."

Bowman let that pass. "I didn't know you were a gun guy."

"I hunt. Leo said this rifle would make me a better chef." Darwin opened the bolt and fished a box of ammunition from a pocket on the side of the case, began pressing long brass-and-copper cartridges into the magazine. It was Leo's Winchester Model 70—"prewar," as he liked to point out—in .270. He'd used this rifle to kill all but the largest of the African animals mounted in the library, and Bowman had learned how to shoot and hunt with the old gun, had killed a mule deer with it himself before he'd switched to more primitive means. The scope looked new. Bowman imagined a gift from Uncle Jeremy.

"I thought you and my father didn't get along."

"We got along fine." Darwin hung the rifle's sling on his shoulder and tucked two extra boxes of cartridges in a jacket pocket, mumbling something about the difficulty of shooting that little drone with a rifle. On his other shoulder he slung marine binoculars with huge bell-shaped objective lenses.

He removed a handheld radio from a charger on his desk and started to leave, telling Bowman to stay here in the office in case Summer or Jeremy called, but Bowman held up the remote control and asked him to turn on the other screens so he could see what was happening.

After a quick lesson on the remote, Darwin left Bowman to watch the screens and answer the phone. Two of the screens toggled every few seconds among various views of the exterior of the house: he watched Darwin walk from the courtyard past the solar panels, stopping on the side of the hill to look up toward the ridge with the binoculars, then after a few moments he walked out of the frame.

The top left screen showed the now-familiar scene of the entrance and the front of the caretaker's house. The next covered the back of the barn behind the caretaker's house and the unprepossessing turnoff behind the barn. That was where the actual driveway started its intentionally poorly maintained progress across the rising sagebrush plain toward the mountain. Another camera watched the fortified gate at the bottom of the switchbacks.

Motion in the first screen caught his eye: a blue sedan hesitating at the entrance before pulling in and parking in front of the caretaker's house. A woman in big sunglasses got out with a handbag and peered around, keeping her back to the camera. Dark hair, medium height, medium build. Tight blue jeans, light-colored tank top, also tight. He decided she was thirties and dressing younger. She moved uncertainly toward the front porch, where Sarge the caretaker opened the front door. She stopped and spoke, using hand gestures, pointing up and down the road. Exasperated, apologetic body language.

Bowman didn't believe it.

He watched, feeling the power of the invisible watcher and at the same time a nauseous hopeless impotence. He considered the possibility that he was letting his paranoia affect his judgment. The woman could be what she appeared to be: a lost tourist. As a sophisticated—that is, self-aware—paranoiac, Bowman had had to learn how to make the right mistakes. Facing uncertainty and the unknowable minds of others, he would evaluate each pair of opposing interpretations of any situation agnostically, gaming out for each alternative the worst possible outcome if that interpretation were acted upon and turned out to be wrong. He would then choose to act upon the interpretation where being wrong resulted in the least harm. If he called Sarge and warned him, and his suspicion of the woman turned out to be wrong, Sarge would think he was crazy. If he went with the more reasonable interpretation that all was well, and it wasn't, then Sarge could be hurt.

He picked up the handset of the phone on Summer's desk. A regular dial tone. It had a small electronic screen and he started pushing buttons, hoping the screen could show the number from Sarge's call earlier. A number came up, and after pushing some more buttons he got the phone to dial, waited, ringing, then his uncle's voice: *This is Jeremy St. John, leave a message.* He hung up.

No notes nearby, no handy lists of numbers. In the top drawer, a tangled mess of pens and paper clips, scissors and staplers and hair ties, business cards, small bottles of lotion, sunscreen. He slammed it shut. On-screen, Sarge smiled and beckoned. The woman was grateful, relieved.

Nothing helpful on the other desk either, just the empty radio charger and a small computer. No other radio, no base station he could use to call Darwin. The visitor was up on the porch, shaking hands. A brief conversation. Sarge opened the door for her. They disappeared inside.

Bowman waited, paralyzed by this electronically mediated experience of a potentially life-or-death drama. He and Summer had never watched television as children—the very idea had been anathema to their father—and when he'd seen it in people's homes and on boats over the past couple of decades, the hold it could have on minds, imagination, attention, and time had always puzzled and distressed him.

Now he realized he'd simply never allowed the flickering electrons to become real.

He found this particular sense of disembodiment disturbing, very different from the effects of drugs, or fever, or ecstatic trance. Those experiences, while not always pleasant or comforting, generally left him with a sense of the larger world, an expanded reality. The utter contentment of his consciousness with a two-dimensional rectangular screen—such a tiny segment of potential experience—left him claustrophobic after only a few minutes, gasping for the smell of leather and faint perfume, the rustling of clothes against his skin, hard pine flooring under his boots, gravity clutching his bones to the earth.

Was this—too much television—why people in America were so surprised and shocked when they discovered they were made of flesh?

New movement on the screen pulled him back in, a battered pickup pulling a trailer stacked high with hay bales shot past on the road, leaving the usual cloud of dust. Before it dispersed, the woman walked out the front door of the caretaker's house and shut it behind her, her posture more resolute, headed for her car with brisk steps, a scarf covering her lower face. She was hurried but not panicked, a cell phone to her ear.

He laid the remote control on Summer's desk and rushed out into the hall and down the first flight of steps, stopping when the big dog stood from where he'd been resting, leonine, on the landing. Marco watched Bowman with the same reserved attentiveness he'd displayed earlier. Broad white head tilted up, jet-black nose and lips, big hazel eyes more than curious, more than cautious. A little afraid, and that was the rub, Bowman thought. He was not a dog accustomed to fear.

"Marco, we got to go find Uncle Darwin."

A low, rumbling growl.

"Did Darwin leave you here to guard me? Are you supposed to keep me in the house?"

Marco said nothing.

Not wanting to crowd a growling 150-pound dog on an eight-by-eight landing, he sat on the steps above, and reached out with his hand.

"I'm not what they told you."

Marco didn't move. Bowman set aside his impatience and took long, slow breaths.

The struggle between trepidation and curiosity played out in Marco's eyes until he gave what Bowman could only describe as a self-disgusted shrug and stepped decisively into Bowman's space, sniffing his hand, his knees, hopping his front paws onto the first step and frankly sniffing his crotch, chest, face, ears, those remarkable eyes watching Bowman's at close range. His fur smelled of sun, pine tar, dust; his breath, vaguely of fish. Bowman's hands cupped his heavy skull, rubbing the powerful muscles attached to a prominent bony knob on the back of his head, like the point of a battering ram. A flash in Bowman's mind, an image, a ferocious bite and shaking without mercy, a powerful capacity for violent action, held in abeyance by a thousand years of breeding and a lifelong love for a particular family of *Homo sapiens*.

Marco's ears came up. He tilted his head, eyes no longer focused on Bowman's face. He huffed like a bear and turned around, bounded down the steps, started again with those monstrous warning barks at the doors. Bowman followed. By the time he got there the glass panes were vibrating with the clatter of a helicopter flying through Panther Gap.

43

Rice didn't bother telling Apryl to get back into cover. She wouldn't have done it, and his voice would only distract her. He dropped the binoculars and lifted the rifle, aiming with both eyes open.

His mind accelerated as everything outside his skull slowed down.

Whom to shoot first?

If he shot, of course, it would alarm his Mojave rattlesnake. Would it bite him in the leg or slide away from the source of the concussion? He figured the odds were pretty good that it would just take off. Better than fifty-fifty, anyway. At least as interesting as the bite-or-flee issue was the question of why the snake had curled up between his legs in the first place. Not seeking warmth like the rattlers in the old cowboy yarn where they crawl inside your sleeping bag. It was hot, too hot. And it wasn't as if the snake didn't realize what Rice was. As he understood it, a pit viper's infrared perception was more than capable of distinguishing his leg from the hot environment. The snake's umwelt, or perceived world, resulted from a synthesis of combined input from the infrared-sensitive pits, the visible light response of its eyes, chemical analyses from its flicking tongue, vibration sensors in its skin and skull, and who knew what else.

So, yeah, Mojave had intentionally settled in between two legs attached to a large mammal, a creature that could be dangerous to it. Yet it seemed to have fallen asleep.

All of these thoughts flashed through Rice's mind in a very short in-
terval. Three of Apryl's steps. He'd experienced this before, as if extreme
pressure brought that famous unused percentage of the brain online, providing an overcapacity of consciousness far beyond what was necessary
to deal with the immediate crisis, leaving space for other considerations,
such as, *Why is a Mojave rattlesnake curled up between my legs? What does it
mean?* He considered how modes of perception were strongly determin-
istic of "reality": any organism's experience of the cosmos was narrow
and incomplete but sufficient for its survival and reproduction. Humans
tend to assume what we perceive is all there is. . . .

The guard on the left twisted his body to point his gun at Apryl.

That's my target.

He noted the guard's good instincts, doing his own split-second
threat assessment: first shoot the woman with the pistol like an extension
of her arm, then what's-his-name . . . Sam . . . holding that big .45 with
somewhat less self-assurance. Summer was there with the other two, unarmed, the three of them spreading out and advancing in a line. It struck
him that Summer was either extraordinarily brave or out of her mind.

Rice slipped the safety off and settled the glowing yellow chevron
on the guard like a hat, then lowered it to his chest—no body armor in
this heat. And no holdover at this range. An easy shot, then the other
guard, then skip Mia, who might be armed but if so her gun was small
and concealed and would take some time to deploy, leaving her to Apryl
because the sniper was the much bigger threat, at four hundred yards a
very long shot for Rice with no time to aim, but he would fire some
rounds in that direction, hoping to distract the sniper long enough for
Apryl and the others to run to cover.

It was, he thought, not a good situation.

"In five seconds I'm going to shoot this fucker closest to you, then
the other guy, then I'm on the sniper." He pressed the trigger through the
take-up. He'd hated the original trigger on the SCAR, rough and heavy,
so he'd replaced it with an aftermarket two-stage that had improved his
accuracy by half.

"Hold up," she said.

"Yeah, no. Three seconds."

A few months ago he'd participated in a madcap nighttime firefight in the desert, all flash and nonsense, his mindset then very different from this slow progression toward methodical homicide. He felt the pure enormity of the partial trigger pull he'd already executed, taking up the first quarter inch of travel, finding the minor resistance of the second stage, but he remained calm, focused dispassionately on the mechanics, the breath control, the minor adjustments with his left hand on the forend, holding the chevron aiming point steady on the guard's upper torso.

Such a small thing, what he now held back: that final deliberate press of the first pad of his right index finger. Somewhere in his suddenly capacious mind it bore down on Rice how little qualm he felt about taking another human being's life. It was disconcerting, this unexpected willingness to shoot someone. Someone he'd probably like, a professional, a coolheaded hard-ass who'd risen above the random mindless murderousness of the cartel foot soldiers and joined the elite who would guard a Mia Cortez. He felt no animosity toward the man, but he also knew he could kill him.

This was something in himself he was going to have to watch out for.

"Hold the fuck up. It's—" He heard a manic, very un-Apryl laugh start up. "It's a Mexic—"

"Don't even say it," he said. She was making jokes now. He didn't shoot. He was antsy and hot, his eyes dry and stinging from staring in the dry air. He decided he wouldn't have made a very good sniper.

Mia finally noticed the three figures oncoming from the U.S. side. Alarmed, she turned right and left to see her bodyguards approaching from behind her and raised both hands, shouting *"¡Detener!"*

They all stopped. Her voice was sharp, and though he caught it through Apryl's radio it was loud enough that a second later it carried to his other ear through the air. Even Jeremy froze. Mia stepped forward, waving her guards back, waving Apryl and Sam to lower their weapons. She leaned in to Jeremy, beckoned him to bend down, and spoke directly into his ear. The two of them held this position for an impossibly long string of moments until the tension in Jeremy's body began to shift, to slacken, though not, Rice thought, with relief. Mia was dropping a bombshell and what Rice read in Jeremy's body was disbelief, shock. Then he looked resigned.

Rice relaxed his finger, allowing the spring load on the trigger to push it back to where it had started. He lifted the binoculars and rested them on top of the rifle scope so he could watch without laying the rifle down.

Mia and Jeremy had broken their clutch but she was still speaking fast, barely moving her lips. Stumping lip-readers. They were far enough from cover that any parabolic microphone would have trouble listening.

Jeremy turned and spoke to the others. Sam nodded and handed the big pistol to Summer. She gave it a press-check and a quick look at the safety lever while Sam walked back to the oak grove like he was marching toward his own execution.

Rice took the opportunity to shift his legs, both of which had started to fall asleep. No rattle. Moving as slowly as he could, he twisted around to see. Mojave was gone.

44

A helicopter flew from the south, low over the lake, a gigantic dragonfly. It turned east when the pilot finally spied the house high on the ridge, slowing as it approached, rising to eye level with Bowman, who stood outside with his hand resting on Marco's shoulder to calm them both.

The machine turned and hovered with the passenger-side window facing Bowman. A palm pressed against the glass, then a hand-lettered sheet of paper: PEACE, MAN.

Bowman gave them an exaggerated shrug and the pilot flew a couple hundred yards to the north, settling down in the saddle where the gravel driveway coming up from the east leveled off before dropping westward into Panther Gap.

As the rotors slowed he walked down from the house, Marco leading. He hoped the dog might give him some measure of security if the sign in the window turned out to be a ruse, and in fact Marco was showing signs of seriousness, his tail curled again, legs stiff, chest rumbling.

A familiar figure appeared in the open passenger door before gingerly stepping down to the gravel. He was smiling. He had a bandage on his head similar to Bowman's.

"Nice place you got here, Mr. Sherman Carver." He gave a theatrical look around at the granitic bluff overhead, huge sandstone pillars nearby, the sweep of green valley and dusky mountains to the west.

Marco lost interest, his tail drooping. He sat and watched a bumblebee trading among the wildflowers that grew alongside the driveway.

"It doesn't look like much from the air," Bick continued, "must be something about the air currents, a lot of dust in the wind, *hell* of a wind, you know, almost blew us into a cliff coming over the mountain down south, would have for sure if we weren't in a Bell 412 and Art there wasn't the best combat pilot to come out of the Corps in the last ten years. But shoot, once you're in here, it's real pretty."

"Who are you and what do you want?"

Bick grinned stupidly, reprising his innocent Samaritan act from the Suburban. Bowman turned away and called Marco, started back up the hill.

"Wait, what do you want me to say?"

When Bowman turned back, he still wore the same grin. Bowman waited.

"Okay, here you go, in a nutshell: a very discreet organization in Switzerland that's been holding a secret account of your grandfather's for thirty-five years hired the outfit I work for to look after your family until you claim the money and can take care of yourselves."

"And who were those people who ran us off the road? They had that big black military truck."

"Yeah, Hummer H1. You don't see many of those." He stopped, looked around again at the scenery with an approving air.

Feeling somewhat unhinged, Bowman held his impatience at bay, his worry about the caretaker. He couldn't be completely sure Bick wasn't somehow behind all of this. Though he obviously hadn't planned the attack by the creek, the wreck, nearly drowning.

Bick finished his reverie, seemed to remember the question.

"Those sonsabitches are worse than I thought," he said. "Prison gang, if you can believe it. Big presence on the outside: drug and weapons trafficking, kidnap, extortion, prostitution, murder for hire, they're into everything. Been availing themselves of the revolving-prison-door criminal ecosystem to build a national organization with political pretensions. They're in forty-two states, growing like a cult, the whole thing led by some wingnut who came up in the old-school Vegas mob, buddy of your grandfather's. They say he's an Odinist. Our intelligence guys tried to warn me they were dangerous."

Bowman took a moment to filter out Bick's extraneous rambling. "Would they send a woman to murder the caretaker?"

"Oh, I'm sure they would."

"If you're not here to help, I need to go." He and Marco again started toward the house, but Bick called out.

"Wait, I brought you a gift." He said this with such an intense burst of trickster glee that he began to glow. A burst of color, pale magenta in the air surrounding Bick, a haloed warning. This first event of synesthesia in a decade or more surprised him, the magenta flagging a complicated and dangerous level of self-satisfaction.

Bick opened the second door of the helicopter and hauled out a large, heavy backpack in military camouflage, tall and narrow and flat, like it might contain a pair of skis, but much heavier. He laid this on the ground and brought out a smaller satchel of the same camouflage fabric. Though smaller, it looked as heavy as the first. Marco was curious and trotted over to sniff the two packages.

Bick stepped back. They both watched Marco investigate. Bowman wished he would lift his leg on these "gifts." Instead he sat and looked expectantly at Bowman.

"What is it?"

"It's a rifle. And ammo! A fucking smorgasbord, you got ball, A-MAX, armor piercing, Raufoss, de-linked SLAPs, a few tracers—"

"I'm not going to shoot anyone."

"I know!" Another outpouring of trickster happiness, magenta shading toward purple. Bickford Rangely enjoying himself this much was triggering potent alarms in Bowman's joints—a jumpiness, a readiness to leap aside.

"I know," Bick repeated, glowing purple now with complicated malice beside the still-hot helicopter pinging and purring and stinking of aviation fuel, the helmeted, engoggled pilot nearly hidden and studiously ignoring the conversation outside, murmuring into a microphone and fiddling with switches overhead, periodically checking a small computer screen on an articulated arm in front of his face.

"You don't *have* to shoot anyone." Bick delivered this with an exaggerated performance of perfect reasonableness, of sympathetic understanding. "It's a fifty-cal, you can shoot *machines*." He paused here, like he was expecting Bowman to catch on, to get with the program. "You shoot *vehicles*. Cars and trucks. Hippies hate machines, right? Here's your chance!"

A rifle shot snapped from the ridge above. They both—Marco too—turned to look in that direction, waiting in shared prescience for the second shot. When it came, Bick said, "I hope that's your uncle."

"He's shooting at their little helicop—their drone."

Bick shook his head at the notion—you couldn't shoot *that* kind of machine—and picked up where he'd left off.

"You're a hippie, Sherman Carver. Despite the good haircut. A tree-hugger hippie, and I hate hippies. Inside that head you're still eighteen years old, an arrogant, naïve, superior punk who's allergic to America, and it just pisses me off." He said this in the same mild, companionable tone he'd used for almost everything else since they'd met, when was it, this morning? That hard-to-place southern accent.

"Plus," Bick continued, as friendly as he could be, "I've been told to be more careful. I've made too many *mistakes*"—here he mimed quotation marks with his fingers—"and my boss says no more extreme measures, he says go by the book. Still, you did save my life, so I'm going out on a limb for you."

Switching into technical mode, he rattled off a series of instructions and descriptions—the rifle was semiauto, zeroed at three hundred meters; in the case were three removable ten-shot magazines, already loaded; there was a night-vision device in a padded pouch he should mount forward of the scope when it got dark; the suppressor was in there too: "Remember to attach it or you'll be sorry."

When he noticed Bowman's incredulous look, he stopped.

"Don't try to tell me you can't shoot. Leo Girard didn't raise a son, or a daughter, who can't shoot."

It was the first time he'd used Bowman's family name. Bowman supposed he should be relieved the charade was over.

"How do you know so much about my family?"

"You people turned into kind of an obsession in the past couple years, I have to admit."

Bowman started to ask why, but another crack from Darwin's .270 intruded on the conversation. Then two more.

"You'd better take that with you," Bick said, meaning the packs. "If they did kill your caretaker they'll be on their way up before long. You've got a hell of a defensible redoubt here, but you have to defend it."

"I'm not shooting anyone, or anything."

"Then you won't be much help to your family." Bick's disappointment was so genuine it was almost touching. "You could always run down into the valley there and disappear. They'll never catch you. That's more your style, isn't it?"

Bowman didn't reply. He jogged up past the house, past the solar array, Marco following. He would follow Darwin up the trail to the escarpment, but Bick was right. Without a weapon, there wasn't much he could do.

45

1990

"Bowman?"

No sign of him, and Leo wouldn't know if the boy had answered. He couldn't hear, not even his own ragged breathing.

The pistol was loud, and he'd just fired a full magazine to slide-lock with no hearing protection. Jeremy had described the weapon, which wasn't even for sale yet, with some excitement: chambered in the FBI's new 10mm round, giving ballistics close to what you'd get from a .41 magnum revolver but in a reliable semiauto with seventeen rounds per magazine. Much flatter trajectory and more reach than the .45, and much more punch than the 9mm. The recoil was sharp but manageable.

He was silently thanking Jeremy now.

Four men lay dead or dying within a few yards of the trail where Leo sat in the mud. This was exactly what he'd been hoping to avoid. With a shocky sense of disassociation he watched himself eject the spent magazine and shove a full one home and release the slide.

He'd been shot before. Once in Korea and once in Africa. He'd had bones broken too. He would be all right. But when he tried to stand, the pain overwhelmed him and he nearly blacked out. After that he sat very still. Reflected on the pain, which was a worse kind than he'd known before, a sense of broken foundations. Something deeply distressing about it. Demoralizing. One of the older operators in Africa back in the late sixties had told him the worst thing you could do to someone with a gun, short of killing them outright, of course, worse even than gut-shooting them, was to shatter their femur with a high-velocity bullet.

These men had been using AKs, and their first shots had been at his legs. The trauma had nearly knocked him unconscious. It absolutely was intentional, and it was their fatal mistake, telegraphing their intention to keep him alive, at least temporarily. Not their fault, really, it was built into the assignment. He noted the men's tattoos and had no doubt they would have overwhelmed him quickly in a fair fight.

Bowman, wily woods creature that he was, had vanished at the first shot, thankfully. Gone before Leo had even hit the ground.

He opened the first-aid kit in his pack and windlassed the tourniquet below his groin, nearly passing out three times before he got it tight enough. At least the bullet hadn't clipped his femoral. He would have to splint the leg before he could move. He would need Bowman for that. He would need him pretty soon, actually, before shock incapacitated him.

He called out again. Had Bowman been hurt? Leo realized he hadn't even considered the possibility until this moment. They were in the forest, his son's natural habitat. He'd assumed the boy would be untouchable here. Not because of any violent tendency, quite the opposite. He'd never been violent, killing animals for food only after proper ceremony. Didn't like guns. Preferred bow and arrow.

When his son had finally walked into camp yesterday he'd been more feral than Leo had ever seen him. They'd slogged miles through the trackless forest before Bowman felt it was safe to make camp again. He'd built a smokeless fire and boiled tea infused with some sort of plant matter—it looked like a mash of herbs and roots—that had cured Leo's intestinal horror show overnight. He should've known Bowman was watching him, had been for a while, and he wished he'd realized before what it would take to bring his son in: his own mortal vulnerability.

He'd tried to draw Bowman into conversation, tried to explain the things he'd disastrously put off—his past, what had occurred in Africa, the future his own father, Martin, had decreed for the family—but the boy said the bandits following them were competent trackers, savvy in the woods, and he was resolute in his insistence on silence.

Leo called out again. He had to consider the possibility that this firefight had spooked Bowman enough that he wouldn't come back. If that was true, Leo would die here. He wouldn't last the night.

A rustling in the underbrush made it through his gradually recovering eardrums, had to be fairly loud, but it took a moment to locate. Coming down the steep slope above the trail. Grimacing, Leo twisted around, leading with the Glock.

A fifth body rolled to rest against the trunk of an oak tree. Bowman leaping down behind, carrying an improvised cudgel, a heavy deadwood branch half as long as his leg, dripping blood from the end.

The dead man had the same clothing and tattoos as the others.

Bowman was shaking, angry. He didn't speak. He took in the other bodies first, then Leo's leg.

"I'm sorry you had to do that," Leo said, a sadness rising up at the inadequacy of what he was saying, the cruel necessity of what he had to tell Bowman next. "Those tattoos, they're symbols of a Guatemalan assassin cult. They mean something that will affect our family. Something we have to talk about."

Bowman looked away. His nostrils quivered. Seeing beyond what was visible. More the wilding than ever, Leo thought. What would killing this man do to him?

"There's a logging road," Bowman said, "a mile west. There are trucks every day. One will pick us up."

46

2009

Sam stood for a moment in the still air under the low oak canopy, staring at Melissa's backpack. He remembered first noticing it leaning against her barstool in the café in wherever-that-was, Arizona. She'd been protective, wouldn't let Mac carry it for her. Now that he thought about it, she'd kept it within reach the whole time, had probably dragged it into the tent when she and Mac had decided to get naked and make all that noise.

No, wait, she'd locked it in the Subaru. He'd given her the keys.

Which had probably saved his life.

If the kidnappers hadn't been able to find the keys, wouldn't they have gone looking? Started breaking bones until Mac or Melissa pointed into the sagebrush thicket?

He saw Melissa smiling at him, imagined Mac burying her at gunpoint. He'd thought she was just high-strung, a nervous sort of person.

It was quiet there in the trees. Still hot in the shade. Insects buzzing, the gentle rustle of leaves moving in a breeze too scant to feel on his skin. He freely admitted to himself that he was terrified. Compulsively gaming out their situation, he'd known for a while that as soon as this cartel woman, Mia whatever, confirmed that Jeremy had brought her the package she expected—and he was sure by now that the million in coke weighting the pack was an afterthought compared to whatever the smaller package contained—as soon as she had what she wanted, there would be no more reason not to shoot Jeremy, and certainly no reason not to shoot Summer and Apryl and last but not least the mostly innocent and now-unarmed tax-attorney-on-vacation Sam Hay.

He imagined himself running back to the campsite and then west on that awful dirt road, flagging down a Border Patrol truck, begging a ride to Douglas.

Pretty funny, how attractive that scenario was right then.

He hefted the pack onto one shoulder and walked back out toward where the others stood waiting. As he emerged from the woods he realized they were all looking at him. He almost stopped. It was a lot of attention from people with guns, especially the unseen sniper, and he could feel it on his face like heat. His skin tingled and jumped. To make himself feel better, he pictured Rice up in the rocks, watching over them with some sort of weapon, a most unlikely taciturn sweaty scruffy-bearded angel.

When Sam reached Apryl and Summer, they fell in with him, one on each side, these women with pistols, escorting him to Jeremy.

Who didn't look good. His shoulders slumped and he seemed to have aged. Sam read deflation, disappointment, defeat in his face.

What in the fuck could have shaken this man? Jeremy's face scared him worse than the machine guns, worse than the imagined sniper with Sam's head centered in the crosshairs of his scope.

Mia stood with a surreal air of nonchalance and confidence, like she'd sucked it out of Jeremy when they were talking. Sam moved closer, slid the strap from his shoulder, set the pack on the ground, and leaned it toward her. She gave him a quick little ironic smile and opened the top to glance briefly at the cocaine, then she reached through the lower sleeping bag section to the divider where Sam had picked away the stitches. After feeling around and tugging and twisting, she pulled out the other package.

Sam willed himself to stand where he was, an arm's length from Mia, though every instinct told him to move away. Mia looked up at him but she didn't step back.

She held the flat package covered with tape close to her face and turned it over in her hands, inspecting it for an absurdly long time.

Then she nodded.

If that was her signal to shoot us, I'm going to tackle her.

Yep, that's what I'm going to do. Tackle this woman.

He waited, trying not to telegraph his intentions.

Nothing happened. She gestured to the guard on her right and he headed back down the hill toward the trees.

"He'll bring the reward." She spoke to Sam. Must think he was the one who found the backpack.

I guess I was, he thought. *Technically.* He let go of his tackling plan. *This reward, how much might it be?*

"Um," he began, but Jeremy spoke over him, said, "No," with some force, like he'd recovered his self-assurance.

Mia raised her eyebrows. "Are you sure?"

"I'm sure. But I do want three things." Jeremy held up his hand, counting on his fingers. "I want the cartel to owe me a big favor. I want you to owe me a big favor. And we need a ride back to Colorado, tonight."

47

Bowman dropped to all fours beside Marco as they crested the windy ridge, and together they eased around a lightning-killed juniper, pausing in its shadow. Far below, the shadow of the escarpment crept eastward over dun-colored sagebrush plains washing past red-lit Rosewater Butte, Smokehouse Mesa in the distance, big open country ongoing a hundred miles to a hazy bluish nothing at the exhausted edge of the world. The vast desert space made him a little woozy, so different from the jungle-and-ocean landscape his eyes were used to.

Another shot from Darwin's .270, close by, the ninth altogether, Marco and Bowman both flinching at the report. There he was, hunkered behind a stone fin farther down, at the edge of a thousand-foot cliff. Bowman searched but couldn't find what he was shooting at.

He and Marco scrambled down a steep slope of loose dirt and gravel, dry bunchgrass and rabbitbrush. Darwin turned, his face pinched with frustration, waved his hand at the dust as Bowman and Marco slid into place beside him.

"Damn thing's been flying all around down there. I almost hit it when it was hovering above the gate, but it's working its way back to Sarge's house. Too far away."

"You see that blue car pull in? About an hour ago?" The caretaker's house was two air miles away. Darwin wouldn't have noticed the car unless he'd been looking for it.

"Nope." Darwin reached out and rubbed Marco's head. Bowman dropped to a knee next to Darwin and scanned the faint line of the public road that ran past the caretaker's house. No vehicles visible in either direction.

"I saw it on the screen in the office. A woman got out and pretended to be lost, Sarge let her in the house, and five minutes later she came out alone."

"How do you know she was pretending?" The question sounded flat, worried.

"I just know."

"I haven't been able to get him on the radio." He picked up the handset and spoke into it, waiting, no reply. "I thought I heard a helicopter."

"You did. It's that guy I told you about. He's still trying to help, and I still don't trust him."

"Forty years without a single real intruder, and today we got a helicopter in Panther Gap?" Glaring at Bowman like this was all his fault, Darwin tried Sarge on the radio again.

"Can't you call the sheriff with that?"

"No, it's only good for a few miles. Works around the ranch but that's it. Sheriff's on a different frequency anyway."

"But you have a cell phone. Everyone has a cell phone now."

"I keep it in the truck. Doesn't work on the ranch."

A family of coyotes started barking somewhere on the shadowed sagebrush plain to the east, and almost immediately they were answered by a large pack on the escarpment, off to the south, howling and yipping, comparing notes on the ruckus the humans had been making, on what might be coming next.

Bowman stood and walked a few steps away from his uncle, surprised at his own reaction to the coyotes' song, clenched throat and a nearly irresistible urge to answer, to howl and yip and bark his sudden glee at the connection, at his presence here on a cliff guarding Panther Gap. He recalled sketchy details of the hours he'd spent wandering that afternoon. How all of the unusual animals from his childhood seemed to have disappeared.

"What happened to the wolves?" Though he wasn't sure he wanted to know.

They listened to the last trailing notes from the pack on the ridge. Darwin was giving Bowman a slightly sad version of the usual disappointed stare.

"There were never any wolves."

"Well, you never saw them."

"Don't get mad. You were a kid. You were always telling us you'd seen some animal nobody else could see, acting like you had special powers. It was your father's fault, all puffed up with the notion of us being Indians."

"The notion?"

Now Darwin looked like he regretted talking so much all at once. "Well, it's possible."

Bowman waited.

"Your grandfather made it up," Darwin said. "Mother was dark-skinned, and she grew up in an orphanage in San Francisco, but she had no idea who her people were. The cowboys who killed her and our father thought she was Indian, though they would've done it no matter where she'd come from. Martin was only stretching the truth a little bit, he said, when he convinced us she was an American Indian who didn't know her tribe. He did it to give us an identity, something to be proud of. He damn near believed it himself, made him feel good to imagine passing this land on to people with Native blood. He said he did it because he was French, but that never made any sense to me."

Bowman returned to squat on his haunches beside his uncle. Marco watched sleepily from where he'd settled on a flat rock a few yards uphill.

"Grandfather Martin told you this?"

"The week before he died. I was twenty-three years old and he told me a lot of damn things."

"You kept it to yourself, then."

"I told Jeremy, and your mother. She laughed, but she made me promise not to tell your father. He was the only one made a big deal out of it back then. He acted like he'd married Pocahontas."

This information made Bowman so dizzy he worried his ciguatera fever might be circling back for another flare-up, which, given the circumstances, would be inopportune.

His quarter-blood Native American (tribe unknown) heritage was not something it had ever occurred to him to question. Naturally he'd wondered what tribe he and Summer and their mother and uncles had come from. At one stage in his early teens he'd annoyed his uncles by obsessively studying their faces, along with pictures of his mother, and comparing them with images in a library book titled *The Big Atlas of North American Indian Tribes.* Results were inconclusive, though he'd formed a never-tested hypothesis, based mostly on the San Francisco site of his grandmother's orphanage, that they were Miwok of one subgroup or another, which in turn triggered a burning desire to visit Yosemite National Park, never realized. Later he'd decided that that level of specificity was both unnecessary and unattainable, but the bedrock fact of his Native blood remained tightly woven into his identity. He caught himself regressing to his fifteen-year-old self, dismissing Darwin's revelation in a desperate, self-protective reflex. Back then he'd been sure his mother's mother must have come from an ancient line of Native magicians, medicine men, powerful witches.

"What are you grinning at?" Darwin asked.

"My own horrified reaction to what you just told me."

Darwin shrugged. "Doesn't mean we're *not* Indian," he offered.

After that, they waited in silence. Coyotes down on the plain started singing again, but the pack on the ridge didn't answer. Bowman scanned the sky, hoping for an eagle returning to roost in Panther Gap. He thought of Alecto, counted the years. She might still be alive. There, low in the shadow, a bulky raptor flying away from the cliffs, nearly invisible, a great horned owl headed out to hunt. He tried to see more, the way he could as a kid, but found he was limited to ordinary human vision. It was enough. Venus had risen, pale in the east. A pair of ravens flew past, oddly silent, turning their heads to watch the two men in the rocks.

Something moving out on the sagebrush plain caught his attention. Vehicles, no headlights. He pointed. Darwin turned with the binoculars.

"Three trucks, coming in the driveway, fast. Half mile past the barn." He paused, and Bowman felt his uncle's dread increasing as the seconds passed. "Sarge should be headed out on his four-wheeler by now. He should've given an alarm on the radio."

48

Three other men besides his father languished on cots in the infirmary tent. The camp had suffered a rash of accidents in past weeks, nearly overwhelming the young medical worker, a man named Gilberto whose training consisted of six months as a medic in the Mexican Army. The foreman had instructed Gilberto that Leo was top priority, that he was to keep Leo alive long enough to generate the negotiated payment, which Bowman knew was as much ransom as reward.

He sat with his father during the day, helping Gilberto when he could, but at night he watched and listened from the forest. His father was safe enough until Uncle Jeremy arrived with the money and a doctor, but Bowman had no illusions about his own safety. He mistrusted these loggers. He'd watched them cutting timber in the old forest higher in the mountains and had seen their occasional brutality. They were rough, hardworking men, and they were looking for someone to blame for the recent accidents, and an itinerant American boy wandering the forest didn't sit right.

So he spent his nights nearby, close enough to watch and listen to the infirmary tent but invisible to the men in the camp. Tonight he hung Leo's hammock forty feet up in a big Mexican Douglas fir and lay on his back listening to the night sounds. When the heavy rain came after midnight, he covered up with an old waterproof poncho from his pack.

His father wanted him to come home. He said the world was always going to be dangerous for their family, and Bowman was putting himself—and, indirectly, his sister—at great risk wandering around alone in Mexico. The men who'd attacked them were professionals, sent by an old enemy to kidnap them both, and this enemy would try again. He tried to explain about the kind of people who would seek them out: powerful, corrupt politicians; organized crime syndicates; the United States federal government. Leo kept mixing up different threats, something from his own past and something in the future that had to do with an inheritance from Grandfather Martin.

Bowman felt sorry for him. The irrational paranoia he'd seen last August had worsened. The distinctive tattoos Leo had pointed out on the gunmen were fairly common—Bowman had a good look at them when he was hiding the bodies, and since then he'd noticed similar tattoos on several of the forest workers. He suspected the men all belonged to the same clan, some local group that was violent and bullying and inclined to banditry. And it hadn't been an ambush, exactly. When two men had stepped into the trail and pointed their rifles, his father had reacted instantly, drawing his pistol and shooting both of them. The others had reacted with surprise, fear, a disorganized retreat, and counterattack. They weren't professionals. They were bandits looking to kidnap a rich-looking white man who'd been pestering the locals, paying U.S. dollars for information about a missing boy. Bowman began to question his own participation in the battle. He knew he'd had to hit that man to save his father from being shot again, but now he thought he shouldn't have hit him quite so hard.

His father had given him his strange pistol and told him to keep it out of sight, but to use it if they were attacked again. Bowman had buried it in the forest. Like so much else about his father, it was nothing he wanted anything to do with. Still, he couldn't abandon Leo in the logging camp. So he stayed, and kept watch—in his fashion—day and night. He knew Uncle Jeremy was on his way, but Gilberto had run out of antibiotics, and the terrible roads into these mountains became nearly impassable when it rained, and on the third day Bowman smelled the gangrene.

The next morning, Leo began to rant. He listed the names of men and organizations that were searching for Martin Girard's fortune, who would still be searching in 2009 when Bowman and Summer took control, when it would be impossible to hide any longer, when Leo wouldn't be there to help them. Gilberto the medic was disturbed by these outbursts, the naming of criminal organizations, shadowy government powers. Bowman told him Leo was making all of it up. That he had been unwell in his mind for a long time.

When Leo grew quiet, Bowman asked Gilberto if he was dying. The answer he gave was, Yes, of course, but who knows how fast? He had to leave the infirmary for a while, and he asked Bowman to watch his father and the other remaining patient, a sick worker, possibly dying. The other two had gone back to their chain saws and skidders and trucks as soon as they could stand.

Bowman sat on the floor beside Leo's bed and spoke quietly in English. He told his father that the world of powerful men, of fortunes and governments and revenge, it didn't exist for him, that it was only froth on the vast surface of human beings' lives and experience, which in turn was froth on the larger world that defied any attempt to encompass it in human terms. He said he wasn't going home, and he tried to explain why.

"We thought we were living close to the earth, close to the bone, as you liked to say. But we could only live that way because of what Grandfather Martin had done. He destroyed and poisoned and exploited until he realized what was happening and used his wealth to buy Panther Gap, to secure a remnant of the old world for himself and his family."

Bowman explained that he was looking for a more honest life. He'd come south through the desert, following the old bones the jaguar had left, to explore wild mountains free of paved roads and parks and recreating white people. He had already been learning from locals who were poor and yet lived full lives, rich in real work and community.

He stopped, mulling over what he'd just said. Summer would object to this. He heard her voice in his head nearly every day, and now she was calling out his romanticism, his penchant for imposing his perspective on complex human beings with their own experience, their own centuries of history and culture. But he'd seen it, felt it. People with almost nothing to share had taken him in and fed him, given shelter. He'd helped out with whatever work was available, trying to repay them, but not because they'd asked him to. It wasn't easy to know the lives of other people, but it was worth the trouble.

He said he hoped his life here would be more consistent with the truth in what Leo had taught him, more honest, closer to the land, the old gods, the Others. In the mountains he'd found bears and lions and wolves, whole new worlds of exotic butterflies and hummingbirds and parrots and macaws, the magnificent imperial woodpecker, and most of all he'd searched out the creature who had visited him in Panther Gap years ago, who had journeyed so far north, leaving a hundred carcasses as his spoor, the bones in the desert that Bowman had followed southward.

He told his father that when he'd finally stopped searching, the jaguar had come to him.

To kneel on the bank of a small river high in the Cebadilla, drinking from cupped hands, and to suddenly understand who was with you: on the far bank a male jaguar big as a bear in the last rays of late autumn sunlight, blazing a fever dream of orange yellow black against the dark forest green, bright yellow eyes locked on Bowman's as the great cat dipped his face to drink from the same stream, not fifty feet away.

Bowman's whole body tingled at the memory.

Leo opened his eyes and smiled.

"You were listening?"

A weak nod, trying to sit up. Bowman reached to help, but his father collapsed back onto his pillow. Closed his eyes, fought off something, a wave of pain. Opened them. Dark blue irises, sandy hair, both from his own mother. Neither Bowman nor Summer got those looks, and Leo had always been pleased both children favored their Native mother.

"I'm proud of you. You've surpassed my every hope. I could never have imagined what you're becoming." He spoke slowly, with random pauses for breath or pain. His focus wandered, swung back in line. "You're right about powerful men, money. It's nothing."

He gathered his thoughts, his energy.

"But family is not nothing. Eventually you'll know."

Bowman waited. His father drifted, mumbling, then he seemed to be arguing with someone, Martin, Leo's own father, Bowman's grandfather. Leo was angry. Martin had cursed the family, hidden his wealth from his enemies, someplace where it would wait like a disease for Summer and Bowman.

Leo opened his eyes, saw Bowman there beside his bed.

"It wasn't what I wanted for you. He was dying, and he hurled everything he had into the unknowable future. His grown grandchildren would become masters of whatever world existed."

Bowman was disappointed, his father still going on about this. "I won't be master of anything, or anyone."

"I know you don't want it. It will come anyway."

"Not to me."

"You can't . . . you can't hide. You don't understand how dangerous it will be. Your grandfather was wrong, about the durability of greed. Those people don't forget, and they pass their grievances along. Summer doesn't know. You should warn her."

He quieted for a while. Peaceful.

More mumbling, then, ". . . and your families, both might be married . . . children. It's hard for me to imagine . . . future so distant."

He was fading. Bowman felt a moment of boyish panic. He looked around the tent for help. No Gilberto. The other occupied cot, a man they called Cantador, the singer. Inert, not singing now.

"I raised you and Summer to be ready . . . your clear, strong, wild minds. I wish we could have more time together."

His father's eyes widened, grew wet, glassy.

"Jeremy won't make it in time. I've heard the rain at night. Promise me."

"What? Promise what?"

"Promise you'll be with your sister, no matter what happens. It comes on the solstice, June, the year she turns thirty-five. Can you remember that? For your sake and for hers. You may need her more than she needs you. Swear it, on your mother's grave. Swear it by the jaguar you follow. Swear on the bones in the desert."

49

2009

Darwin handed Bowman his heavy binoculars.

"Tell me if they're the ones ambushed you."

Bowman rested his elbows on the stone and watched a bright image of the black Hummer leading the silver dually pickup and another light-colored pickup truck, all running out in front of an impressive cloud of dust billowing into the calm evening air.

"Yeah, that's them. Plus one."

The trucks slowed as they approached the first intersection. The driveway branched a half-dozen times in the three winding miles between the barn and the gate, false roads circling around or dead-ending in the sagebrush to throw off unwelcome guests. They turned onto the left branch and accelerated.

"They know where they're going," Bowman said.

"That's 'cause they scouted the way with the drone."

"You know who they are?"

"Do you?"

"The guy in the helicopter told me they're from a prison gang led by someone who knew Grandfather Martin."

"Jake Salifano. That sonofabitch."

The name meant something, had been talked about when he was

young. "Who—" he started, but the rifle went off as the trucks slowed at another intersection and Bowman nearly dropped the binoculars. Marco whined and ran back up the slope to stand at the lightning-struck juniper, where he glared down at them.

"Tell me if you're going to do that." He could barely hear his own voice. The cottony aftereffect of the concussion drained away and his ears sang a high-pitched glassy note.

"Was I close?"

Bowman looked through the binoculars. The trucks were accelerating again, headed toward the gate. He guessed the range was well over a thousand yards.

"I don't think they noticed."

"You're supposed to tell me where the bullet hits."

"You should wait until they get closer." His uncle didn't respond. He cycled the bolt on his rifle and watched through the scope, but no more shots followed.

Eventually the trucks passed out of sight behind a massive stone pillar, reappearing as they slowed and parked in a line facing the formidable steel contraption guarding the road up the escarpment. The distance from Darwin's high shooting eyrie was probably six hundred yards by air, but the horizontal distance was half that.

"It's a steep angle," Bowman said. "You have to aim lower than you'd—"

"I know what I'm doing. Hold your ears."

"Wait a minute. Let's see what they think they're going to do with the gate."

Grandfather Martin had originally built the gate during the Great Depression, and Bowman remembered at least one overhaul in the eighties at Uncle Jeremy's insistence. Preposterously overbuilt—a D9 bulldozer would have trouble battering its way through—the gate was set in a narrow gap between two house-sized slabs of sandstone.

Three men unloaded boxes, might've been metal ammunition tins, from one of the trucks, while four others, all carrying military-style weapons, stalked around keeping watch. An eighth man, holding what looked like a small computer screen, stood in front of the gate, his attention moving from the computer to the gate itself to the rock walls above on either side. The drone must still be flying around down there; the screen must be the controller for the drone. The men with the boxes set them next to the gate and started pulling out smaller packages.

"They're using explosives," Darwin said. "I'm shooting now."

Holding the binoculars with his left hand, Bowman managed to plug his right ear with a finger just before the shot cracked. A plume of dirt jumped next to the man with the controller. He fell backward, scrambling low for cover as the men unpacking the charges dropped what they were doing and followed. The armed men sprinted to the right, disappearing behind the rock pillar.

"Are you trying to kill him?"

"Not really."

"Then what were you aiming for?"

"His left knee."

Bowman stopped himself from asking his uncle if he'd ever actually hit anything with that rifle. He turned around to check on Marco, but he'd disappeared. Bowman got on all fours and climbed a few yards farther up the steep slope, trying a different view of the gate. No activity.

"Maybe they'll leave," he said. "They might assume we're calling the sheriff right now."

"Maybe."

"I don't see what they think they can gain by breaking in like this."

His uncle looked away to the darker sky in the east. Bowman loved that about his uncles; even as a teen he'd understood they were poor dissemblers.

"What is it? You know what they're after?"

"They're after you. You and Summer. Your fingerprints. So they can take control of your grandfather's bank account."

Bowman considered that for a moment. "How would anyone have my fingerprints?"

"You wouldn't be able to remember it, but Martin talked Anna into letting him fingerprint both of you, he got prints of your whole hands. He'd already had us done, me and Jeremy and Anna. Your father never knew. Summer was a baby. They say your fingerprints don't change."

Bowman stared at his palms, his fingers. The light had failed on the lower slopes, but the afterglow was still bright up on the ridge and the scars and calluses were clear, a half-dozen white lines, bars, and crescents on each hand.

"That's hard to believe. After all that time. Did you know he was involved with these people, with the one you mentioned, Salifano? That he was a criminal?"

"He was an investor, where he put his money after he got out of the timber and the mining and all. He didn't go 'round shooting folks. A man like your grandfather, he was complicated." Darwin hesitated. "When we were young, before your father moved back, would've been the early sixties—" He stopped again, uncomfortable revealing Martin's secrets. "Sometimes he'd tell us to stay in our room, Anna in there with us, while he entertained important guests. Of course we snuck out to see. He would send Macey Torv, he was the caretaker back then, to the La Plata airport, and he'd pick up a bunch of well-dressed men—mostly men, sometimes there were women—he'd load them up in a van and make 'em all put on blindfolds, drive the whole group up here in the dark. Then they'd all have dinner and sit and smoke and drink in the library most of the night and then Macey'd blindfold everyone again and drive 'em down to the Strater to sleep it off. I guess they'd fly back the next day to wherever they came from."

"You think they were organized crime?"

"We always made up stories about them. Mobsters, movie stars, politicians."

Bowman pictured the three brown-skinned children huddled in a stairwell, or standing on overturned buckets at an outside window, spying on the important white grown-ups.

"Did he ever introduce you?"

Darwin shook his head, his face impassive. "Your grandfather did right by us," he said. "He told me he was going to hide away some money, that it would be a long time. . . . He asked me to stay, to make sure the family kept the ranch until . . . until now." The air had gone out of him. "He left some for the time between, for me to manage, but it wasn't enough. The taxes . . ." He seemed to lose heart, didn't finish his sentence.

Bowman was stunned. The notion that this man, his mother's brother, had come back, had stayed on the ranch for decades, to fulfill a mad promise made to mad Grandfather Martin. He doubted Summer even knew.

"You didn't want to be here, to live here, all that time."

"That's none of your business." Darwin's voice had regained its sardonic bite. "You don't get to know about that."

A familiar high-pitched whirring approached from below.

"Get down," Darwin said, opening the bolt on his rifle to eject the spent casing, pressing more cartridges into the magazine. It was hard to tell exactly where the noise was coming from, and Bowman searched for a while before he found the drone, moving fast, laterally along the face of the cliff, climbing at an angle.

They both crouched behind the stone fin like duck hunters in a blind, Darwin readying the rifle, a fierce look on his face. The sound grew louder, then faded, then it was louder again as the drone searched the nooks and ledges along the cliff face. Finally it appeared a hundred feet to the south, slowing and hovering, whining louder as it encountered the wind at the top of the ridge and halted, struggling to stay in place. Darwin rose to a kneeling position with the rifle already at his shoulder and took his shot quickly, the blast nearly deafening Bowman again, but he heard the smack of bullet on plastic and metal. The drone spun around and flew into the cliff below, pieces falling off, bouncing once before falling out of sight.

"Ha!" Darwin said.

Bullets began sizzling overhead as automatic gunfire opened up on them from the sandstone pillar east of the gate. They ducked back behind their barrier, the experience of actually being shot at sobering them both instanter.

"Shit," Darwin said. Bowman remembered Jeremy as the more gifted swearer of the two brothers. Darwin only cussed in extreme situations.

Bowman crawled a few yards to the north with the binoculars, keeping low, to a point where he could see the gate without exposing himself to the shooters on the pillar. Two of the men were already placing explosives on the right hinge of the gate. They worked quickly, and by the time Bowman called Darwin over with the rifle, bullets still passing over them, a few pinging into the rocky slope above, a bright flash at the gate was followed by the rolling sound of the explosion, then another flash and explosion. Then a third. Bowman felt sick, a surprisingly emotional response: Grandfather Martin's massive gate, protecting the family from shadowy threats these seventy years, looming in his imagination since childhood as perfect, invulnerable, impenetrable, was being destroyed.

"Switch places with me." Bowman scooted backward and let Darwin lie prone with the rifle poking out from behind the rocks to their right.

Bowman sat up with the binoculars for a quick look. "They're hooking up a cable."

"I see 'em."

"Shoot the black vehicle, they're going to use the winch."

Another blast from Darwin's rifle, and the sound of the bullet hitting something metal, but Bowman didn't see any effect on the Hummer. The only response was more intense firing from the guards, with ricochets coming off a small rock ledge above them. Were they doing that on purpose?

Darwin shot again, then yelped and reached back to grab his leg. Bowman crawled forward, found blood already pooling in the dirt while Darwin cursed with his brother's eloquence. Borrowing Darwin's pocketknife, he cut away the leg of his uncle's jeans at the knee. Blood surged up from the calf muscle. He wiped it away with the cutoff denim, glimpsed an oblong hole in the left calf before the blood obscured it again. The bullet must've been tumbling when it hit. He pressed gently on the skin around the wound with his fingers.

"Bullet's still in there. I can feel it, not that deep, but it damaged a blood vessel and we have to stop the bleeding."

Darwin sat up and started fiddling with his belt buckle.

"Hang on, you might not need a tourniquet. Belt's no good anyway. That's cowboy first aid. You guys still slicing open your snakebites?" He took off his father's shirt, cut off both long flannel sleeves, and returned the pocketknife. Then he folded one of the sleeves to press on the hole in Darwin's leg. Blood seeped through the fabric and he added the second sleeve, leaned on the makeshift compress with his left palm over his right.

"Ow, shit!"

"Sorry. It's a nasty wound. We should get the bullet out tonight."

"You gonna poke around in there with my knife? Give me a stick to bite on?"

"I meant we should drive you to a doctor."

"That seems unlikely." The shooting had stopped. Darwin twisted around, trying to see the gate. "What are they doing?"

Sound of engines straining, going fast uphill. Bowman raised up to see over the stone rim and glimpsed a white pickup truck as it passed through the gaping right side of the gate and disappeared behind a bulge in the rock face.

"They're driving up."

Darwin tried to push his hands away. "My leg's fine, you have to stop them, take the rifle."

"I'm not leaving you before we stop the bleeding."

He pressed hard on the makeshift dressing while they listened to the sound of the engines rise and fall, speeding up the switchbacks. Bowman wondered what sort of violence was coming to Panther Gap. What they were going to do about it.

Then, a heavy *crack-whoosh,* followed quickly by two more, then a pause, then another pair. They sounded less like gunshots than world-ending blasts from some futuristic artillery piece.

The engines quieted.

"What the hell was that?" Darwin raised himself up again, but Bowman gently pushed him back down.

"Stay low. They might've left a shooter in place on the pillar."

"Was that a gun?"

"I think so." He checked the leg again, felt blood seeping out but not as fast. Placed his uncle's left palm on the compress. "Stiff elbow," he said. "Keep your weight on it. Don't let go." He put on his father's now-sleeveless shirt. "I'll be right back."

50

"I hear you fly. You're licensed."

Summer watched the man's face, gradually understanding he was offering her the copilot seat.

"Do you need me?" They were flying straight to Whitespring, where they planned to pick up Darwin and—she hoped—Bowman, then on to Denver, landing at a municipal airport around midnight. A milk run for a guy like this; he wasn't going to care about a copilot.

"Not really." He was her height, probably her uncle's age. He clearly enjoyed talking to women. He wore pressed khakis, new trainers, a starched off-white oxford tucked in. She'd expected the Hollywood version: young, bearded, unkempt, a natural genius, a misplaced barn-stormer reeking of pot. But he was an airline pilot, the traditional kind, before they all started looking like high school kids. Based in Tucson and moonlighting, literally.

"You fly much at night?" He gestured toward the cockpit. It was an interesting plane, the smaller and probably faster version of Andrew's King Air, and there was a certain get-back-on-the-horse attraction, but she needed to talk to Jeremy and Sam. This would be their first time alone since Apryl had driven them away from the damaged Cessna in the afternoon. Plus, she was picking up a serious lechery vibe from the pilot and didn't have the energy to deal with that right now, so she headed for a window seat in the spare four-passenger cabin, explaining she'd already crashed one plane today and needed a little downtime before taking the controls again. As she took her seat her ribs fired again—the cramped, uncomfortable ride in Apryl's Jeep to the hangar in Douglas hadn't helped. She grunted a curse, drawing a frown from Sam, who followed and took the seat next to her. Then Jeremy, stowing her bag, Sam's pack, and the pistol case behind the seats in an empty cargo space she imagined would be packed solid on a more standard assignment.

"Ninety minutes in the air," the pilot announced. Then he slid into the pilot's seat and put on his headset.

Jeremy and Sam held their phones to their ears, her uncle frowning in frustration. All three of them had been trying to make calls since they'd first picked up a signal in Douglas. Summer had left a message for Andrew, saying they'd be in Denver tonight, late, and she'd call him in the morning. She and Jeremy had both tried to reach Darwin on the landline and on his cell to let him know he, and Bowman if he'd showed, should meet the plane in Whitespring. Jeremy was calling Sarge, the caretaker. He'd already talked to dispatch at the sheriff's office. No bomb had been found at the Whitespring airport after all.

She leaned her head against the warm windowpane. They were taxiing toward the runway. The airport was small, poorly lit. A glow in the distance that must be the border. She'd given in to an impulse and hugged Rice goodbye in the parking lot, then she'd hugged Apryl too, and given the younger woman her cell number, insisted she call if she needed anything. She hoped she wouldn't regret doing that. They were professional smugglers working for a famously ruthless Mexican drug cartel. But she rarely met people she actually liked, and she tried not to question serendipity.

As the plane accelerated, Jeremy dropped his phone in his shirt pocket. Summer caught his eye and he shook his head. The plane lifted off and climbed at a steep angle.

"We're about to lose our signal," she shouted over the engine noise. "This plane flies a lot higher than the Cessna." She dialed the landline at the ranch again. No answer. Darwin's cell. No answer. Sam was telling someone goodbye, and after he lowered his phone the three of them simply looked at one another.

"Anything about your brother?" Sam asked. "You get Darwin? Your fella at the bank?"

"Nope."

"I got Mac at home. He keeps seeing bogeymen, but he's okay. I told him to stop worrying, that we fixed things with the rightful owners of the backpack."

Jeremy sighed and looked down at his big hands in his lap.

Sam noticed the gesture. "We did, didn't we?"

Jeremy nodded miserably, and then seemed to rouse himself, like Sam's question had broken through the self-absorbed worry that had gripped him since that weird tête-à-tête with Mia Cortez. He actually smiled.

"We sure tried."

Summer and Sam both waited.

"I'm starting to see the humor in it." He glanced around the cabin. She could imagine the paranoid wheels turning: Pilot was wearing his headset, plenty of white noise, but who knew about hidden microphones?

He leaned forward, eyebrows arched, and she and Sam leaned in as well until their foreheads nearly touched. Smell of salty dried sweat, stale breath from a day of mortal stress and empty stomachs.

"She's DEA, undercover," Jeremy whispered. "Why she didn't bring a honcho. DEA set me up. Recovering that packet of whatever it is will move her up in the cartel. Called it a real coup. She said if I out her, she'll tell them we were all in on it before they torture her to death."

They looked at each other for a moment, their faces too close together. Summer could feel herself sweating again even in the cold pressurized cabin.

"They're going to think that anyway," Sam said, voicing Summer's thought as well. "If she gets caught."

Jeremy sat back in his seat. "So you see why it's funny."

Sam and Summer said *No* at the same time, but he didn't explain.

"Did you tell Apryl and Rice?" she asked.

He looked uncomfortable. Jeremy took pride in being forthright even when it was against his own interest. But he wasn't going to betray a fellow law enforcement officer either.

"Sort of. I told Rice not to trust her."

They sat quietly. Summer mulled over the implications. Eventually the cartel was going to find out who Mia was, one way or another. Would they remember her "coup," and how the backpack had been recovered? Would they forget who'd been involved? Maybe, if enough people were arrested, there wouldn't be anyone left who cared. It was too far off to worry about, she decided. Plenty of more pressing problems. The loud vibrating plane was a powerful soporific. She was tired, sore. She'd brought a bottle of aspirin in her satchel but couldn't imagine getting up and finding it. Jeremy stared ahead, his eyes glassy. At her side, Sam was nodding off. It'd be okay to rest her eyes for a few minutes. She reclined her seat all the way back. She fell asleep.

51

Four more concussive blasts issued from what Bowman assumed was the rifle Bick had bragged about earlier, now answered with spitting bursts of automatic fire from the intruders. He was winded and couldn't hold the binoculars steady at first, and even with the big light-gathering objective lenses he struggled to see details in the gloom, but at least four different men were reaching full-auto carbines out from behind the rock at the final hairpin turn, firing blindly and without discipline. The wide Hummer sat inert and smoking in the turn, blocking the way. Three bodies lay beside it like discarded rag dolls, ripped open and tossed.

He crawled another fifty feet before he could see two figures on a rock ledge below his position, near the top of the driveway, one lying prone behind a large scoped rifle resting on a bipod, the other sitting cross-legged to his left, watching through binoculars. They'd clambered up to a wide ledge on the inside wall of the canyon and piled loose rocks into a fortification on three sides. Their tactical advantage was stark: the ledge overlooked the final hairpin turn at a quarter mile, well within the range of the big rifle, but they were too distant for the intruders to target accurately with their carbines, especially in the poor light. The last leg of the driveway passed through a twenty-foot-deep trench cut through the rock, all of it exposed to the rifle.

The shooter was Bick, and the spotter had to be the helicopter pilot, still wearing his helmet, the goggles pushed up on top. Two more military rifles with curved magazines leaned against the rock face behind the men, handy but out of the way: AK-47s, the *cuerno de chivo* triggering unpleasant memories of military checkpoints, bandits, armed drug traffickers.

Bowman felt exposed on the slope, too visible in the waning light from the afterglow, but no one in the battle below seemed to notice him. He waited, hunched over with his uncle's binoculars next to a gnarled, shrubby piñon rooted to the steep rock and gravel, instinctively mimicking its shape with his stance, disappearing like a stick-beetle.

Bick fired two more shots, the recoil of the rifle shoving his shoulder backward. He had to be at least mildly concussed from the wreck earlier, and shooting that thing couldn't be pleasant, though the recoil looked less violent than Bowman would have expected. The reduced recoil—and the strange report—must be due to the thick cylindrical suppressor attached to the muzzle.

Downrange, the Hummer started rolling backward. No one was pushing it, so they must've hooked up a cable, probably it had a winch on the back as well as the front. Trying to clear the way. Then it stopped moving. Looked like the rear bumper had hung up on a bulge in the rock wall.

After a moment, the white pickup drove forward from behind the shelter of the turn for a better angle on the cable, guards firing their automatic weapons to provide cover, but two quick shots from Bick slammed into the pickup's front grille, steam and shrapnel exploding up and to the side. The truck stalled and the driver's door opened, tumbling out a man, clearly injured, crawling on his elbows toward cover.

One of the others ran out to help, but Bick's shot caught him in the center of his chest, destroying with a sharp crack whatever hard steel or ceramic plates he wore in his protective vest. He spun around to lie facedown.

A follow-up shot hit the still-crawling driver in the thigh, a horrific impact that nearly removed his leg. He screamed and tried to keep crawling, his arms too weak now to pull him forward. Two more shots, each landing a sparking yellow flash on the side of the pickup behind the cab, then a third found the gas tank and the truck exploded in a fireball that lit the canyon orange in the shadowy dusk.

A whoop of triumph from either Bick or the pilot was followed by more screaming from the hairpin turn, someone caught fire, and when Bowman looked, Bick and the pilot were climbing down from their shelter with the assault rifles. They jogged toward the fire, hugging the inside wall of the driveway at the turn, leapfrogging twice, then one of them stepped out and fired three short bursts with his AK and the screaming stopped.

Bowman scrambled backward and ran to where he'd left Darwin, who had taken off his belt and used it to strap the compress tightly to his leg. He was sitting up, cradling the .270 and peering out at the pillar where the automatic gunfire had come from earlier. Marco had returned and was wagging his tail, forcing his head between Bowman's thighs, nearly lifting him from his feet. Bowman gently pushed the dog away and checked the tension of Darwin's belt with his fingers, felt for fresh bleeding.

"It's not a tourniquet," his uncle said, a little defensively. Bowman's quip about cowboy first aid must've stung.

"No, it's fine."

Marco sniffed at the dried blood on Darwin's leg, black against the paler skin.

"The ones who were shooting at us must've left."

"They're all dead," Bowman said.

His uncle's face turned toward him.

"The helicopter, Bick, the guy who I told you about and his pilot, they brought guns. . . ." He felt his voice trail off. He couldn't explain it. "We need to get back to the house. Can you walk?"

They both stared up at the steep slope of loose gravel above. The way they'd come. Darwin wasn't going to make the climb back to the top of the escarpment, the only way to reach the usual trail that would take them down past the solar panels to the courtyard and the house.

"Let's not go that way. There used to be an old game trail leading around the hump to the saddle."

He didn't know if it would still be there, but they found it—steeper and more exposed than he remembered—and descended in the rising dark, following Marco's ghostly white lead, Bowman carrying Darwin's rifle and binoculars and struggling to support his uncle's injured side without losing his own footing to bring them both tumbling down the gravel slope.

Darwin didn't complain, but their progress was slow, halting, and it was full dark by the time they scrambled down the last few yards to where the driveway crossed the saddle into Panther Gap. A light played on the helicopter, someone with a headlamp standing in the open passenger door, twisting a wrench or applying lubricant or something.

He must've heard them, or sensed someone near, because the light turned their way and brightened. The metallic clacking of a rattletrap AK hastily deployed. Bowman shaded his eyes, resisting the urge to grab for his uncle's rifle. The light subsided and a low voice, not Bick's, called out.

The light came toward them. Stopped when Marco growled.

"You must be Bowman and Darwin. I'm Art. I'm with Bick."

"Marco," Bowman said. The dog sat, still rumbling in his chest.

Art slung the AK on his shoulder and moved to Darwin's other side, supporting, encouraging him, guiding them toward the open door of the helicopter. Darwin was quiet, nearly given out, but he let the man turn him to sit facing out with his feet resting on the skid.

"You got hit." The light brightened, a variable headlamp of some sort, illuminating Darwin's leg, which had bled more than Bowman liked during their descent.

"Yeah," Darwin said, then added, "Ricochet."

To Bowman, "You dressed it?"

Bowman nodded.

"You mind if I take a look? I have some experience as a combat medic. This right here," pointing at Darwin's leg, "is in my wheelhouse."

Bowman heard the smile in the man's voice. And in his heartbeat, an equable rhythm. "Up to Darwin," he said, and stepped back. "What you and Bick did, back there. Those men driving in . . ." He stopped, not sure where he was going. Unless the two men planned a dastardly double-cross, Bowman and the rest of the family were unequivocally in their debt.

Art opened a medical kit on the seat of the helicopter in the light from his headlamp. "Part of the job."

The job, Bowman thought. They'd been hired to protect the family. He had questions for Bick. He asked Art where he was.

"In the house. He carried some equipment up there, and he wanted to keep an eye on your surveillance feeds in case more of those clowns show up."

Bowman started to ask how Bick knew about the video screens or where they were, but he was struck with a sudden sense of Summer's presence nearby. Wasn't sure he could trust it. Though he'd gone a solid half day without any ciguatera flare-ups. Hard to say. Summer might be on the property, or she might be somewhere in Arizona.

"He's waiting for you," Art said. "I have a radio. I'll let him know you're on your way. So he doesn't shoot you."

52

1990

The prefect came for her in fourth period, physics. Knocked and scurried in, handed a note to Mr. Stacks, and left without looking at the class. Summer was needed in the headmaster's office. She stuffed her textbook and notes into her daypack, the teacher and class all tense waiting and silent, the attention and curiosity uncomfortable.

Had to be about her brother. She'd heard nothing directly from her father since the airport in Hermosillo in January, her weekly conversations with one or both uncles relaying only the sketchiest reports of the ongoing search for Bowman.

Was he hurt? She reached out with her mind, scraping the cosmos for presentiment of bad Bowman news. Nothing. Still, her feet were numb as she climbed the steps, and her stomach dropped away when she saw the only person in the headmaster's office was Uncle Darwin. He looked stricken, and her first thought was to comfort him: he'd carried whatever this catastrophe was all the way from Colorado and now was charged with laying it on the tender sixteen-year-old heart of his only niece. She dropped her pack on the floor and hugged him, her eyes already wet with pity, for whom she wasn't sure.

It was her father. He'd been shot. Bowman was with him, somewhere up in the Sierra Madre. Jeremy had been on his way with a doctor, but—Darwin just got this news an hour ago, in the airport—Leo died of his wound before Jeremy could get to him.

She stopped herself from melting down, for her uncle's sake. He wouldn't know what to do with her, which would make everything worse. She remembered Bowman telling her how their father and uncles had reacted to Summer and Bowman's mother's death: in front of each other they'd hidden their heartbreak completely and it was like Anna's death was a problem to be solved, a practical challenge to be met with clearheaded efficiency. "Very cowboy," he'd said.

So she said to herself, *You have to cowboy this, Summer.* She lowered her voice half an octave, asked Darwin practical questions. She offered practical suggestions. She pressed him on exactly what had happened, but the details were scant. She imagined Jeremy giving his taciturn report on a staticky line from Sahuaripa. They would have to wait for Jeremy and Bowman in person to tell the story.

Darwin said they should leave soon, to catch their flight out of Bradley. The headmaster had come back in and offered the usual condolences; she asked if Summer needed help packing, but Summer didn't need to pack. She walked out with Darwin and they drove away in a light snow squall, the wet New England cold cutting through her sweater, an insistent reminder that she was alive, that her father had left her behind, that she had been charged with responsibilities, though she wasn't clear yet on what they were.

Darwin was quiet, relieved by her lack of histrionics, subsiding into a deep musing. She imagined he must feel the weight of his own responsibilities. Her father had relied almost entirely on Darwin to manage the family's finances. Would there be enough money without her father's pension? And she wondered what conflicts or tensions or misunderstandings between Darwin and her father might now be left unresolved, unresolvable. For now, at least, she resisted dwelling on the memory of her own parting with her father. He hadn't been himself, and she refused to allow that time to poison her.

They flew west in the dark. She rested her forehead on the

cold plastic window and watched the lights below: towns, cities, highways, lights wherever she looked. People everywhere. Then clouds obscured the view and she shut her eyes. They would spend the night in Durango and pick up Jeremy and Bowman—and her father—at the airport tomorrow. No sense driving all the way to the ranch to sleep for a few hours and turn right around. She pictured the empty house, the African animals in the dark library. Were they bereft or rejoicing? Did they know? Why on earth would she even think that? She sat in the chair beside the fireplace reading, watching over the top of her book, her father in the chair opposite with a book open in his lap, staring at the flames. He felt her attention, turned to her and smiled.

She was overwhelmed, then, not by her own loss but by a powerful empathic experience of her father's: Anna, her mother, dead eleven years ago at twenty-five. Cancer. Up on the ridge, where the wind blew without ever letting up, her father's crushing realization as they laid the stones: *However long I have left to live, I will live without you.*

Her breath caught in her throat, and a convulsive sob bent her forward like it would break her back.

No no no, none of that, look out the window. Clear now; flat country, snow-covered and pale in starlight. The lights more sparse here but patterned: geometric roads, farmsteads, grain-elevator towns at regular intervals.

What now? she asked her father. He began speaking as she finally wept, a steady stream of tears she allowed to run down her cheeks and drip invisibly into the space between her armrest and the window. He spoke of what he wanted for her, for Bowman, for their uncles, the ranch. She wept but she felt better, so she urged this conversation forward, speaking with the version of her father she'd known before Bowman left.

He said he needed her to become the center of gravity. She would hold the family together, protect the ranch, the land. Another generation would come along, and she would pass it down. He was depending on her. *You're the one who has to do this. Your brother and your uncles need you. All right,* she said, *all right,* vaguely

aware that this ongoing conversation with her father was an elaborate trick she was playing on herself to hold her grief at arm's length
until she could handle it. Someday she would willfully step into that
interstellar cold, that world of loss, of absence, but not now.

She and Darwin waited behind a low metal fence for the flight
from Dallas with a young mother gripping the hands of two tod-
dlers, a cold breezy March morning, snow on the mountains, high
icy cirrus clouds stealing the sun's warmth. Jeremy appeared in the
doorway and walked slowly down the steps. When he saw them he
walked across the tarmac without waiting for Bowman. Summer
watched the door for her brother, the lost one she and her father
had searched for only a couple of months ago. But he didn't appear.
Jeremy noticed her looking. He embraced her over the fence and
spoke quietly into her ear.

"He stayed there."

"Why?"

"He didn't say. He just vanished."

"What *did* he say?"

Jeremy gently untangled himself from her hug. "We'll talk on
the way home. I'm so sorry."

She started to hyperventilate when the rough pine casket appeared on a cargo forklift, but Jeremy squeezed her hand and she
began again a repetitive conversation with her father, an internal
mantra in which he told her over and over: *Take care of our family.*
She was able to observe with some detachment the fact that the
family was already down from five to three and she was failing
before she even had a chance to get properly started.

I'm technically an orphan, she thought, though she didn't feel like
one.

The forklift driver set the head of her father's casket on the open
tailgate of Darwin's pickup and got down to help her uncles shove
the thing off the forks and into the truck bed. Even pushed all the
way against the cab, the foot of the casket hung out over the tailgate, so they couldn't shut it.

"You got straps?"

Jeremy glanced over and Darwin nodded. The four of them stood there for a long moment as the forklift motor idled in the background. Like they were all, including the forklift guy, unsure what would come next. Then he said he was sorry for their loss and drove away. Still, Summer and her uncles stood at the back of Darwin's pickup truck, staring at Leo's casket. Not quite believing what had happened, unready to move into a future without him, hanging on to a few more moments of the time before. Summer imagined cottonwood seeds floating away and wanting to run after them, follow them wherever they drifted.

Would her uncles leave again, like they had after her mother's death? Without Bowman here to help, how would she keep the ranch? Would she have enough money? Would she even be able to go back to school? She surprised herself with a powerful desire to do so.

A breeze swirled off the tarmac, carrying a whiff of stink, one she recognized and, after another moment, understood. Her eyes widened, and her uncles must've caught it too, because they were suddenly bodies in motion, rifling behind the seat in the cab for cargo straps, muttering darkly about this being no time for lollygagging at the airport.

53

2009

By the time Summer turned off the main highway, headed south on a straight gravel road, Sam could barely see Jeremy's taillights ahead in the distance.

"I didn't think his truck would go that fast."

"It goes exactly as fast as he wants it to." She stepped on the accelerator. "I can catch him." She tossed her phone into his lap. "Try the last three numbers again before we lose the signal."

Sam found her recent calls and called the first number. This would be the fifteenth, maybe twentieth time they'd tried the ranch, Darwin, the caretaker. As they'd landed in Whitespring, Summer and Jeremy had both called several times and failed to reach anyone, their concern ratcheting up by the minute. Jeremy said he could handle whatever was happening at the ranch and that Summer and Sam should continue on to Denver—they had a free flight, after all—but Summer refused, said there was little point anyway without the whole family going. She'd sent the helpful cartel pilot on his way and they'd all jogged out to the parking lot.

Ten rings, no answer, no voicemail. Same result with the second, but the third number eventually connected with an unfamiliar male voice, *Andrew Coates of First Denver Bank and Trust, please leave a message.* Sam ended the call.

"Your boyfriend sounds like he's from Texas."

He felt her starting to object, but she must've seen his smile, because she relaxed. "He is, supposedly. We dated for a year and he hardly ever talked about his family, said his dad was a broke wildcatter and he didn't have much to do with him. He sure never introduced me."

Sam nearly asked what happened, why they broke up. Instead, he said, "You're worried about him."

She didn't answer for a while. They had left the lights of Whitespring behind, the huge sky ahead dense with stars, still so surreal to Sam's city eyes. Jeremy's taillights rose up in the distance before disappearing again.

"I am worried about him," she said, "and I'm worried about Bowman, and I'm worried about Uncle Darwin, and Sarge. Something's wrong. It's not just that we can't get them on the phone."

A jackrabbit shot into the road, the desperate full-body stretch-bunch-stretch. Summer swerved a few degrees and the nauseous thump didn't come. She accelerated out of a slight fishtail and drove on.

"For some reason, knowing Bowman is on his way, knowing I'll be seeing him soon for the first time in so long—" She stopped for a moment, struggling with how to put it. "Something's been triggering Bowmanesque phenomena."

"What's that?"

"When I spotted Rice up in the rocks from the Jeep? That was Bowmanesque. Then I kept seeing him later on, when we were at the border. Not seeing him, but seeing through his eyes. That was Bowmanesque. Now this gut certainty that something's wrong at the ranch and Bowman's in the middle of it."

They topped a rise and Jeremy's taillights appeared again, slightly closer. The road was rougher and they hadn't passed any cars since leaving Whitespring. The clock on the dashboard said 11:17. Summer drove calmly but the vehicle swam side to side, lifting and dipping, vibrating like it was about to shake apart, at the very outer limits of her control. He leaned over to see the speedometer: seventy-two miles an hour.

"Are you going to catch him?"

"Not before we get there. He's out of his mind." She laid off the gas a bit, slowed to sixty-five.

"Jeremy's worried too."

"Yeah."

"What do you think he meant when he told Mia Cortez the cartel was going to owe him a favor?"

"He said that?"

"When he told her he wasn't taking the reward. I guess I was closer than you were. He told her she would owe him a favor, and the cartel would owe him another favor. Plus our flight home."

"Maybe the favor is the cartel won't hunt us all down and kill us."

Summer slowed and turned in to the entrance, catching Jeremy in the headlights as he jogged from the barn to the caretaker's house. She pulled around back and through the open door into the lit barn. Jeremy's truck, parked next to Darwin's, smelled like it was about to catch fire. They'd put their bags in the back of the ATV when Jeremy appeared, carrying a military carbine and a walkie-talkie. His face was stone. At his truck he unlocked the toolbox in the bed, began jimmying it open.

"Sarge is dead," he said.

"What?" Summer came around from the other side of the ATV. "Oh my God. How?"

"Shot in the back of the head. Small-caliber. Sam, come here and take the HK." He turned toward Summer. "I called up to the house. Your brother's home."

"He's all right? You talked to him? What about Darwin?"

"They're both fine. But it was your friend from the bank who answered."

"Andrew? What's he doing here? How'd he even know—"

"I asked him, he said it wasn't easy to find the place but he managed. Said to bring you up to the house right away. He didn't know about Sarge, but he said there was an attack earlier and it's under control now. I called Sheriff Sartoris, he's on his way. But we're not waiting."

He handed Summer the carbine he'd brought from the caretaker's house and the larger scoped rifle he'd used at the ransom exchange. Before he jumped into the driver's seat of the ATV, he tossed a folded blue plastic tarp to Sam.

"Lie down in the back and cover yourself with this until we're away from the camera out back."

"Why?" Summer asked. "What are you thinking?"

"He's useful because no one knows about him. Andrew is expecting you and me. Let's keep it that way."

"You don't trust Andrew."

"Never did."

The engine fired up and Summer slid into the passenger seat with both rifles, Sam seeing no alternative but to stuff the big pistol under his belt in the small of his back and climb into the bed, kneeling on the rough boards where Marco had ridden on the way down yesterday morning. He hid under the tarp as Jeremy accelerated out of the barn and onto the rutted driveway.

54

Bowman found Bick in the office, paying less attention to the video screens on the wall than to a bulky portable computer on Summer's desk. A grimy wood-stocked AK-47 lay on the floor next to an open plastic suitcase with electronic gadgets seated in foam cutouts, wires running back and forth to the computer and several other inexplicable black boxes arranged on the desk. He looked pleased when Bowman walked in, followed by Marco, who barely glanced at Bick before padding over to sit on a horse blanket under the window.

If he doesn't like you he ignores you.

The bandage on Bick's head was grimy, stained with sweat and dried blood and dust. Bowman reached up to touch the gauze and tape on his own cut, which had been throbbing. He imagined he looked a lot like Bick. He laid his uncle's old Winchester in its case on the other desk, set the binoculars down too.

Bick was giving him a self-satisfied grin. Waiting for congratulations, thanks.

Bowman moved toward the phone on Summer's desk. "I need to call the sheriff."

"You're welcome. And your uncle already talked to the sheriff. The other uncle, the scary one, I think. Can't ever keep them straight."

"Uncle Jeremy? Where is he?"

Bick nodded at the surveillance screens on the wall. "He and Summer just drove in like a house afire. They're on their way up now. Be here in, ah, well, they have to get past that mess we left. Half an hour? He did mention the caretaker was murdered, just like you said. Condolences. Though of course you wouldn't have known him. Sarge was his name."

He stood and waved his hand at the equipment on Summer's desk, as if presenting it to Bowman.

"I set this up for you, thought we'd have to do Summer in Denver, but now"—he looked over at the screens again—"it's much better for you to be together. Time for a family reunion."

The inheritance. Of course that's what the equipment was for. It was always about Grandfather Martin's money. Bick seemed happy—not the malicious glee from earlier, no synesthetic colors. These were genuine good spirits.

Bowman couldn't decide which was worse.

"We're not going to have anything to do with the money." He felt his anger stirring, steadied himself, leaning against his uncle's desk. He wasn't angry at Bick so much as at his grandfather. "That's why I'm here. To stop it." He was growing stronger, more resolute. Things were starting to make sense. "Everything that's happened today, our wreck, the caretaker, the attack, those men dead down there"—here Bick started to object, something about how he should be very goddamn glad they were dead, but Bowman spoke over him—"all of it says my father was right. Grandfather Martin's money is dangerous. And that's what I'm going to tell Summer."

This set Bick to thinking, making a decision.

"Okay." He bent and lifted a black backpack from the floor behind Summer's desk, rifled through it, produced a roll of black duct tape and a figure eight of black plastic zip tie. He set these on the polished mahogany. "You don't look so good, my man, come have a seat."

Bowman refused. Bick reached inside his jacket, removed a smallish pistol from a shoulder holster. He squeezed the grip, a quiet cocking sound, pointed it at Bowman.

"Come on over, sit in this chair." He patted Summer's chair with his left hand, his voice as pleasant as ever.

The overt physical threat from Bick was so unsurprising that Bowman felt he had foreseen it down to the smallest detail. Of course. His job. The boss. This made more sense. He'd killed the men in the driveway so he could steal Grandfather Martin's money for some other organization.

"You need my fingerprints."

Bick bugged his eyes in response and waved the pistol toward the chair.

"You think I care if you shoot me?"

Bick pivoted to point the pistol at Marco, already asleep on his blanket.

"Wait." Bowman suddenly felt giddy with relief, a wash of irony. "This is stupid. You're trying to steal what I don't want. You can have it, I'll give it to you."

Another exasperated sigh from Bick, and a louder click as he relaxed his hand on the grip and the pistol de-cocked. Bowman reached out with his mind. Marco, dreaming, running alongside a paint horse, frozen grass and hoarfrost crunching under his feet. *Wake up.* Marco opened his eyes and looked at Bowman, his ears perked. *Go.* The dog stood and walked out of the office, down the stairs.

Bick had turned his back to the dog and didn't seem to have noticed this exchange.

"You still have no idea what's going on, do you?"

"I know you were about to shoot Marco."

Bick shrugged. "I like dogs as much as the next guy. But you need to understand. I'm not taking any more chances on what's about to happen. You and your sister are going to take possession of your goddamn accounts so I can recover my good reputation with my employer, collect my bonus, and retire to Baja."

"You're actually telling the truth now, aren't you?" Bowman found this realization not much of a comfort, given Bick's willingness to deploy violence to get what he wanted. "Why not tell me up front? You went to a lot of trouble following me around, pretending not to know who I was. What was the point, why all that performance?"

"Told you, I hate hippies," Bick said, somewhat absently. As if that were obvious and explained everything. He holstered his pistol and leaned heavily onto Summer's desk, rested his weight on outspread hands. Examined those hands, thinking. Then he glared at Bowman.

"I was absolutely sure there was nothing you could do that would surprise me, but here we are. Just to clarify: If I tell you I'm going to steal your money, you'll sit in the damn chair and cooperate?"

"I would've," Bowman said. "But not now. You missed your chance."

Without any change in their positions or facial expressions, the tension between the two men spiked. Bowman considered his options in the event of more violence. Darwin's rifle lay in its open case on the desk behind him; Bick's eyes flicked there too. Unfortunately, he'd unloaded the rifle at the patio door—a reflex built when he was a boy—the handful of .270 cartridges heavy in his jeans pocket. The *cuerno de chivo* lay on the floor, but it was farther away, and he wasn't familiar with its mechanism, and Bick could draw that squeeze-cock pistol from his shoulder holster.

He met Bick's hostile stare. His mind quieted, emptied itself of words. He settled into an open waiting readiness.

55

With nothing to hang on to in the bed of the ATV, Sam nearly bounced out several times on the ten-minute ride in. He covered himself again with the tarp as they neared the camera above the gate at the base of the cliffs but pitched forward to catch himself on the back of Summer's seat when Jeremy slammed the brakes, cursing as he swerved around some obstacle and sped upslope toward the first switchback. Sam lowered the tarp and saw in the red taillights a section of the heavy steel gate lying on the ground.

"What the hell could've done that?" he asked the two in front, but they didn't answer.

They drove another half mile, climbing gradually, turning on another switchback, higher now, speeding along the drop-off that had spooked Sam on the way down twenty-four hours ago. Now it was beautiful and dramatic, the world falling away into the mysterious dark below. Jeremy slowed as they approached the final switchback, then stepped hard on the brakes again. The burned-out husks of several trucks smoked in the headlights, bodies on the ground, blood, people had been shot, set on fire, a couple looked like they'd been turned inside out.

Jeremy shut off the headlights and backed up fifty feet in the dark.

"Out," he said. "Up against the rock."

The driveway here turned into a narrow passage between the face of the escarpment and a massive slab of stone leaning eastward that must've broken away eons ago, and the dark was relieved only by faint starlight that found its way down from the band of sky far overhead. A flashlight lit the rock wall and the ground around them, Jeremy calling Summer and Sam to follow, whispering commands: *Stay close to the rock and keep behind me, hand me my rifle, wait here.* At the bend in the rock wall, he passed his flashlight back to Summer and dropped into a crouch.

"Wait," she said. "What are you doing?"

Jeremy moved ahead, then dropped to his knees and elbows and inched around the bend, cradling the rifle with the night-vision scope.

"Turn the light off."

She clicked it off but shout-whispered, "We're not your damn SWAT team. You have to explain."

Jeremy sighed, and grunted, then came sounds of backward scuffling and a barely discernible form at their feet, a boot bumping Sam's shin.

"Whoever did this could still be up there. It wasn't my brother. It sure wasn't your brother. I doubt it was Andrew. So maybe they're on our side, and maybe they're not. I'm going to have a look with my scope before we walk out into the line of fire. Will that work for you two?"

"Yes," Summer said. "Thank you." In the pause that followed, Sam understood Jeremy was waiting for his reply, though in the dark he couldn't tell if this consideration was petulant or ironic or genuine, so he just said, "Yeah, good plan," prompting Jeremy's dismissive snort, and more scuffling as he crawled back into position.

Two full minutes passed before Summer's patience ran out.

"Come on," she whispered. The flashlight lit up again, but she'd slung the caretaker's carbine on her shoulder and her off-hand was cupped around the light's lens to limit its throw to the ground at their feet. They eased around the bend, close enough to the unseen corpses that Sam smelled blood and viscera and scorched flesh. They found Jeremy's rifle lying in the gravel, the man himself standing out in the open with his hands up in surrender. The narrow canyon was quiet, no sound other than the distant voice of the wind always blowing way up high on the escarpment.

"Now what are you doing?" Summer walked out to stand beside her uncle. Sam picked up Jeremy's rifle and raised it to his shoulder, peered through the scope. A bright greenish image of vertical rock walls on either side of the narrow road leading toward the house. He didn't notice any snipers or armed guards. Along the cliffs and slopes higher up were dozens of places for defenders to hide.

"I'm drawing their fire," Jeremy said. "Getting it over with, just in case."

Point being, Sam gathered, there was no sense trying to sneak up from here. He took a breath and carried the rifle out to stand beside the others. His legs didn't shake even a little. Jeremy's arms fell to his sides and Sam handed him the rifle.

"Did you ever think," Summer asked, laying her hand on her uncle's arm, "we'd be the ones walking this stretch, expecting to be shot at any moment?" Then she stepped past him with the flashlight and led the way up the driveway.

56

Static crackle from a handheld radio in the plastic suitcase. Bowman and Bick both looked at it.

"Yo, Bick." Sounded like Art the pilot-slash-medic.

Bick walked around Summer's desk and picked up the radio, a wary eye on Bowman.

"Yeah."

"They're here, walking up the road. They're both carrying."

Bick waggled his eyebrows at Bowman. "I told you she could handle her firearms." Then, into the radio, "Shoot the uncle."

Before he knew what he was doing, Bowman lunged forward and caught Bick's right hand as it moved toward the holster, clamped his other hand on Bick's throat, pushing him back into the desk. The surprise on the man's face was so extreme as to be comical, nearly shading into fear, and it took him a full second and a half to club Bowman in the head with the radio.

After the second blow, blood ran into his eyes, stinging, blinding him. Bick had aimed at his bandage. Before a third blow could land, Bowman lifted Bick completely off his feet by the throat and wrist and threw him over the top of Summer's desk. As he fell he knocked over the chair and landed on his back on the far side, sliding several feet along the floor, the pistol in his hand and pointed at Bowman before he even came to rest.

Bowman held very still. His whole body tingled.

Art's voice from the radio on the floor where Bick had dropped it, "What do you want me to do?"

Bick coughed twice before he could speak. "Jesus wept, what was that? I was kidding." Keeping the pistol on Bowman, he reached over and picked up the radio. "Hang on a sec, I'm having problems with Sherman Carver in here." Then, to Bowman again, "See, if I don't press this button on the side, the person on the other end doesn't hear what I'm saying."

He got to his feet, shaking his head, rueful, more performance, mumbling something about concussion, the wreck, shooting the god-damn fifty, now this. Righted Summer's chair.

"You're a lot stronger than you look," he said. Bowman got the sense he was putting some effort into this nonchalance, controlling an anger that threatened to overwhelm his studied offhand cool. Bowman himself was shaken by his own sudden violence. Not like him. Or was it?

Bick glanced at the video monitors on the wall, all dark. *Watching for police,* Bowman thought. As if Uncle Jeremy really had called the sheriff.

Bick spoke into the radio. "Okay, bring her on up, but Art?"

"What?"

"I need them both disarmed."

"Yeah, I figured."

Bick set the radio down. "Last chance to do this the easy way, hippie man. Come sit or you'll wish you had."

Bowman didn't reply. If Bick was going to shoot him he would've done it by now, and indeed Bick holstered his pistol. But he started to glow again, his aura skipping magenta and going straight to malicious purple as he reached into the pack on Summer's desk, came out with a blocky black plastic toy gun, had to be a futuristic weapon of some sort. Bowman took a step back. Smiling happily, Bick pointed the thing at Bowman and confetti blasted into the air between them. Two darts trailing tiny wires appeared in his belly and his thigh and a racking convulsion took him, his body shaking and cramping, major muscle groups seizing up, everything out of control. He started to topple sideways, but Bick moved fast around the desk and as the current shut off he caught Bowman in his arms, helpless and drained. Heaved him into Summer's chair and zip-cuffed his hands in front of him, then pulled a length of tape ripping from the roll and wound it around Bowman's torso and the chair back a half-dozen times. When he'd finished, Bick tugged on the two darts one by one, but left them embedded in Bowman's skin.

He stood back. "Now, *that* . . ." he said, eyes wide, leering, delighted. "That was fun."

57

Sam leaned his head back against the cool stone and stared at the band of stars, but what he saw was the ruptured and burned bodies at the wrecked vehicles. Smelled the cooked flesh as they'd moved past in the dark.

Jeremy had said to hang back. He wanted Sam to stay hidden until he gave the all-clear signal, which he didn't describe. He said the situation was "a little hinky," apparently law enforcement slang for suspicious. Summer and Jeremy both wanted to hurry, and Sam found his hanging-back assignment frustrating and a little bit insulting. At least Jeremy had let him keep the pistol.

He pushed away from the wall and stared into the darkness, looking for a glow from Summer's flashlight and hoping he hadn't missed the signal from Jeremy, when everything lit up at once, the reddish walls of the passage, the open gravel flat ahead, Summer and Jeremy caught in the open, hands coming up to shield their eyes from a floodlight off to the right that Sam couldn't see.

He was sure they were about to be shot but a voice over some sort of PA system called out their names, asking them in firm but respectful tones to set aside their rifles and lie facedown with their hands behind their heads, fingers interlaced. Sam flattened himself against the wall and kept still as a figure jogged out to where the others lay and secured their hands behind their backs. He zip-tied Summer's ankles, then picked up the rifles they'd dropped, slung one from his shoulder, and prompted Jeremy to stand. They both walked out of sight toward the light source.

Nothing happened for an excruciatingly long several minutes. Sam crept forward, staying within the shadow cast by the cliff to his right, and when the light went out he started running blindly toward where Summer lay, but someone with a headlamp jogged out before he covered much of the distance. He stopped and crouched, watched as the man cut the binding on her ankles, helped her to her feet. Sam was close enough to hear Summer's angry questions and objections, but the man responded in a calm, quiet voice he couldn't catch. After a moment, the man cut her hands free from behind her back and she held them out in front for him to resecure with another zip tie. Then the two figures, barely visible against the glow of the headlamp, walked up the hill toward the house.

He counted to sixty before sneaking ahead in the dark, holding Jeremy's heavy pistol out in front with both hands, pointed at the ground, hugging the right-side wall until it ended, the starry sky opening up overhead. He walked as softly as he could, stopping every twenty steps to listen. His eyes had readjusted to the dark after the intrusive floodlight, but the world continued its subtle brightening and he realized the moon must have finally cleared the butte to the east. An alien shape looming up in the dim light startled him: a helicopter, long blade overhead, glass panes reflecting stars. Must be where the floodlight and the PA had come from. Something shifted inside the open door. He pointed the pistol.

"Don't move."

"We *can't* move," Jeremy said. "We're handcuffed to the goddamn helicopter. What took you so long?"

58

They triggered the motion sensor and the footlights around the upper courtyard switched on, illuminating Marco's huge white head staring out at them through the French doors. He whined, wagging his tail at Summer, then changed his mind and growled. The man who'd introduced himself as Art had his hand on the door handle but didn't open it.

"I met that dog earlier. He bite?"

"Maybe." She didn't know what Marco would do. He'd always been less protective of her than Jeremy, an absurdity that her uncles pretended to find unsurprising, though she had to concede that here she was, unhurt, escorted to the house by a handsome helicopter pilot, and it was Jeremy, according to Art, who was "tied up in the chopper for now" along with Uncle Darwin. Who, by the way, had been shot in the leg, a wound Art had dressed, but he would need a doctor in the next twelve hours or so. Summer's outraged objections to being trussed up like a heifer had drawn Art's sincere-sounding apology followed by his explanation that he and someone named Bick were only making sure they could "control the situation, as a precaution, after what happened earlier." He'd said this in such a reasonable tone she'd almost agreed it sounded like a sensible plan, which meant she was too tired to deal with this situation effectively.

She assumed by "what happened earlier" Art meant poor Sarge, and the carnage back there at the switchback. When she'd asked about Bowman and Andrew, Art said they were fine, that's where he was taking her. As to who he and this Bick person were and why they'd flown a helicopter to the ranch and who were those bodies in the driveway and what the hell exactly was going on, Art had been less forthcoming.

He stepped back and shifted the AK-47 hanging from his shoulder around in front where he could get to it.

"Why don't you open the door, let him out?"

"And you'll shoot him? No way."

"I won't shoot unless I have to."

"You shoot this dog and there's nowhere on God's green earth you can hide. Just so you know."

She'd barely turned the door handle when Marco pushed his head out and gave her a searching look. She said, "It's okay, boy." The rest of him came through the door and he barely glanced at Art before galloping through the courtyard and down the hill.

She watched him disappear into the night, held up her hands in front of her. "He must not have noticed I'm handcuffed."

"You did tell him it was okay." Art gestured for her to go first. "Bick said they're in the office. I don't know where that is."

She led the way down the hall and up the steps. The door was open. She stepped in.

Bowman was taped to a chair, dressed in a flannel shirt with the sleeves cut off, his wrists bound in front of him. His bloody, bandaged head lolled forward and he looked sick, and so thin, even for him. Andrew stood nearby, fiddling with electronic equipment she'd never seen before. There was no one else in the room.

"What have you done to him?"

Andrew turned, a stained bandage on his forehead too, but somehow it wasn't Andrew. A bubble expanded uncomfortably inside her chest, as if her body knew something was terribly wrong well before she could articulate what it might be, a nauseous, slightly panicked sense of fundamental reality shifting and reordering in unpleasant new configurations. Andrew watched her with an air of expectation.

She managed to blurt, "*You're* stealing our money?" before moving toward him with her bound hands raised and clenched into two fists, ready to club him, but something stopped her. Andrew still hadn't spo-

ken, but his barely contained glee—his smug satisfaction—felt dangerous. She lowered her hands, conscious of Bowman's eyes on her now. She
was afraid to look at him again.

"No," Andrew said. "Of course not. Exactly the opposite, in fact."
Even his accent was subtly different. Still Texas, but less refined. "I'm
glad you're safe, glad you're here instead of in Denver. You didn't do
what I asked, big shock, but it worked out."

"Summer," Bowman said, his voice weak. "You know this guy." It
wasn't a question.

She nodded slowly but in truth she wasn't sure.

"You're all right?" she asked.

"Of course he is. He's fine. We're all fine. I only need you two to
prove your identity to these machines here, claim your inheritance from
your grandfather, and Art and I will be on our way."

"You're not really a vice president at First Denver Bank and Trust,
are you?"

"I sure am. Was, I guess. They've fired me by now."

Bowman said, "He and Art killed those men." His voice was still
flat, without affect. She couldn't tell if he was approving, disapproving,
or simply stating a fact.

Andrew held out his hands in a please-be-reasonable gesture. "Those
men were coming to kill you. *And* steal your money. They shot your
uncle in the leg, for God's sake."

Summer struggled to orient herself, to decide who were good guys,
who were bad guys. "Didn't look like they had much of a chance."

"Eight against two? They had a chance." Andrew paused, letting
that smug grin sneak onto his face. "Okay, yeah, they had no chance at
all. Prison-scum militia shitbags. Think they're hard 'cause they stabbed
someone with a sharpened toothbrush. Think they want a civil war. But
learning how to quick-change magazines in your fucking M4 doesn't
make you fucking mujahideen."

One, two, three beats of stunned silence. A significant fraction of
Summer's brain was furiously reevaluating her relationship with Andrew: he'd certainly liked guns, and was a little too conservative in his
politics, but he had an edgy intelligence she'd found fascinating. He
talked a lot, made her laugh, was worldly and cosmopolitan in a carefully

calibrated low-key smooth-Texas manner that someone like Summer was likely to find attractive.

"Who even are you?" she asked.

Andrew blinked. "Right now, Summer, I'm your fairy godmother. Have a seat next to your brother."

59

"I should've stopped him from taking her."

"No, you did right." Jeremy sat in the open door of the helicopter and rubbed Marco's ears. Maybe it was because his dog had shown up healthy and happy, but Jeremy had set aside his earlier pique with Sam. Apparently the man who'd captured Jeremy and Summer—and it had been only one man, the pilot of the chopper—had relieved both uncles of their knives, and Jeremy had maintained a running critique of Sam's innate failings as a red-blooded American male—*What kind of guy walks around knifeless? Not even a little Swiss Army knife?*—while Sam fumbled around in the dark until he came up with a pair of surgical shears from the helicopter's medical kit, left open on the copilot's seat, and cut Jeremy's zip ties.

"If you'd run up to them in the dark with that pistol he'd have shot you, would've thought you were another intruder, you'd be another body lying in the driveway. Summer might've got hurt too."

Sam decided to take him at his word and stop worrying about it. Jeremy moved out of the way and Sam crawled in with the shears to where he could reach Darwin, who grunted a curse as he leaned forward so Sam could reach his plastic cuffs.

"Sorry," Sam said.

Jeremy heard this and leaned back in the doorway to tell Sam his brother had refused the morphine he'd been offered, but Sam couldn't tell whether he approved of the decision. Darwin grunted again as Sam helped him to the doorway. He got his legs to the ground and tested his weight.

"You walk?" Jeremy asked. He'd found his rifle and a walkie-talkie he said was Darwin's. He stood nearby watching the path to the house through the night-vision scope.

"Yeah." Darwin lunged forward and fell to the left. Sam caught him, got his arm under Darwin's shoulder, and stood him up. Jeremy made no comment, but his impatience buzzed like a bee swarm. They managed a few steps away from the helicopter.

"You're not putting any weight on it," Jeremy said. He seemed unaccountably angry with his brother.

"It'll loosen up."

Jeremy stood there breathing, then turned and walked on, checking the way ahead through his scope every ten seconds. Sam and Darwin made slow halting progress up the hill.

"Do you know what's going on?" Sam asked.

"Nope."

When Jeremy came back to check on them, Sam noticed in the moonlight he had Summer's—the caretaker's—carbine slung on his back. Which reminded him.

"Shit, Jeremy, I'm sorry, I left your pistol in the helicopter."

"No, I got it, here." He handed it over to Sam. "Safety's on. Look, Dar—"

Darwin interrupted. "You two go ahead," he said. "I can make it." He shook off Sam's support and showed he could stand on his own.

Jeremy muttered something that sounded like encouragement. He started jogging up the hill and Sam hurried to keep up.

"Do we have a plan?" Sam asked.

No answer. Then, "I'm thinking one up. We have to avoid the cameras."

60

"Summer."

Bowman's voice carried more force than before. She turned to him, took a couple of steps, stopped.

"We can't take the money," he said.

There was too much dried blood on his face, but his eyes had brightened, recovering from whatever Andrew had done to him.

"This is why I came back. Dad warned me before he died, and I didn't take him seriously. I never told you. But look what's already happened. If we take it, there'll be more violence, more people trying to steal it. We'll all be targets for the rest of our lives."

Andrew groaned. "Now you see why I had to tie him up?" This might've been directed at either Summer or Art, who was still waiting quietly behind her in the doorway. "You're going to be targets anyway." He spoke in a patronizing tone she'd never tolerated when they were together. "You need the money to protect yourselves."

Summer knew she was exhausted, and she'd already seen herself accept the unreasonable as reasonable, but this argument between Bowman and Andrew struck her as farcical. She spoke to her brother. "You're beaten up and duct-taped to a chair, Bowman. Do you really think Andrew's *not* stealing our money?"

"Who?" Bowman asked.

"Him!" She pointed angrily with her bound hands, aware of Art lurking behind her. She'd already mentally located several weapons stashed in the office, none of which she would be able to get her hands on before Art grabbed her. "He told you his name was Bick, I guess." Then, to Andrew, "Which is it?"

But Andrew was distracted by the monitors showing the feeds from the security cameras. Three vehicles with flashing blue and red lights had pulled in front of Sarge's house. Instead of answering her question, he approached and palmed her elbow, urged her toward the chair he'd placed next to Bowman's. When she resisted, he nodded to Art, who padded across the room to stand on her other side, not touching her.

"We all have lots to talk about," Andrew said, "but now is not the time. For obvious reasons, Art and I have to be gone before any of those police make their way up here. Summer, I'm sorry, but I can't risk any delays in your cooperation."

He reached inside his jacket and came out with a pistol. He waved it toward the empty chair.

She felt her mouth fall open. As many problems as the two of them had had, she was pretty sure that Andrew pulling a pistol on her had never materialized in her wildest paranoid imaginings.

"He won't shoot you," Bowman said. "He's still in love with you."

Andrew gasped, affecting drama, deflecting. "Whoa. Whoa whoa whoa. That voodoo mind-reader shit is just not called for." He glanced around the room. "So maybe I shoot that dog you like so much."

"We let him out," Art said. "Sorry."

"Okay. I'll send Art down to bring up the uncles. I can shoot the scary one or the gay one, you choose."

"The gay one?" Summer and Bowman said this more or less simultaneously.

"Oh please, don't even try to tell me—" He stopped in midsentence, staring at the video screens again. Two more police vehicles had pulled up to Sarge's house, looked like state troopers. The intensifying law enforcement presence at the caretaker's house put Andrew in a more serious mood. He pressed a switch on the largest of the black boxes on the desk.

Lights flashed and it made a whirring sound. The top was a plate of glass about a foot square.

On the video screen, floodlights from the police vehicles lit the care-taker's house. Figures moved back and forth between the vehicles and front door.

"Good news is," he said, "all that police'll keep any more bad guys away so we can get this done."

He slid the box on the desk in front of Bowman.

"Hands on the scanner."

Bowman shook his head. "No."

Andrew sighed and moved behind Bowman, grasped an elbow in each hand, pressing thumbs into his forearms, feeling for nerves.

"Andrew! Stop it! What are you doing?"

She started toward them but Art held her shoulders. She stepped out with her left foot, ready to twist her upper body and land an elbow in the man's face, but he was too fast, wrapping his arms around her sore ribs under her breasts, holding his head to the side to avoid her backward head-butt.

"Hold on, Summer," he whispered, his scent of sweat and a vaguely familiar deodorant enveloping with his arms, the embrace still too tight, Summer hissing a curse. Art sensed he was hurting her and loosened his bear hug, which became strangely calming. They watched together as Andrew struggled with Bowman.

Andrew's frustration was obvious, Bowman sitting calmly, smiling, his zip-cuffed wrists lying relaxed in his lap while Andrew tried again to force them up and onto the plate glass of the scanner.

"Goddammit, Andrew. Leave him alone."

Andrew cursed and let go of Bowman's arms, picked up what looked like a plastic dart gun from the desktop. A Taser. Two wires ran to blood spots on Bowman's shirt and jeans she hadn't noticed before.

"You know what this is, right?"

"Don't," she said.

"Then tell your hippie brother to cooperate."

Bowman laughed. "It doesn't affect me," he said. "He's bluffing."

The expression that flashed across Andrew's face was not one she'd seen on him before. Hatred, fear, cruelty all at once.

"Time's up." He pulled the trigger on the Taser and Bowman went rigid in his chair, back arched, straining against the duct tape, a moan from deep in his gut, his grin pulled obscenely into something like a death mask.

61

1996

Summer eased the backpack from her shoulders and laid it on the salt-crusted, fish-scaly planks of the dock. The sudden lightness, her bones and joints and ligaments rejoicing. Pleasurable in a stupefying, low-consciousness way. Her favorite part of backpacking. She watched the oil sheen on the water, watched a school of minnows flash and vanish in unison.

Sitting on the pack, she took off her boots and sweaty socks, stretched bare legs out in front of her. She was tired, content. The sun was still a couple of hours from sunset, a corrugated metal bait shop casting its shadow far enough to shade her. A dozen boats glowed in warm light, gently rocking in the harbor, sailboats and motor yachts all apparently vacant. In this unfashionable port town on the Yucatán, none were big or fancy. She wasn't a boat person but she found the scene peaceful, pretty.

This was the off-season and she imagined it would be busier with tourists in the winter. The few locals who passed by paid her little attention; they'd seen her type before. She knew she stank, sweaty from walking all day, and she didn't care, had gotten used to it. Dirtbag. Saul had said he was tired of living like a dirtbag. Last week, she'd walked with him to the bus station in Boca del Río and regretted it because he'd tried again to talk her into going back with him, said she wasn't going to find her brother, that searching for him had been an excellent pretext for a few months of postgraduate footloose adventuring but he, Saul, had never thought she was completely serious about it. He'd affected concern, a worry that she might be a little bit delusional. Walking away, she'd felt relief, but also some sadness. Saul was beautiful and smart and they'd been together through most of their senior year at Northern Arizona. He pretended to Bohemianism, and had claimed to want to live rough. She smiled at that now.

She was thirsty and left her pack on the dock, stepped into the bait shop, and bought three Modelo Especials. Beer was cheaper than bottled water, and sweet sodas made her sick. Sitting on her pack again, she drank the first beer quickly, aware of the modest buzz on her empty stomach, and sipped the second, thinking she would offer the third to Bowman if her instincts were right, if the tall American she'd learned was crewing on the French research boat turned out to be her brother.

All three beers were gone and she'd fallen asleep with her head on her pack when she woke to the sound of an engine approaching and, over the noise, loud polyglot voices. Lights had come on around the harbor, even on the boats at anchor she'd thought deserted. A much bigger boat, almost what she would call a ship, was motoring her way. The *Marion Simon* had been collecting biological data of some sort somewhere in the Gulf for three weeks and would be docked here for several days before heading back out.

She carried her pack closer to where the boat was headed. A single weak floodlight lit the dock, swarming with insects, and she didn't want to miss, or mistake, her brother in the poor light. Instinctively, she stood in the darkest shadow she could find. More shouting in French, then Spanish, a loud diesel churn as the engines reversed, cut off. Ropes were tossed, men leaping to the dock and wrapping complicated knots onto cleats bolted to heavy posts. An air of release, excitement. Two young men and a woman, all carrying backpacks, hurried onto the dock and out of sight, talking among themselves in Spanish. Summer waited. She tried not to rehearse what she would say to her brother. Better to let the surprise sink in, let him decide what to say to her.

She realized she knew for certain he was on the boat. That hadn't happened before.

They'd last seen each other more than six years ago. Would he even recognize her? Then, his voice, unmistakable, saying good-bye to someone in French. A thin, slow-moving silhouette against the throw of a dim yellow light on the boat, graceful as a heron, embracing a tall, dark-skinned woman. It was more than friendly, which made Summer happy for him. The woman turned and left quickly, walking away on the dock toward shore.

Bowman watched her go, quiet, in his posture a tinge of regret. He probably wouldn't see her again. He would miss her. He stood there looking left and right for a moment before reaching a long leg across the two-foot gap to the dock, pausing again, shifting a heavy duffel on his shoulder, both feet on the solid unshifting boards, savoring this new sensation of stillness.

He turned directly toward her.

"It *is* you," he said. "I thought I was losing my mind."

He dropped his duffel and rushed to her, lifting her off the ground in a bear hug. He smelled of salt and sweat and the Gulf, and while he was still thin his strength was surprising, a man's strength, muscles standing up in cords on his arms and back. He was asking how she'd found him, sounding pleased rather than angry as she'd half expected.

He put her down, still smiling at her.

"When did you decide you like boats?" she asked.

"It's not the boats, Summer, it's the water. Do you remember when Dad first let us look through the microscope?"

"Invisible wildlife in a drop of lake water, yeah." They'd been ten and twelve, and it had made a hell of an impression. They'd gone on to discover more tiny creatures on their skin, in their guts. The notion of symbionts complicated the notion of self in ways that they'd both found troubling at first. Their father had delighted in holding back life discoveries and then laying them out for his children in a way that surprised and shocked and shook their conception of reality, forcing what he called "a violent expansion of consciousness." She wondered now whether it had been all that great an idea.

"It's the same," Bowman said, "like you're looking through the microscope and you can't believe what you're seeing, but out on the reefs, the Others aren't microscopic. For me, what was I when I came to the coast? Twenty-two years old, discovering a new universe . . ." He didn't finish his sentence. Summer noticed he still used their father's term for nonhuman life. He seemed happy, as enthusiastic as he'd been when they were younger.

"I have a campsite," he said, "outside of town. Let's get some food and head out there. After three weeks on a boat with other people, I need quiet."

They bought fish tacos from a street vendor who knew Bowman, and more beer at the bait shop right before it closed, and they set off walking, leaving the houses and shops and street signs behind, eventually turning off the gravel road onto a dirt footpath. She pulled the flashlight from a pocket on her pack's belt and turned it on. Bowman stopped so suddenly she bumped into his back. He asked her to turn it off, though the moon was dark. He said he would tell her when to step carefully, when there were roots or rocks.

"I was thinking more about a fer-de-lance," she said.

"Ah, right, *Bothrops asper,*" he said, as if she'd mentioned a mutual friend, "beautiful snake, especially the big females. You're right, you don't want to step on one. She doesn't mix well with the human population. I've only seen a few in this forest." He continued walking. "There are jaguars, though. I can walk from here to the best jaguar habitat in Mexico." His voice had grown excited again, unselfconscious, and in the dark she could imagine this was the Bowman of their childhood, telling her about the rare and imaginary animals in Panther Gap.

"I know. How do you think I found you?"

He stopped again, puzzling, then gave a kind of satisfied, approving laugh before he walked on. She followed close behind as they descended—it felt like descent, though the landscape here was relentlessly flat—into a humid, fecund jungle where her brother's aspect grew more and more feral and, it struck her with a mild shock, powerful. She knew this was her imagination, and the beer, and the velvety dark, and her brother's obvious familiarity with an ecosystem that to her was exotic and vaguely threatening, but even his shadowy form ahead on the trail looked taller, darker.

The path led to an opening in the canopy—she imagined a forest giant had fallen here a long time ago. In the ambient light she made out a fire ring of pale stones and several heavy logs set up as benches or tables. A hammock hung ten feet up in the branches of a huge spreading tree, the species a mystery to her. Bowman set about starting a fire with his bow drill while he asked Summer to catch him up on her life, school, college, their uncles, the ranch, the wildlife in Panther Gap.

She gave him only the vague outlines, somewhat put off by his blithe assumption that he deserved to know these things. She unwrapped the paper from her taco, the snapper spicy and flaky. Yellow flames climbed the tepee of twigs as Bowman snapped sticks in his hands, laying them on, reprising a tableau she'd seen hundreds of times when they were young.

"I had a dream after Jeremy left," he said, "when he took Dad's body home. I was a marmot in that rock outcrop on the ridge, watching you and Darwin and Jeremy bury Dad next to Mom."

"Did you watch us carry him up there?" She blurted this out with her mouth full. "Could've used your help."

Bowman didn't reply. She saw their father in her own dreams, several times a year, and in each dream he had come back, or had never really died, but there was always something horribly wrong with him.

She asked Bowman if he would tell her what happened when their father was killed. He didn't say anything at first.

"You told Uncle Jeremy it was a team of elite assassins sent by an enemy of Dad's from Africa."

"I told him that's what Dad said. It's not what happened. Those guys were local bandits who planned to kidnap us, and Dad started shooting first. They shot him in the leg not because they were trying to keep him alive for interrogation but because they were poor shots. He wasn't a superman."

She'd expected something like this, but the implication caught in her throat. A sadness for their father.

"When I was with him, looking for you in the Sierra Madre, I decided you were right, that he was suffering from some form of mental illness. Maybe for a year, more, gradually advancing, becoming delusional. It sounds like by the end he was hallucinating."

"Yeah. He had a bad fever before he died, which made it worse. But yeah."

"You know he wasn't in the CIA, don't you?"

"He never said he was."

"He implied it. Always so mysterious about Africa." She described how last summer she'd talked Uncle Jeremy into helping her investigate Leo's career. They'd found someone who'd worked with him in the State Department in Central Africa in the sixties. Apparently the lines between State and CIA were blurry over there at the time, and Leo had an impressive military background, but he was never an agent. The guy she and Jeremy talked to was old-school, told them Leo "went native" in '66, '67—he didn't realize he was talking to mixed-blood Native Americans—and over the next few years he'd spent months at a time living in the bush with several of the more "primitive" tribes, helping them file grievances with the central government to stop a local strongman who was pushing into their territory, poaching bushmeat, forcibly conscripting boys from the tribe into his militia.

"Dad got frustrated, and tried to defend his friends, and he went too far, killed some people. Not that the CIA wasn't killing people back then, but what he was doing didn't suit the plan. They hushed it all up, and his superiors recommended early retirement."

This story seemed to throw Bowman. He frowned, and Summer felt him processing new news about their father, recalibrating his opinion in a more positive light. This sort of thing would appeal to him, their father standing up for indigenous people fighting to protect the land so they could continue to live in the old way. Focusing only on that slice of indigenous struggle was, to her, narrow-minded and a bit romantic, but she couldn't deny the appeal.

Another lengthy, quiet interlude followed, her brother's unorthodox conversational rhythms unchanged since she'd last spoken with him.

Welp, she thought, *enough dancing around the elephant in the forest clearing.*

"So why haven't you come home?" she asked. "No postcard, no phone call. It's been six years, Bowman. Six years." Her voice rose despite her determination to keep it otherwise, and the show of emotion had the effect she'd feared: more silence. Which she met by doing what she'd told herself she wouldn't: she let loose with pent-up frustration and hurt and recrimination, describing how hard it had been on her and their uncles without him, how they'd tried to find him, not knowing if he was even alive. How she'd tried a dozen times to quit school, quit college, not go back in the fall after working with Darwin and Jeremy every summer, each time succumbing to both uncles' insistence that Leo had wanted her to finish school and experience life beyond Panther Gap. But it was too hard now, even with Jeremy and Darwin working their lowland hay farm, and their jobs in town.

Her brother didn't appear to be listening. Dark eyes shining and faraway, long dark hair on his shoulders. A Hollywood Indian, the heroic version. Tall and strong, pleasing to a white audience, Anglo-handsome with just enough flavoring from their grandmother to hint at the indigenous. A vaguely insulting observation she hadn't been capable of the last time she'd seen him.

"Grandfather Martin left an endowment that's supposed to cover ranch expenses," she said, "but the county has increased the taxes so much Darwin says the money won't last five years. I'm going back to help, to live at the ranch. But I had to find you first. To let you know what's going on. To see if you'll come back with me."

"Jeremy and Darwin are good men," he said. "You should listen to them."

"They're good men and they're killing themselves trying to do what our grandfather and father asked them to do. It's not fair."

"There's something in our blood," he said. "On both sides. Or maybe it's something about the place itself."

"What are you talking about?"

Instead of elaborating, he reached for the paper bag with his fish tacos. He'd ordered five, his teenage appetite apparently unabated. He unwrapped the first, took a huge bite, opened a can of Modelo while he chewed, watching her. He'd offered to buy their dinner, said he'd been paid on the ship, had the cash, but she'd insisted reflexively, wasn't going to have her itinerant brother spending his hard-earned money on her. Though now, as they watched each other in the uneasy light from the fire, she remembered he had more than she did, his bank account from Dad's life insurance sitting there earning interest while she'd blown hers on college, on a BS in environmental studies with anthro minor that was going to be exactly useless on the ranch.

"You have an education," he said, apparently reading her mind. "Use it. Venture out in the world. Don't retreat from it."

"I'm not retreating." She felt like a defensive girl, the two of them already falling into the old back-and-forth where he acted superior and she fumed.

"You must see the pattern," he continued, as if she hadn't spoken. "Grandfather Martin started it, moved up there to Panther Gap and barely left the place for fifty years. Then, after half a lifetime away, Dad ended up back there. Mom died there. Our uncles tried to get away but were drawn back when we were kids. Now you?"

She tried again to explain her reasoning, how it was the right thing to do, how she—they—couldn't blithely seek their own purpose in life while their uncles took care of the family's land. She was about to actually call him selfish when he interrupted.

"Why not sell it? You and our uncles would be wealthy."

For a moment she thought he was joking. She started to laugh. But he wasn't.

"You can't mean that. Do you know what would happen to the place?"

"The same thing that has happened, is happening, will continue to happen to every place in the world that doesn't enjoy the protection of the wealthy and powerful. I've seen it in the Sierra Madre."

"And that's okay?"

"No, it's a tragedy, it breaks my heart. The people gain nothing, and the land dies. Illegal logging is destroying jaguar habitat in Sonora. Land that's supposed to be set aside. The local Indians, people I know, are trying to stop it and they're getting killed." He stood quickly, couldn't sit still, couldn't contain what he was feeling. "There's nothing okay about that."

Anger was not an emotion she remembered seeing in Bowman very often. Even at the end, when he and their father were arguing, Bowman rarely showed real anger. Worried, distant, desperate to leave the ranch, but not angry. And even now he wasn't demonstrative, wasn't crushing his beer can or kicking the stack of firewood. But she felt his mind flare hot—the uncanny sibling connection they'd always had. There was bitterness too, and a heedlessness.

She let what he'd said settle, let out a breath she hadn't realized she was holding.

"Why not go back there, help stop what's happening?"

He gave her a quick glance and a rueful head shake, must be readjusting to the connection, her ability to read him. This was something he'd been thinking about. "I was a kid when I was in those mountains," he said. "I thought I could just show up, join their world. Mistook kindness for connection. I was presumptuous. But you're right. Maybe I could help."

"And if Panther Gap faced something similar?"

This time he reacted like she'd thrown something at him. Which she supposed she had.

"It's already an island," he said. "You know what that means, over time. As the country around is developed, disturbed, as the climate heats up—"

He was coming up with this on the fly, an ex post facto rationalization for rejecting his family and the magical place he used to love as a part of himself. She interrupted him.

"That's right, and we'll do what we have to. Save what remains. Whatever it takes."

She knew he was frustrated with her, thought she was missing the point.

"The problem you're presenting," he said, "is the Girard family running out of money to hold on to their property. You're willing to give up whatever you might accomplish in the world to go back and try to prevent that from happening. I'm not."

"You know damn well we weren't raised to think of Panther Gap as 'our property.'" Their father had deconstructed the Euro-American concept of land ownership for them at an early age. This land owns us, he'd say.

She was tempted to ask Bowman what he thought he was accomplishing here, crewing on a boat, sleeping in a hammock in the jungle. He was so wrong about all of this.

He sat back down on the log, the fight draining away from him.

"We have an obligation," she said. "The land's bigger than we are."

But he just stared at his beer can for a while before he looked up at her, his face sad.

"I'm sorry, Summer. I'm not going back."

62

When the current stopped flowing through the barbs in his stomach and leg, Bowman slumped in his chair and would've fallen out if not for the duct tape.

At the same time, Bowman stood and walked away from his body.

Summer was yelling at Bick, or Andrew, "Stop, he's sick, you're killing him!"

Bowman thought she might be right. Something was going on with his heart. Art the pilot held Summer, but he was frowning and Bowman got the impression he didn't approve of what Bick was doing.

"Bullshit, he's not sick, he's faking. The hospital in Costa Rica said he'd recovered."

Bowman was only so surprised that Bick had talked to the hospital. He'd worked undercover at the family's bank, would've seen the wire.

Bick leaned in close to Bowman's body, reached out with the plastic electric torture-gun, and lifted Bowman's chin.

"Are you faking, Sherman Carver?"

From behind Bick's back, Bowman said, "Nope," but they couldn't hear him.

"What did you call him?" Summer asked.

"That's what he told me his name was." Bick slapped Bowman's face, hard. "Wake up."

Out-of-body Bowman perceived the smack as a low-frequency vibration. He still couldn't understand why Bick hated him so much. Another slap, then Bick held up the electric gun and grinned, about to pull the trigger a third time. His cool had left him—rattled by Bowman's resistance, he was lashing out, indulging a hidden cruel streak. Enjoying this.

Summer shouted again and, as if to answer her, a loud bark sounded somewhere nearby in the house, and a tall man Bowman had never seen before ran through the door into the office holding a large pistol in both hands.

He pointed the pistol at Bick and shouted, "Drop it."

Art let go of Summer and grabbed for his AK where it hung behind his back, but before he could raise it, Uncle Jeremy stepped into the room with a military carbine, Marco beside him.

"Don't," he said. Art shrugged in surrender, handed his rifle to Summer.

Marco trotted over and began licking Bowman's face.

Bick and out-of-body Bowman spoke at the same time to the man with the pistol: "Who the hell are you?"

Instead of answering, he asked Summer if she was all right. She nodded, holding Art's AK in her cuffed hands, not sure what to do with it. Uncle Jeremy removed Bick's pistol from his shoulder holster, forced Art and Bick to lie prone on the floor so the new guy—Summer had called him Sam—could bind their wrists and ankles with their own zip ties.

Jeremy picked up the plastic gun from the floor where Bick had dropped it, realized what Bick had been doing to Bowman—he called it "tasing." For a moment Bowman was sure his uncle was about to kick the man in the head.

"Thanks, Uncle Jeremy. It's good to see you."

But his uncle couldn't hear him.

Summer found a pair of scissors in a desk drawer and cut her own wrists free as she hurried to Bowman's body, spectral Bowman stepping out of the way, not ready to allow his sister to pass through whatever he had become.

"He's alive, he's breathing," Summer said. "Pulse is faint." Sam was helping her cut Bowman free of the chair and lay him down on the floor.

Not dead yet, then, Bowman thought.

"He's fine," Bick said. He and Art had rolled into sitting positions on the floor in the center of the room, arms behind their backs, legs straight out in front of them. "This is ridiculous. You people need to focus." He was back in character, unfazed by the turn in his fortunes. "There's not much time. The cops are going to see what happened in the driveway and come busting in here with guns out and curiosity piqued. They'll find out about your grandfather's accounts. You don't want that."

This started a three-way argument among Bick, Summer, and Jeremy that only paused when Uncle Darwin limped in. Bowman had been worried about him, was glad to see Art really had re-dressed his wounded leg, though his uncle was pale, obviously in pain. He sat heavily in a desk chair and propped his injured leg on one of the boxes Bick had brought in. After a moment, he pulled Bick's open computer toward him and started examining it. Jeremy got in touch with someone at the sheriff's office and bought them "maybe an hour" with vague assurances that things were under control at the house, and he would make a copy of the security tape showing the woman who'd driven away after apparently murdering Sarge.

Summer described Bowman's objections and suggested they consider whether he might have a point. Maybe they should decline Grandfather Martin's money.

"Thank you," Bowman said, speaking only to himself.

Jeremy favored Bowman's approach, but Darwin didn't.

"We'll lose the ranch," he said.

Bick saw an ally in Darwin and rushed to back him up. "That's what the bank shareholders were after all along, why they sold you out to Salifano. They're going to jail but the debt's still there. You can't service it with your little cattle operation."

"Why not take the inheritance and report it?" Sam suggested. "The IRS has a voluntary disclosure program. You'll pay twenty percent plus back taxes, but you can repatriate the accounts."

"The guys in Switzerland are doing that already," Bick said. "They're not money launderers but they've been accumulating clean funds over the years in a special account. I don't know how much, but it should be enough to pay off your note and cover expenses for a while."

He checked the screen on the wall again, the police milling around at Sarge's house still making him nervous.

"You need to hurry. Once you claim the account, Art and I'll clear out. We'll fly Darwin to a hospital. Bowman too, if you want."

Summer sat on the floor with Bowman's body, which was laid out under a blanket next to Marco, his head resting on Summer's folded jacket. She clearly liked the sound of clean funds to pay off the ranch debt. Bowman saw what Bick was doing.

"There's more to it," Bowman said. "It's not all clean." He tried shouting, but no one reacted except Marco, who perked his ears and looked over in his direction.

Summer said, "All right, then."

Darwin pointed to the glass-topped scanner on the desk. "How do you use this thing?"

"It's automatic," Bick said. "You just put your hands on it."

Sam propped up Bowman's body into a sitting position, and Summer grasped a forearm in each hand, almost exactly as Bick had only a few minutes ago. Bowman tried to stop her, but he had no control over his body. She pressed his palms onto the scanner they'd set on his lap, cords stretched taut from the desk. A bright bar of light passed back and forth.

When Bowman's body was reclined again, Summer laid her own hands on the glass. Again the bar of light, and after a moment Bick's computer chimed.

"Congratulations," Bick said. "You're both who you're supposed to be."

Watching over Darwin's shoulder, Bowman saw a page materialize on the computer screen, with a message asking for wire instructions. Arrangements had already been made with the IRS, and the balance in the account was net of the penalty and back taxes. His uncle froze, and when Summer asked him what was wrong he said, "Nothing. It's almost twelve million dollars."

Bowman felt nauseated, which he knew was strange for a ghost, and decided he couldn't stay in the room any longer. As he walked out, he noticed Marco watching him with a perplexed expression. Bowman waved to the dog and made his way downstairs. He could barely feel the steps under his feet and the air had gone shimmery, the light from the wall fixtures dim, underwater.

He had failed completely. Worse than failed: by coming home he'd brought his hands to be scanned, allowing Summer and his uncles to claim the entire inheritance, which, he was sure, included more than the "clean" account. His family, already fortunate, had been made wealthy. They would keep the ranch. And a murderous prison gang would hunt them forever. Maybe this was Grandfather Martin's curse: the family would have to insulate themselves even further, they would have to hide, the old multigenerational paranoia confirmed and deepened. They would live the same way Martin had, probably forever, until they died out.

He'd never had a chance. Summer's determination to use the money to save the ranch she and the uncles had worked so hard to hang on to would never yield to Bowman's cursed-money arguments, their father's deathbed pronouncements of doom.

He stood at the top of the stairwell leading down into the tunnels. He should go down there, see what might happen. He was pretty sure he was dying. Maybe he would find the passage to the underworld. He thought of the were-jaguar he'd faced beneath Teotihuacan. It could be waiting for him here. This might be a special way people like him experience death. Or maybe this was how everyone dies.

There were no visions now to inspire him. He couldn't save himself with herbs and a kayak and a roll of hundred-dollar bills. There was only the descent into the tunnels. He would find the lake underground, the shining metal balls, the glittering stars in the stone roof of the cave.

But when he started down the steps, a jaguar was walking up. It was no were-jaguar. This was an animal pure, free of human perversion. A big male, like the one he'd seen first in his dreams as a boy, then later on the bank of the river in the Sierra Madre, a dozen times in the Yucatán and Belize and Costa Rica, each one a memory as vivid and real as any of his life—some had been visions, some the cat himself, some he couldn't say which.

The jaguar's face and huge front paws were soaked with blood from a recent kill. He knew this particular cat, from later in the Sierra Madre. They'd shared a branch in an ancient oak during a violent thunderstorm.

He looked Bowman in the eye and brushed past. The fur on his side was warm and rain-wet, the black-spotted orange rosettes undulating with his stride. He walked down the corridor toward the front entrance hall, leaving bloody paw prints on the stone flagging. He stopped and looked back. Not a threat, and not imploring either. Waiting for Bowman to make a decision. Bowman looked away. He worried what he might find if he descended into the tunnels. What sort of hell had been wrought, upon whom.

"What did we do?"

The jaguar didn't answer. He padded away, disappearing down the corridor. The tracks remained, dark red flowers painted on stone.

Bowman hesitated. He could go into the tunnel and find out what had happened, or he could leave the violence in the past and face whatever was coming next. Face whatever this animal from his dreams and his life wanted to show him. Neither option, he sensed, would be pleasant.

At the front door, he found the jaguar waiting like a gigantic house-cat, asking to be let out.

"You can't just walk through?"

He turned the doorknob and pulled the heavy door aside. The jaguar stepped out into pale moonlight.

Bowman followed.

63

Summer had to push Marco away because he kept resting his heavy head on Bowman's barely breathing chest. That the dog had decided to fall in love with her brother in one day was as unsurprising as it was annoying.

"Tilt his head back," Art the pilot said, referring to Bowman, not Marco. She and Art had developed a rapport that belied the preposterous, violent circumstances. She sensed he had skill as a healer.

"You need to support his neck," he said. "Roll up another jacket or something."

"I don't know what's wrong with him. He . . . his bladder let go."

"That's not unusual when you get tased. How's his pulse? Still steady?"

She checked again, nodded. So weak, though. She stood and found a clean towel in the bathroom down the hall, folded it under her brother's neck.

"I can help," Art said. "My kit's in the chopper."

Uncle Jeremy overheard this and said, "Forget it." He and Sam were hovering behind Darwin, looking over his shoulder at Andrew's computer screen.

"I know where it is," Sam said, and left the room, still carrying Jeremy's pistol, before anyone could stop him.

"You know," Andrew said, "it would make a hell of a lot of sense if you just untied Art and me. We're on your side."

Jeremy had threatened to duct-tape Andrew's mouth twice now, and Summer almost wished he would do it. Darwin had scheduled an $11.87 million wire to the modest checking account they kept at the local Whitespring community bank. It would land first thing in the morning, and some minds were going to be blown, but they'd all agreed with Andrew that they couldn't safely use First Denver Bank & Trust. Andrew had explained how Grandfather Martin had helped set the three shareholders up in legit banking when they wanted out of the life, and forty years later they'd betrayed him when Jake Salifano's people came sniffing around. Coveted the ranch. Had big plans, high-end resort development. Of course, Andrew took credit for stopping them, dropping dark hints about one shareholder having mysteriously disappeared after providing evidence implicating the other two.

Summer asked him why he was still pretending he hadn't planned to steal the accounts himself, and Andrew actually looked hurt for a moment, a flash of the man she'd known last year. Then he regressed to smug, amused, defended.

"Think of it this way, Summer: the bonus I expect from successfully completing this multiyear assignment is generous enough that I'd much rather accept said bonus than try to extort money from you and then be on the run from my employer for the rest of my life."

"Was it part of your multiyear assignment to date me?" she asked.

"Oh God no, that's what got us into all this trouble. Strictly against the rules. For good reason."

Darwin cleared his throat. Uncomfortable with the conversation. "There's a message. They're asking about multifactor security. For the other accounts."

"That's good," Andrew said. "I brought an iris scanner. We'll use that and long-form passwords to go with your handprints, and—"

"What other accounts?" she asked.

"The offshore accounts. I've never seen them, they'll be hidden, titled via shell entities scattered across various jurisdictions with protective secrecy laws. You'll be able to access them remotely, but you can't bring the money into the U.S."

"Andrew, what are you talking about?"

"Most of your grandfather's fortune. It's dark money, criminal provenance. I don't know how much, but it's going to be a lot. The Swiss custodian is tight-lipped by definition but I got the impression your grandfather gave them carte blanche to invest, given the distant time horizon. They're taking this whole thing seriously. Why they hired the security company I work for to look into the threats your grandfather warned them about."

"If it's criminal, why should we have anything to do with it? So you can get a bigger bonus?"

"Well, yeah, but it also has something to do with you all living more than another few weeks. Salifano's gang's not subtle, they'll torture you until you transfer the accounts, then they'll kill you."

"The money for the ranch is enough. So we give them the other accounts and they'll go away." This, she thought, might help to appease Bowman. As soon as he woke up. He was going to wake up. He'd started to twitch every few seconds. She wished Sam would hurry back with Art's medical kit.

"Summer. Hey." This was Andrew. He'd said something to her but she'd missed it.

"What?"

"Jake Salifano is not a rational criminal mastermind. He's as committed to destroying your family as he is to stealing the money, and he's not going away no matter what you give him."

"What do you know about Salifano?" Uncle Jeremy had been listening quietly, unhappily, but now he closed with Andrew, squatted down in front of him, eye to eye.

"He wasn't just some hit man," Andrew said, happy to show his superior knowledge of their family history. "He was a secret partner in a mob offshoot your grandfather screwed somehow back in the day, and he never got over it. All these years, even in prison, he's been searching for the Camboust fortune like it's the Lost Dutchman Mine. Now he controls this criminal gang. He is absolutely fucking dangerous, more than I'd realized." He twisted around to speak directly to Summer. "You have to hire sophisticated security, and the safest way to do that is through an offshore account. Don't use the money in the ranch account. You can hire my company, and you'd have the best, and don't worry, it won't be me, I'm retiring, and they wouldn't involve me after this mess anyway."

Uncle Jeremy looked thoughtful, even distracted. He turned to study the screens on the far wall. At Sarge's house, the ambulance had come and gone, leaving a forensics truck and a handful of police cruisers, the sheriff's blue Tahoe.

"They're not going to try anything with the police there," Andrew said, also looking at the screens.

"You agree with Andrew?" she asked. "Uncle Jeremy?" He nodded. "Darwin?"

Darwin had swiveled around in his chair to look at Summer. He nodded as well.

"Shit," she said. What had Grandfather Martin done to them? The others waited. She wished Bowman were conscious, but even if he were, this decision was hers.

"Shit," she said again.

64

When Sam walked into the office with Art's medical kit, Andrew was still trussed up, kneeling on the floor, but it struck Sam how he seemed to be in charge, barking instructions at Summer and the uncles. *Bring the laptop over here, get her iris scan, come up with a long password.* Jeremy held an electronic device, like a binocular with no objective lenses. He plugged it into some sort of hub, handed it to Summer. She looked into it.

Sam laid the kit beside Bowman, who was shivering violently enough that Sam worried he was starting to seize. Without thinking much about it, he walked over to Art with Summer's scissors and cut his legs free while the others were distracted. Art smiled reassurance and followed to kneel next to Bowman.

Summer saw what was happening and joined them. Sam pulled items from the bag on Art's orders while Summer applied a blood-pressure cuff. Eventually she reached around with the scissors and cut Art's hands free too. They started an IV saline drip and got an epinephrine infusion prepped. Bowman gradually quieted. Art turned to look at the others, Darwin typing on the laptop, arguing back and forth with Andrew, Jeremy hovering behind and looking over his brother's shoulder.

Art offered his hands and whispered, "You'd better handcuff me again or your uncle's gonna freak."

"He'll be all right," Summer said.

Sam glanced at Jeremy, but he wasn't paying any attention to them. He and Darwin and Andrew were bickering over something or other.

"What did I miss?"

Summer sat back and started explaining about the hidden offshore accounts, Andrew's argument that the group who'd tried to break in posed a long-term existential threat to the family, and her decision to take control of the accounts, a decision Sam had trouble accepting. She stopped midsentence.

The uncles and even Andrew had grown quiet, all staring at the laptop.

"What is it?" Summer asked.

None of them responded.

"Hey!"

Darwin stood unsteadily with Andrew's computer and carried it over, trailing cords, limping, a glassy uncomprehending look on his face. Turned the laptop to show Summer the screen, Sam and Art each taking a knee behind, looking over her shoulder. Three lists, eight accounts each. A total sum at the bottom. They all were shocked into silence. No gasp, no incredulous laughter.

"Now are you scared?" Andrew asked. "Now do you see why people are after you?"

Jeremy muttered something about needing to go for a ride. He checked the display on his burner phone, reached into Andrew's plastic suitcase and pulled out a night-vision headset, switched it on. He had Sarge's carbine on his shoulder, a handheld radio clipped to his belt.

"Now?" Summer asked. The stakes had been multiplied a thousandfold, and the danger along with them. Sam agreed that Jeremy taking off right then didn't sound like a good idea.

Jeremy read their faces and managed a half smile, looking pale, determined. "Trust me."

"Of course," Summer said. Jeremy did Sam the courtesy of looking for a response. Sam nodded.

Addressing both of them, he said to stay alert if they went outside, and to keep an eye on the screens while he was gone. He gestured toward the two AKs leaning against the wall near the door. "Use those if you have to." And he was off, Marco trotting after him.

"Can you please untie me?" Andrew was kneeling on the floor where they'd been accessing the accounts on the laptop. "I've been working for you, for your family, you all have to know that by now."

"No," Summer said, "you're working for you, for your goddamn bonus. You tortured my brother and you won't be forgiven for that." She'd told Sam and Art she wanted Art to fly Bowman and Uncle Darwin to a hospital. She would go with them. She hadn't mentioned what she wanted to do with Andrew.

"Okay," Andrew said. "But at least listen to me. This changes things completely. I had no fucking idea." He rolled to a sitting position and inched his way toward Summer, pulling with his heels and trying to drag his butt across the floor. Sam stepped in between but Andrew didn't get far before he gave up, frustrated, all bravado drained away.

"Summer, your whole family is going to have to become invisible. My company can help with that. You'll need foreign passports. It's called global citizenry, there's a super-elite class, people who share a healthy fear of kidnap and ransom, extortion, capricious law enforcement. Not CEOs or Silicon Valley plutocrats, I'm talking about the families of top drug lords, former dictators in exile, stateless Russian oligarchs, the underground one percent of the one percent. All of their money is offshore like yours. They exist in a parallel universe, living on giant yachts, private islands, luxury jets, a penthouse in Singapore, I've seen it, or I've had glimpses, life for these people is an international, anonymous, itinerant parade of invulnerability—"

She cut him off. "Andrew, shut up, we're not doing that. Don't be ridiculous."

"You have to. You have to leave this place, you're burned here."

"I said we're not doing that. Any of it. And we're definitely not leaving the ranch."

"Please don't be stupid!" Andrew shut his eyes, a theatrical effort to calm himself, though Sam thought he might not be faking. He also was afraid he might be right. Andrew opened his eyes and continued.

"Salifano will learn from his mistakes, he'll hit you again, much harder, when you're not expecting it. Even my outfit wouldn't be able to protect you if you stay here. You can buy property somewhere else. Buy a ranch in Alberta, buy one in Chile, one in Kenya, New Zealand, wherever. But you can't stay here."

65

2002

The organization behind the logging in the old forests had recently made it known in the region that whoever might happen to kill or capture him would receive a monetary reward. They'd started low, a modest price, much less than they could afford, because most people who lived in the northern mountains were poor. Still, rumors had circulated, what had happened on the Sirupa, whispers about the black magic that Bowman must have deployed against the missing men.

He still felt his own residual power, jittery and uncomfortable, something he didn't want. Other people, or some of them, could feel it too.

And so no one had tried him, and they'd raised the price.

Tonight, a man about his age had followed him from the cantina into the street. Bowman had noticed him inside, staring, and he knew he was there now, but he didn't turn around until the man called out. A generic greeting, in a belligerent tone. Testing. Bowman might be armed. Bowman watched his eyes. They weren't drunken, or crazed. They were careful. The man had heard some things, but he was brave, and hungry, and used to killing, and he took a few steps closer before he stopped and pulled a .32-caliber pistol from his boot.

Bowman thought it must be uncomfortable to carry a pistol, even a small one, in your boot.

When the bullet hit him in the chest it felt like someone had punched him, not very hard, and he didn't fall down. He stood still and blinked. He barely felt the second shot.

The two of them stared at each other for a long moment.

Shoot me again, goddammit. Get it over with.

"Otra vez," he said. *"Una vez más."*

But the brave man with the pistol was a little bit superstitious after all, and instead of shooting Bowman a third time he dropped his pistol in the dirt like it burned his hand. He backed away, walked backward all the way to the door of the cantina, and disappeared inside.

Bowman's chest began to ache. Since it seemed he wasn't about to die, he walked to the town's medical clinic. The bullets had entered between ribs and slid harmlessly past lungs, heart, arteries, veins, major nerves, and lodged under the skin of his back. The young doctor examined him quietly. He told Bowman that if this had happened in Mexico City, where he'd gone to school, he would call his colleagues, and they would all examine the wounds, try to understand what had happened. They would write a paper. His religious colleagues would be nervous, they would mutter darkly about inquiring with the Church. To declare a miracle. Or request an exorcism. But here, in the Sierra? The doctor shrugged. These things happen. It's usually the Indians, though. Never an American. He made two small incisions, removed the bullets, and gave Bowman a bottle of oral antibiotics.

He'd barely put his shirt back on when the local police chief entered with two heavily armed men and wouldn't let him leave the clinic. Bowman knew this man was paid by the same organization that had tried to have him killed, but the chief had been born and raised in the town and he was afraid now to murder the American who may or may not be a powerful warlock, but who surely had a number of formidable mountain families supporting him. He confined Bowman to a room in the clinic, and insisted a member of his family collect him and take him far away, preferably back to the U.S.

Bowman recited the phone number at the ranch, and the chief wrote it down.

He was pretty sure his family wouldn't have changed it, even after so many years.

Summer flew to Chihuahua, and drove to the town in the mountains, and asked around until she found the clinic. The fact that two police guards with rifles were posted outside his locked room gave some credence to the chief's dark hints about the awful fate coming for Bowman if he didn't leave Mexico *inmediatamente*.

In the room, three Tarahumara men sat in chairs with huge antique revolvers in their laps, smiling, as if they'd recognized her already.

Bowman opened his eyes and rose up from his bed and hugged her, thanking her for making the trip as if another six years hadn't passed them by. He'd grown even stronger, and a troubling residue of violence lay on his skin like an acrid oil. Beneath the weird strength and violence, a deep melancholy.

He introduced the three men in Spanish as they stood one by one and watched her with a friendly curiosity. They all walked out, one of the men in front, two following. The two police had already left.

A boy ran down the street, sandals slapping, eyes wide, headed for the leader of the Tarahumara guard detail. He whispered in the man's ear and as he did the man grew still. Bowman frowned, went to the man as the lanky boy sprinted away on other awful errands. They spoke low in a language Summer couldn't follow. The stillness passed from the guard to Bowman. Then rising anger, arcing like electricity to her mind. The violence she'd sensed, surging now. She stared, alarmed, her brother suddenly unfamiliar.

The Tarahumara man placed his hands on Bowman's shoulders, speaking fast, calming him. The heat of his anger receded, leaving an aching sadness.

In the car, Bowman was numb, hollowed out, like that bizarre wave of pent violence had scorched him on the inside. She tried to interrogate him: Why had he been shot, why was he so sad, and what was this terrible news from the boy? All he would say was friends had been murdered because of him. When she told him he would have to leave Mexico, he nodded and said that was probably best.

On the ten-hour drive to Hermosillo, she gradually managed to pry loose, in bits and pieces, through fits and starts, Bowman's story, or as much of it as she was likely to get. He reminded her she'd suggested the last time they were together that he come back and help his friends in the Sierra Madre. He'd eventually decided she was right, left the Yucatán to offer his service to several families who had been kind to him. The logging, it turned out, was sponsored by one of the drug gangs, and the situation had become untenable for the Tarahumara. Dozens had been murdered by outsider gunmen with no consequences for the perpetrators, so local leaders started looking for international assistance. Bowman had picked up a good bit of the Rarámuri language during his time there as a teenager, and while most of the Indians also spoke Spanish, Bowman's English, French, and German made him a valued interpreter. He became associated with a handful of locals who served as guides, and whose knowledge of the forest where their people had lived for hundreds of generations bordered on the supernatural.

He'd worked with these men for three years of relative quiet, helping to safely guide foreign scientists, media, politicians, and tourists in the forest. There'd been belligerent outsiders, some bullying violence, but nothing deadly until last month. He was translating for a pair of brothers, Tomás and Martimano, guiding a group of European Union scientists and a documentary film crew from Germany, a big international charity working with the Tarahumara to highlight threats to primary forests of global significance. They were driving to a campsite in one of the forests near dusk, rushing so they could set up camp before a line of thunderstorms overtook them. But a pickup truck was waiting, men with AK-47s, not locals. They were rounding up the group—it wasn't clear to Bowman what they planned, probably they would shoot the locals and ransom the foreigners, eventually shooting them too—when a fantastic storm hit, lightning and wind and heavy rain and hail, broken branches dropping out of the trees. The men with the guns saw they were losing control of the situation and started shooting, killing two of the film crew, and in the near-zero visibility the others ran into the forest, where Bowman and the two guides tried to gather them, calling to each other like scattered turkeys.

"The gunmen didn't follow right away, didn't want to leave the road during the storm. We headed deeper into the forest. Tomás and Martimano knew the way to a cliff with overhangs where the group took shelter. The three of us separated and waited in the forest nearby. We planned to intercept the gunmen if they showed up, lead them away from the others."

He stopped for a long while. Summer drove on through the night, thinking she knew where this was headed. She resolved not to point out to her brother that he was repeating their father's mistakes.

"I'd climbed a tree," he continued, reciting his story in a distant monotone. "It was a big strong oak, but the wind threw the branches back and forth like they were bamboo. The thunderstorms rolled through the forest one after another, and I knew the weather was protecting us, but the men with the guns would eventually come. I had no weapon. None of us did. The storms finally let up, and in one of the last big flashes of lightning, I saw that a male jaguar was lying on the same branch I stood on. He was soaked with rain, his huge head resting on his paws. Watching me."

"He wanted to eat you."

Bowman didn't respond. When she looked over, his face was turned away, looking out at the rocks and trees on the side of the road passing by in the headlights.

"I'm sorry. Was it like the were-jaguar, the one under Teotihuacan?" She'd meant this half-seriously, hoping to prompt the rest of his story, but it sounded patronizing even to her.

"No," he said. "He had no human component. Just Jaguar. A forest god. Or he could've been a regular jaguar, I don't know."

"So what happened?"

"I waited in the tree with Jaguar for the men with the guns. I don't think I could have slept without falling out, but I had dreams." He stopped again, she could feel his mind turning away from this part of the recollection. Couldn't bear it.

"Later in the night, something spooked the Europeans. They

panicked and left the cliffs. One man, an older biologist from Sweden, drowned in a river a half mile away."

"And the gunmen?" She asked this with some trepidation.

"They disappeared. All of them. Their truck was found empty, back at the campsite where we'd run away. We—Tomás and Marti and I—were accused of killing them, and the gang that had sent them promised revenge. What the boy told us back in town was both of my friends, and their families, were murdered last night by another group of gunmen."

He sank back into silence. Summer tried consoling him, but he hardly stirred. She kept talking, filled him in on the family, the ranch. She did this in part to beat back the quiet, to push against her brother's palpable heartache that was morphing into a profound hopelessness that frightened her.

She told him she'd lived at the ranch with Darwin and Jeremy for six years, and despite their best efforts, the endowment for the ranch had run out, forcing them to borrow money from their grandfather's old bank to start a limited cattle operation. When Bowman didn't react, she pressed on, explaining that restaurants in all the ski towns were looking for grass-finished beef from Colorado ranches, so they'd fenced off the valley's best grass and ran stockers in the summers, young steers that would gain weight and could be sold before the winter.

She reminded him he had some money he'd inherited from Dad sitting in a bank account. Of course she'd spent hers on school, but she'd taken over Darwin's role at their grandfather's charitable foundation and was accepting a modest salary. She tried to interest him in her work there, the new directions she was taking the foundation, supporting experiments in enlightened grazing practices, sustainable forestry, implementing some of these ideas on the Girard ranch. She told him it felt like she was making a difference. He didn't say anything. It was hard to tell if he was even listening.

She asked if he'd heard about the tunnel found recently at Teotihuacan, under the Temple of the Feathered Serpent. She glanced over, careful, unsure whether it was okay to bring this up. He looked at her, more interested now. Shook his head.

"It was like a diorama," she said, "a miniature landscape with

mountains, and pools of mercury. The Teotihuacans had stuck pow-
dered pyrite on the walls and the ceiling, so in torchlight it looked
like a sky thick with stars. Metal balls scattered around. Jaguar bones,
jaguar sculptures. The archaeologists think it was intended as a model
of the underworld. It's eighteen hundred years old, completely undisturbed all that time. How did you see that stuff? We weren't near
that temple, so I don't understand how you knew."

"The were-jaguar showed it to me," he said, apparently unsurprised by the discovery. "He wanted to take me there. I'm glad I
didn't go."

The flash of the camera for his passport photo seemed to startle him,
to wake him up. He blinked a few times, then looked at Summer
and said, "I can't go home with you."

She was almost relieved. For the past thirty-six hours he'd been
as tractable as a lamb, agreeing to ride with her to Hermosillo, sub-
mitting to the medical evaluation she'd insisted on, signing without
question all the paperwork she'd brought, tolerating the tedious
passport renewal process in the U.S. consulate. She'd already called
a psychiatrist she knew in Denver and made an appointment for him
the day they were scheduled to fly back.

"Well," she said. "I can't force you."

"So I don't need this passport."

"Yeah, you do. You don't have to come home but you do have
to leave Mexico. Where do you want to go?"

He thought about this, apparently for the first time.

"I want to go back in time. To the Pleistocene."

"You and Dad both. But failing that?"

He looked like he was about to object to the comparison with
their father, but must've decided it wasn't unwarranted. They
walked together out to the waiting area in the consulate. Sat side
by side in plastic chairs.

He turned and looked at her, wide awake and almost smiling.

"South, I guess."

66

2009

A great horned owl flew up from the dark valley and lit on the roof of the house in the rocks. The hunting was no good near the house tonight. There'd been too much activity, humans coming and going, and the usual rodent scurryings in the brush were quiet. Why was he here? He watched the noisy flying machine down the hill, quiet now, and the human walking toward it. Then, closer, more humans, a male and a female carrying another male that was unconscious or dead. They laid him on his back on a low stone wall. The male went back inside, leaving the female speaking softly to the dead male.

The owl didn't enjoy the sound of humans speaking. He raised his head to the night, several bats fluttering almost inaudibly overhead. The bats were prey, but he perceived their erratic flight as something beautiful, thinking, *The last bat now cruises in his sharp hieroglyphics.*

That's not right, he thought. *That's from a poem.*

Something was off.

He listened to the human again, the female. *She's speaking to me.*

The owl dropped from his perch and set his wings in a steep glide.

Summer's face, dim in the moonlight, looked down at him, saying words he still couldn't understand. The pain of waking forced a moan from his lips. He wasn't quite in control of his body. His jeans were wet, clammy.

"Bowman? No, hold still. Don't try to move."

"I was an owl. I watched you and someone else carry me out here."

She reached down and kissed him on his forehead. "God, Bowman, I've missed your crazy bullshit. I knew bringing you outside would wake you up. We're going to fly you to the hospital. Art's prepping the helicopter."

"I was angry. I walked out of the office—" His memory was filling in. "There was a jaguar in the house."

"Of course there was."

He tried to relax but the jaguar's bloody face and paws filled his mind. They'd stood together in the center of a meadow while thousands of Others spun around them in the moonshadows at the edge of the forest. Alecto was there, and the wolf pup from when he was a boy. He couldn't remember clearly. Wasn't sure what it meant.

He raised himself on an elbow. From there, with Summer helping, he sat up on the edge of the rock wall, rested the soles of his boots on the flagstones. Dizzy, light-headed. Deep breaths.

"I'm fine. I don't need to go to the hospital. I'll rest up a couple days and get out of your way." He was almost certain this was what he should do. He would go off-grid again. Back to the Osa, the palm trees in the cove.

He eased to his feet, took a tentative step, and fell into Summer. She stumbled and grunted with pain but held his weight, got him seated again. "Are you okay?" he asked.

She laughed. "Me? Andrew shocked you with a Taser, twice." She sat down next to him, kept a hand on his shoulder like he might topple over. "You had a seizure. You're flying with Art to the hospital if I have to tase you myself. And I don't want you to get out of the way. Where do you think you're going? You can't leave now."

"I'm going back to Costa Rica. Coming here was a mistake. I accomplished nothing."

Again, though, as he said this, the ambiguous vision with the jaguar and the Others in the meadow took shape in his mind. Something about that, something important. He would remember later.

She let go of his shoulder, folded her arms. Regarded him without speaking. All of this was so familiar to him, his sister's repertoire of persuasion unchanged in two decades.

"You said you came to stop me from accepting our grandfather's money, you said Dad made you promise to be here."

Whenever Summer began an argument by reciting something he'd said, he knew he had to be careful in how he responded.

"You think I came home for some other reason." A distant moaning drifted up from the valley, mournful, out of place. After a moment he remembered the cows he'd encountered earlier. "There's money for the ranch now, will you get rid of the cattle?"

This seemed to amuse her. She must think he was channeling their father, predictably complaining about the cows.

"I haven't had time to think about it. Maybe not all of them. We're using rotational grazing, temporary fencing, we keep them away from the water. They're not hurting anything. I'll show you."

He recalled the swarms of biting flies at the lake, the stench, the noise, all so different from when they were young. But he wasn't ready to argue with his sister about cows.

The upper courtyard lit up. Darwin had stepped through the door and was limping toward them. He carried one of the AK-47s slung on his shoulder.

"How's the leg?" Bowman asked.

"Hurts like hell. We thought you were dying."

"Not yet."

"We need to get to the chopper. I'll tell Art to come back up and help with Bowman." Darwin turned to go, held up his walkie-talkie. "Jeremy says the sheriff drove up and saw the bodies and now a whole convoy of police are on their way in."

"He's up on the ridge?" Summer asked.

"Yeah, he rode Star up there. Sam's bringing Andrew out. He's making him drag along on his butt with his legs tied." Darwin waved and set off down the slope toward the helicopter.

"Where did Sam come from?"

"He just showed up in East Canyon," Summer said. "Yesterday, or two days ago, I guess. He's a lawyer."

Bowman was digesting that unlikely information when Sam himself and Bick appeared in the courtyard. Bick inched along, sending what sounded like an unbroken stream of curses toward this Sam person, who, based on his body language, was enjoying Bick's predicament more than the situation strictly called for. He carried the other AK on his shoulder and held the same pistol he'd brandished when he'd burst in earlier to save Bowman from the Taser.

Summer called out to Sam, "If the police are on the way, maybe you should go ahead and cut his ankles loose?"

"Up to Bowman, I think," Sam called out. "Glad you're awake," he added.

"Thanks," Bowman said. "He did save our lives."

"Finally," Bick said. "A little appreciation. Saved your lives and, by the way, made you the wealthiest family in Colorado."

Bowman frowned at that, but he didn't know much about money. Sam pulled from his belt an enormous bowie knife that must have come from Uncle Jeremy's collection and cut the zip tie from Bick's ankles. Bick stood without further comment, wrists still cuffed behind his back, and marched stolidly down the hill in the dark, Sam following.

"I'll be back up in a minute," Sam said.

When they'd gone, Summer turned back to Bowman. He could feel her building a case, working up reasons why he should agree to stay at the ranch.

"We had to take custody of Grandfather Martin's offshore accounts, and Jeremy agrees with Andrew that the people who're trying to take the money from us are dangerous. They have some old grudge against Martin and they're determined to destroy the family. So yeah, we are all in danger, like you said. Like Dad said."

"You can hide out in Panther Gap. Our family has done it for three generations."

"Maybe," she said. "Andrew insists we can't be safe here anymore, he says we should use the money to disappear, live on yachts, travel in foreign countries."

"I have trouble imagining that."

"I do too. We'll stay here, and I want you to stay with us. You have to help us decide what to do."

"Uncle Jeremy will figure out how you can stay safe."

"Not what I'm talking about. It's more than survival. We're being given this fortune at a historical hinge-point. Everything we were raised to care about is being destroyed."

Where was she taking this? She seemed to be struggling with it herself.

"You think you could use the accounts," he said. "To try to change things."

"*We* could. I *know* we could. I can't do it without you. Think about it, Bowman, the irony. It's too delicious to pass up. We'll take what our grandfather did and turn it around, use it against him and the people like him, the people who have all the power, they've been plundering the world for hundreds of years, amassing wealth like it's their—"

"Thousands of years."

"Thousands, then. That's not the—"

"It's too big. So much bigger than greedy rich people, or capitalism, Western culture, industrialization. You can't change it with money."

Sitting beside him on the rock wall, she reached out and grabbed his hand. Squeezed it.

"You didn't see the offshore accounts." She shuddered with something like horror. "It's so much money it's not even money."

Bowman didn't know what to say to that. Wasn't sure what she meant. He'd spent years searching for a meaningful gap between humanity's capability to destroy and exploit on the one hand, and its heedless compulsion to do so on the other. But he'd never found one. There wasn't anything you could do about it.

"What you're saying you want to change has been in place since the Promethean leap, since before the first African diasporas. Over the past hundred millennia, humans have conclusively demonstrated our collective inability to restrain ourselves in any meaningful way over a meaningful period of time. When you stand back, the whole of human history looks like the inexorable fall of a river toward the sea."

"Not always."

He smiled at her quick-draw disagreement, the old reflex.

"No, not always," he said. "But counterexamples only prove there's a choice to be made. That's why it's tragic. You look at that river of human history and you see these beautiful eddies, backwaters, big oxbow lakes, but the river flows on down."

He heard her breathing catch. She paused.

He waited.

"Then let's make an eddy," she said.

For a while, neither of them spoke. The noise of the helicopter warming up rose and fell with the wind. The eastern sky had grown pale, a false dawn. Bowman was not optimistic that the Camboust-Girard-St. John family could break free of their niche, that they would choose well. But he supposed they could try.

Summer had let go of his hand and now she stood in front of him, forcing him to tilt his head up to see her face in the dim light from the house.

"When you let yourself get shot in Mexico, in the Sierra Madre, I should never have left you. You were trying to change things and you'd done something extreme, maybe something you regretted, and it didn't even make any difference. It backfired, got your friends killed. You'd given up, and I didn't know what to do with you. I'm sorry. But now we've been handed this tool, this . . . sledgehammer, right before the end. We have to use it."

We are at the end, he thought. New forces had been unleashed by the stresses and dislocations of the late Anthropocene, destructive gods whose power dwarfed those who'd come before. The catastrophic river of humanity's adventure on the planet suddenly a cataract, a Niagara. Only the most radical, subversive acts would make Summer's eddy.

He saw the jaguar, his bloody face and paws.

Was that what his sister wanted? He tried to see her mind, but was still too weak.

He'd given up any real hope, so long ago.

She reached out, a strong hand gripping his shoulder again. "You know what Uncle Jeremy says about despair."

He felt his sister catching him as he fell, though neither had moved. "I don't recall him talking about that."

"He says when you despair you're just admitting you fell for the happy horseshit in the first place."

67

A raft of cumulus clouds moved in from the west, obscuring the moon and forcing both Sam and Andrew—or Bick, Sam still didn't know which name to use—to step carefully along the path down to where Art was starting the helicopter.

"Thank God you didn't bring the flashlight like I suggested," Andrew said. "We might actually be at the chopper by now, and you could scurry back up to help bring Bowman down so we can get the hell out of here before the multi-jurisdictional police force swarms the place."

"Hang on a minute. Wait here." Sam had refused Andrew's flashlight because he felt it would make them too easy a target, and now he thought of something. He turned and walked back up the path, ignoring Andrew's declaration that he wasn't going to wait here or anywhere else and he was going to keep walking and Sam could shoot him in the back if he wanted, and so on.

At a pile of tall stones leaning together below the courtyard, he worked the pistol under his belt in the small of his back next to Jeremy's bowie knife. Jeremy had fetched the knife for him from a trunk inside the French doors before they'd crept up the steps toward the office, obviously on impulse, a tongue-in-cheek gift for the putz who doesn't carry a pocketknife. The plan had been to wait outside the door until they could assess who was in there, who was armed, etc., then Jeremy would step in first and neutralize the pilot—that was the word he'd used—but Sam had charged ahead without thinking when he'd heard Summer yelling. Jeremy had so far declined to berate him for this breach of tactics.

He felt around in a natural crevice in the stones, found Jeremy's rifle where he'd hidden it before they entered the house. He found the power switch for the scope, switched it on, checked for snipers underneath trees on the steep slope above, or hiding in the rocks to the north.

Nothing.

He hoped he was channeling his fear into Jeremy-style tactical awareness. Those offshore accounts had spooked him. He'd seen numbers like that in his practice—multinational corporate tax returns, major bond issues—but he'd never seen twenty-four numbers like that, all stacked up together, controlled by a single family. He wondered what that kind of power would do to you. He'd seen something in Summer's posture. There was shock, and a little fear, but the wheels were already turning.

And Andrew was right about one thing: In order to use those accounts, the family was going to have to internationalize their lives and disappear. You couldn't do anything with accounts like that in the U.S. If they were very, very careful, they might be able to launder a tiny fraction each year, giving up 50 percent, but even then it would be a risk. Eventually, accounts that size were going to attract unwelcome attention.

He found Andrew with the scope, saw he was a good hundred yards ahead. The crosshairs on his back made Sam queasy despite the fact that he disliked the man. He made sure his finger wasn't near the trigger. The second AK-47 was hanging from his right shoulder, so he slung Jeremy's rifle on his left and retrieved the pistol from his waistband, where, along with the bowie knife, it was pulling down his shorts despite his tightened belt. He caught up with Andrew, who laughed when he noticed the rifle.

"What are you going to do with that? You look ridiculous carrying all those guns. Have you ever even shot before?"

"Not much," Sam admitted.

"You also don't seem like a serious contender for the affections of the lovely Summer Girard."

"And you are?"

"Obviously not. Where'd you come from anyway? The family usually uses Knight and Armstrong in Denver, but you're East Coast."

Sam didn't answer, annoyed he could tell that.

"And I doubt any of the Knight and Armstrong attorneys would come charging blind into a room waving around a Mark 23 like it's a fucking ham sandwich. Not in the job description. You're incredibly lucky Art didn't shoot you."

"I know how to use this." Sam held the pistol down by his leg. The two rifles bounced against his hips with each step, and the hilt of the bowie knife dug into his lower back. He did feel a little ridiculous, like a twelve-year-old boy arming himself against zombies.

Andrew walked ahead to the helicopter, where Darwin and Art were preparing the cargo area behind the seats to transport Summer's brother. They worked in near-darkness, Art switching on his dim headlamp only intermittently, which Sam felt confirmed his decision not to use a flashlight. The engine was running but the rotors weren't turning yet. As he walked under them he noticed Darwin's face was lit from below by an illuminated signal meter on his walkie-talkie. Jeremy's voice, scratchy and turned up loud: *I'm not going to make it in time.*

"Then we're leaving," Andrew said. He turned and reached his hands down to the bottom corner of the open front door of the helicopter. With a quick upward jerk he popped off the plastic zip tie Sam had applied earlier.

"What's going on?" Sam asked.

"Jeremy's on his way down but the state police are too close," Darwin said.

"Which means time's up," Andrew said. "Art, let's go. Uncle Darwin, get in if you want a ride to the ER. Offer's still good."

But instead of jumping into the pilot's seat, Art walked around the nose of the chopper to stand close to Andrew and Sam.

"Bowman was seizing, Bick. I don't know what's wrong with him, but if he dies before they get him to a doctor you're looking at manslaughter."

"And if we're arrested before we can take off? What are we looking at then?"

"I'll go talk to them," Sam said, surprising himself. "You guys run up and help Summer bring Bowman down. I'll stall the cops until Jeremy gets there."

He handed the AK and the knife and Jeremy's pistol to Darwin and, once he got himself oriented, jogged in what he hoped was the right direction. He found that if he didn't stare directly at the ground in front of his feet he could see better.

Jeremy's rifle bounced on his shoulder, so he unslung it and held it against his chest. Was this called port arms? He'd seen a dozen old war movies where men marched with their rifles like this. A rock wall loomed and he stopped. Using the night-vision scope, he found the mouth of the driveway forty yards to his right.

In the deeper dark of the rock trench, he slowed. Stopped, listening. No blue flashing lights yet, though Jeremy had said the police vehicles had arrived at the switchback turn. He used the rifle scope again to look ahead, seeing that there was a final curve in the trench that he didn't remember from his walk up with Jeremy and Summer. That was good, he would be able to intercept the police at a spot where they couldn't see the helicopter take off.

He held the rifle at port arms again and walked on. The driveway was dark, too dark to see the ground even in his peripheral vision, but the gravel surface was even, and he could orient himself by the lighter belt of sky overhead and keep from walking into the walls on either side.

As he walked he rehearsed what he would say to the police, or the sheriff, whoever, something along the lines of, *My name is Sam Hay and I'm an attorney for the family. Deputy Jeremy St. John is on his way and he asked me to reassure you that everyone is fine and the intruders were stopped by the heroic intervention of two employees of a security company hired by a third party to protect the family. Deputy St. John wants us to wait here until he arrives so he can escort you to the house. He's been riding along the ridge guarding the property and is reasonably certain no more hostiles are on the property.*

He hoped that last bit was true.

Something made a noise in the dark ahead. Still no blue lights, no flashlights or police radios. Just a scuffing sound in the gravel. He listened. Nothing. He raised the rifle and scanned left to right. There, up against the right-hand wall, two human figures.

Several things happened at once. A fast *clip-clop clip-clop* approached from behind. Jeremy yelled, *Sheriff's Department! Stand down now!* Two flashes appeared in front of one of the figures in the scope. And Sam was punched twice in the stomach.

More shouting. Jeremy identifying himself, "This is Deputy Jeremy St. John of the Mirador County Sheriff's Department, hold your fire, goddammit!"

Sam understood he was lying on his back in the gravel. A shape loomed above him, impossibly huge, snorting, stomping, the horse, then a cool wet nose touched his, Marco. Licking his face. Jeremy called his name. Someone was saying over and over, "It was a good shooting, Deputy. He was pointing that rifle at us. It was a good shooting."

He was being lifted up. A stab of hot twisting fire erupted in his abdomen and shot through his chest, back, spiking into his head. He moaned. Couldn't help it. Jeremy saying, Tell Sheriff Sartoris to call Mercy Regional, they have patients inbound, one's a friendly fire incident, abdominal gunshot wounds.

More jostling, hoofbeats, the pain flaring and spinning, a living thing detached to swirl around him, and then a cold washing wetness in his belly that was worse than the pain itself.

68

2010

Bowman had insisted on using his bow drill, but he was out of practice, and Summer tried to be patient, to maintain a level of seriousness that Bowman was implicitly asking for. Tried and failed. Complained out loud she should've brought a book and a flashlight. She was relieved to hear him laugh. He hadn't been laughing much. Finally a tendril of gray smoke lifted past his face in the twilight, and a moment later he'd managed to ignite the tinder at the base of the signal fire.

He stepped away from the reaching flames and sat beside her cross-legged on the familiar flat stone outcrop. As the fire grew, roaring and crackling, hot on their faces, she watched her brother sidelong, wondering if he would hear the old voices.

So many things from their past had been resurfacing.

Yesterday Apryl Whitson had used the phone number Summer had given her a year ago: Rice was in a Mexican jail, and Apryl had stumbled into something she wouldn't describe except to say she still had trouble believing it was real. She was driving up to Whitespring next week so they could talk about it in person.

Darwin was in New York, had been since last fall, but he'd surprised everyone when he'd reinvested the proceeds from the sale of his and Jeremy's alfalfa fields in a building in downtown Durango and announced he was opening a restaurant. Jeremy was still a deputy with Sheriff Sartoris and lived at the ranch, where he was head of a vastly expanded security apparatus. He'd been asked about running for sheriff when Sartoris retired and he said he was thinking about it. As sheriff, he said, he could lock down family security even tighter. They all knew Jake Salifano's gang wouldn't be the last criminal organization to find out about the family's dark money, and not the last to try to take it by force.

At Bowman's urging, Summer had sold off all the cattle and pulled up the fencing in Panther Gap. While they were at it, they'd also removed the remaining boundary fence with the Weenuche reservation and told the tribe they were welcome on the land, asking only respect. She'd hired an executive director for the family foundation, and now she spent her time researching ways to deploy the offshore accounts in the service of whatever scheme she and Bowman eventually came up with. They'd given themselves two years to establish security and develop a plan. She'd been traveling: Central and South America, Africa, Indonesia. There were places in the world where the powerful were again inserting themselves, looking ahead to the coming disruptions, securing resources in advance. A creeping postcolonial imperialism. Summer was feeling around for pinch points, places where the accounts could be leveraged. She'd come to understand that the almost complete invisibility of Grandfather Martin's fortune multiplied its power.

Bowman heard the voices in the fire, but he let them wash over him, knowing now they were untranslatable music, not mysterious lyrics. He faced the flames but he was looking out into the night, through the Old Ones' notch in Rosewater Butte to the ancient signal site on Smokehouse. Where he'd stood with Jeremy's flashlight twenty-two years ago today, relaying Summer's ambiguous signal.

An answer was finally coming back. A fire burned brightly there, thirty-six miles away. To the west, another fire blazed on Comb Ridge.

He flew up into the night sky. More fires burned in the south, a line of signal fires from far into Mexico, tracing the jaguar's trail of carcasses, the broken bones dry and moldering in the desert. An urgent warning from the distant past, from the near future.

"Bowman."

His sister. Sitting beside him. He wrenched himself from his vision. "What?"

"Where did you go?"

"I'm here."

For a year, he'd doubted the accounts Summer was so sure of, those numbers flickering on a computer screen, their power and their curse passed down from Grandfather Martin, transforming Bowman into a plutocrat in possession of exactly the kind of power he'd dismissed, denigrated, fought against. He suspected such massive concentrations of notionally material wealth would soon be rendered irrelevant, burned to cinder in what was coming. But until then, were there ways to marshal that power, to use the sledgehammer as Summer hoped?

The rich and powerful people and institutions, companies, governments, they were smart, and they knew as well as anyone what was coming. With climate breakdown as the accelerant, they would lash out preemptively, deploying their wealth, technologies, militaries, weaponry, exploiting whomever they need to exploit, destroying whatever they need to destroy, all to prolong their comfort, convenience, and ultimately their existence.

Summer saw his grin.

"What?"

"Macbeth," he said.

She was used to his obscure pronouncements and she waited for the explanation.

"To be thus is nothing."

"But to be safely thus," she finished for him. "You're channeling Grandfather Martin."

"That's what I thought was funny."

"It's not funny. It's horrifying."

"I guess it's both," he said. "Do you remember when Dad told us about the cave in South Africa? The false saber-tooth? I think he got it from Chatwin's book."

"Yeah. I read C. K. Brain in college, and Dart, Vrba. That's where Chatwin got it. His version's more metaphor than science. Dad called it the Great Unshackling. One of the major discontinuities in the history of life on this planet. I think I asked him about beavers. What does that have to do with anything?"

"Beavers!" he said. "I'd forgotten that."

As their father had told it, paleontologists dug up millions of years of sediment from the floor of Swartkrans Cave, and once they'd analyzed their findings, arranged them according to strata, they marveled at the story told. From the oldest levels at the bottom, every layer contained the broken bones of animals, the remains of prey left by whatever formidable predators had lived in the cave. More than half of the bones they found were of primates—our ancestors and relatives—and there was some reason to suspect that the predators were large cats of the now-extinct genus *Dinofelis*, and that these cats may have specialized in killing primates.

This arrangement continued through the ages, through the layers of deposition for hundreds of millennia until, suddenly, in the upper levels of the dirt floor of the cave, there was charcoal, and hominid artifacts, and charred bones of *Dinofelis*. Then the great cat was gone.

Ancestors had risen up against the Beast, fought it to the death with fire and spear. The Promethean leap: the universe gone topsy-turvy in a heartbeat. For the first time, a species had broken out of its ecological niche, the inescapable prison that had held it and every other species that ever existed. With *Dinofelis* gone, a spectacular feedback loop ensued as hominid brainpower suddenly multiplied, small bands of men and women embarking on their first wide-awake journeyings on a wild earth. Africa first, then the great African diasporas followed, people making their way into every habitat on the planet. Leo had believed that was the apogee, when *Homo sapiens* became its most peculiarly beautiful, magnificent self.

Summer had asked their father whether contemporary beavers look back with pride on the day when an ancestor discovered the damming of water, calling it a great moment in the history of life on the planet, the one great breakthrough in niche modification. . . .

"Dad loved that stuff," she said now. "*Homo sapiens* becoming itself by suddenly transforming into the ultimate hunter, changing the world forever through courage, ingenuity, small-group cooperation. The good old days, before the invention of agriculture, and sedentary lifeways, cities, overpopulation, all the other mess of civilization."

"Well, I think it's about to happen again. Another reversal."

"What?" She was smiling at him, and he felt the old bond, the back-and-forth. "Humanity gets put back in its box? The cats win this time?"

"Not the cats. Something bigger."

"So what do you want to do, try and stop it?"

"We can't stop it."

They waited on the cool stone. The fire grew hotter, throwing sparks into the night that gathered around them. Together, as if they'd agreed, they turned to face east, looking over the darkened country, the warmth on their backs now. It was a while before her brother spoke again.

"You know he's out there."

"I know," she said.

"What do you plan to do if he doesn't leave?"

"I have no idea."

Sam would have realized what they'd done, she thought. Or, more precisely, what Uncle Jeremy had done, and the rest of them had reluctantly learned to live with. It had been an utterly surreal experience, chilling and nightmarish, nothing she'd ever want to repeat: your mortal adversaries, along with all of their associates, suddenly disappear, like it's the Rapture and they were the Chosen.

The negotiated price was, on the one hand, head-spinning. On the other, it had consumed only two of the smaller accounts.

Uncle Jeremy had said not to worry about Sam making trouble for them. Sam's solid, he said.

Her fire-blind eyes adjusted to the night, but it was too dark now to see the road, the place where Sam would be parked.

As she watched, the sky to the east filled in with stars.

And in the southeast, the dark bulk of Rosewater Butte looming. . . .

She gasped. Reached out, grabbed her brother's arm.

"Bowman."

"What?"

Her eyes watered, staring at the impossible. A bright orange warning that burned in the dark.

"Do you see it? Look."

He didn't reply, but she knew. Of course he saw it. He'd seen it all along.

69

Sam sat on the hood of his rental car, two beers into a six-pack of Sierra Nevada. The bonfire on the ridge to the west flared against the last of the afterglow.

He didn't remember the flight in Art's helicopter, but Summer had flown with him in an air ambulance from Mercy Regional to the Level 1 trauma center in Colorado Springs. In the ICU she had kissed his cheek and said goodbye, and he'd been prepped for emergency surgery. He hadn't seen her since. Six months with a colostomy bag and three follow-up surgeries in D.C., and he never got a bill for any of it. When he checked with his insurance company, they had never been contacted. The hospitals only would say his bills had been fully paid.

In March, when he was recuperating from his final surgery, he'd received his first and only communication, postmarked in Denver: a handwritten note thanking him for helping the family through a tough couple of days, wishing him a quick recovery and no more surgeries, and warning him to forget about the family. Beneath Summer's signature, *Hello Sam* and *Hope you're back on your feet soon* and *Try to stay out of trouble from now on* from Darwin, Bowman, and Jeremy. At the bottom of the card, the name of a bank in Grand Cayman, an account number, and a password hint: *Jeremy's dog.*

It was, after all, a get-well card.

He'd told Mac there was no way he could keep the money, and Mac had laughed.

"What the hell are you going to do with it, then? You can't find them to give it back. If you try to give it to charity the feds will swarm you like hornets. Leave it there," he'd said. "You and I can fly down once a year and spend the interest."

He'd resigned from the firm in May and dropped the asking price on his house to fair market value. Told Mac the money from Summer had nothing to do with it. He was moving out West. Arizona, maybe. He was pretty sure he wouldn't mind the heat.

Two months ago Mac had emailed him a link to an online news report with the message, *Meet me at Orinoco's tonight, eightish.* He opened the link. There'd been a sudden, incredibly ruthless gang war. More of a slaughter than a war. The entire leadership structure of a notorious prison gang, and two-thirds of the membership, inside and outside prison, had been obliterated in a three-week coordinated attack by what appeared to be the combined soldiers of at least two Mexican cartels, an outlaw motorcycle gang, and various associated street and prison gangs. A few arrests had been made, but law enforcement agencies were having trouble generating a lot of outrage.

At the bar, Mac's first comment was, "What a coincidence." His second was, "I told you they were fucking scary." His third was, "You better be glad they're on your side." A number of martinis and old-fashioneds followed. Sam had never told Mac about the scale of the offshore fortune the family now controlled, or his suspicion that they would try to do something drastic and subversive with it. Before they left the bar, though, he did confess his infatuation with Summer had only grown, that he was still trying to find her. Mac told him he was a fool.

Not that he had much of a chance. She'd resigned as director of the charitable foundation her grandfather had set up, and no one he contacted—the new director and trustees of the foundation, college classmates, local business owners—had any idea where she was or what she was doing. He'd left messages for Jeremy with the sheriff's office in Whitespring, all ignored.

Yesterday he'd flown to Durango, spent the night at the Strater, and this morning he'd driven to the ranch entrance. He'd knocked on the door of the caretaker's house. The guy who came to the door said he'd moved there in February. He'd bought the house and twenty acres, got a pretty good deal, he thought. He didn't know much about the land on the mountain. He'd heard some company from out of state had bought it.

Sam knew this friendly, down-to-earth fellow, who said he "hailed" from northern Nevada, was almost certainly an employee of the family, or of a security company hired by the family. Maybe even Andrew's company. Almost certainly he was armed and well trained. He would pass along Sam's intrusion, his curiosity. The pictures from the hidden cameras would confirm who he was. He'd resisted the impulse to wink at the Nevada man as he made apologies for bothering him.

From the caretaker's house, Sam had driven along the eastern boundary of the property and parked next to the POSTED sign he'd ignored before and hiked all the way up to the canyon. He carried enough water this time, but he tired more easily than he had before the shooting, and he stopped often to rest, hoping for another coyote encounter. He made it to the grove of old cottonwoods and entered the canyon. The AP village was there, but the elk skull had disappeared and new stones had been piled at the edge of the alcove, blocking any view of the door leading to the tunnels through the mountain. The newly placed stones appeared ancient already, blending into the old stonework and the canyon itself. After resting awhile in the shade, a meditative interlude among the silent stones, he'd returned to the road and driven to the gravel pullout where he and Mac and Melissa had camped one year ago.

Sitting on the car with his beer in the cooling desert evening, he felt liberated, relaxed, his expectations modest. He hadn't known it at the time, but the last shred of hope he'd had of reconnecting with Summer and the family had drifted away when he'd seen the stones blocking the door in the alcove. Something about that smooth, unclimbable wall, with no prospect of a knotted rope thrown down.

Now he was content to watch their fire on the ridge. This was close enough, after all.

Epilogue

2011

In the early spring, on their way to visit the stone mounds where Anna and Leo and Grandfather Martin were buried, they found a fresh coyote carcass. Marco had run ahead and was sniffing at it, tail curled upward in his usual expression of intense engagement.

The coyote was laid out on its back, the abdomen opened below the rib cage.

Summer let Dove nibble a tuft of dry bunchgrass while Bowman dismounted to squat beside the carcass, the new paint gelding—Summer couldn't pronounce his name—nervous at the scent. He spoke to the horse, calming him in a language Summer didn't recognize.

Bowman found a stick and poked around in the coyote's abdominal cavity.

"The heart and liver are gone." He turned the coyote over. With his knife, he made a cut through the skin across the back of the neck, peeled the skin partway down the coyote's back. "Three deep punctures behind the shoulders."

Then he stood and scanned the monstrous sky of the Colorado Plateau.

When they were kids, he used to tell her he could pull his eyelids back over the top of his head and watch the whole sky, all at once.

She humored him for as long as she could.

"I know what you're doing," she said. "Stop it."

"I'm looking for her."

"I know, but it's weird. Your eyes go back in your head and it looks like you're having a fit."

"You can do it too."

"I don't want to do it."

More than a year and a half had passed since that night he'd decided not to walk into the tunnels under the house, and instead had followed the jaguar's bloody tracks to the door. His memory of what happened next had filled in over time. The cat had led him to an open grassy place surrounded by forest, a meadow in Panther Gap he'd never seen. They'd stood together in the center.

In the moonshadows cast by the forest at the edges, other animals began to gather, old friends and acquaintances from before. Alecto came first, then the wolf pup born in the valley, grown now. Then a small grizzly, a wolverine, black bear, lion, bobcat, lynx, species appearing more quickly: bald eagle, all three accipiters, four falcons, a half-dozen buteos, wild turkey, turkey vulture, black vulture, bison, elk, moose, mule deer, raven, fisher, fox, magpie, weasel. . . . They circled the meadow, running walking flying, hard to see in the shadows, dozens of them passing in and out of his perception. More came, so many he lost track: jackrabbit, vole, chipmunk, pika, marmot, blue grouse, prairie chicken, a dozen warblers, ten hummingbirds, a half-dozen woodpeckers, rattlesnakes and coachwhips, cutthroat trout swimming the air, staghorn beetles, bumblebees, fireflies, vespid wasps. The trees themselves leaned forward, fir maples juniper oaks spruce cottonwood pines, their branches animate and thrashing in the wind of the other creatures' passing. Hundreds, then thousands of Others whirling around Bowman and the jaguar in a great circle, at first a soft whoosh of footfalls and wingbeats, but growing faster, louder, now a cacophony of vocalizations, rising to a deafening primal roar, suddenly silenced.

They were passing judgment. They were asking for help.

They were saying goodbye.

He'd made a promise to the jaguar then. A promise to the Others.

He hadn't told Summer about that. Not yet.

But he would.

He searched the sky for a while longer, his sister and Marco and the two horses watching him. He knew they all thought him strange.

"She's not around now," he said. "She'll be back."

"It could be another eagle. She'd be about thirty. Do eagles even live that long?"

"Yes. Longer." He called to Marco and swung back up into the saddle, let the paint quick-step past the carcass. "It's her."

Author's Note on Made-Up Places

Most of the setting for this story is my fanciful invention (Panther Gap, Red Creek Range, Whitespring, Los Robles, etc.) set down in the real landscapes of southwest Colorado and southeast Arizona. In particular, I sincerely apologize to the Ute Mountain Ute Tribe for distorting the geography of their homeland and reservation to make room for Panther Gap.

Acknowledgments

First mention goes to Kirby Kim, for topflight agenting and editing skills, and Zachary Wagman, for more fine editing and for sticking with me and believing in my work under challenging circumstances. The loyalty, kindness, and patience of these two go way beyond any sane measure of professional obligation. Thanks, guys. Thanks also to Eloy Bleifuss and Maxine Charles, for providing invaluable assistance to (me and) Kirby and Zack, respectively.

Thanks to the talented Sara Wood, for another killer cover (with help from Keith Hayes), and to all the folks at Flatiron for taking me on and for their incredibly high-level work bringing this story to readers, especially Bob Miller, Megan Lynch, Malati Chavali, Marlena Bittner and Alexus Blanding, Nancy Trypuc and Katherine Turro, Omar Chapa, and sharp-eyed Dave Cole, who caught more than a few otherwise-invisible mistakes in the manuscript.

For moral support and wise counsel, thanks to friends and fellow writers Dabney Stuart, Michael Knight, and Jordan Fisher Smith.

For reading the manuscript and providing technical background expertise, as well as amazing stories from the outback of the American West, thanks to Alec Cargile, who is emphatically not to be blamed for the innumerable and often extreme liberties I have taken with reality in this book.

For her kindness and generosity and for important boosts to this aspiring writer over the decades, thanks to Margaret McLaughlin Grove.

Thanks to Peter McLaughlin, musical muse, Sonoran Desert sage, and friend of Mojave rattlesnakes.

For material support during my long writing process, thanks to Taylor Cole and the rest of the crew at Conservation Partners.

Thanks to Gee McVey for steadfast friendship and a constant stream of anecdotes I will always steal shamelessly.

Thanks to my siblings and sibs-in-law, for their love and support and for allowing Nancy and me to spend so much absolutely crucial time at Maxwelton in the past few years.

Among the myriad domestic and wild Others who have provided companionship, motivation, hope in the face of hopelessness, and (mostly) healthy distraction, special thanks to canids Little Bear and Odin (RIP, boys); felids Sam and Roman; equids Cisco, Trouble, Catcher, and the rest of the Maxwelton herd; and the peregrine falcons on the Rock, whose names we'll keep to ourselves.

Finally, and most of all: boundless, loving gratitude to Nancy Assaf McLaughlin. None of this happens without your love and inspiration, your always brilliant ideas, and your stubborn faith in your husband.